THE SECOND BOOK OF *THE WELLBORN CONSPIRACY*

Knights of the Sea

~A GRIM TALE OF MURDER, POLITICS, AND SPOON ADDICTION~

PAUL MARLOWE

SYBERTOOTH INC
SACKVILLE, NEW BRUNSWICK

Litteris Elegantis Madefimus

The moral right of the author has been asserted.
Cover design copyright © Sybertooth Inc. 2010.
Pippin portrait copyright © K.V. Johansen 2010.
Cover by Artemisia. Lunar phases font by Curtis Clark. Proofreading by Tutivillus.

The publisher would like to thank Martina Loebl for providing the seascape that was the starting point for the cover design.

First published in 2010 by   Sybertooth Inc.
                                 59 Salem Street
                                 Sackville, New Brunswick
                                 E4L 4J6
                                 Canada
                                 www.sybertooth.ca

The paper in this edition is acid free and meets all ANSI standards for archival quality.

Library and Archives Canada Cataloguing in Publication

Marlowe, Paul, 1969-
      Knights of the sea / Paul Marlowe.

(Book II of The Wellborn conspiracy)
Sequel to: Sporeville.
ISBN 978-0-9739505-9-5

      I. Title. II. Series: Marlowe, Paul, 1969- . Wellborn conspiracy ; bk. 2.

PS8626.A757K65 2010   jC813'.6   C2010-901183-X

PRAISE FOR *SPOREVILLE*,
THE FIRST BOOK OF *THE WELLBORN CONSPIRACY*

"Fans of Philip Pullman's *His Dark Materials* trilogy will certainly enjoy this novel. In fact, readers who like Gothic literature, science fiction, fantasy, and history will all relish this book... I cannot wait for the sequel... It was absolutely the best, most delicious thing I have read in some time."
– Bonnie Campbell, *Resource Links* (Selected for *Resource Links*' 2007 Year's Best list)

"*Sporeville* is an exciting, well written, fast paced story which captures the atmosphere of the times." – Mary S. Moffat, *Historical Novels Review*

"I recommend this mystery for teens who enjoy a Gothic feeling read... the times described, and the mystery, is similar to the feel of Philip Pullman's *Sally Lockhart* mysteries." – Jenn Stephen, *Mad Tales*

"A fun read!" – *Teens Read Too*

"...the characters are all quite odd and there's lots of deftly delivered dialogue, with none of the trappings of most modern literature. In other words, it isn't boring."
– Craig Pinhey, *Here* Magazine

"Anyone who loves science fiction, mystery, or history will enjoy this read, which is a great novel on its own as well as a terrific start to the *Wellborn Conspiracy* series."
– *What If?* Magazine

PRAISE FOR PAUL MARLOWE'S SHORT FICTION

"[an] instant classic" – *Sonic Society* (on the radio play of "The Resident Member")

"...an entertaining and thoughtful story."
– *SciFi UK* (reviewing "The Mudmen of Tower Tunnel")

"Gritty and realistic, Marlowe achieves his goal with deft prose stokes and clever dialogue." – Marshall Payne, *Tangent* (reviewing "Night of Sevens")

"The story is optimistic without appearing naïve, and offers a complex treatment of difficult political and economic questions. The touch of humor remains light and kind." – Ekaterina Sedia, *Tangent* (reviewing Marlowe's "Krasnaya Luna")

TABLE OF CONTENTS

Hear, then, attentive to my lay,
A knightly tale of Albion's elder day.
❧Sir Walter Scott❦

THE CAST OF CHARACTERS

or

DRAMATIS PERSONÆ

Of the following New and Original Novel of Modern Life

A Tragical-Comical-Historical-Pastoral-Satirical-Political-Nautical-Mongrel
Entertainment entitled

Knights of the Sea

~A Somewhat True Story~

Being the sequel to the Gothic novel *Sporeville* (lately delivered to the public), wherein (if we may be allowed to recap in brief the events of that shocking foretale to *Knights of the Sea*), the sleepy town of Spohrville became still sleepier when beguiled by the somnambulism-inducing fungal spores of that depraved villain & master of perverted science, Professor Strange, who was thwarted by three plucky youths, Elliott, Paisley, and Denis, who triumphed in spite of (respectively) their hay-fever, their lycanthropy, and their low socio-economic status, in addition to divers related impediments including, but not limited to, spore-zombies, parental disapproval, hired goons, eels, the tidal forces of the moon, and the like.

And now, returning to *Knights of the Sea...*

TIME

Shortly before and during the Golden Jubilee of Her Imperial Majesty, Queen-Empress Victoria.

PLACE

Principally the village of Baddeck (Victoria County, Nova Scotia, Dominion of Canada, British Empire), with several thrilling scenes in the port of Halifax, some upon the railways, and still more upon the high seas.

The Players, in no particular order

Elliott Graven : A traveller prone to misadventure. Aged sixteen, but often feels much older. From Kingston. An aficionado and sometimes practitioner of scientific romance and the medical arts.

Paisley DeLoup : A maiden of curious ancestry with certain lupine predilections. A citizenness of the Reevedom of Spohrville, and a reader of novels & other subversive materials. Noted for her skill at the artistic depiction of fungi. Also sixteen.

Sniggler : A cat and devotee of fish who was named for a technique of eel-catching, to whom Elliott will shortly be indebted for his life, and vice versa. Age: unknown.

Miss Claudia Hayward : An aunt. Also, a devotee of Fabianism, spiritualism, women's suffrage and other eccentric modern enthusiasms. Age: a matter of contention. She has taken a summer house in Baddeck and named it *The Hypatium*, after the ancient mathematician, Hypatia, who was murdered by religious fanatics.

The Honourable John Sparrow Thompson : A Privy Councillor, Queen's Councillor, former Premier of Nova Scotia, former Supreme Court Justice, etc., etc. Eminent statesman & great legal mind. Minister of Justice & Attorney General of the Dominion. Future Premier of Canada. Trencherman and stout fellow (in various senses).

Captain Iarik Starko : An excitable seafaring foreigner from the Tsar's dominions, with a passion for shellfish and a talent for enraging landladies.

Mr Garrity : A cabby and sometime journalist of Irish tendencies.

Alexander Graham Bell : A Scottish-American inventor of electric speaking tubes, magnetic bullet locators, and other instruments of Progress. Amateur eugenicist & sheep hobbyist. Part-time resident of Baddeck.

Lady Beauchamp : Pronounced 'Beecham' for reasons best known to the English. A young widow, a Fabian, and a vegetarian theosophist.

ALISON STILES : Lady Beauchamp's personal gentlewoman & long-suffering companion in her travels & spiritualist explorations.

CAPTAIN RAWLINS : An officer of the Royal Engineers. In his spare time, a rogue & purloiner of unearthly artefacts.

OSWALD SLACK : Alias 'Professor' H. Strange. Experimental eugenicist, vivisectionist, war criminal and villain of the lowest water. Nemesis of Elliott Graven in particular, and of all right-thinking persons in general. Wanted for his enslavement of the village of Spohrville, and for countless other abominable crimes.

DR RAFE MADDOX : A genuine professor & practitioner of the Etheric sciences. A lecturer on such matters to genteel audiences. Founder of the Etheric Explorers Club. Confounder of prophesies & diabolical machinations when the need arises. Grandson of the notorious pirate & philhellene, John 'Malabar Jack' Maddox.

MRS SOWERBY : A gentlewoman from the upper echelons of the so-called charitable organization known as the Wellborn Trust.

DENIS LUDLOW : An entrepreneur & eel expert. Budding magnate. A purveyor of lemons and other goods vital to public well-being & the smooth operation of democracy.

ADELMO VON HASSELBERG : A young industrialist of the German Empire. Anti-slavery advocate & benevolent imperialist. Displays a tendency to race about in motorwagons, submarine boats, and such unnatural contrivances. Claimed by some to be dashing; by others to be a dashed nuisance.

MUNGO MCKELVIE : A local carpenter, werebeastie tutor, and Scots impersonator.

MRS MCKELVIE : A genuine Scotswoman of keen memory. Dubious of kilts, caber tosses, and kindred Celtic tomfooleries.

MRS LEONOWENS : A whirlwind of organization in human form, formerly in the employ of the court of Siam. Benefactress of the arts, founder of the Victoria School of Art, and booster of women's suffrage.

Wallace Gibson : A de-badged United States Marshal, once charged with the apprehension of Professor Strange, now in reduced circumstances due to the spore-addling of his mind while staying in Spohrville, which resulted in an unreasonable and inconvenient yearning to collect other persons' watches and clocks.

Monsieur Percheron : A citizen of the *Troisième République*, and agent of the *Deuxième Bureau*, who has to experience his *première* performance as a pendulum in order to appreciate the gravity of his situation.

George : A telegram delivery boy, and would-be Saviour of the Empire.

& SUNDRY MINOR villains, heroes, servants, spouses, spies, politicians, assassins, and members of the great public.

Prologue:
September 1886.

Under the metropolis of London.
Sort of.

"Thrimby!"

The call echoed down the cavernous sewer until it was smothered up in the blackness of a turn. Rawlins raised his lamp over his head. All he could see was glistening brickwork and a ribbon of water like black tar.

"Thrimby, where are you?"

Under a dripping waterproof, his Wellington boots stuck in the muck, it required a sharp-eyed observer to detect any of Rawlins' customary military neatness; even his moustache drooped, and if he had any pipe-clay about his person it wasn't whitening his belt.

Droplets splashed down from the ceiling into the foul, noisome canal, but no-one replied. Rawlins searched left and right, trying to get his bearings; sewers all looked the same. Bricks. Tunnels. Squeaking, scuttling rats. Stench. Blast Thrimby! Of course, only *he* knew the way out.

Trapped. Trapped here forever. It had been madness to come at all. And they hadn't even anything to show for it.

Rawlins stiffened. Something... a splash... had sounded down the tunnel. Behind him. He strained his ears. There was a *plosh, plosh* of feet, impossible to say how far off. Hurriedly, he shuttered the lantern, scorching his fingers. He fumbled blindly in the dark, struggling through the buttons of his overcoat. As the steps grew closer, louder, his hand made a wrong turn, finding his pipe by mistake. "Blast it!" He almost hurled the briar into the waters before he struck cold steel. With no time to spare, he drew out his revolver and cocked the hammer. The ploshing was near now. Every so often the man would pause, puffing, as if to listen or catch his breath. *Plosh, plosh, plosh...* If the *Sûreté Impériale* had found them...

11

Plosh, plosh. Rawlins held his breath. The man in the dark stopped again, close, almost within reach... who could tell in the dark? The man coughed, and spat into the stream. "Bloody Rawlins," he said. "Where is that nitwit?"

Rawlins uncocked his pistol before he was tempted to do anything else with it. "That nitwit was about to blast you into the next world."

"It's not so easy as that," said Thrimby.

"Where's your lamp?"

"I fell in back there. Lost it."

"Never mind," said Rawlins, opening his own lamp to reveal the dour face of Thrimby. A man is never at his best after a ducking in a sewer. "Just get us out of here. This whole business has been a complete washout."

"Which is what I'm going to need when I get home."

"Yes, you do reek, rather."

Thrimby took out a flask and swilled some brandy around his mouth, gargled horribly, and spat the brandy into the sewer. "Probably get typhoid," he muttered.

"Just get us out of here."

It really was too bad, thought Rawlins on the repulsive trek. All this way, and nothing. Not a sausage. In the diced light below an iron grating, he half considered climbing up to the gas-brightened streets to find some prominent statue he could knock the head off of, just to relieve his feelings. Fortunately, Thrimby kept up a punishing pace, following a mental map and the odd marks he'd left on the masonry earlier.

"We could have timed it better," complained Rawlins. "Waited for some rain. This place wouldn't be half so disgusting, flushed out with a bit of rain."

Thrimby disdained to turn 'round, continuing his steady ploshing. "We would've drowned."

Even Rawlins began to find the labyrinth familiar when pipes appeared alongside the curving brickwork walls.

"Ah."

Another couple of hundred yards, or metres, and the pipes converged where an iron pillar stood in the centre of the tunnel, supporting a thrumming tangle of wires, pipes, brass boxes and ironmongery protruding from the ceiling like a rather ill-conceived chandelier. Rawlins halted, considering it.

"What is this thing, anyway? Never seen anything like it. Except the first time we went by. Part of the waterworks?"

Thrimby puffed impatiently, then thought. He looked overhead, as though peering through the brick and earth and cobbles above to examine the hidden city. He nodded slightly several times as if counting.

"It's under the fountain. Triumphal Square. It must be the apparatus for the fountain."

"That thing. But that's bloody huge! Shoots water up as high as the dome of Saint Paul's."

Thrimby nodded assent.

"And this little thing does all that?"

"Seems to."

Rawlins regarded the jumble in a new light.

"I'll be *having* that."

Thrimby looked aghast, but Rawlins shook his head. "I'll not let this journey be an utter waste of time."

"But…"

"But nothing," said Rawlins, recovering a bundle of tools from the pocket of his Mac. He took a hard look at the mess of tubes, wires, and valves with the calculating eye of a Captain of the Royal Engineers.

"But," repeated Thrimby, "we don't have time for a major plumbing job."

Rawlins turned a wheel, listened to the vibrations of the machine, and kept turning it until it squeaked closed.

The ceiling attracted Thrimby again. "It's the greatest fountain in this world. Someone will notice."

But Rawlins was already unscrewing the bolts that secured the brass cases. "Mind the live wires," he cautioned.

Chapter One
INFERNAL MACHINES

JUNE 1887. HALIFAX EXPRESS.
WESTMORLAND COUNTY, NEW BRUNSWICK.

AFTER SEVERAL FALSE starts, Elliott was finally starting to appreciate travelling. True, the Halifax Express was just as bumpy, smoky, and hot as it had ever been, and the scenery was mostly boring, but he was journeying on his own — not counting his scrawny tortoiseshell cat, Sniggler — and he was heading to a destination of his own choosing. That made all the difference. On top of the freedom, he was buoyed up by the fact that it was June, the weather was splendid, he had recently celebrated his birthday, and for the first time in months he didn't have to worry about telegrams, or criminal conspiracies, or any of the other tiresome concerns of day to day life. He could just sit back in the chair of his plush private compartment aboard the first class sleeper carriage, loosen his collar, and watch the country roll past the open window, where occasionally a tall black steeple would obligingly rise like a witch's hat from the endless ranks of trees to break the monotony. A chair, a desk with a view, two bunk beds to choose from — except that Sniggler had laid claim to the upper bed — what else did he need?

All things considered, it was the telegrams that Elliott was happiest to have escaped. Ever since Paisley's father had opened a telegraph office at his store in Spohrville, he'd gotten carried away with the novelty of the thing, sometimes sending Elliott four or five telegrams in a single day. Each one bore some new earth-shattering announcement, such as STILL RAINING HERE, THE TELEGRAPH KEY HAS GOTTEN MOULDY, or DID YOU RECEIVE MY LAST TELEGRAM. The delivery boy in Kingston developed an almost permanent smirk, probably from the deepening of Elliott's grimaces with each

14

successive communication. It wasn't in Elliott's nature to be rude without a good cause, so he endured all of this electric pestering and even put up with the bankrupting tips for the telegram boy, rather than squelch Mr DeLoup's obvious enthusiasm for instant messaging. Still, it came as a relief to be out of reach of the telegraph wires, which were harmless now even if they accompanied him the whole way, strung on poles alongside the rails.

Elliott slumped in his chair, remembering the botheration of it, and took a deep breath. He coughed. Coal soot was blowing back from the engine.

"After all, we're on holiday. I'm not going to think about piles of unopened telegrams," he told Sniggler, who was squinting at him sceptically from the upper of the two bunk beds, overlooking the desk where Elliott sat. The cat was right to be doubtful. Now that he'd recalled the constant telegraphic pestering, Elliott couldn't seem to think of anything else. Every passing pole reminded him of it. Even the ta-ta-tum, ta-ta-tum, ta-ta-tum of the train clattering over joints in the rails sounded in Elliott's ears like a Morse key tapping out an accusing u, u, u — *you haven't answered those blasted telegrams yet.*

"Well, it's too late now. And anyway, it's too expensive," Elliott complained to Sniggler, who merely narrowed her eyes a little more.

Ignoring the poles, he watched the clouds instead, which had the advantage of offering a less dizzying, more relaxing view. Life — out here in the wide world — seemed brighter than he remembered it being for a long time. Away from the gloom that hung over home. Sometimes it was the slightest thing; when his mother spoke of his father and called him *professor* instead of *doctor*. Other times it was the scream in the dead of night, when she woke from one of her dreams. There were times when she forgot where, or when, she was. And the black, silent moods when she remembered too well.

Professor Strange had spent much time and labour moulding her mind, reforging it to his liking; bending it back would be no easy task. Nearly a year had passed since Strange had been driven out of Spohrville, but the man's shadow still lay across Elliott's family as it did across so many others. Here, in this little moving world on the train, the shadow lightened. It was a selfish relief. With the shame of it, Elliott sensed the clouds closing in again. He might have stayed home. Helped. Somehow. Talked with her. Explained things for the hundredth, the thousandth time. Who she was. What had happened. That it was all finished now.

It was, wasn't it?

He should have stayed. But they had both urged him to go away for the summer, and he'd not protested too much.

Seeing Paisley again...

Elliott had spent so long worrying about his parents, it was impossible to stop now. Perhaps they'd wanted a holiday of their own from seeing that worry in his face every day.

As a distraction, Elliott cast about for something to read. He'd already pored over the latest volume of *The Proceedings of the Etheric Explorers Club*. Which reminded him not to be late for the lecture that evening in Halifax. Rafe Maddox, one of the founders of the club, was going to be speaking on the subject of clairvoyance. For a few minutes he occupied himself in studying a chart of the moon's phases for the next few months that he'd drawn in order to compare with Paisley's behaviour. A full moon tomorrow. It would be interesting to see whether the moon really had any affect on her. Thank goodness her hair didn't fall out and sprout again every month, like her father's.

Digging into his coat pocket, he pulled out a letter from Paisley; the last one he'd received before he left Kingston, and he'd read it half a dozen times already. No harm in reading it again. He flattened it out on the desk and weighted one corner with his best, and heaviest, fountain pen to keep the paper steady in the breeze from the window.

> *Miss Paisley DeLoup*
> *c/o Miss Claudia Hayward*
> *"The Hypatium"*
> *Crescent Grove, Baddeck*
> *Cape Breton Island*
> *Nova Scotia*

> *May 26, 1887*

Dear Elliott,

The "wanted" posters for Mr Gibson to distribute are finished, and have been despatched to New York. I hope the likeness of the so-called Professor Strange is good enough. Drawing from memory, it is hard to tell.

How is your mother this week? It was awful, the way Strange twisted her mind with his fungi, and mesmerism, and whatever other horrible things he used. Does she understand yet the truth about what happened on her voyage, and in Spohrville? And that she no longer has to worry about it?

Papa is plaguing me with telegrams also. You would think that being the town's reeve, organizing the new school, the constables, the mine, and so on, would fully occupy his time.

I am so glad that you will be joining us here soon. The house that Aunt Claudia rented for the summer is agreeable. There is much to admire in Aunt Claudia, but, not having met her before, I should prepare you; she can be an inconveniently large personality at times. It will be a relief to have

16

*someone sensible to talk to at last. Be further forewarned, though: we are
expecting an influx of spiritualists, suffragists, vegetarians, politicians, and
who knows what all else. Apparently...*

Before Elliott could read any further, a distraction arrived in the form of
four paws landing on the letter. Fangs clacked onto his good pen, and then
it, and the beast, leapt away, Paisley's letter flapping off to the ceiling on
the wind.

"Hey!" His reflexes couldn't better the cat's. Sniggler dove under the
lower bunk where, from the sound of it, she began to gnaw her way into the
pen. Getting down onto his hands and knees, Elliott peered cautiously into
the dark gap. A paw whisked out, raking a hair's breadth past his nose. As
he lurched back, something else caught his eye. Beside the cat-shaped silhouette bent over his unfortunate pen, there was a box. Elliott reached under the bed and dragged it out, forgetting for the moment the demise of his
writing instrument.

It was a plain brown suitcase. No monograms, or tags, or labels of any
sort. From the weight of it, it wasn't empty. As he heaved it onto the lower
bunk, though, he also noticed it was ticking faintly. Elliott wrestled with the
latches to get the case open.

"Just my luck. Some fool leaves his luggage under my bed with an alarm
clock in it. Probably would have gone off just as I was taking a nap and
scared me half to..."

There was, indeed, an alarm clock inside. For a moment, it seemed to
Elliott that the clock was an electrical contraption that someone had jury-
rigged together, since it was wired to a big oozing battery that smelt of
sulphuric acid. A second later, he recognized the dozens of grey cylinders,
filling the rest of the case, as dynamite.

A bomb.

Tick, tick, tick.

It's a bomb. On my bed. On MY bed.

Tick, tick, tick.

Think! What's one supposed to do in a situation like this?

Looking over the collection of tangled wires and explosives, Elliott
couldn't seem to bring his mind into focus. Instead of presenting a solution,
his brain kept seeing the bomb as just a confusing and deadly muddle of
stuff. He looked at the round clock-face, and the half-dozen wires attached
to the hands, the bells, and the clock case. Quarter to twelve, and the alarm
set for noon. Good. That was good. A whole fifteen minutes before the
sleeping car was blasted to pieces, and the train was derailed. Plenty of time.

His hands hovered over the bomb, trying to pick out some vulnerable spot that would let him render it harmless. Water… That was it! Soaking the dynamite would keep the fuses from setting it off, surely. Elliott sprang to the service button by his door and jabbed it five or six times to summon a porter. After ages of ticking, one appeared.

"Water," Elliott squeaked, not realizing how dry his mouth had gone at the sight of the bomb. "Please bring me a glass, no better make it a pitcher, of water."

Elliott paced as he waited. He'd soak the dynamite. That would work. Though, actually, now that he thought of it, dynamite was made of nitro-glycerine, not gunpowder. Water might not keep nitro-glycerine from going off. Worse still, it could short circuit a wire. And that might be bad.

The porter knocked, and Elliott opened the door.

"Your water, sir."

"Um, on second thought I don't think water would be such a good idea," Elliott told him, and shut the door again just as the porter's mouth was dropping open.

Clammy with sweat, Elliott returned to his bed. Seven or eight minutes left. His heart froze as a new noise started up. A scraping, crunching noise. But it was just his pen being eaten under the bed.

Think!

Then it came to him, that the bomb wouldn't work without electric current to set it off. Gingerly, he prodded one of the wires that ran into the battery. Soldered on. He rummaged through his pockets and drew out a clasp knife.

"I hope this works," he said.

Elliott cut the wire. Nothing obvious happened once it had been sawn through. The clock was still ticking. On an impulse, and wondering why it hadn't occurred to him before, Elliott decided the safest thing would be to toss the whole case off the train. He didn't think his nerves could stand waiting for the alarm to go off, even if the bomb wasn't working any longer. He shut the case and hefted it towards the window. On the way, sensing that something was afoot, Sniggler pounced onto Elliott's shoelaces and set to work shredding them.

"No! Out!," commanded Elliott, dancing away from the cat and clutching desperately at the bomb, the train's rocking and swaying making it difficult to keep his balance. "Get off! Pssst!"

Sniggler slunk back under the bed, drooping in disapproval, leaving Elliott to get on with his bomb disposal. He first stuck his head out of the window and into the rushing wind to make sure they weren't coming into a station, or passing someone who might object to forty pounds of dynamite landing on their head. It looked clear. They were racing across a broad, flat field near a reddish river, with no-one in sight but a few cows, the engine coughing out clouds of black coal smoke far forward at the head of the train. Perfect. At the last minute, Elliott undid the latches, trusting that all of the bomb-bits would fly apart on hitting the ground at whatever speed the train was going. He shoved the case out the window with all his strength, and dropped to the floor.

Seconds passed, unmarked now by the alarming clock. Elliott's own heart was an unreliable timepiece at the moment, but it seemed that the bomb really was inert now, and nothing was going to happen. At least, nothing worse than Sniggler trotting out from under the bed and licking Elliott's nose thoroughly with a very sandpapery tongue.

"If that's a thank-you for saving all nine of your lives, then you're welcome."

It had to be Professor Strange who was behind the bomb. After all, Elliott didn't have any other enemies. At any rate, none who wanted to kill him badly enough to blow up his train.

He gave his cat a quick, if shaky, pat and slipped out into the narrow corridor. If the bomber hadn't already left the train, it was likely he'd investigate why Elliott's compartment hadn't blown up. Especially if Elliott was conveniently out. And Elliott didn't particularly want to be in when a homicidal maniac came calling.

As he'd hoped, Elliott ran into a railwayman at the far end of the car. The porter was a very tall, aristocratic-looking fellow who, when Elliott previously crossed paths with him, had displayed that cheerful sort of confidence that one invariably finds in porters and conductors on trains. Even now, Elliott had the feeling that if he had made a remark along the lines of "There's an extremely large bomb in my compartment, and it seems it's about to go off," the conductor would have smiled affably and replied, "Really sir? That's against regulations. If you would like to proceed to the dining car, I'll see that the device is taken care of before you finish taking your luncheon." Of course, at the moment the explosive situation seemed to be under control, and so Elliott settled for slipping the porter a fiver and asking him to keep an eye on his compartment.

"Let me know if anyone suspicious is, you know, acting suspiciously. Around my door."

"Ah. Yes," the porter agreed. He was looking at Elliott in a rather wide-eyed way, for some reason. Elliott hoped the story of the water pitcher hadn't already started circulating amongst the train's crew.

"I'm just going off to get some luncheon. Can you send a," Elliott winced, "a telegram, from the next station we stop at?"

"Yes..." said the porter. He was staring even more fixedly now. Elliott ran a hand through his hair in case sticking his head out the window had made it stand on end. "Yes, of course," the porter continued, drawing a pad and pencil out of a pocket, though he still took a furtive look at Elliott from time to time as he scribbled.

Elliott cleared his throat. "To Paisley DeLoup, care of, um, Miss Claudia Hayward. The Hypatium, Crescent Grove, Baddeck, Cape Breton. DEAR PAISLEY STRANGE BUSINESS INFERNAL MACHINE BUT AM FINE BE VERY CAREFUL ELLIOTT. That's it. No, add an extra 'very' in there, would you? Oh, and you might warn someone that there seems to be a lot of dynamite spilt alongside of the tracks, about a mile back. Someone ought to look into that," Elliott said. "Is that enough," added Elliott, indicating the five dollars, thinking that the porter's hesitation came from a desire for a bigger tip. Then again, it was about a quarter the cost of his ticket.

"Enough?" asked the porter, seeming lost in thought. "Yes, sir. Thank you, sir. I haven't met such a generous gentleman since a few years back when Mr Oscar Wilde rode on this very train."

"Oscar Wilde, eh? The writer?"

"Yes, sir," said the porter, seemingly entranced by Elliott's nose. "A great gentleman for witty *bon mots*, was Mr Wilde. I recall him saying that there was only one thing better than being in Moncton."

"And what was that?" asked Elliott, not really paying attention.

"*Not* being in Moncton. Of course, that was shortly after he'd been *arrested* in Moncton."

The porter went on to relay further samples from his favourite Wilde epigrams, which hardly registered in Elliott's consciousness, for he was already moving unsteadily through the door and edging across the noisy, jiggling platform between the cars. He steered clear of the edges, where the tracks, and the cows, were hurtling past the barrier with disconcerting speed, and he passed through the door of the next car.

After winding his way along another first class sleeping car, he came to the dining car, where the third seating of lunching passengers was underway. It hardly seemed like a popular meal: Elliott was the only diner, and so received the full attention of the waiter, who, from his impertinent sniggering, had definitely heard of Elliott's water pitcher incident. Ignoring it, Elliott ordered two salmon fillets — one for him, and another for his cat to have later.

It finally sunk in then, as Elliott waited for his food to arrive, that Professor Strange really wanted him dead. Not with just a wistful some-day sort of death wish, of the kind that most people, at one time or another, harbour for a rude neighbour, or a salesman, or an exceptionally pompous civil servant. Rather, Strange wanted him dead in the most severe and definite way possible: the blowing-up-the-train-car-and-everyone-on-it sort of way. Despite the serious nature of the previous year's events in Spohrville, in which Elliott and his friends had not only frustrated Strange's plans, but had humiliated and bankrupted him, Elliott had never felt seriously in danger afterward. Even when Elliott and company spent all of their spare time trying to track down Strange and bring him to justice — or paying others to do so — he always felt that Strange was on the run, he was in pursuit, and it was only Strange who was in danger. Staring out the window, at racing forest now, Elliott no longer knew who was chasing whom. His very presence might bring destruction to everyone around him, as it almost did on the train. He shivered. If not for Sniggler's annoying mischief, he'd be atomized instead of sitting down to lunch.

Too absorbed to notice anything, Elliott was startled when someone pulled out the chair opposite him.

"Do you mind if I join you?" asked a heavyset man in his mid forties. He had long sideburns, and wore a black suit with shiny black silk lapels. "I hate to eat alone when I'm travelling."

"No, I don't mind," Elliott mumbled. A dreadful feeling arose in him that he was going to be lunching with the man who planted the bomb, but there didn't seem to be any way to innocently escape, what with his fish choosing that moment to arrive. It was just the sort of thing one of Strange's cronies would do — stroll boldly up and introduce himself. And this one had the cunning eyes of a criminal mastermind. Or perhaps this was a different assassin who hadn't even been told of the bomb; Strange was ruthless enough to send a man to certain death, just to ensure his revenge on Elliott.

"Fellow bluenoser, eh?" The villain said heartily, chuckling a little.

"What? No," said Elliott, recollecting that this was a nickname for Nova Scotians. "I'm from Ontario. As I'm sure you already know," Elliott added, a little bitterly. It was bad enough to have eat with his assassin, but having him play silly games was too much to put up with.

"Upper Canadian? Hmm," said the man, nodding to himself as though that explained something. "My name's John Thompson."

Elliott frowned. John Thompson. At least Strange had used some imagination when inventing his alias. "John Thompson" was positively feeble as a false name.

"Really?" asked Elliott. Mocking the whole ridiculous charade, Elliott grinned foolishly and stuck out his hand with exaggerated friendliness. "And of course I'm the infamous Elliott Graven. How perfectly wonderful to make your acquaintance!"

Thompson seemed a little non-plussed at this, but shook Elliott's hand anyway, though only in the most perfunctory manner. "Are you feeling all right?" Thompson asked, apparently with genuine concern.

Elliott didn't bother replying, concentrating instead on separating the bones from his salmon. Presently Thompson's steak and kidney pie arrived, and the two ate in silence as the train stopped to pick up a few university students at Easter River, the second last station in New Brunswick, and then continued across vast, flat hayfields, over the Missiguash river, and into Nova Scotia. Finally Thompson, who was seated with his back to the engine, gestured out the window to his left and cleared his throat.

"That's where Ketchum is building his ship railway," he commented, pointing to some activity out on a messy-looking mudflat near the bay. "Before long, huge ships will ride over the isthmus on double rails, from the Fundy to the Northumberland Strait. Amazing, isn't it, what you can do with steam and steel."

Elliott looked up from his fish, and out the window at the churned-up mud of the construction site, and then back to Thompson. He couldn't fathom why the man was nattering on about dragging ships from place to place. Was he trying to get Elliott's guard down, or was this some obscure allusion to the attempted assassination? Elliott decided it was about time he let Thompson know he was on to him.

"I suppose they must use a lot of dynamite to do all of that construction," Elliott said, eyeing Thompson to catch him twitching in surprise.

"Dynamite? Yes, perhaps they do," he said, vaguely. "I'm afraid I don't know anything about the technical matters. Not much of practical turn of mind, myself. My interest is in the law."

Elliott gave a little nod, and considered that it made perfect sense for an arch-criminal to be concerned about the law. "I'd say it was quite practical for a man in your, ah, line of work, to take an interest in law," he said, and mentally counted himself a coup in the banter. While Thompson's face was registering amusement, followed by slight confusion, Elliott stood and wrapped one of the salmon steaks in his napkin, depositing it into his jacket pocket. "Well, it's been great chatting with you Mr, ah, Thompson, but I really must be making like a fine day and clearing off, as a friend of mine once said." He turned and trotted off at double time, hoping to make it back to his compartment soon enough to lock the door before Thompson decided to pursue. At the end of the dining car he dragged open the heavy door and crossed the landing to the next car. It was only a few hours to Halifax, and then he'd be off the train and safely into a hotel for the night. Surely he could avoid Thompson until then.

Elliott flattened impatiently against a window in the corridor to allow a couple of elderly passengers to slowly creep past him on their way to the dining car, and then he jogged the rest of the way to the next door, lurched through it and onto the connecting platform, nearly colliding with someone in a bowler hat who was already occupying the narrow space. Not that he was likely to have suffered from being run into, since he was about a foot taller than Elliott and filled out his suit in a way that suggested muscle rather than fat.

As Elliott began uttering an apology, the man stared for a second and tossed away the cigarette he'd been smoking. Without offering any reply, the man stepped forward and struck Elliott so hard on his ear that Elliott flew sideways and crashed into the waist-high steel wall that surrounded the platform. He groped for the wall, head ringing and vision fading back from a starry night. The wind sounded like water in his ears, but before he could shake his head his jacket was grabbed from behind. He was being lifted up. Desperately he flailed for a handhold, kicking at his attacker at the same time. Half upside down, he caught hold of something on the barrier with his left hand and clawed at the man's face with the other, causing a bellow as he managed to tear an eye, or something. This earned him another blow on the back of the head, and stars again. There was no way Elliott could overpower the brute. Any moment, he knew he'd be thrown over and dashed to pieces like the bomb. The ground was a speeding blur. He kept madly thrashing in the losing wrestling match, even as his right arm came close to dislocating, and he grimly gripped whatever it was he had in his fist. Until suddenly the lever turned, and the barrier wall swung out into empty, roaring space.

O

Chapter Two
THE UNFORTUNATE ESCAPE OF THE PROPAGANDIST

THERE WAS A bright solarium full of orange trees and fuchsias on the south-east side of *The Hypatium*, and beyond its windows lay a spectacular view of the round, green-black bulk of the hill behind Red Head, jutting out into the waves from the left side of Baddeck Bay. To the right, and farther still — about four miles over the brackish blue expanse of the Bras d'Or Lake itself — dark hills loomed hazily over the shore between Grand Narrows and Shunacadie. Anyone would find it an inspiring vista, at least anyone who took a look at it. Paisley, on the other hand, was bent over a beeswax-covered copper plate that was clamped onto an easel. She gripped a fine engraving needle, poised to scratch another thin line in the soft wax that was filling the solarium with its sweet smell. Oblivious to the sunshine and greenery, Paisley screwed up her face in concentration and blew a stray strand of auburn hair away from her eyes. She pared away a little more wax to add a some lines of shading on one side of the figure taking shape on the plate, and puffed out a blast of breath again, this time to remove the little shavings of wax.

From the other end of the house, the clang of the doorbell brought Paisley's mind back to world. She stood and stretched, her eyes still on the plate, scanning it to gauge the overall effect. It was for one of Aunt Claudia's election posters. The picture showed — in reverse of course — the classic image of Britannia. Seated, wearing a toga and a Roman helmet, she had beside her a shield emblazoned with the Union Jack. Instead of a trident, though, she had an umbrella tucked into the crook of one elbow. Her other arm reached upward, clutching a paper with the word "vote" on it, or "ɘɟov". If Paisley's Britannia was a trifle cross-eyed, she considered it a matter of artistic licence. Probably Aunt Claudia wouldn't even notice, at least not until the posters were all printed. The acid etching could be postponed for Elliott to do when he arrived. He'd enjoy messing about with concentrated sulphuric acid. Paisley couldn't stand the stuff; it burned the nostrils like smelling salts.

She worked the kinks out of her neck and took in the view properly, feeling a quiet thrill at his coming visit. It had been months and months since she'd last been with Elliott. She hoped they'd still be good friends, like last summer. They'd written so many letters in the past year. It was such a *blasted* shame that he knew about the family history. If only...

The doorbell clanged again, more insistently, followed by a piercing bellow from on high: "Paisley!" Aunt Claudia, immured upstairs with the maid, Mary, at work with some dressmaking, or bunting production, or some equally vital activity.

Paisley set down her engraving needle and went to see who was behind the jammed front door. Aunt Claudia seemed to regard the door as some kind of initiation test of character. Those who were upset by it were obviously inferior specimens of humanity. Claudia herself relied on the maid to open it for her. Likely the visitor was one of her cronies, come to discuss politics or communication with the dead. There had been a time, not so long ago, when spirit boards and other accoutrements of the occult had been of keen interest to Paisley, but each time she met one of Aunt Claudia's friends it made her more squeamish about the whole business.

"Oh, it's you again, George," she said, after pounding on the door to get it unstuck. Outside, on the door mat, there was a boy in a navy blue coat and peaked cap. His sunburnt face fell in disappointment. "I suppose you were hoping Mary would answer the door," said Paisley.

"What?" he exclaimed. "'Course not. Is she here? Anyway, it's for you." He handed over a telegram envelope.

Paisley plucked a couple of pennies from a bowl of coins kept next to the calling-card salver on a table by the door for the sole purpose of tipping George. "Here," she said, passing them to the delivery boy. "But Mary's busy. Maybe next time," she added wryly, as George turned to go.

It was almost galling, the way Mary remained oblivious to the frog-eyed admiration of practically every masculine creature of even vaguely marriageable age. What Mary imagined was going on, Paisley couldn't guess. Perhaps the girl thought everyone in Canada behaved strangely.

Paisley didn't even bother to look at the telegram, since she'd been receiving several each day from her father, and none of them had been worth the effort of opening, much less worth the two-penny tip. She tossed it into a basket filled with identical little envelopes and was starting back to the solarium when her aunt bellowed again.

"Paisley! Paisley? We require a volunteer to serve as a dressmaker's dummy!"

Paisley groaned at the thought of being stuck with such a tedious task. And with numerous pins. She backed towards the front door again and speedily laced on a pair of tall boots, grabbed a straw hat, stuck her dark glasses on her nose, and twisted desperately on the doorknob.

"Hello? Are you down there?" her aunt called.

Foregoing stealth, Paisley gave the door a sharp kick. It thumped open, and she darted out, sprinting for the yard-high rose hedge that separated her aunt's property from the neighbours. She took it in one bound, and flattened to the earth on the opposite side.

Now that she was well hidden behind the roses, Paisley began crawling uphill on her hands and knees towards the even better hiding-place of the woods, occasionally sparing a second to glance over her right shoulder as she went, for a quick look at the peculiar state of the house next door. The Bells had decided they needed more room, and so they'd had the whole house raised on posts while a new ground floor was built beneath it. This architectural marvel had been the main topic of conversation in Baddeck for weeks. Some thought it a wonder of the century, in the same league as Bell's telephone, or the Eaton's catalogue. Now that Paisley's aunt had decided to get into politics, though, the House on Stilts was all but forgotten, and there was also growing curiosity about the strange boat that a foreign visitor had moored in the bay.

Hollow-sounding bellows from inside *The Hypatium* sent Paisley flattening herself to the ground. Evidently her aunt had not given up yet. Paisley was pretty sure she couldn't be seen, though. A whiff of pipe tobacco caught her attention, and she looked about to see where it was coming from. About a hundred yards away, in the Bells' vast vegetable garden, a thin man in a grey suit was marching to and fro in good square-bashing fashion, puffing on a briar. It was that Captain Rawlins, a guest of the Bells. She knew his tobacco's distinctive spicy-woodsmoke scent. Probably a Turkish blend. Perhaps he was investigating the ghostly lights that had been scaring workmen away from the half-finished house. Dr Bell had even had a spectral visitation from his wife. Which was all the more bizarre, considering that his wife was still alive. Paisley was trying to make out whether anyone else was with Captain Rawlins when her Aunt hollered out of one of the upstairs windows.

"Paisley! Where are you, girl? Are you out gallivanting someplace?"

Captain Rawlins stopped in mid-stride and span sideways to see what all of the ruckus was about. To Paisley's dismay, Rawlins immediately spotted her. His head was dipping up and down slightly as he looked from Aunt Claudia, craning out of the window, to Paisley, cowering under the shrubberies. Paisley was just about to mime a pleading message — that he should act as if none of this were happening — when luckily his pipe dropped out of his mouth, showering the grass, or possibly his shoes, with burning embers. While Rawlins was dancing about in a little cloud of sparks, stamping out the flames, Paisley crawled discretely, and hurriedly, towards the tree-line, noticing with irritation as she did that another face had appeared in a window. Paisley's own window. It was Miss Stiles, that lady's maid of the peculiar Lady Beauchamp. In *Paisley's* room... looking out through *her* spyglass, now. She had half a mind to storm back and tell the girl off for taking such liberties, but prudence demanded escape. Besides, the girl, Alison, seemed to be studying Rawlins next door, not Paisley. She continued crawling, and in a minute or two the house and her aunt were far enough away to risk straightening up, stiffly, with some more groans.

Safely enclosed in the dense hazel and blackberry bushes at the edge of the shadowy forest, Paisley removed her sun hat and took a deep breath of needles and leaf mould. And something else, heavier, muskier. She was sniffing, trying to think of what the smell was, when a deafening *crack!*, like a sheet of lake-ice snapping, made her every muscle go taut in alarm. Something huge and brown sprang past her in the bushes, and she felt a burning wasp-sting ache on her calf. She reached a hand to her right boot. When she looked down at it, it was covered in blood.

O

Chapter Three
OYSTERS & THE HONOURABLE ASSASSIN

A S THE PLATFORM gate swung away from the train with Elliott clinging
to the top edge, his face pressed to the wrong side and feet pulled up
for fear of catching them in the wheels, he had a wild hope that his assail-
ant might overbalance and fall through the gap. But the man, though surprised and a little the worse for wear, only glared hatefully at Elliott through
his remaining uninjured eye. He steadied himself with deliberate effort and
kicked hard at the swinging gate, and at Elliott's fingers, missing them but
sending the gate in a painful arc that bounced Elliott off the side of the train
before it pivoted back into place for a second kick. The villain was grinning
unpleasantly now, the deadly sport taking his mind off his eye. This time
the boot caught Elliott's little finger, but his howl of pain was cut off when
the gate crashed into his face. Mercifully, his nose just felt numb, and hot. It
was the salty flow past his lips that told him a good deal of blood was coming out. Kicking his legs, more in panic than anything else, Elliott managed
to keep the gate from swinging back to be struck again. Unfortunately, this
left him dangling helplessly off the speeding, rocking train. He scrambled
for a better hold on the gate, and looked about for a handle or anything
to grab hold of in order to climb away onto the next car. There was nothing. The thug was re-positioning himself to pound methodically on Elliott's
fingers when, behind him, the sleeping car door flew open. If Elliott had
any hopes of someone — perhaps the conductor — saving him from being
torn to pieces under the steel wheels of the train, they were dashed when he
recognized the face emerging from the door. It was the so-called Mr John
Thompson, evidently done with his lunch.

"Come to finish me off, have you, *Thompson?*" Elliott said, between
gasps.

Thompson, short and heavy-set, stood still gripping the door handle, drinking in the scene before him. "What? What in God's name…" he said, and started towards them. It was only when Thompson spoke that Elliott's attacker noticed the new arrival. He wheeled around, aiming a fist at Thompson's face. But whether it was from no longer having the benefit of binocular vision, or from Thompson's quick dodging, the blow went wide. As if from reflex, Thompson's right fist, then his left, connected in two quick jabs with the man's jaw, snapping his bull-like head back and sending him toppling through the gap in the barrier. Elliott caught a sickening glimpse of the whites of the man's eyes a second before the body crumpled into the blurry railway metal and fell away out of sight, past a curve in the track.

LYING ON HIS bunk in the sleeping car, with a damp cloth over his face and only a hazy recollection of how he'd gotten there, Elliott slowly came to. His head was throbbing. His breathing felt laboured, as if a heavy weight was bearing down on his chest. The weight began to purr. With a start, he remembered his struggle on the landing between carriages, and sat up sharply. It was a mistake. Immediately he flopped back onto his pillow with a whimper, and Sniggler leapt away to the foot of the bed. At the sight of Mr Thompson standing next to the window Elliott tensed, but then it came back to him. Thompson had saved him. Thompson turned to regard Elliott with a look of concern on his big jowly face.

"Uh, thank you," Elliott said weakly. "Thought I was a goner there."

"Good grief, son! What is this all about? Why on earth was that man trying to throw you off the train?"

With his head still whirling and singing like a bell with an overzealous ringer, Elliott had trouble putting thoughts in any sort of order. It was hard to know where to begin. "I think he was the same one who put a bomb under my bed."

"What?!"

Elliott shifted the cold cloth onto his forehead and tried to recount the history of his conflict with Heywood Strange, and the other criminals who were in Strange's employ. Beside the bed, Thompson pulled up a chair and listened, agog, to the tale of Spohrville's enslavement by Strange, the effort to defeat him, and the failure of the judiciary to take any action afterwards. Once Elliott had worked the story up to the present, Thompson sat back and puffed out his breath in amazement.

"I would call that account pure poppycock, had I not been an eyewitness to your near-murder. You're a lucky lad!"

Elliott sat up and tried to snort at the idea of being fortunate, but found his nose too blocked with clotting blood. Instead, he sank down miserably into his bed again.

"Thought you were with *them*," Elliott mumbled, remembering his idiotic behaviour toward Thompson in the dining car. "Ugh… I'm too young to have a nemesis."

Thompson withdrew a card from his jacket and passed it to Elliott. "Perhaps I should have introduced myself more fully, but I'm afraid that your peculiar manner at luncheon left me a little confused."

To avoid moving his aching head, Elliott lifted the card up to his eyes, finding in the process that his arms were as sore as the rest of him. Reading the print required more effort than he felt capable of. It sank in after a few moments.

The Honourable John Sparrow Thompson, QC, MP, Minister of Justice
Room №64, East Block, Parliament Hill, Ottawa

Queen's Council. Member of Parliament. The Minister of Justice.

"You're the Minister of Justice?" Elliott asked, incredulously. "What are you doing here?"

"What am *I* doing here? I should be asking you that, perhaps. I am *from* Nova Scotia. My riding is in Antigonish. It's you I'm concerned about. Something will have to be done about this outrage. You can't just go about hurling people off trains. It's… it's not commensurate with public order."

Elliott could see that Thompson was quite nettled by the whole affair. Perhaps his life in politics didn't usually deliver to him this much excitement.

"I don't mean to seem ungrateful, sir, but really it was *you* who threw *him* off the train."

Thompson sprang out of his chair, which was quite an achievement for a man of his stoutness. "Good grief!"

"I suppose," Elliott continued, a little deliriously, "it's not good form for Ministers of Justice to go about killing people, or hurling them off trains. I mean, it might alarm the voters, mightn't it, sir? What would the Liberals say?"

A look of pure horror passed over Thompson's features. Whether it was dismay at having brutally, if justifiably, taken a human life, or the thought of the bespectacled opposition leader, Edward Blake, accusing him of bloody murder in the House of Commons — or rather on a train — Elliott wasn't sure. Then Elliott had a bolstering thought.

"It's okay, sir. Mr. Blake just resigned, didn't he? So he won't be able to stand up in the House and demand to know why a Minister of the Crown is tossing fellows off trains. To die horribly. Torn to bits."

Thompson's mouth dropped open slightly in response to this terrible vision of the future. Or the vision of the past. Either way, it seemed to Elliott that he hadn't quite succeeded in calming the Minister's nerves.

"Probably it'll really be Wilfrid Laurier who ends up accusing you of going on murderous rampages, sir. Looks the type, doesn't he, to make an unfounded accusation like that? I mean, that big bald head, and those beetly little eyes."

For a moment, Elliott thought Thompson might continue in his new career of ejecting people from moving trains. His alarming expression faded to mere sombreness, though.

"I think that knock on the head has scrambled your brains," Thompson said, charitably. "See a doctor, once we arrive in Halifax."

"But I am a doctor." Elliott thought about this for a moment. "I mean, my father's a doctor. I'm sure he wouldn't let anything happen to my brain."

"Yes…"

"Anyhow, it's just scrapes, cuts, contusions, haemorrhages, concussion…"

"Yes, have those looked at as well, why don't you?"

After some more persuading, Elliott agreed to seek medical attention in Halifax if he hadn't by then "recovered his senses", as Thompson put it. Elliott had to admit the wisdom of this advice; all of this blithe levity in the face of assassination was most likely the result of concussion. Or hysteria. The Minister also suggested that, while the business on the train would have to be reported to the proper authorities, it might be best to handle things quietly, to prevent alerting the network of conspirators who were obviously involved.

"I know the Attorney-General of the province. I'll pass the matter along to him for his opinion. I am too closely involved to be impartial. Perhaps, temporarily, if the newspapers assume that the attacker was some sort of… anarchist, we will avoid correcting their error. It will keep the principal criminals off guard while we track them down. Most likely they *will* assume that he was an anarchist. Perhaps bent on attacking Dorchester Prison…"

"Now, alas, merely bent into a variety of curious and unpleasant shapes," Elliott added.

"Yes. Do see that doctor, won't you? And wash that blue ink off your nose. You can contact me if you find yourself in any further troubles. I shall be staying at the Telegraph Hotel in Baddeck. That's in Cape Breton."

Elliott was puzzled by Thompson's remark about ink, until he noticed that Sniggler's paws were blue where she'd been licking them; it reminded him of her licking his nose after the bomb incident. Then he stared at Thompson, astonished, now that he'd considered the rest of his words. "But

31

I'm going to Baddeck too!"

Thompson, as it turned out, was an advocate of votes for women, and was travelling to Baddeck to observe the coming by-election there, where Paisley's aunt was planning to bring the issue to prominence in the campaign. Thompson was slated to deliver an address on the subject as well. He lectured Elliott about his views on suffrage, legal reform, rebellions, fish, corruption, and other random topics, in a distracted manner until they pulled into the station at Halifax, but his attention evidently lay on the matter of the attacker, and the bomb. Perhaps he was waiting until the dynamite was found to confirm Elliott's wild tale, but by the time they parted ways Elliott believed he had gained an ally.

The Intercolonial Railway Station was an ornate Second Empire-style place that looked to Elliott a bit like the Mackenzie Building at the Royal Military College in Kingston, only not so square, nor so limestoney. The station had copper-green Mansard roofs, with a clock in the central tower which Elliott compared with his watch, and it was conveniently located just across Campbell Road from Admiralty House, next to the naval cemetery. At least, it would have been convenient had Elliott been a sailor, and rather more gravely injured. As it was, he merely wished that someone had taken the trouble to build a hotel there instead of a mansion full of admirals.

There was no shortage of cabs in the areas at any rate, even if Elliott's battered face made the drivers less than enthusiastic about soliciting his business, compared with their exuberant haranguing of other potential fares. With waves and nods Elliott tried to catch the eye of one, without any result. They seemed universally disinterested in him. But if cabdrivers are found to be lacking in curiosity, it can no doubt be attributed to that faculty having been lost amid the innumerable other curiosities cabmen find themselves surrounded by every week. In fact, as a general rule, one can say that things are most easily lost amongst similar objects, which is why seamstresses avoid the society of haymakers. But as all rules have an exception, so Elliott's cabman stood out from the crowd of his fellows, not least in his willingness to take aboard a lad who looked like the last-place contestant in a ten-round bare-fisted boxing match.

"You'll be wantin' the Infirmary on Barrington and Blowers?" the cabby asked, setting down the newspaper he'd been reading and adjusting his moth-eaten derby hat. His amiable, ruddy face pinched up slightly in concern, or sympathy.

"What?" Elliott massaged the back of his neck. Looking up at the man perched atop the cab was making his cervical vertebrae ache. "No, I need to find a hotel."

"If you say so. Which one is it?"

"Which one? I don't know. Just take me to the closest one."

The cabby tilted his hat onto the back of his head. "No reservation?"

"Not really, no."

The driver raised his eyebrows, as if in a lifetime of odd travellers Elliott was already shaping up to be one for the memoirs. He explained, once he'd descended and helped Elliott load his luggage onto the cab, that there weren't likely many rooms available in the city.

"The Jubilee, you know. Lots o' folks in town for the next few weeks. You might find a room, but..."

With this unwelcome news Elliott climbed into the cab, carrying Sniggler's basket and moving like a rheumatic centenarian with a migraine. He was discovering pains in muscles previously unknown to him except as diagrams in anatomy textbooks.

Due to her suspicion of such things, Sniggler generally grew melancholy in any sort of wheeled conveyance. It was her habit in such situations to slink deep into the bowels of her basket for a consoling yowl. Nothing if not a creature of habit, she made no exception on this occasion. Passersby were now stopping to enjoy the spectacle of The Mutilated Boy and His Howling Baggage. But to be fair to the advocates of the wheel, Sniggler would have objected as strenuously to legged transport had Elliott ever cared to take her riding on horseback, and the horse most likely would not have been much happier than she.

At the top of Halifax, the Citadel squatted on its hill like the sort of acropolis one finds hanging above any of the better class of Greek city states, only without so much marble and style. Below the old fortress, with its zig-zag walls and ditches and its cannon ever aimed at the sea, Halifax's brick and granite temples of commerce were arrayed in neat rows like terraces, cascading towards the busy harbour. Through gaps between buildings Elliott caught glimpses of slips and yards as his cab progressed along Water Street, past the navy docks. Shipping facilities, that is. The sorts of slips people might hang in their yards on clotheslines weren't approved of by the city aldermen. They only allowed laundry on certain days, for the sake of public order and decency.

The harbour looked prickly with ships' masts. Elliott's cab turned up Cornwallis, onto Brunswick, down Buckingham, and across Granville, by which point he no longer had any clue where he was. Now the cabman halted outside the Central Hotel and threw a meaningful look at his passenger. Elliott heaved himself painfully out of the cab, only to find that his relief at putting a period to his journey was short lived. In the hotel window a handwritten sign bore those words most dreaded by weary travellers: "No Vacancies".

The cab-horse trotted off again and carried Elliott away through the maze of streets, going up and down more often than a weather glass on a typical day in the Maritimes. Wherever they went there were yet more grim signs, variations on the theme of "No Rooms", or "Full Up". Coming after a long day of train travel and assassination attempts, this paucity of accommodations had the effect of dampening Elliott's spirits still further. He was mentally calculating the cost of simply paying the cabby to drive him around continuously while he slept in the back, when the carriage drew to a stop across from the Royal Nova Scotia Yacht Squadron, at the far end of Pleasant Street. A vast, rambling wooden house-like structure greeted them with a black and white sign saying "Ivanhoe Inn". Without much enthusiasm, Elliott dismounted again and trudged up the walk to the hotel.

At least there was no sign in the window, though from his recent education in the ways of hotels, Elliott had learnt that this had little to do with whether they had any vacancies. This latest one was certainly a *lively* hostelry. The moment he crossed the threshold, Elliott found his already raw senses assaulted by the racket of an argument at the front desk. A handful of bystanders had gathered around, displaying mixed embarrassment and fascination, as the lady behind the desk exchanged words with a mountainous, bearded creature in a vast navy-style pea coat and peaked cap, whose communication was alternating between broken English, violence, and some barbarous-sounding language that was completely alien to Elliott. The two continued their altercation as Elliott cautiously approached the desk, though some of the audience seemed to be looking with greater interest now at Elliott as he slouched uncertainly behind the sailor. The front desk lady was so red in the face that Elliott considered warning her of the dangers of apoplexy, but he decided that presently she was too busy to take his medical advice. For his part, the sailor seemed fairly umbered as well, from what could be seen of his face through the beard. It gave the impression of a rather angry devil peeking through an irregular hole cut in a poorly-groomed beaver.

"You're not having your bags 'til I have my money, and that's that!" the landlady declared. "And to think," she went on, "*him* staying in Mr Oscar Wilde's room!"

The foreign person stamped his foot and uttered what must have been expletives in his native tongue, unless it was a criticism of decadent dandies and aesthetes like Wilde. His hand smacked the desk where a few tattered and unfamiliar banknotes fluttered from the impact. "There! Money! Take money, give luggages!"

His opponent folded her arms and shook her head defiantly. "I've told you, we don't take your strange foreign money here. For all I know, that could be a pile of fancy Chinese laundry tickets. Go to a bank and change it if you like, but until I have proper legal tender your things stay here, in lieu of payment."

While the sailor was raving and thumping and pulling his hair in his rage and despair, Elliott edged up to the desk. The landlady was grimly standing her ground. She started a bit when she got a good look at Elliott's face.

"And what might you want?" she asked, looking him up and down. Even the sailor stopped ranting for a moment to see what Elliott would say.

"I don't suppose you have any rooms available," he said, hopelessly.

She seemed to make up her mind that Elliott was slightly more respectable than the other customer. "No. I'm sorry, but until this... person... settles his account, the last room will be occupied by his belongings. *Until we can pawn them*," she added, with a menacing glance at the sailor.

At this the sailor picked up his rambling at an even more furious pace and volume. The landlady pointedly ignored him. It seemed like the end for Elliott. Perhaps he could... no, they wouldn't let him sleep at the station. He hoped the hotel argument wouldn't degenerate into killing. He'd had quite enough of that for one holiday.

Incensed at being disregarded, the sailor began smacking his open palm repeatedly onto the desk bell, making an even more irritating sound than his angry gabbling. The sheer misery of it made Elliott clamp his hands over his swollen ears until the landlady hit the sailor with a curtain-rod to make him stop. They went back to verbally assaulting each other with what Elliott thought were rather coarse terms to use in public. It was maddening. Everywhere he went, people were either crazy or trying to kill him.

"How much," he began to say, but no-one was paying any attention. They continued carrying on as if he had already given up in favour of another hotel. Which he would have done, except that the cabman had taken him the length, and possibly the breadth, of Halifax. There was no place left. Unless he slept in Point Pleasant Park like a hobo. But no, he wanted a real bed. He deserved it. It wasn't every day that he went on holiday and nearly got murdered. He needed a good night's rest.

"How much," he tried again, a little louder, shaking a trifle with exhaustion and frustration. The landlady was shouting now too, in a shrill shriek that made Elliott's head feel like hot nails were being driven through it. Elliott took a deep breath, and howled.

"Aaaaaaaaaaaa!"

He winced at the pain of his own voice, but drew breath again in the stunned silence of the lobby.

"That's better. Now, how much does he owe?" Elliott asked, drawing out his wallet.

TEN MINUTES LATER, the previous resident's goods had been shifted out — all except for a tall brass samovar the sailor had pressed on Elliott by way of thanks — and Elliott's luggage was installed in their place. At last, at long last, something had gone right. Or would have gone right, had Elliott been able to do what was uppermost in his mind, which was to collapse on his bed like a boneless jelly and sleep until his train left the next day, even if it was going to be a pain-filled, nightmare-haunted sleep. But his will-power had utterly evaporated. Instead of being blissfully unconscious, he found himself back in the cab with the erstwhile occupant of his room, who had been so exasperatingly grateful that he insisted they have dinner together. Or a late lunch. It would fill the time before Elliott's scheduled dinner with his uncle.

"Should never have come here," the sailor said as he guided Elliott out of the hotel. "Thought was Russian hotel. From name. Ivanhoe."

Needless to say, the cabman took this latest turn of events with the customary equanimity of his breed. Nevertheless, he showed a certain gleam of the eye that suggested an eagerness to learn how it was all going to turn out. "Where to now?" he inquired.

"Take us," the sailor rumbled, "to oyster bar."

"Any preferences? The Admiral Shovell?"

The sailor grunted something like assent, and so they spun away again down Pleasant Street, back towards the centre of town.

"The admirable shovel?" Elliott asked, wearily.

"*Admiral*," the cabby corrected. "Cloudesley Shovell. He and the *Association* sank off the Scilly Isles." He twisted around in his seat to see what affect this string of errant silliness would have on Elliott, getting glowered at for his trouble. "S'true," he said, sounding a little let down.

"As long as have oysters," the sailor said, and that settled the matter. The hairy stranger cogitated awhile, perhaps on molluscs, before suddenly stamping his foot hard enough to rock the carriage. He turned to swat Elliott on the arm, adding to the bruises. "What goose I am! Have not introduced. Iarik Starko," he said. "Am Russian sea captain."

To Elliott, "Iarik Starko" sounded rather like another foreign curse, but he assumed it was the man's name. Starko took Elliott's hand in a great, meaty fist and shook it. "Elliott Graven," Elliott said.

"You are generous fellow, Eeliott," said Starko. "And wealthy," he mused, swivelling his head about to gaze witheringly at the mere pedestrians on the pavements around the cab. "Perhaps you are English milord?"

"What? No," Elliott said. He waved a hand at the traffic to draw the cabby's straying attention back to the horse, and the road. "My money's from…" Elliott continued, "… from silver mines."

The Russian nodded and stroked his beard. "Ah. Industrialist. Capitalist. Still, you not bad sort, I think."

After a few minutes driving they found themselves in the slightly seedy, dockside region of Lower Water Street, where every second door seemed to belong to a warehouse, if not a grog shop or oyster bar established for the comfort of visiting mariners. Or, if the sailors were of a more elevated turn of mind, they could go around the corner to visit the Lieutenant-Governor's residence, or the Academy of Music. Starko appeared to be more of the oyster persuasion, for he descended eagerly from the cab as it slowed to a halt in front of the *Admiral Shovell*.

"Shall I wait here?" the cabby asked while Elliott was picking through change for the fare. "I don't mind," he added, hopefully.

"Well..." Elliott thought. It might be easier than trying to find another cab later. Then again, it would be more expensive. On the other hand... He couldn't seem to get his mind in order enough to make even so simple a decision as this.

"Now I think of it," the cabby said, "I'm a bit peckish myself. Maybe I'll nip in for a bite as well."

If restaurants can be judged by their clientele, the *Admiral Shovell* was the kind with patrons who believed that a bath was what happened when you fell overboard, and that spittoons were for girls. When people called it a "low establishment" they weren't referring to the ceilings.

The interior of the *Shovell* was homey enough, with a cold black fireplace at one end and a scattering of tables, several of them occupied by a motley cross-section of dockyard denizens. Elliott aimed for the least greasy-looking table, but Starko selected one by the window instead. Presently the waiter arrived.

"Oysters," Starko told him. "For three." Starko looked pensively at Elliott and the cabby for a second. "You English all like beer, eh?"

"Actually, I'm Irish," replied the cabby, "but..."

"I've never had..." began Elliott.

"Good," declared Starko. "They will have beer. For me, vodka."

"Rum or whisky," the waiter offered.

"Rum," said Starko. "Is better than vodka. But always ask for vodka. Is tip of hat to Russian nationalism."

The waiter returned with heavy white china plates and cutlery, followed by rum and pint glasses of pale ale. Elliott looked dubiously at the drinks, while the waiter looked expectantly at Starko.

"I forget," Starko said. "No Canada money. My friend, Eeliott. He will pay."

Elliott gloomily dug out his wallet yet again and handed over some money, discovering in the process that he had a pocketful of smashed salmon leftover from Sniggler's lunch. They all then turned their attention to their glasses.

Starko was the first to seize hold of his, raising it for a toast. "To our new friend, Eeliott!"

Elliott turned to the cabby after grimacingly taking the expected swig of ale. "Who *are* you, anyway?" Elliott inquired.

"Ah. Name's James Garrity," he said. "I'm your cab driver," he added, in case Elliott had forgotten.

As they sat quenching their thirsts — except for Starko, who had downed his rum with the first toast — Garrity explained that he had ended up in Halifax after emigrating to Canada to follow his childhood sweetheart, whose family had come out earlier.

"Fell through, though. Met someone else, she did. My own fault, I suppose, for not acting sooner."

They sat for a while in silence, sadly contemplating unrequited love. Eventually the waiter brought a great tureen of steaming oysters, along with some bottles of sauces, and another round of drinks. Elliott was about to protest that he hadn't finished the first one, when he noticed that he had.

"You toast next, my friend," Starko instructed Elliott.

Elliott squinted up at the filthy ceiling beams, finding them for some reason blurry as well as grubby, and tried to think of something to toast. "To Starko"? No, not inspiring enough. "To your health"? Too commonplace. Then, like the gentlemen of that renowned Whig-filled pie shop of yesteryear — the Kit Cat Club — he resolved to toast the merits of a lady of beauty and accomplishment who held the highest place in his esteem.

"To Paisley DeLoup," he said, raising his pint.

"Ah," Starko said, grinning, "You have young lady. What she like, this Paysle-ee?"

Elliott plunked his chin down on his first pint-glass, upturned and empty, and stared as if at something wonderful far beyond the pile of flabby hot oysters. "She's wonderful, Ivan."

"Iarik," the Russian corrected.

"Iarik?"

"What?" asked Iarik.

"What?"

Iarik cleared his head with a quick shake. "Paysle-ee?"

Elliott sighed and his eyes glazed over again. "I've missed her, Iarik. Haven't thought of anyone or anything else since we parted, a whole year ago, almost. Well, 'cept for thinking about my mother. An' 'bout astronomy. And cats. And medicine. And travelling to the moon. And revenge."

The Russian whistled through his teeth. "Pff, you complicated fellow, Eeliott. Still, is good to be in love. Except for horrible things." Iarik shook his head again at some dark thought. The Russian pounded the table to attract the attention of a waiter, who delivered more rum to Starko, a little reluctantly. "So, you marry this Paysle-ee?"

"Thassa tragic thing, Ivan, er Iarik. She's prob'ly not old enough to get married yet. And even worse, neither am I. In fact, I'm not entirely sure I'm old enough to be drinking this delicious India Pale Ale."

"Drink! In Russia, mothers give babies stronger drink! Pff, age mean nothink. Look at Iarik. Went to sea when twelve. Was terrible. Still, better than family."

"Really?" Elliott said, picturing a tiny gnome-like Iarik in a crib drinking rum. In Elliott's mind's eye, even the baby Iarik had a beard like a frazzled raccoon. He turned to Garrity. "I mean, I've heard stories about Guinness and the Irish, but..."

"Anyhow, is jubiloo," Starko said. "Must toast British Empress, Victor-eeah."

They raised their glasses to the monarch and clinked them, except for Garrity, who forgot to join in. Instead, he speared an oyster on his fork.

Iarik now began downing shellfish at an alarming rate, and rather than seem unfriendly, Elliott tried one too. It was rather like... No, it was definitely not like anything he'd ever eaten before. The only thing that came to mind was that it was a bit like how he imagined swallowing his tongue would feel. That is, if his tongue smelt like Halifax harbour. Which, now that he had eaten the oyster, it probably did. He shook a bottle of brown sauce over the remaining oysters in the hope of rendering them more edible.

"She's wonderful, Iarik," commented Elliott. He screwed up his face, trying to remember if he'd said this already. Whatever the case, it was worth saying again.

"Wonderful. Likes mushrooms."

"Mushroom! We need mushroom for these oysters," Iarik declared, and began shouting for the waiter again. "Mushroom! Fried in..." he turned, puzzled to Elliott. "What is... fat stuff, made of milk?"

"Cheese?" Elliott suggested, jostled from his love-sick reverie.

"...in cheese!" hollered Iarik. "No, that not right."

Garrity laughed. "Cream?" he said.

"Butter?" offered Elliott.

"Mushroom fried in butter!" Starko bellowed.

Elliott sighed, fondly remembering Paisley from the previous summer, when she was in a steam-filled mine, rain-soaked and covered in spores.

"An' she's got nice teeth. Big teeth. You know, Iarik, and, er, Garrity, sometimes I think, I think Paisley's a werewolf?"

"What is ware-woof?" asked Starko.

"It's…" Garrity said, winking to Elliott to let him know that he could play along with a joke, "a sort of person who turns into a wolf."

"Paysle-ee is *oboroten*?" The Russian looked genuinely baffled over this, until he brought his huge hand around in a smack that sent Elliott sprawling half over the table. Iarik roared with laughter and pounded the already suffering table until the plates clattered together. "You wery funny fellow, Eeliott! Ha!"

Iarik rose to his feet for some reason and wheeled around, hurling his glass into the stone hearth at the other end of the dining room, where it smashed spectacularly. The oyster bar went strangely quiet, and Iarik glared at the clientele, wordlessly inviting any who wished to, to follow his example, or else fight him if they objected. No-one did.

"We go now," he declared.

Elliott caught sight of a clock over the hearth and jumped up too, remembering the lecture he'd meant to attend at the college. "I'll be late!"

Chapter Four
"GOT 'IM, HIMMEL!"

A SECOND OR TWO passed before Paisley connected her bloody leg with the bang and understood that she'd been shot. She dropped to the ground in alarm, clamping her hand back over the hole that ran through her boot and the back of her calf. Footfalls, fast and close, were approaching as someone ran across the crackling forest floor towards her. Paisley pressed herself to the earth, hoping her silence would keep her invisible. Beyond the bushes, the person paused, then crept closer. The sour smell of black powder smoke preceded him like perfume announcing a debutante. There was a rustle of leaves, and the gunman emerged into the clearing in front of Paisley. Perhaps twenty or so, he wore a hunter's wool suit and a feathered hat that he was just now replacing after the bushes had dragged it off of his short flaxen hair. The young man saw Paisley lying at his feet and recoiled, eyes wide.

"*Gott im Himmel!*" he exclaimed. He sprang forward and into a crouch beside her. Paisley flinched away, wondering who "Himmel" was, and feeling a little indignant at being referred to as 'im. Then she grasped that he was speaking German. "What have I done?" asked the man. Paisley relaxed a little, now that it all appeared to be an accident. She sat up to better apply pressure to her leg. That sounded like the sort of thing Elliott would have advised under the circumstances.

"You shot me, that's what you've done," explained Paisley, frowning.

The man threw his rifle away in one direction and his hat, for some reason, in the other. His hands danced in the air over Paisley, torn between modesty and necessity. "Where…?" he said. "Are you…dying? Oh, if I haff killed you I shall not let myself live von minute longer!" said the man, in an overwrought German accent. His steely eyes were vatering with emotion. Or watering, rather. As he knelt there beside her, Paisley thought he could easily pass as a pre-Raphaelite knight grieving for a mortally injured lady, if only his Harris tweeds were turned into armour.

"It's just my leg," Paisley told him. She didn't want the poor fellow weeping, or shooting himself over what she was pretty certain was a mere flesh wound.

"Only her leg! Brave maiden!" He drew a long, horn-handled hunting knife from his belt. "Vith your permission?" he asked. Paisley wasn't sure what exactly he was asking permission to do, but hoped he didn't mean to gut her like a deer. She nodded.

He held her boot in one hand while the other sliced through the lacing in one neat stroke. He slipped her leg gently out of the boot and cut away her stocking to expose the wound, and a shocking quantity of naked ankle. The German's fingers delicately kneaded her calf, testing the bones for breaks. His eyes narrowed in concentration and compassion, twin blue pools of limpid…

"What?" said Paisley, becoming aware that he had spoken.

"I think that there are no fractures, thank *Himmel*. But I must bring you to a physician. Your house is near?"

"It's just down the hill."

No sooner had the German produced a clean white handkerchief from his coat pocket and tied it over the wound, than he thrust an arm under her knees and another about her back, lifting her up like a leaf on a breeze.

"I shall bear you there at once," he said, and set off at a trot, swaying this way and that to avoid branches until they came out of the woods and onto the pasture that sloped down to *The Hypatium*.

Paisley was about to point out that it was inadvisable to move injured people, according to Elliott at least, but there seemed little point now that they were already in motion. Instead, she relaxed and enjoyed the ride as much as possible, which was rather more than might be expected considering that she had a bullet wound. *So this is what it's like to be swept off one's feet and carried away in a man's arms. It's not so bad, except for the shooting part.* For a moment she rested her head on his chest and felt his heart pounding, but it seemed far too intimate a thing to do. He was a stranger, after all. Guiltily, Paisley stiffened her neck to look downhill instead. They were almost at her Aunt's house now. Captain Rawlins next door, at the Bells' cottage, had evidently gotten his pipe under control, for he had it clenched and smoking between his teeth as he watched the German returning Paisley like a wayward lamb recently captured.

He was probably still watching as the German struggled to grab the doorknob with one of the hands supporting Paisley. He couldn't quite get enough purchase on it to overcome the door's reluctance to open. He tried knocking, but wasn't able to make much noise without either dropping Paisley, or using her as a door knocker.

While he was looking from side to side, in search of some piece of furniture on which to deposit her with dignity, Paisley cranked the doorbell. The clanging eventually summoned the maid from some corner of the house. She stood, staring blankly at the pair on the door step.

"Mary, this gentleman..." said Paisley, before realizing that she didn't know his name. She looked to the German, who began his introduction with a sharp nodding bow that sent his forehead colliding rather painfully with Paisley's skull.

"Ow!"

"Miss, I am most profoundly sorry! I am unaccustomed to being introduced whilst carrying a young lady."

Paisley rubbed the crown of her head. "Please continue, without the bowing," she suggested.

He nearly nodded again, but checked the instinct in time. "How do you do," he said. "I am Burggraf Adelmo von Hasselberg."

"Mary," said Paisley, "Herr von Hasselberg recently shot me, in the woods. I wonder if you might make us a pot of tea."

The girl, a trifle stunned, moved aside to allow them to enter, but it seemed to Paisley that she then disappeared in quite the wrong direction for the kitchen. Hasselberg followed Paisley's directions to the front room, where they considered and rejected a variety of chairs and chesterfields, finally settling on a chaise longue as the best place for her to recline. But before Paisley could work herself into a suitably tragic pose, her aunt Claudia swept into the front room like a gale wrapped in a bronze-silk gown.

"Young man!" she said, as Hasselberg leapt to his feet from where he had been kneeling, fluffing Paisley's pillows. "Are you aware that I am attempting to effect great social change?"

"Ah!" said Hasselberg. He bowed after hesitating for an instant to check that he was unencumbered by any stricken girls. Rather than attempting to make sense of Aunt Claudia's baffling remark, he wisely chose to ignore it. "Do I haff ze pleasure of making ze acquaintance of ze young lady's elder sister?"

Paisley leant out from the couch, a little incredulously, to see if she could tell by Hasselberg's face whether he was trying to be obsequious. He appeared to be sincere.

"Sister!" said Aunt Claudia. "Sister! Young man, do you imagine me to be a mere child?"

Hasselberg somehow forced his spine into an even more erect posture than it had previously suffered. He glanced pleadingly to Paisley. "*Nicht*, no, not over head. I mean, not at all. Miss, ah, Madame is, ah, obviously a mature voman…" he said, lips curling into a slight smile of satisfaction at having mastered both English and etiquette in a tight situation.

"Mature? Mature!" said Aunt Claudia, whom Paisley firmly believed to be an ancient of nearly thirty. Aunt Claudia blew menacingly up to Hasselberg. "I like that!" she informed him, from a distance of a few inches. "Young man, were I of so venerable a season as to deserve such a title, I would have entered this world in an age when poorly chosen words led to duels, and I would be of a mind to make such customs familiar to *you* as well."

Hasselberg recoiled slightly at this convolution of hypotheticals. "I apologize most humbly, Madame. Mine mother tongue *ist* German, und I zometimes have difficulty vith your English."

Paisley thought Hasselberg had been doing all right with *her* English, but declined to comment.

"Ah," said Aunt Claudia, as if finally she had received something like a civility. She strode across to the chaise longue where Paisley was recuperating. "But what have you been doing to my poor niece?" she asked Hasselberg.

"Then you are an aunt," he concluded, winning a somewhat vexed expression from Aunt Claudia.

"Burggraf von Hasselberg shot me in the woods," supplied Paisley.

Hasselberg looked pained at this explanation. "Please," he said, "call me Adelmo. And I have never shot a young lady before today."

"It was a novel experience for us both," said Paisley.

Aunt Claudia peered into Paisley's eyes. She took Paisley's pulse, and felt her forehead. "You seem febrile, my dear."

"I *am* feeling warm all over," admitted Paisley.

"No doubt the blood is rushing to your extremities."

"How," wondered Paisley, "does the blood know what to do when it finds itself in an extremity?"

Aunt Claudia looked stern. "I am certain that it has had the necessary emergency training, Paisley. And your chest is heaving," she added.

"Is it?" Paisley checked, and it was. She adjusted the pillow at her back to make the most of the heaving.

"Please," asked Adelmo, peering past the chesterfield, "vy ist zere a servant behind ze furniture?"

A fair head rose past the back of the chesterfield. "Oh," said Alison, the liberty-taking lady's maid who had so recently availed herself of Paisley's spyglass without permission. Alison stood and directed an accusing finger towards Paisley's leg. "The blood. I must have swooned."

Paisley found this most unlikely. Aunt Claudia waved dismissively at

Alison — who curtsied before scuttling out the door — and then addressed Hasselberg. "And you, young man, why are you not fetching the doctor?"

"Indeed, Madame, I shall go zis instant!" said Hasselberg, when he paused. "If I might, before I depart, ask the young lady's name?"

"Very well," conceded Aunt Claudia, with a magnanimous motion of the hand.

"It's Paisley," said Paisley. "Paisley DeLoup."

"DeLoup..." said Hasselberg. "Is this from the French, 'loup', meaning 'wolf'?"

"Oh... ah." Paisley laughed nervously. "Who knows where these old surnames come from? It might mean anything." *Mustn't mention wolves. Anything to do with wolves. He mustn't ever find out, as Elliott did. He only needs to know me, not my genealogy. Only me.*

Hasselberg seemed gratified by Paisley's nebulous prattle, for he gave a quick, nodding smile, and left the room with long, purposeful strides. Paisley and Aunt Claudia both watched him depart, in thoughtful silence. When the distant sounds of struggling at the front door subsided, Aunt Claudia turned to Paisley.

"I do hope he knows where the doctor lives," she said.

Just then, the doorbell clanged again. Aunt Claudia inclined her head and awaited the German's reappearance to ask directions. But instead, Mary arrived with a bit of paper in her hand.

"Excuse me miss, madam. A... person, delivered this for Miss DeLoup."

Paisley accepted the grey, grubby bit of torn paper. "Who left it, Mary?"

"No-one of my acquaintance, miss. He didn't seem a gentleman, if you take my meaning. Smelt a big gamey, miss."

"Gamey?" said Aunt Claudia.

Paisley unfolded the uneven scrap of paper. It was covered in such an illegible scrawl that she wondered if the writer had used his opposite hand as a writing desk.

To the lassie in the wudd when the forainer fired his fusket: she should return to that place at nine tomorrow night, to lairne a thing that's to her profit. From a frend.

"Even if he is a friend, I don't think much of his spelling," said Paisley.

Chapter Five
WOULD THE LATE ELLIOTT GRAVEN PLEASE STAND UP?

BACK ON THE pavement outside *The Admiral Shovell*, Elliott was dismayed, and not just from having to pay for Iarick's glass in addition to dinner for three. Now that Elliott was running late for something, the cabby, Garrity, had decided to stop cabbing.

"Had a few, you know," Garrity explained, hooking a thumb back to the oyster bar of recent memory. "Shouldn't really be in charge of a cab. Then again, I don't really want to leave it here," he said, drinking in the dockyard neighbourhood like a pint with a fly in it. "Tell you what, why don't we leave the cab around the corner, in front of Government House, and I'll take you up to Dalhousie on foot. It's just up Spring Garden — we'll be there in no time."

Having no other choice available, as there were no more cabs about, Elliott grudgingly agreed to the plan. So they followed Garrity as he led his hack horse and cab up Salter Street and over to a hitching post in front of the Lieutenant-Governor's residence.

"Maybe the Lieutenant-Governor would help me," mused Elliott, starting towards the squat vice-regal mansion.

The others took him gently by the elbows and turned him around to face the more sobering view of the graveyard on the opposite side of the street.

"It's not very nice, you know, being assassinated. Almost. Over and over."

"No," agreed Iarick. "Isn't."

"You know what Paisley would say, Yorrick?"

"Iarick," corrected Iarick.

"She'd say, 'Now is the winter of our discontent,'" declaimed Elliott, a little more boomingly than Paisley would have done on a public street.

"'cept it's Spring," corrected Garrity.

"Listen," commanded Elliott, which several passers-by were taking to heart, not to mention the guard at Government House. "Listen, 'Now is the winter of our discontent made glorious summer by this son of York.'"

"Iarick," corrected Iarick.

The guard relaxed, recognizing them as merely a troupe of actors, or some such harmless riff-raff.

A puzzled expression fought through the gaps in Iarrick's beard. "How you know I have son?"

"Hadn't we better be getting along," suggested Garrity. He was watching an alert constable proceeding up the street towards them at a saunter.

"True," said Elliott.

They dodged through the traffic on Pleasant Street to the gates of a cemetery filled with trees and old sandstone grave markers, across from Government House.

"Short cut," explained Garrity. He guided them around an immense brownstone triumphal arch with a lion standing on top, above the word *Sebastopol*. Elliott stopped to gaze up at the thing.

"What's this?" he asked Garrity.

"This? The Crimean War Memorial."

"Crimean? The war against Russia?" Elliott turned nervously to Iarick, in case the war was a sore point. "Well, we're all friends now, I suppose."

Iarick stroked his beard and looked up at the monument too. "Ah, Crimean. Was only boy when war ended. Wery embarrassing defeat. Still, took British Empire, French Empire, Ottoman Empire, and Piedmont to beat Russia."

"Piedmont?" asked Elliott. He'd never heard of an empire named Piedmont. He resorted to Garrity again, who seemed well versed in Crimean history, but the cabby just shrugged. "Did a lot of men from Halifax die in the war?"

This Garrity did know. "These two did." He pointed out the names on the two legs of the arch: Welsford on the left, and Parker on the right.

Staring up at the memorial was making Elliott's head spin, so he stretched out an arm to steady himself against a tombstone. It had been a truly tiring day. Luckily, he spotted a convenient table-like slab nearby, supported on little pillars. He staggered over to it and lay down on the cool stone. Closing his eyes had little effect on the curiously unpleasant impression of spinning. It was as if the world had grown suddenly fed up with people ignoring the fact that it spins at a thousand miles per hour, and decided to make the whirling more obvious. Elliott gripped the edge of the slab.

"They've poisoned me," mumbled Elliott. "The assassins... the oysters."

Starko and Garrity had wandered over to investigate Elliott's demise atop the gravestone, where he was trailing one arm into the grass and wearing a rather stricken look on his battered face. Garrity removed his derby and looked mournfully down at Elliott. On the other side, Starko likewise took off his cap.

It was at this point that a white-headed man in his sixties wearing a clerical collar puffed up to the grim tableau, carrying a trowel. He perceived Elliott's body with distress and began babbling.

"Dear me," he said, "has there been an accident? I was just planting a rhododendron by General Ross' resting place. Mr Alexander Graham Bell was most interested in the General when he was here last week. He burnt Washington, you know, in the War of 1812. The General, I mean, not Bell. Bell *lives* in Washington. At least, when he is not in Cape Breton. Then I noticed you here. My! he looks terrible! Was he run down by a tram, or an omnibus? Such hazardous conveyances. I keep writing to the council about them, but they never listen."

Through a crack between his eyelashes, Elliott could see Garrity shaking his head sadly. "Poor boy," the cabby said. "So young. He was just going to attend an improving lecture, when…"

Elliott's eyes popped open. He sprang up — miraculously recovered — and almost bowled over the astounded reverend gentleman, who dropped his trowel in his astonishment. "Late!" said Elliott, and sprinted for the far side of the cemetery, pursued by Garrity and Starko.

A little way uphill, outside the court house, Elliott allowed Garrity to catch up, sensing dimly that he needed the cabby to show him which way to go. The three of them proceeded to Dalhousie, where they were able to seat themselves in the auditorium only a few minutes after the commencement of the lecture which, to the mystification of both Starko and Garrity, was entitled "Clairvoyance as the Intuitive Apprehension of Multiple Etheric Probabilities."

"That's Dr Rafe Maddox at the podium," Elliott whispered to Garrity, seated on his right. Dark haired, dark suited, and dark complexioned, Maddox almost disappeared into the shadows. "He's one of the founders of the Etheric Explorers Club. I'm a member myself."

Elliott made no effort to explain anything to Starko, as the Russian had been looking drowsy since before they were even seated. He tried to concentrate on Maddox's lecture, but after a quarter of an hour Starko, sedated by a colossal meal of oysters, began snoring intermittently, bringing disapproving glares from the learnéd citizenry of Halifax. Elliott was forced to elbow Starko occasionally in the ribs, or at least where he guessed ribs lay hidden beneath the Russian's mammoth coat. Starko snorted and muttered.

Following Dr Maddox's concluding remarks, and the applause, there were a few questions from the audience before Maddox produced a paper that he consulted in the light of the podium.

"It has been our pleasure," Maddox said, "at the Etheric Explorer's Club, to welcome a number of new members from the Dominion of Canada in recent years. Now I realize Canada is a *somewhat* large land" — he paused for a titter of laughter from the audience — "but I wonder if any of the Canadian membership has been able to join us tonight...Mrs. Henry? Ah, there you are. Good of you to come. The Honourable Mr Whibberley? Good evening, sir. Miss Hayward? Miss Claudia Hayward? No, of course, she was unable to attend. Dr Elliott Graven?"

An uncanny sensation stole over Elliott, rather as if he'd been petrified while somehow retaining the ability to sweat. It suddenly came back to him in a mortifying flash. He'd been reading a copy of the *Proceedings of the Etheric Explorers Club* that Paisley had sent him. She'd gotten it from her aunt. After poring over the bizarre and fascinating studies of inexplicable phenomena, he'd come to a notice at the back, inviting applications from prospective members, particularly those who had some acquaintance with unnatural occurrences. Elliott had written up a brief account of his experiences in Spohrville, but at the last minute had gotten cold feet. After all, they wouldn't accept a mere boy in such a club, would they? It seemed harmless enough at the time to grant himself an academic title. Who would mind? And it wasn't as if he was likely to be travelling to the club quarters in London any time soon. But now...

"Dr Graven, are you present?" Maddox asked again.

In panic, Elliott looked to Garrity for help, but the cabby was barely controlling his sniggering. There was nothing for it then — Elliott prodded Starko into consciousness.

"Quick! Say you're me!" he whispered in Starko's ear.

Instantly the huge Russian shot to his feet, eyes blazing. "I am me!" he shouted, to the terror of several adjacent ranks of the audience. An elderly woman seated immediately behind him wailed briefly and feebly before being calmed by her companion.

"He!" Elliott corrected, whispering a little more urgently now that the Russian was standing up.

Starko surveyed the audience menacingly, daring any who were bold enough to contradict him, and nodded. "He is me," he declared, in the sort of grave tone one might use to inform the Tsar of the unexpected arrival of a million armed Frenchmen in the suburbs of Moscow. As an afterthought, Starko pointed helpfully at Elliott, who cringed lower in his seat. On the other side, Garrity sounded as if he was choking. But it was too late to turn back now. Elliott frantically tried one last time to drive the proper line into

Starko's addled brain.

"Elliott... Graven," he prompted.

Starko was looking distinctly confused now that he was fully awake, with a hundred gimlet eyes skewering him like Saint Sebastian.

"A lot given...?" hazarded Starko, now as thoroughly at sea as when his ship was in full trim.

Then, without warning, inspiration struck the Russian. He beamed at the onlookers and addressed them with more confidence. "Excuse me," he said. "I am hard to be hearing." He tapped his head a few times somewhere in the vicinity of his ear. At the podium, Maddox pursed his lips thoughtfully and went on to the next name on his list. Elliott sank as low in his seat as he could possibly go.

A NIGHT AT the Ivanhoe did little to improve the state of Elliott's mind or body. By the time he was aboard another train heading east to Cape Breton, burdened by a sense of universal humiliation and by Starko's samovar, Elliott was simply praying for a few hours of peace to sleep off his headache. And all of the other aches. No bombs. No murderers. No friendly Russians. Rest was looking like hard work, though. Trains, and the world in general, were making him nervous. It remained to be seen whether hired killers or dying of embarrassment was to be the greatest danger on this leg of the trip.

After checking his baggage at the station, Elliott thought he'd caught a glimpse of the lecturer, Dr Maddox, so at the last minute he snapped up a copy of *The Morning Chronicle* to hide behind. His bruises had grown an even ghastlier motley of blues and purples, so hiding would also be an act of mercy to the feelings of his fellow passengers; he didn't want any of the frail-hearted to faint away at the sight of him. Apart from anything else, he was in no condition to apply first aid.

No doubt it was the lively palette of his face that drew his fellow travellers' attentions in the section he'd been forced to share, there being no convenient corners in the packed carriage to slink away to.

"My word," said the woman, somewhere in her fifties, sitting opposite Elliott. He hadn't been quick enough in raising his newspaper. "Have you suffered an accident?"

The man with the curling moustache and golden pince-nez on Elliott's left looked up sleepily from his *Evening Herald* and started violently at the sight of Elliott's face. He ducked back into yesterday's news.

"Spot of trouble on the Halifax Express, Ma'am," explained Elliott. Generally, he found that people were happy to get an explanation. Whether or not it made sense rarely mattered.

"You *must* be careful, young man," the lady advised. "There are some *strange* characters about Halifax."

"Yes?" Elliott relaxed slightly, now the conversation was drifting safely away towards the city.

"Yes, indeed. Why, only last evening I was attending a *respectable* lecture, when a huge, barbarous-looking villain stood and rambled like a madman. He called himself... let me see... Dr Elliott Craven. Though if he was a *Doctor*, I'll spread a tube of crimson lake on my toast and have it for breakfast. He was more like an *anarchist*."

"So you must be..." Elliott began, about to say "interested in the Etheric Explorers Club", only stopping himself at the last second. It wouldn't do to let on that he'd been at the lecture too. 'A painter' occurred to him as a possible substitute ending for the question. The question was moot, however, as the lady grew weary of waiting for Elliott's cogitations to reach a conclusion.

"Mrs Anna Leonowens. I am organizing the new Victoria School of Arts."

Too late, Elliott realized he would be expected to introduce himself, now. His mind went blank. In its dark, aching recesses, only ridiculous false names appeared. Nemo Jimmerson. No. Montagu.... Van Buren. No, that would be as bad as using his real name. Desperately, he smiled and scanned the *Chronicle*. The smile seemed to worry Mrs Leonowens.

His eye alighted on 'William Fielding'. That sounded like a real name. Of course, it probably was. It was in the paper. Wait. No. Impersonating the premier might only make matters worse. Especially as Fielding wasn't very popular at the moment, having failed to fulfil his election promise of seceding from the country.

Elliott sweated a little under the pressure of Mrs Leonowen's expectant gaze.

"Ah! Speaking of anarchists, it says here that one was found on the railway line near Dorchester."

"Indeed?"

"Yes," he continued, "it says here the fellow was planning to blow up the prison."

Mrs Leonowens shook her head in disapproval of this outrage. "Shocking. And such a fine, new, Gothic-style penitentiary. And so necessary for the Elliott Cravenses of this world."

He was so relieved to duck the issue of his name that he couldn't stop himself. It was like jumping out of the path of a locomotive, only to notice too late that it was a jump off a cliff. Touched by poor Mrs Leonowens' concern for Her Majesty's latest contribution to the art of prison architecture, he felt compelled to reassure her.

"Not to worry. He was really trying to assassinate me, not explode the prison."

Mrs Leonowens turned her eyes incredulously heavenward, or towards Sniggler in the overhead luggage rack.

"Assassinate him!" she exclaimed.

The man in the next seat crushed his paper in surprise, then shook his head gloomily at Elliott, apparently under the impression that the lady was addressing him rather than the Powers Above.

"By Jove," he said, in an unusual accent.

"Assassinate!" Mrs Leonowens repeated, apparently enjoying the opportunity to employ a word from beyond the bounds of her everyday vocabulary. "Oh, these young boys and their wild imaginations!"

Elliott frowned. Finding that too painful, he tried to force disapproval into his blank glare at Mrs Leonowens. Instead of being relieved at having the matter laughed off, Elliott actually found it a trifle offensive that his horrifying brushes with death were being dismissed so casually by grey-haired old ladies, however venerable.

"No doubt," said the woman, "it was some rough and tumble play that gave you those bruises. When His Majesty king Rama V of Siam was a boy, I remember he came to me for his lessons one day quite disarrayed after a boyish tussle of some sort."

King of Siam? Elliott hadn't previously set the woman down as a lunatic, but surely this was some type of maniac confabulation. He elbowed the quiet gentleman, who started again as if he could never quite get used to Elliott's looks.

"King of Siam!" exclaimed Elliott. "These ladies of a *certain age* and their imaginations! What will they invent next? I blame novels. They inflame the brain."

For the remainder of the trip, Elliott sensed a certain coldness emanating from the direction of Mrs Leonowens. He read the paper very thoroughly.

AT IONA THEY reached the end of the railway line, with antlike navvies in the distance still laying rails for future trains. Most of the remaining passengers transferred to the *Blue Hill*, a steamship that bore them across the Bras d'Or Lakes to their final destinations. Elliott was relieved to find that none of them looked particularly murderous. He didn't feel up to life and death struggle, not just at the moment. Not only was his cranium throbbing, but hours on rocking trains and now this swaying boat were not helping his nausea. He couldn't be too careful, though. At least Elliott was spared Mrs Leonowen's society, as she had perched herself on a seat in the cabin while Elliott paced about the deck in the bracing breeze. The cold air was, if not filling him with a salubrious sense of well-being, at least making him feel slightly less violently awful.

With a mere few miles to go before setting foot safely on the soil of harmless, remote Baddeck, with its promise of a long-awaited reunion with Paisley, Elliott could at last relax a bit, and survey with his spyglass the wooded hills that ringed the briny lake. Perhaps not the best pass-time; the jiggling, inverted landscape seemed to be making his head and stomach spin faster, in opposite directions. Ahead, a small island bearing a lighthouse guarded the lakeside of the town. Rather like... But no. He lowered the telescope. Lots of towns must have lighthouses, on islands. Just a coincidence. Baddeck wouldn't be anything like Spohrville. Paisley would have said something. It would be nice. Quiet. Restful. That's what he needed. Rest. Paisley would understand. Not like Uncle Frank. It had been hard enough getting past the doorman at the Halifax Club the previous night, where Elliott had been invited by his uncle for a late supper. The doorman had seemed to think Elliott was an accident victim who'd stumbled in off the street. Possibly because he'd stumbled on his way up the steps.

"Councillor Westbrook's table," Elliott told him. "I'm expected."

He was passed to another club servant, who led Elliott through the main dining room, past a table of heavily bewhiskered city patriarchs. The men laid aside their cigars and conversation to goggle at Elliott as he went by.

"Don't you know it's vulgar to stare?" growled Elliott in passing.

At his uncle's table, Elliott's relation stared as well.

"Had a bit of trouble on the train," explained Elliott.

"Did you? You know, that was the Mayor and the Executive Council that you just snapped at."

"Really?" said Elliott. He turned in his chair for another look at the men. Then, facing his uncle once more, "No excuse for them having no manners, then," he added, loudly enough to carry across the dining room.

"Yes, well *I at least* have to work with them," Uncle Frank said through gritted teeth, "so if you wouldn't mind showing a little common courtesy, I would be most grateful."

Naturally enough, when a semblance of normality had been restored to the club, Uncle Frank's mind came around to his sister, Elliott's mother.

"Extraordinary business, Jessica turning up last year in Spohrville, of all places. All those tales of sleepwalkers, slave labour in a mine, piracy, and that fellow, Strange. Absurd as anything I've ever heard. Like some lurid

Gothic novel. I wouldn't have credited them with so much imagination in an out-of-the-way spot like Spohrville..."

"Oh no, all fanciful tales," agreed Elliott. "All those scores of unexplained graves? Just a prank. And the disappeared ship? The mountain of silver bars, and the town suffering antimony poisoning? All talk and tittle-tattle. This," Elliott added, indicating his black eye and swollen nose, now dripping slightly with blood, and requiring the use of his napkin, "This is simply a day-dream of yours, Uncle. No-one tried to beat me unconscious and throw me off a train. And certainly no-one tried to blow up the Halifax Express with dynamite. What a preposterous notion, eh?" Elliott noticed that the dining room had fallen strangely silent again.

His uncle winced. In an angry whisper, "I suppose you have evidence of this wild tale?"

"Ask Thompson, if you don't believe your own nephew."

"Thompson?"

"The Minister of Justice for the Dominion? Perhaps you've heard of him."

No, IT HAD not been a very successful dinner. But he'd soon be in Baddeck. And Paisley would believe him. She was from Spohrville, after all.

"Elliott Graven?" said an English voice.

Elliott span around, startled out of his holiday reverie.

"Weren't you at my lecture last night?" asked Dr Maddox.

"I...," Elliott began. Just in time, he lurched to the railing to be sick.

"I'm sorry, sir," he told Maddox, when he was finished. "Not quite myself today."

"Or last night, it seems."

Elliott blushed, but felt too ill to care.

"There was a bit of a muddle with names, I'm afraid. I'd be most grateful, sir, if we could just pretend yesterday never happened."

Maddox smiled faintly, cocking an eyebrow. "I've had a few yesterdays of that sort. Very well. Dr Rafe Maddox," he said, offering a hand.

"Er, Elliott Graven. Just... Elliott Graven," said Elliott, pulling back his own hand just in time, as he remembered it was holding the handkerchief that he'd been wiping his mouth with. Maddox nodded instead.

"I would be interested, Graven, in hearing more about your experiences in, what was it? Spohrville?"

"Spohrville. Yes, sir. I was just thinking about it, actually. I was looking at that lighthouse on the island," said Elliott, using his spyglass again, "and thinking how it reminded me of the place. Only coincidence, of course," he added quickly, with a slightly forced laugh. He scanned the hilly, wooded peninsula passing nearby on their right. But really, there were hardly any similarities. Something blurred past the telescope. Elliott swung it back to see what.

"I'm told Baddeck is a simple, peaceful place," said Maddox.

"I..." Elliott fiddled with the spyglass, trying to focus. There was a man on the shore. Sitting on a rock, eating... a sandwich. With no clothes on.

"I... oh Lord..." said Elliott. Another weird little town.

Chapter Six
KNIGHTS OF THE ELECTRIC FISH

PAISLEY WAS RECLINING in the front room on the chaise longue, with a cup of tea in one hand and a massive bouquet of flowers in the other, her bandage-swaddled leg resting on a cushion, when the distant knock sounded. Aunt Claudia broke off her interrogation of von Hasselberg concerning the minutiae of submarine boat construction and operation and glanced towards the door.

"That will be one of our distinguished guests arriving," she said.

The handsome Burggraf von Hasselberg had been valiantly trying to insert one of his fingers into the Lilliputian handle of his tea cup for some time. "Ah," he said, before returning the cup to its saucer on the end table, and his sympathetic gaze to Paisley. At least *someone* was being sympathetic.

"Assuming that it is not another of your father's telegrams, Paisley." Aunt Claudia sniffed. "I do hope you will not be monopolizing the telegraph and the furniture for much longer. As you know, I am expecting a number of visitors in the coming days. Some of them may wish to be seated, or to maintain contact with the outside world."

"I *must* convalesce, Aunt Claudia. I hope to be on the mend soon." Paisley was also hoping to avoid, for as long as possible, being Shanghai'd into service as her aunt's propagandist or dress-maker's dummy. Even being an invalid made for a better holiday than that.

Aunt Claudia sipped her tea. "Stuff and nonsense. You know quite well, Paisley, that only an hour ago your were dashing up and down the stairs two at a time trying to find that bit of ribbon for your hair."

"I must have been giddy from the pain," said Paisley. She reached up and patted the ribbon guiltily, smiling at Hasselberg, who was following the conversation with the polite, uncomprehending expression of someone watching a tennis match under the impression that it was actually cricket. "The doctor said I was *most* lucky. An inch to the left and the bullet would have shattered the bone, necessitating an *amputation*."

"*Himmel verbieten!*" said Hasselberg, going suddenly pale before mastering his emotion. However, the appearance of the maid at the door forestalled any further expressions of distress.

"Master Elliott Graven," she announced, followed presently by Elliott.

Elliott looked a bit... odd. *Frumpled* was the only word for a tweed suit in that state. And his face...

Aunt Claudia's cup halted half-way to her mouth. She squinted at Elliott.

"Perhaps Master Graven would like to wash up before tea?" she suggested.

Elliott sighed. "It isn't dirt, Miss Hayward. They're bruises."

"Oh dear. As accident-prone as Paisley."

"Elliott!" exclaimed Paisley.

Seeming to take in Paisley's elevated leg for the first time, he rushed over to her couch. "What happened!" they both said together.

"Strange again," explained Elliott. "His assassins. I nearly died. Twice. Even more, if you count dying of shame. You got my telegram, to be careful? Too late," he decided, looking at the bandages.

"I was shot," said Paisley. She slid her leg to the floor to allow Elliott to drop onto the couch. He was looking long overdue for a collapse. He examined her tightly-wrapped leg with apparent professional approval, then noticed von Hasselberg for the first time.

"Then this is your doctor?"

"No, no," corrected Paisley. "He's the one who shot me."

"What!" Elliott shot to his feet.

"It's all right," said Paisley, waving Elliott back onto the couch. "It was only an accident. "You're not an assassin, are you, Burggraf von Hasselberg?"

"Vot is assassin, please?" asked Hasselberg.

"It's someone," said Elliott, glaring rather unfairly at Hasselberg, "whose occupation is killing people."

"*Einer Meuchelmörder!* No, vot an extraordinary thought."

Elliott continued glaring. "Not connected in any way to the Wellborn Trust, then, are you? Or an Oswald Slack, alias Professor Strange?"

Aunt Claudia raised an eyebrow.

Hasselberg blinked in astonishment. "I am merely a tourist. *Ja.* Seeing your lovely country. Very nice," said Hasselberg, nodding approvingly at a lampshade.

Paisley smiled at Elliott. It was good to have that settled. It would be beastly having the summer spoilt with a lot of conspiracy theories, espe-cially just as it was becoming *interesting*.

"Nothing ever happens here, does it, Aunt Claudia?"

"Not generally, Paisley, no. It is possible that this season may be live-lier than usual." Aunt Claudia sipped her tea. "The by-election, you know."

"Burggraf von Hasselberg brought his submarine vessel," Paisley told Elliott.

His expression suggested that he was trying to count backwards from a thousand in thirteens.

"He... *what?*" Elliott said at last.

"Brought his submarine vessel." She waggled her hand though the air to illustrate undersea travel.

Elliott wilted back into the couch. "I only wanted a holiday. And to..." he turned, looking pitifully at Paisley for a moment before staring blankly into the distance again.

"... to have a holiday. Instead, it's been nothing but murderers, and bearded madmen, and," he added, glaring again at Hasselberg, "... subma-rine ships."

Paisley pursed her lips amid the now conspicuous ticking of the man-tle clock. Clearly travel hadn't agreed with Elliott. This gloominess wasn't like him at all. A submarine boat should have been just the sort of thing to buck him up a bit. Or perhaps he didn't believe there really *was* a submarine boat? It wasn't, after all, the sort of boat that one normally found people pot-tering about in on their summer holidays.

"Adelmo is a shipping magnate," explained Paisley. "Heir to one of the biggest shipyards in Kiel."

"The Hasselbergwerke," said Adelmo. "*The* largest, in fact, it is."

Elliott gulped down his tea, and poured himself another cupful with the air of an apothecary doling out a dose for a desperate case. He searched in vain for a spoon. The fact that everyone was stirring tea with a butter knife was doing nothing to alleviate Elliott's apparent disorientation. Adelmo was even stirring his ostentatiously, as though he'd mastered some revered lo-cal custom.

"And he's taking me to see the submarine boat after tea," continued Paisley. "He's been so kind about shooting me, and all." Paisley paused to sniff her bouquet. "We're going to travel in his carriage, which moves with-out horses."

"My motorwagon," corrected Adelmo.

Paisley grinned. "That's right, his *motorwagon*. Adelmo has all sorts of interesting things."

"Does he," said Elliott, not sounding as though he really wanted Paisley to expand upon the issue. He muttered something under his breath that sounded like "Adelmo", and raised a hand to his cheek. "I think one of my teeth is loose."

"Oh, you'll be fine," Paisley assured him, adding to Adelmo, "Elliott is always worried about medical things. It comes from being a doctor's son, I suppose."

"Ah," said Adelmo. "Fortunate, that you know a physician. They seem very dangerous, the trains here. I always am refreshed after having rail journeys on German trains. Very comfortable, trains in Germany." Adelmo regarded Elliott for a moment. "You do not appear to have been very comfortable."

"You seem to have gotten a scratch yourself," said Elliott, gesturing to the mark on Adelmo's left cheek.

"That's Adelmo's duelling scar," explained Paisley. "They're very fashionable in Germany."

"Unfortunately," said Elliott, "duelling is considered a crime in this country. But as for my trip, no. I found train travel... not altogether satisfactory. Though the flux of blood through my nose seems to have helped my allergies."

Now that he mentioned it, Elliott did sound as if he had a cold. More so than usual. "Perhaps it would cheer you up to come see the submarine boat with Adelmo and me?"

Elliott wrestled silently with this simple proposition for a considerable time before destiny, or practicalities, or Adelmo, intervened.

"The motorwagon," said Adelmo, "can seat at most two persons."

Elliott nodded, grimly.

"More tea, anyone?" asked Aunt Claudia.

IT WAS JUST as well that there was no room for him in the motorwagon, for Elliott was not really up to an outing. There was no room for a chaperone, either, for that matter. Paisley had asked Aunt Claudia for one, albeit not very enthusiastically. Aunt Claudia had merely cocked an eyebrow and dismissed the idea.

"Are you not a rational creature, Paisley, as capable as any man of swaying the fates of nations?"

Always thinking about politics, was Aunt Claudia. A radical, too, and for the first time since the start of her visit, Paisley thanked Providence for the fact. At the door, she poked through the umbrella stand and pulled out the *Peabody's Patented Parasol* belonging to her aunt. Then, on second thoughts, she stuffed it back into the wicker urn. If she limped, she could always lean on Adelmo's arm for support. A straw hat would do to keep off the sun. She slipped her dark glasses onto her nose.

At the back of the carriage, or *motorwagon*, Adelmo was pouring something that smelt like kerosene into a brass drum. When she looked back, up at Elliott's window, Paisley saw him glowering down, his face not only a mask of bruises but also of awe. Or possibly dismay. She waved cheerfully to him, as did Adelmo, when he'd emptied the fuel tin. Definitely dismay. It was unlike Elliott to be so suspicious of machines. And so generally baleful.

"Can we be back by six?" she asked Adelmo. "I have to attend dinner. You're welcome to dine here, of course," she added quickly.

Adelmo wiped his hands on a rag. "Six? *Ja*, certainly! No longer are we confined to the pace of beasts of burden, not with the Benz Motorwagon. Regrettably, I have a previous engagement, or I would be pleased with you to dine." He stooped to insert a crank into the engine that sat at the back of the motorwagon. He cranked manfully. The engine stuttered and coughed clouds of blue smoke before settling into a roar and chatter like an angry clockwork toy about to explode. Then he assisted Paisley onto the raised bench at the front of the little carriage.

"It all looks rather complicated," said Paisley. It was her first time riding on an oversized, deafening, spoke-wheeled tricycle. Adelmo joined her on the bench.

"Oh, no, you see? One simply releases this lever, and this one here, and depresses the clutch, advances the gear lever, adjusts the choke and throttle, and turns this," he said, indicating a knob on a post in front them. "This steers the machine," Adelmo explained, as Paisley assumed a vice-like grip on the bench against the lurches and shudders of the motorwagon. Elliott, Paisley noticed, now had his mottled face pressed firmly against the window pane.

"Are these machines very popular in Sleswick-Holsatia?"

"This is one of the first. My friend, Herr Benz, gave me this. You are not frightened?"

"Pardon me?" asked Paisley, taking her fingers out of her ears.

"Not frightened?"

"No, it's lovely." It was a new invention. One had to expect a certain amount of smoke, and din, and peril, Paisley decided, watching the spokes blurring around a few inches from her whitening knuckles.

Leaving a trail of stares, spooked horses, hysterical dogs, and oily smoke as they went, they proceeded noisily up Baddeck Bay for a mile or so to a clover-covered meadow by the shore, dotted with waving buttercups as glossy as fresh yellow paint. When the engine juddered to stop, they sat in the quiet sea breeze listening to their ears ringing, and to the ticking of the hot motor.

"Well?" announced Adelmo, with a proud smile. "Zere she is."

Paisley removed her sunglasses to examine the bay. She wasn't sure what submarine craft looked like exactly, but most probably not like the pair of ducks that were paddling past.

"Is it...?" Paisley looked harder. Adelmo was beaming. There must be something there. That thing? Out from the shore, a couple of tiny red flags were flapping, a short distance apart. A small grey box was barely visible between them at wave level.

"That is only the hatch," said Adelmo.

"Ah. Of course. How big *is* it?"

"Twenty metres. That is nearly twenty-two of your yards. Six men can travel comfortably."

"As comfortable as a German train?"

Adelmo considered. "Perhaps not so comfortable as that."

"Would you... take me for a ride in it, too, sometime?"

"Anything for you, my dear Miss DeLoup."

"It must have a name, mustn't it? All ships have names."

"*Ja*, she is the *Paradoxo*," said Adelmo proudly.

"What a curious name." It sounded like something out of Jules Verne, or a clever allusion to the paradoxical nature of a ship that travelled beneath the waves.

"I named her," explained Adelmo, "after a species of electric catfish. The *Paradoxoglanis*."

"Oh." Perhaps some names were better if one didn't know where they came from. "Motorwagons... submarine boats... it must be an exciting time in Germany, for inventors." Not for the first time she cast an admiring eye over Adelmo, who resembled some noble archangel come to proclaim the new age of machines. *O brave new world, That has such people in't!*

"Indeed, Miss DeLoup. The Empire is young. Only nearly so old as yourself. But, if you will permit me to say, as thrilling and full of promise as yourself."

Paisley had never been compared to an empire before. It was slightly confusing, though not at all disagreeable. She hoped Adelmo would expand on the subject, wherever that line of discussion might lead. If she were the German Empire, it might be natural to refer to her head, metaphorically, as the Emperor, even if she didn't entirely fancy the comparison. If she recalled correctly, the Kaiser looked something like a dyspeptic Basset hound, with huge drooping whiskers like a pair of furry jowls. No, much better if her head were like... like the imperial crown. Jewels were nicer than jowls.

Reluctantly pulling his eyes off Paisley, Adelmo's face became suffused with concern. He strode away a few paces, towards the shore, and scanned the waters with a fist held pensively to his lips. Paisley wondered if perhaps he had forgotten to anchor the submarine vessel. Adelmo glanced back at her, smiled, then frowned, and looked back across the lake. He paced, running a distracted hand though his fair hair, looked to her again, and marched over, seeming to have reached a decision about something. He took her hands, and faced her.

"Miss DeLoup," he said.

"Please. Paisley."

"Paisley. I…"

Clearly something was on his mind. Something important. *Good Heavens… He's going to propose to me…* Paisley held her breath.

"Paisley, may I… trust you?"

Paisley blinked in surprise. And a little disappointment. *Trust?*

Adelmo shook his head. "Of course I may. How could I imagine one so pure capable of violating a trust?"

Still puzzled, Paisley allowed him to lead her to a slight grassy rise in the field where he removed his jacket and threw it down, beckoning Paisley to be seated on it. Despite being accustomed to staining herself with ink and mud on a daily basis, Paisley still appreciated the gesture. Once they had both sat, Adelmo collected his thoughts and began to explain.

"You have," he said, "perhaps heard of my country's interest in East Africa?" Paisley hadn't, but nodded vaguely to avoid interrupting. "Now we are an empire, many in Germany wish to have overseas colonies, as you British have. And the French, the Dutch, and the other nations — the Russians, with their vast East, and the Americans conquering their West. East Africa is yet open for colonization. I have myself invested in the *Deutsch-Ostafrikanische Gesellschaft* — the German East Africa Company. Also, I am a member of the *Gesellschaft für Deutsche Kolonisation*, a society that aims to encourage German colonization…"

So *that* was it. Marriage, and then moving out to the colonies. Giraffes, and… and things. Pith helmets. And so on. Paisley's heart beat faster at the prospect of an adventure on a faraway continent with… her husband. But perhaps it would have to be postponed until she was a little older?

"…you are very pink, Miss, ah, Paisley. Are you sure you are not too hot here in the sun?"

"No, no, please continue."

"Good. As I was saying, our two peoples are nearly one. The Saxon and the Anglo-Saxon. Your Queen's daughter, the Princess Royal Victoria, has married our Crown Prince Frederick. Soon they will rule Germany together. Of course, we all pray that His Imperial and Royal Majesty Wilhelm I may reign for years to come, but he is already ninety years of age. It will not be long before Frederick and Victoria are Emperor and Empress. His Royal Highness, Prince Frederick, is a great admirer of Britain's liberal constitution, and of democracy. There will be many changes when Prince Frederick assumes the throne, changes for the better for Germany. Do you know what His Highness said? He said, 'I do not like war... if I should reign, I would never make it.' A man of peace. So, you see, our two peoples are like cousins! There is no need for us to ever be concerned about conflict, or war. We must work together! It is only natural that we work together."

In fact, Paisley had one or two cousins with whom she could imagine going to war. Regardless of that, there was a good deal of sense in what Adelmo said, even if it contained more political rationale than was entirely necessary for a marriage proposal. They weren't royalty, after all.

"It will all be announced in but a few days, but please, tell no-one until then."

What would be announced? The reading of the banns? Paisley adjusted her glasses.

"But you haven't told *me* yet," she pointed out.

"Ah," said Adelmo. "You are correct." He sprang to his feet, looking about ready to burst with suppressed energy. "It is a new age of co-operation, Paisley. Britain. Germany. American philanthropists. Ve have been vorking in harmony for von purpose..." he said, losing control of his accent in his excitement. "... *to end slavery*."

"But wasn't slavery more or less ended, when the civil war in the United States was won by the abolitionist states?" And didn't this sound almost entirely unlike a betrothal?

"Yes, yes, *in America*, it ended. But in Africa, ze Arabs have long carried out a slave trade, in ze east. Vith Germany's new colonies, and ze help of Britain, ve vill end zis foul trade forever."

"With submarine ships?"

"Ja!" exclaimed Adelmo, aiming a finger and a wild grin at Paisley. He lowered the finger, perhaps realizing that it was impolite, but continued. "Vith American investment and patents, and my shipyard, and several innovations of British science, ve shall have a superior vessel, able to follow even small slave ships with stealth, and board or sink them. Ve shall silently cruise ze Indian Ocean from Arabia to Zanzibar, like... like knights of ze sea... like ze crusaders of old."

"You did remind me of a knight, when we first met." It was a noble vision, to be sure. Paisley could well imagine Adelmo's fair head emerging from the submarine boat into the hot African sun, to give some filthy gang of slave-merchants what-for, and then tow the erstwhile slaves home to safety. It did raise one question in her mind...

"Why on earth are you going to announce such a momentous thing in a tiny town in Cape Breton? Surely London, or Berlin, or somewhere would be more appropriate."

"Ah. You see, Dr Bell, the scientist, he acts as intermediary in the discussions here, and in America. He has many technical interests. He understands patent law, and is very concerned for the future of mankind. Also, it is very quiet here, without the newspapers, and the public watching."

Paisley leant back on her elbows in the sun, considering. It wasn't a proposal. Not yet. But it was certainly more interesting than her aunt's by-election.

Chapter Seven
ANOTHER DINNER WITH INTERRUPTIONS

THE SPECTACLE THAT Elliott's bedroom looking-glass offered should have been a rewarding one, considering the money he'd spent on it. Especially as the money hadn't exactly been his. A perfectly-tailored tail-coat with black silk lapels, immaculate white tie, starched wing-collar shirt, white gloves, and white waistcoat spanned by a gold watch-chain. Shoes — glossy black, two. Trousers, black, suspended from braces. Everything present and correct. Then there was the face. No matter how he looked at it, perched atop his spiffy collar that face still looked like an old russet apple that someone had spent the day kicking around the streets.

"I hope they're right about the clothes making the man," he told his reflexion, before picking up a ribbon-wrapped red box and heading downstairs to a dinner that he expected and hoped would be mercifully dull; the sort that was an hour or so of tranquil clinking, silverware against expensive china, with the only excitement being an occasional utensil that one couldn't remember a use for, and no greater demands than passing the pepper. His nerves weren't up for much else. Whirling as his mind was with dark thoughts of submarine craft, assassins, and haberdashery, Elliott hardly noticed the girl coming towards him up the stairs until they were about to collide. She stopped, apparently to admire his dinner-wear. Fair-haired, with purposefully-narrowed eyes, she looked a few years his senior.

"Um," said Elliott. He stepped aside to let her by.

She stayed rooted to her stair. "I'm Alison, sir," said the girl, in some flavour of British accent Elliott couldn't identify. "Lady Beauchamp's lady's maid." Wisely, under the circumstances, Alison offered her hand instead of curtsying. He shook it, though the way she was looking at him was making Elliott feel conspicuous enough to entertain second thoughts about dining. She was still scrutinizing him even after letting go of his

metacarpals and phalanges, and he couldn't make out whether he was providing an amusing, puzzling, pitiable, or satisfactory object for consideration. Several conflicting emotions seemed to be wrestling with Alison's
risorius, zygomaticus, and various other facial muscles. Elliott cleared his
throat, and tried not to think of anatomy.

"Ah, Alison. Do you think... I mean, do I look all right? I don't want to
put anyone off their dinner." Elliott laughed feebly, and touched his battered
face. "I could eat in my room."

"Honourable wounds are always decorous."

"Oh. Thank you. And, uh, would you know if Paisley... I mean, Miss
DeLoup... is back yet from... is back yet?"

"Yes, Master Graven. Miss DeLoup was in the library when I passed it
a moment ago."

He thanked Alison, thinking as he did that there was something a little odd about her. Continuing downward, he stole a quick glance over his
shoulder at the maid. She was looking back at him, too. He accelerated towards the library, avoiding the excited conversations welling out of the parlour from the other guests.

At the library door he halted for a last bit of fiddling with his collar. Submarine boats and motor carriages were all very well, Elliott reassured himself, but there was something in a snappy set of clothes, too. Re-
inspecting his face in the hall mirror, he found that, unfortunately, what was
in a snappy set of clothes was the same old decrepit Elliott. He checked that
the cuts on his stiff upper lip weren't bleeding, and sauntered into the library. *Honourable wounds*, he told himself.

As libraries went, it was a modest one. There were a couple of bay windows with seats to read on, a few chairs, a stuffed owl. Still, Miss Hayward
was only renting the house, so it wasn't a bad collection for a summer cottage. Paisley was reading in one of the wing chairs by a window.

"Good book?" asked Elliott.

Paisley lowered the volume she was reading and inclined her head.

"Yes, but what a bother to get it. I went to the local library as soon as I
arrived here to look for it, but they weren't very encouraging. There were
two women running the place. I asked one of them, a Miss Chamberlain.
She had pleasant, dim-witted eyes, like you might see on a deer, or a rab-
bit," said Paisley, acting out the gormless part with a silly face. "'Poe?'
said Miss Chamberlain. You would have thought I'd asked for a shrunken
head, the way her eyes got even wider. 'So gruesome,' she said. 'Wouldn't
you rather have a nice book about sewing, or... or... something morally
uplifting?' No, I told her. Poe. *The Murders in the Rue Morgue*. She started to sway. 'But that is more of a *boys'* book, dear. Perhaps...' No, thank

you. *The Murders in the Rue Morgue*, please, I told her. 'Oh dear. I think, I think I shall have to lie down a moment,' she said, and took her vapours home, mumbling 'gruesome... gruesome...'. So I tried the other woman, Miss Rivers. She, at least, looked awake. But she turned out to be the bossy sort who has her opinions and won't let mere facts stand in the way of them. '*Murdering Rumour*?' she barked, getting the title all wrong. 'No young people would read that. Too many long words. And it is not realistic. It is only trying to make a dull period of French history more interesting. And real Frenchmen are not as clever as that Mr Lupin,' she explained, getting Monsieur Dupin's name wrong also. 'It is only a watered-down copy of this new play I saw.' She went on about plays rather a lot. In fact, I don't think she ever mentioned books. Probably she doesn't read them. I suppose she prefers watching plays. You know, Elliott, I don't think either of them were proper librarians, *not at all*."

Elliott didn't think so either. They sounded more like a proper pair of pills to him. He took the chair facing Paisley's. "I'll confine myself to your aunt's library, if I can find anything without index cards."

"That's what I've done, at least since her books arrived with the rest of her things. But you know what Pope says: *How index-learning turns no student pale, Yet holds the eel of science by the tail.*"

"The Pope said that?"

"Not *the* Pope, *Alexander* Pope. Anyhow, I was able to find books at the public library even through their catalogue is a mess, so it shouldn't be too difficult here." She seemed to pluck her mind's eye from the iniquitous anti-librarians and noticed her present surroundings again.

"You're looking very formal," said Paisley.

"I just thought, you know. Dinner with all of these important people. I could change," he said, and started to rise.

"It's all right." She ran an appraising look over Elliott's sartorial splendour. "You look very... that is, it suits you. You may put the other gentlemen to shame, that's all."

Elliott began to relax.

"Of course," said Paisley, "were *Adelmo* dining with us, I'm sure he would be well dressed. He's planning to bring German culture to Africa, you know."

Elliott tried to imagine millions of Africans eating sausages and dancing polkas in lederhosen to tuba music. Then he tried not to.

"He's very dashing," said Paisley, "don't you think?"

"Hmm," muttered Elliott. "I'd need a lot of dashes to describe *him*."

Changing was a moot question in any case, as Miss Hayward's maid appeared in the doorway to announce the imminent serving of dinner.

Rising, Paisley asked, "What's that?" reminding Elliott of his box.

"It's for you," he said, passing it to her. Paisley sniffed the yellow ribbon and yanked on it, releasing the lid.

"Chocolates," said Paisley, popping one forthwith into her mouth.

"Liquorice cream chocolates," said Elliott, perhaps superfluously, now that Paisley was chewing one with the dreamy expression of a girl who, having just received a cheque, has, on closer inspection, discovered a few unexpected extra zeros on the end of the amount payable.

"Mmm," agreed Paisley, swallowing a little reluctantly. "I didn't know they made liquorice cream chocolates," she said, looking into the distance as though a mist had suddenly parted, revealing where Alph, the sacred river ran, through caverns measureless to man, down to a sunless sea.

"They're what you might call bespoke chocolates. I had them made specially. At a confectioners in Kingston called *Angelina Fortune*."

"They're *so* good. We had better go, though, or I'll spoil my appetite," said Paisley, eating another after flashing a long-canined smile that left Elliott a trifle giddy.

It had to be love. Unless it was concussion.

"Are you feeling unwell?" she asked. "You look flushed. You could skip dinner and rest."

Elliott felt his skull for cracks. "Perhaps I need some trepanning..." When Paisley failed to recognize the term, he described the process of drilling holes in the head to relieve excess pressure. She wasn't favourably disposed to the idea.

"I hope not. Your head has seen enough trouble as it is. We'd better go..."

They merged with the stream of chattering guests flowing from parlour to dining room. Elliott had hoped to get a few words of warning, or introduction, from Paisley before encountering them *en masse*. He nodded to Mr Thompson. At least Thompson had believed his story. Probably. Mrs Leonowens was almost certainly a lost cause as a social acquaintance.

His luck being what it was, when Paisley's aunt pointed out his seat to him, Elliott found that it was between Mrs Leonowens and a slender young woman with gold hair and a green satin gown. Mrs Leonowens glared at him just long enough for Elliott to feel her mentally selecting a chunk of India rubber and erasing him, pastel face and all, from her world. He turned, more optimistically, to the other woman, already seated to the left of Elliott's place.

"Good evening," he said.

The woman swivelled to squint at him. "Thank-you, but I do not require the services of a butler at this time."

Elliott, having gone so far as to plan on sitting down as his next move, was now reconsidering. "Excuse me?"

Paisley's aunt cruised past, in her ongoing sorting of the guests according to gender, or social status, or height, or however it was done. She paused to make introductions.

"This is Elliott Graven, Lady Beauchamp. He will be dining on your right."

Understanding dawned on Lady Beauchamp's clouded, if perfect, brow.

"But what a wonderful idea, my dear Claudia! Having your butler dine with us. You are so advanced in your thinking. I must tell the other Fabians. In fact, let us have Alison join us as well. She's fairly presentable. *Égalité, Fraternité*, and... whatever that other French thing is. *Livrée?*"

"I do not keep a butler, Lady Beauchamp," said Paisley's aunt.

Elliott, sandwiched between them, was wishing he had followed the wiser counsel of his own misery and stayed in his room. Lady Beauchamp now frowned.

"But then, whose butler is he? You don't mean to say that he simply wandered in?"

Miss Hayward leant over and spoke slowly and distinctly before going about her organizing. "He is a *guest*, Lady Beauchamp."

"I *am* sorry, sir," the lady told Elliott. "Do be seated. It was merely your clothing, you see. You were so well dressed, I naturally assumed you must be a servant." Once settled, a comforting satin-gloved hand fell lightly upon his arm. "I am gratified, sir, that *someone* is cognizant of the proprieties of civilised society. They dress so coarsely in the colonies, don't you think?"

Elliott smiled nervously, first at Lady's Beauchamp's beautifully haughty face, and then at Dr Maddox who, seated opposite in the same suit he'd been wearing on the boat that morning, was presumably included among the coarse colonials. Though he was from Kent, England. Perhaps Lady Beauchamp felt that everyone outside her immediate wardrobe was on the borders of barbarism. Not that it wasn't fetching. Elliott had never paid all that much attention to women's attire before, apart from noticing with disappointment the way in which girls' dresses grew longer and longer the older they got, the hemlines ceasing to lengthen about the same time the girls did; in formal gowns, they'd always looked to him like some sort of mermaid-like chimeras, with the top half human, and the bottom half a set of drapes. He had it on good authority (a medical text) that grown women did still have legs, somewhere. Lady Beauchamp, though, didn't resemble any drapes he'd ever seen. In green satin, with a wasp-thin waist, she was, well...

"From what part of the Empire do you hail, sir?" asked Lady Beauchamp.

"Where? From Ontario, Lady Beauchamp."

"Is that in our Indian possessions?" Apparently she took a personal interest in Imperial affairs. "I suppose you must be one of these fabulously wealthy Rajas we hear so much about?"

"Rajas?"

Raising a set of spectacles on a golden stick — a lorgnette — she inclined her head for a careful examination of Elliott's face. "Oh, I see now. That dusky colouring is not natural. Or even. Or becoming. My word. Even your eyes are different colours."

"The eyes are natural, Lady Beauchamp. It's called *heterochromia iridum.*"

Elliott reminded himself to be cautious in the future with his vocabulary. While Lady Beauchamp was all right, he did occasionally encounter people who were asinine enough to think that a lad his age shouldn't use such big words.

"My dear, your poor face! I expect you were being a *preux chevalier* to some damsel in distress, were you not?"

Elliott was by now losing his grip on Lady Beauchamp's conversation and wasn't sure what to make of this. Did she mean some maiden had punched him for making unwanted advances? "No, no," he assured her.

"So gallant. So modest, Lord Graven."

Elliott squirmed. He shook his head slightly at Dr Maddox, across the way, trying to convey his assurance that this new imposture was none of Elliott's doing, not at all like that business of pretending to be a certain *Doctor* Graven. He looked to Paisley. Yes, Paisley could explain it all away innocently.

Innocence, or a rather forced impersonation of it, was just what was fully occupying Paisley at that moment. One of her hands disappeared towards her lap. It went suddenly to her mouth bearing a chocolate. The chocolate disappeared. She chewed, innocently.

"Um," said Elliott, already too late to clear up anything. He noticed that Lady Beauchamp had extended a hand to him. He shook it. She blinked at him, and turned his palm upwards. She edged closer and peered through her lorgnette at it.

"I suppose, Lord Graven, that Claudia has told you of my abilities?"

"Not… not as such, no."

"I have learnt the secrets of palmistry, you know."

"I didn't. What does it, you know, foretell?"

Looking into his open hand, she drew one finger over it. "This line," she said, her face darkening, "is very bad."

"Is it?" Elliott waited expectantly. All he needed now was to hear that destiny was queued up with everyone else to have a kick at him. Not that he would have been surprised.

"It is," Lady Beauchamp assured him grimly. "It signifies that you have neglected to iron your gloves."

Elliott pulled them off and presented his hand again.

"Hmm," mused Lady Beauchamp. "Even worse." She traced her finger silkily over the lines. "I see great danger."

Danger? That sounded like yesterday's weather forecast to Elliott. "Are you sure it's not post-cognition? I've already had the great danger. I don't think danger gets much greater than what I went through yesterday."

Lady Beauchamp shrugged elegantly, and patted his hand. "It is not a precise art."

At this, Dr Maddox felt moved to join their tête-à-tête. "It could be, however. My colleagues and I hope to apply scientific analysis to such phenomena."

"I am sure, Dr Maddox," said Lady Beauchamp, "palmistry would not be of interest to you. My mediumistic talents, on the other hand..."

"You communicate with the spirits?" asked Elliott, who knew all about the phantasmagoric realm, having encountered it in Paisley's attic. "I suppose you use a spirit board."

"Oh, no. They come to me in a trance. That is to say, when *I* am in a trance. Not the spirits. I have no idea what happens to a spirit when it is in a trance. Perhaps the living communicate their secrets to it. Yes, my talent is confined to the trance state. Except for the spirit of my aunt. When communicating with Aunt Charlotte, I use the post."

"What," asked Elliott, " you mean you write a letter?"

"Indeed. The method is invariably effective. She nearly always writes back, often complaining that I have used insufficient postage. Spirit writing, I suppose. Some," said Lady Beauchamp, looking meaningfully up the table to where Paisley's aunt was now seated, watching the serving dishes arrive, "believe that Aunt Charlotte is yet among the living. But I assure you, Lord Graven, that had you ever read her correspondence, there would remain no doubt in your mind that such cannot be the case."

It was difficult to know how to respond to this latest intelligence of Lady Beauchamp's supernatural prowess. She was quite mad, of course, but she was turning out to be a harmlessly amusing dinner companion. Paisley was not entirely unaffected either; she was, by now, suppressing a smirk with such effort that her eyes were beginning to cross. Fortunately, Dr Maddox was more than willing to leap into any breaches in the conversation.

"Has your interest in the spirit realm been a long one, Lady Beauchamp?" he asked.

"Indeed, Dr Maddox. It is my faith in the transmigration of souls that has led me to what some consider an unconventional diet. One would hate to devour someone whom one had met socially."

Elliott's attention wandered to Lady Beauchamp's maid, who had arrived with the first dishes, as he pondered the meaning of this talk of transmigration. Perhaps it meant she was opposed to eating passenger pigeons? They migrated. Were famous for it, in fact. Just as well, if so — there weren't many left.

With the appearance of the first of the food, Paisley wrinkled her nose. Quite adorably, thought Elliott. He was drinking in the sight with such relish that he didn't at first notice the sour odour that had followed the maid into the dining room. Paisley lifted the lid of a china serving dish and found it full of steaming Brussels sprouts. They smelt remarkably repellent.

"Pickled, of course," said Lady Beauchamp.

Another tray contained asparagus, mercifully fresh. Merciful, too, was the ebb of conversation as everyone tucked in — some less enthusiastically than Lady Beauchamp — to the repast. Paisley and Elliott reached together for the butter dish, in a forlorn hope of making the sprouts edible, only to find it full of a mysteriously pulpy orange paste.

"Squash chutney," said Lady Beauchamp. "Very wholesome."

Then their glasses were being filled, and Elliott quickly stuck a hand over his, asking for water instead of the white wine — a departure from the menu serious enough that Lady Beauchamp had to lay down her cutlery to give her full attention to Elliott.

"Wine is made from vegetables, Lord Graven," she assured him.

"Thank you. I know."

Lady Beauchamp continued to regard him suspiciously. "You are not a Mahometan, are you, Lord Graven? Or," she continued, looking even more aghast, "a Baptist?"

"Merely temperance," said Elliott.

There was no way he would make an embarrassing spectacle of himself with alcohol again. Thank goodness Starko and the Irish cabby had stopped him before he had wandered into Government House to harangue the Lieutenant-Governor, or give him an impromptu performance of *King Lear*. That would have made the newspapers.

Any further question of Elliott's religious propensities was forestalled by Paisley's aunt guiding the general conversation towards the coming by-election, and other uplifting topics of social progress. Paisley, meanwhile, was surreptitiously resorting to her chocolate box with increasing frequency, a process Elliott followed mournfully through the steam from his Brussels sprouts. Seeing him watching her, Paisley's face gradually altered from blissful, to sympathetic, settling at last on a visage of devious cunning. Elliott watched, entranced, as she very slowly wriggled lower in her chair over the course of a minute or two. By the time the next course was served, she would be safe below the table cloth, beyond the reach of vegetarianism. Elliott was musing on joining her when something cracked excruciatingly into his kneecap. Reflexes came inconveniently to play and bashed his knee again, this time into the underside of the table, rattling the dinnerware. "Ow!" he shouted.

A sprout that Mrs Leonowens had been cleaving shot away into the crystal water pitcher and floated there, like a green eye in one of Professor Strange's horrible specimen bottles. All of the other eyes in the vicinity swivelled in Elliott's direction, while Paisley's slow decline halted as she stared at Elliott's facial contortions.

"Excuse me," said Elliott, forcing the words through gritted teeth. "Old injury. Acting up."

"Table rapping," said Lady Beauchamp helpfully, when the guests had grimly returned their attention to their respective vegetables, "is commonly held to be a method of spirit communication. In my experience, it is rarely genuine."

"What causes it then? Muscle spasms?" inquired Elliott. Something had just landed on his other knee, and he was hoping to keep Lady Beauchamp talking long enough to find out what.

"Charlatanry. Pure charlatanry. You would scarcely credit the chicanery perpetrated by some so-called mediums."

Elliott probed cautiously towards his knee. There was a box. The chocolate box. Paisley winked at him.

"Shocking," said Elliott. He pulled his napkin under the table and grabbed a chocolate with it. "Tell me, Lady Beauchamp, who are our other guests? I missed the introductions." He dabbed his lips with the napkin, popping the chocolate into his mouth as he did.

"I believe you know Miss DeLoup," she began.

"Mmm," said Elliott. Paisley snickered. They really were excellent chocolates.

"Next to her is Dr Maddox. Founder of the Etheric Explorers Club, are you not, Dr Maddox? And in passing, I must ask, is an Etheric Explorers Club one of these places one hears about where persons gather to inhale ether and act peculiar?"

"No, no," said Dr Maddox, "Though on one occasion Milford... but that's beside the point. No, the ether referred to in the name is not the anaesthetic fluid, but rather the etheric medium which permeates space and transmits a variety of..."

Lady Beauchamp carried on, tiring of the etheric realm. "To your own right is, of course, Mrs Leonowens. I believe she experienced brief celebrity some time ago as a result of her passing acquaintance with a heathen potentate, serving, if I recall rightly, as a governess, or tutor; one of the professions pursued by distressed gentlewomen."

This statement aroused Mrs Leonowens. "The king and I," she said, "were..."

"And opposite to Mrs Leonowens," continued Lady Beauchamp, "is Mrs Sowerby, the American philanthropist. Mrs Sowerby, what was the name of your charitable organization?"

The stocky woman on the other side of the table was conservatively dressed and looked to be in her forties or thereabouts. She finished her spear of asparagus before replying. "The Wellborn Trust, Lady Beauchamp."

Delicious as the chocolates were, Elliott regretted having taken another one. He choked. Coughing, he groped for his water glass and drank desperately. Paisley was just as alarmed. Professor Strange, in Sporhville, had been connected somehow to the Wellborn Trust. He'd mentioned it.

They mustn't show any special interest in her. Not yet.

"And, uh, the other guests?" asked Elliott, catching his breath again.

"Mr Thompson is a Minister of the Crown in the Dominion Parliament."

"And the bearded gentleman?" Elliott could only see him obliquely, but he looked somehow familiar.

"A neighbour of Claudia's. Makes electric speaking tubes, or something of that sort. Tolerably well dressed, though he doesn't hold a candle to you, Lord Graven."

She sipped her wine, giving Elliott a few seconds to get a better look at the gentleman. He *was* familiar. He was the man lunching in the nude whom Elliott had seen from the steamboat.

"I'm surprised he's wearing anything. The last time I saw him, he was picnicking in, um, *puris naturabilis*, on a wooded promontory hereabouts."

"My word," said Lady Beauchamp. She raised her lorgnette to study the bearded gentleman. "Doesn't have the figure for it, I would say. You might give Dr Bell the address of your tailor, Lord Graven, so that he is better supplied with excursion-wear for his picnics in the future."

"Bell? Is that Alexander Graham Bell?"

"I believe that is his name. He was discussing eugenics with Mrs Sowerby in the parlour, earlier. Apparently he believes that a deaf branch of the human race may form if the hard-of-hearing intermarry. He has some plans for a superior breed of sheep, also. One with more... well... attributes, shall we say."

Bell. So Alexander Graham Bell was the naked lunatic snacking in the woods.

"I wonder if he is related to Dr Bell, of Kingston," said Elliott, Dr Bell being a patent medicine quack who had vexed Elliott's father for years.

"Still," said Lady Beauchamp, "what an inspiration Claudia is, sitting down there at the low end of the table, with the politicians and tradesmen. So democratic."

"Inspiration?" asked Elliott. "Do you mean, she inspires these Fenians you belong to?"

"*Fabians*, Lord Graven."

Feeling that he was depriving Paisley of her chocolates, he started shifting the box towards her with his leg. He connected with her knee and nudged it to get her attention. She was obviously trying not to give any sign that anything was happening. He nudged her harder.

Suddenly Lady Beauchamp's eyes widened. She produced an ostrich feather fan from somewhere and waved it demurely, seeming overheated. She whispered to Elliott behind the fan.

"Not now, Lord Graven! The others... we must suppress our passions and comport ourselves with decorum!"

Fortune, always either coming or going with Elliott, delayed his comprehension of what this meant until Paisley's feet recovered the chocolate box. And intervened again with an altercation at the door.

"It is *my* mistress's house," Paisley's aunt's maid was complaining.

"The recipient is *my* mistress," retorted Alison.

The latter producing a convincing argument, or having hold of the object, she entered and curtsied, bearing an envelope.

"Telegram for you, Lady Beauchamp," said Alison. She looked surprised to see Elliott. Perhaps it was the way he was blushing.

"Do read it, would you Alison?" said Lady Beauchamp.

Alison shuffled. "It seems to be from your *grandfather*, madam."

"Dear old Grandfather. I do hope he is in good health. Do read it, Alison."

"It could be personal, madam."

The guests were by now all not listening very intensely.

"Go on, girl," sighed Lady Beauchamp, turning a suffering look on Elliott, who as a Lord presumably shared her exasperation at the strange whims of the below-stairs help.

Alison rolled her eyes towards the chandelier for such a long interval that Elliott though she must be rehearsing for the role of Tattycorum, counting to five-and-twenty. When two or three decimal-places worth of silent counting was done, she tore open the envelope. The contents seemed to first confuse, then worry her. She appealed silently one last time with a beseeching look at her mistress. Lady Beauchamp waved her lorgnette impatiently.

"Very well, madam," said Alison. "The telegram reads AT CHRYSOPOEIA REVELATIONS JOB CALIGULA DIES GRANDFATHER."

Lady Beauchamp considered this. "Poor Grandfather has always been a trifle eccentric."

It was a good thing for her, thought Elliott, that the trait did not run in the family.

Paisley's aunt and the guests at what Lady Beauchamp had called the "low end" shifted their conversation from high-sounding theories of government to more practical complaints about the terrible state of the world, and the mess politicians were currently making of it.

"It is very sensible," declared Mrs Sowerby, "to have a property qualification for the vote. It confines power to those who have proven themselves superior. Of course, we can achieve much the same result by controlling voter registration through poll taxes, literacy tests, good character requirements, and so on. It is vital that we keep the wrong sort of people from holding sway over government. No end of monkey business could come from letting the inferior vote."

"We will not have any more debacles once we win the vote," declared Paisley's aunt, pointing a finger heavenward in one of those gestures that politicians are so fond of, "and put some women in Parliament to straighten things out, instead of these buffoons and patronage-appointees we have now. I do not include you, of course, Mr Thompson."

Paisley held out her spoon for attention. "Aunt Claudia, who *does* have the right to vote?"

"Well Paisley, until Sir John's 1885 *Franchise Act*, every province had its own rules. Generally speaking, anyone had the right to vote who wasn't poor, female, insane, feebleminded, a school teacher, an Indian, a judge, a Chinese, a civil servant, or guilty of treason. Or anyone working for a political candidate. So, as you can see, practically *everyone* could vote."

"And now?" wondered Paisley.

Paisley's aunt shook her head. "After Macdonald's reforms, it became complicated."

"But," said Paisley, rubbing her temple thoughtfully with the spoon now, "I'm certain you mentioned voting recently."

"Yes," said Elliott, "aren't widows and spinsters allowed to vote?"

Paisley's aunt winced, possibly due to the word "spinster", and puffed dismissively. "Municipal elections... what do they really matter?"

"So..." said Elliott, "you can vote in some elections, but I can't vote in any until I'm twenty-one."

"You see, Elliott," said Paisley's aunt, as though explaining matters to a six-year-old, "it is a question of reason. You are too young to exercise your faculties of reason. But there is no reason why anyone of the age of majority, man or woman, shouldn't be entitled to vote."

"If they're the right sort," said Mrs Sowerby.

Elliott remembered another electoral law. "Unless they earn less than three hundred dollars per year."

"Hmm?" said Aunt Claudia.

"I mean, doesn't anyone earning less than that have the faculty of reason?"

"That's not the point, Elliott..."

"Will you be campaigning for the poor to get votes too?"

"The poor," said Lady Beauchamp, apparently delivering a sermon to her asparagus, "will always be with us."

"Now Elliott," continued Paisley's aunt, "we have quite enough to do to get ourselves the vote."

"The laws in this country are a scandal!" complained Mrs Leonowens. "What can they be thinking in government?"

Elliott didn't think Mrs Leonowens was quite being fair to the Minister of Justice, Mr Thompson, who was too polite to bicker about the issue over dinner. Unless he had become mute from the shock of the food; Mr Thompson liked a hearty meal, judging by his lunch on the train. And he seemed quite fair and progressive, from what little Elliott remembered of his talk when they met. Not to mention Thompson being a trusty fellow in a fight, with a sound left hook. "I wonder," mused Elliott, poking his spoon suspiciously into his dish of stringy stewed rhubarb, "if the only reason women haven't made such complete asses of themselves as men have in politics, is that the women so far haven't had the opportunity." He ate some rhubarb, somehow noticing as he grimaced at the flavour that everyone was staring at him. After the chocolate, the unsweetened rhubarb tasted like the sourest, foulest crab-apples he'd ever been foolish enough to bite.

"Sugar," observed Lady Beauchamp helpfully, "is very bad for the body."

Elliott forced himself to swallow. He shuddered. At the opposite side of the table, Dr Maddox quickly laid aside his spoon and napkin. Maddox looked a trifle alarmed, as if he had just remembered the sight of Elliott leaning over the side of the steamer earlier that day, vomiting into the lake.

"Perhaps we gentlemen ought to retire to the veranda for cigars, and leave the ladies to discuss politics."

Elliott nodded with enthusiasm, gulping. They escaped as rapidly as good manners would allow and settled into some wicker chairs on the far side of the house, overlooking the Bells' peculiarly incomplete residence, to which the owner had repaired with apologies. Mr Thompson, too, had set off briskly towards the nearest restaurant to console his digestion, promising news for Elliott after he'd done some campaigning elsewhere in the county.

Elliott watched expectantly as Maddox extracted a finger-length cigar from a silver case, but he wasn't offered one.

"A cigar might not be exactly what your digestion needs at the moment," said Maddox. He struck a match and tossed it into the grass beyond the veranda after getting the cigar lit. "It has changed a little since I first came to Nova Scotia."

"Really? When was that, sir?"

The chair squeaked and crackled in response to Maddox's settling in. "Some time ago — back about the time you were born, I would suppose. You are, what, about sixteen? There weren't so many railway lines then, and much of the time I had to ride about in Royal Mail stages. Horrible, rattley things, like something out of *The Pickwick Papers*, only with more mosquitoes."

"Were you lecturing then as well?"

There was more creaking as Maddox shifted against the wicker. He lifted his cigar and blew out a stream of smoke. "Not exactly, no. There was a… a confluence of circumstances that led me to come here. A family matter. A scientific matter. To Sable Island, to be exact. Do you know it? Some distance south of Halifax, far out in the Atlantic," said Maddox, after Elliott had shaken his head. "Just a huge sand bar, really. It was for a kind of… experiment. Arrogance, and loss, and desperation led me there. And nearly led to, well, something rather unfortunate."

Maddox noticed Elliott about to inquire into the event, and quickly shifted the subject away from the whatever the unfortunate consequence almost was. "Met my wife out there, actually. On Sable."

"How did you meet? If you don't mind my asking."

Maddox waved away the thought with his cigar. "It was simplicity itself. She was the only woman on the island. Her father was the light keeper."

"I suppose there weren't any *Germans* on the island," muttered Elliott, with a touch of bitterness. "Or motorwagons. Or undersea boats."

Maddox laughed, and puffed his cigar thoughtfully. "Why don't you stroll into town tomorrow, to lunch at the hotel where I am staying? The Telegraph Inn." Maddox leant across the gap between their chairs, conspiratorially. "That is, if you can drag yourself away from Lady Beauchamp's cornucopia. You could, ah, invite Miss DeLoup along as well…"

Yes. Paisley wasn't actually ill-disposed towards him, after all. Just smitten by this dashed, dashing German. Elliott had hardly seen her alone in ages. They just needed to get re-acquainted. Elliott sensed that some ray of hope yet dwelt in the fading day.

Chapter Eight
A Wolf in No Clothing

A<small>SPARAGUS</small>," MUTTERED PAISLEY darkly, as she tramped in the golden evening light up the hedgeline towards the corner of woods she'd met Adelmo in the previous day.

A summer of asparagus would hardly be bearable, plant of many virtues though it was. Just because that... vegetarian... was visiting, it hardly meant the whole household needed to forsake fish, flesh, fowl, eggs, sugar, butter, milk, cheese, and — for some reason — bread. Events were, indeed, taking a *dire* turn.

Even as the field fell into shadow, the westering sun lit the cloud banks brilliantly — great mounds of them, piling up in the sky like celestial cauliflowers. No! No more brooding about vegetables. Later, when the guests were distracted with philosophy and weighty matters of policy, or playing whist, she could raid the pantry for a ham sandwich. Huge slabs of bread. With butter. And mustard. And... How could she be expected to recover her strength on asparagus? It was inhuman. And Aunt Claudia had forbidden her from taking the *Peabody's Patented Parasol* to lean on and, to be truthful, Paisley's leg was throbbing, even if it was healing at a phenomenal rate, as usual. Luckily she had found in the cellar, if not a walking stick, then at least a foot of lead pipe which, in its canvas bag, she swung merrily now that she was contemplating a snack. Whoever the man was who had left her the note — instructing her to return to the location of the shooting incident — she was going to take no chances, even if he did call himself a friend. Not after Elliott's brushes with death on the train. She hoped the note-writer would have his say and let her get home before the rain started. It wouldn't do to get drenched in the woods, like last summer in Spohrville. Apart from anything else, one wasn't supposed to get bandages wet.

Finding roughly the right place, Paisley failed to find anyone lurking. She resisted the siren song of the sandwich and sat gratefully on a fallen tree trunk to rest her calf, waiting for the mystery man. ...*Lairne a thing that's to*

79

her profit... What had the man been trying to say in that note? Would he be offering advice on investments? Surely it wasn't going to be some warning, about Adelmo. That would be just... annoying.

Paisley sniffed. Over the smell of pine and sweet fern there was something else, that reminded her of a damp dog. It...

The tap on her shoulder sent Paisley lurching off the log and clutching for her lead pipe. She hefted it up to head level, bag and all, and jinked around.

"Ah, ye've come. Good," said the man.

He was at least six feet tall, and had a long axe leaning against one shoulder. His red beard was full of lichen and sticks. Paisley didn't lower the pipe.

"Who are you?" Paisley demanded. "And what do you want?"

The fellow was slightly nonplussed by Paisley's suspicion, or perhaps by the bag she was brandishing so menacingly. Following her eyes to the axe, he leant the tool against a tree and stepped back.

"Calm yersel, lass. A'm nae here to do ye no skaith."

"Skaith?"

"Hairm, lass. A mean ye nae hairm."

"All right. But what do you want? Were you watching yesterday, when Adelmo was hunting, and shot me?"

"Aye, lass. T'was *me* he was huntin."

Paisley looked sceptically at the man. "I think I'd have noticed you. What ran past me before the shot was a great furry..." Paisley scowled and didn't complete the thought. She wasn't sure she wanted to.

"Aye. And if ma nose disna google me, ye're one that kens somethin aboot..." The man scratched his beard. Some leaves fell out. "Aboot men becomin beasts, and vice versa." With the elaborate effort of someone who's heard the activity described, but has rarely tried it, he winked.

Paisley lowered the lead pipe a little, but still gripped it firmly. She didn't like the way this conversation was heading. This wasn't something she was supposed to talk about with anyone, not according to her father.

"So you are...?" said Paisley.

"That's richt, lass. A'm a werewoof. Like *ye*, A think."

A werewoof. A werewolf named Mungo McKelvie, if Paisley could take him at his word. According to him, not only did she smell like a werewolf, but she had the eyes of one too. To confirm this he — after Paisley had done flinching — opened one of her eyes very wide with a calloused thumb and forefinger, announcing that she had "a trace o' the extra eyelid". She was certainly going to check *that* in the mirror when she got home.

For a few minutes they followed a path through the trees — McKelvie explaining himself further along the way — until they arrived at a small house in a clearing, with a rough road on the far side extending away into the forest, or more likely towards Baddeck. The chimney was smoking, filling the glade with a sweet scent, and something about the scene put Paisley in mind of a fairy tale. She couldn't work out which one, exactly, but it seemed to her that it was likely one of the stories that had a surprisingly unpleasant role in store for the girl out wandering the woods at night.

"It'll tak some fetchin oot," McKelvie had told her on the way, "but ye've got the werewoof in ye, nae dout aboot it, though the blood be thinned oot a bit."

As far as she could follow the man's accent, he was offering to teach her more about her family's unusual heritage, remote though the connection was. He'd done this sort of thing before, supposedly, when not busy with his real occupation, of working at a sawmill and helping the Bells refurbish their house.

"Mainly work wi' selkies — seals, ye ken? That come ashore, an lay aside their skins to become ladies. Or men. One o' me selkies gaed on tae become a member o' the Executive Council i' Halifax. A've his skin aboot the place somewhere. But as a werewoof masel, A ken a thing or twa aboot thaim, too."

"Used tae gae tae Halifax," said McKelvie, when he'd shown her into the house and introduced Paisley to his wife, "ev'ry December fool moon tae haw a wild nicht on the town, nae lang syne, when the gas lamps was off tae save on the gas on account o' the moonlicht." Mungo sighed sadly. "But noo they've got the electrics in the streets, on all o' the time, even on the fool moon."

"Aye," said Mrs McKelvie, pouring them some strong, cheek-puckering tea, "*fool moon* was about the size of it."

Paisley waited politely but in vain for some biscuits, or tea cakes. Even some bread and butter would have been received ecstatically. A thin, ginger-haired woman of Aunt Claudia's advanced years, Mrs McKelvie chortled when, during Mungo's brief absence to find some book or other, Paisley inquired as to when the couple had emigrated from Scotland.

"Emigrated? Well," Mrs McKelvie said, in an accent that was more of a slight musical lilt than the dense brogue of her husband, "A've been here for ten year or so. Mungo though, he's no more Scottish than this house is. Been here for generations, his family has. Only since we met, he's gone Scots-mad. It's been tartan-this, and thistles-that, an' where's me haggis ever since. Just when A thought A'd left all that daftness behind in the auld country." She lowered her voice, conspiratorially. "An' he's nae really called 'Mungo', neither. His name's 'Bill'. But don't let on ye know — he enjoys it all too much."

"Ah, here she is," said "Mungo", re-appearing with a fat bundle of paper covered in tattered leather. He smacked the volume with some satisfaction.

Wondering if she were about to be signed into the man-beast registry, Paisley imagined some weird version of *Burke's Peerage*. Perhaps *Burke & Hare's Peers* would be a more appropriate title.

"It's the book, "Mungo explained. "Bought by me great-grandfaither from the man himsel. In his ain hand, it is."

"Whose hand would that be?"

"Why, Sir Walter. Sir Walter Scott. It's his *Beastmen of Glen Glammoch*. A maisterpiece."

"I've never heard of it." And as Paisley had a complete set of Scott's *Waverley* novels at home, she found the existence of an unknown work both intriguing and unlikely.

"Nay, ye wouldna have, would ye, lass. Ne'er published. Ne'er saw the licht o' day, did *The Beastmen*. Sir Walter sent it awa to the publishers, o'course, but they'd nae print it. 'Too fanciful' they told him. 'Not *proper* literature'. 'Oh, the public won't buy *fantasy*', they said. Publishers! What a load o' useless bloody ninnies they all are, bleatin like sheep aboot things they ken naught aboot!"

"Now, Mungo," said Mrs McKelvie, resting a restraining hand upon her husband's arm. He sucked in a deep breath.

"Oh, aye, don't let me get started aboot the publishers, lest we be here all night. But, to be brief, Sir Walter set doon a thinly-fictionalized account of his ain true experiences with the beastmen. Changed the names, o'course. Best collection o' practical werewoof lore ever set tae paper," he declared, smacking the manuscript again.

"And how exactly did your great… whatever it was… obtain this lost Scott novel?" asked Paisley.

Mungo looked suddenly downcast, as though forced to describe a personal tragedy. "Money, lass. Puir Sir Walter was hard up then, hard up indeed. Sold the only manuscript for five Guineas. Still," he said, brightening up a bit, "What a bargain, eh?"

Paisley cast a covetous glance over the book. Come what may, she would find some way to read it. "There's a long history, then," she said, "of…uh…our sort, in Scotland?"

"Aye, lass. A long, long history. The werebeasties were a part of the Auld Alliance."

This, at least, was a bit of familiar territory. Paisley had heard her father talking about the Auld Alliance on several occasions, the alliance between the Scots and French against their mutual enemies, the English. She mentioned this, and her French Huguenot ancestry, to Mungo. Mungo shook his beard in the negative.

"Nay, lass. The *other* Auld Alliance. Of the Scots, and the werewoofs. Against the *other* Scots."

"Which others?"

"It disna matter. Whichever clans we doont like. That Cameron, f'r'example, doon the lane, takin me goose... puir wee Wayzy'd doon nae harm... Wandered ontae his property, my eye... Why, if A only had four or five good werewoofs an' a broadsword, A'd go doon there an'.... cook *his* goose right well, that bloody..."

"Now Mungo..." said Mrs McKelvie, soothingly. Her eyes flicked to the window. "The gloamin's comin on, Mungo."

"Enough talk. We'll go now," said Mungo.

Paisley rose from her chair as Mungo headed for the door, and followed him. Mrs. McKelvie lunged suddenly for a cupboard.

"Mind ye tak the blindfold, Mungo," she said, handing it to him.

"Oh, aye," he replied, turning as he stepped outside. "Almost forgot. A fine memory ye have, dearie."

"Aye, Mungo, and don't ye forget it."

In their trudge up the road — Paisley limping slightly, trying to keep up with Mungo's long strides — she couldn't help being a trifle mystified. She'd been expecting a rambling lecture, with occasional ranting asides, drawn from the purported Scott novel.

"Mr McKelvie? Why the blindfold? Are we going to some secret place, somewhere with mystic powers, that I'm not allowed to know the location of?"

"Well," he said, twirling the black cloth bashfully around his massive hands, "nae exactly."

A little farther along, where a stream passed under a crude wooden bridge, they left the road to follow the watercourse. Just out of sight of the road, at a rocky bend in the stream, Mungo halted.

"Now, lass," he said, withdrawing a flask from his coat, "Tak a wee swig o this."

Paisley looked dubiously at the flask. "Why?"

"T'will reveal yer true nature." Detecting Paisley's anxiety, he waved dismissively. "Doont worry yeself, lass. A've drunk of it more times than A care to remember. Recipe straight from Sir Walter."

Paisley frowned, but summoned up her resolve. Fortune had thrown her an opportunity, perhaps a once-in-a-lifetime opportunity, to discover the full truth of her werewolf heritage, even the things her father wouldn't speak of. She uncorked the flask and tipped it back.

"Ach!" she said, after spitting the stuff out all over the moss at her feet. "It's like vitriol!"

Mungo looked dumbfounded, then rummaged in another pocket. "Sorry lass, that'll be me whisky. Try this one."

With redoubled cynicism, she drank from the second container. It tasted of herbs. Mostly. When Mungo had re-stowed both flasks into their appointed pockets, he began solemnly strapping the blindfold around his face.

"What?" Paisley wondered. What now?

"Now lass, ye need to... well... remove yer garments."

"What? You can't be serious."

"In aboot five minutes, ye're gaun t'have the body of a woof. Ye'd be surprised how awkward it is, to git a panickin woof oot o' a dress." Mungo folded his arms, and kneaded his forearms. Perhaps he still had the scars?

If so, it served him right. Paisley started fuming in outrage until it sank in that Mungo was addressing a spruce tree rather than her, and that he had just pushed his pipe through his beard. Perhaps he really couldn't see. She sighed, a sigh that seemed to go on forever, and then retreated behind some bushes.

Coming as it did, hard on the heels of a disappointingly vegetarian dinner, this latest turn of events found Paisley morally and constitutionally unprepared. It was certainly not turning out to be an exploit worthy of record in the chronicles of the family DeLoup. At least, Paisley *hoped* it would never be recorded. Neither, Paisley suspected, would her current attire — one leg bandage — be the sort of fashion advised for a summer country outing in *Miss Cramp's Manual for Young Ladies*. It was not warm. It was, in her estimation, not suitable for polite society. It was... Paisley slapped her knee... blackfly season.

Thunder rumbled distantly. The full moon had yet to rise, and twilight must have stolen into the clearing without Paisley noticing, for all of the colour had gone from the light. She looked thirstily towards the grey, burbling brook; McKelvie's elixir was tasting worse and worse in her throat as the seconds crawled past, worse even than the Brussels sprouts at dinner, almost as if someone were pickling radishes in her sinuses. The taste might almost have been bearable, had she not also had to contend with McKelvie's singing.

> *"Her cutty sark, o' Paisley harn,*
> *That while a lassie she had worn,*
> *In longitude tho' sorely scanty,*
> *It was her best, and she was vauntie..."*

Paisley cleared her throat. "Will you stop singing that, please," she said through the bush.

"Sorry, lass. Just passin the time. Is no verra interestin, sittin in the woods blindfolded."

"You have my sympathies. Now, can you please tell me..." Pain stabbed behind Paisley's eyes, like the worst headache she'd ever known. "Ohh. Tell me how... mush. Ow long... thime..." Now the horrible drink was making her tongue swell. More than that. She groped for words but they slipped from her head like eels. Horribly cramped, she fell to her knees and stretched with a groan.

"Well, coud be no much'll happen," admitted Mungo, "this bein yer first shot and all. An the blood's thin. Still, ye might find ye're gitten a wee bit furrier. And... Ah!" he exclaimed, as Paisley bowled him over with a growl and splashed into the brook on all fours, gulping water that frustratingly fell out her cheeks and went up her nose. She shook her head, snuffling, and then shook all over, her pelt soaked now.

"Crivens!" muttered McKelvie, who'd cast aside his blindfold.

Paisley regarded him coolly for a moment. Not food, she decided. She began to step towards the bridge and the road, slipped on the wet stones, and caught herself, getting the measure of her legs. She set out again, leaving the water, picking up speed until she fairly flew along the bank, onto the lane, through the near-dark. Nearly silent on the earthen road, she found the night full of sound, of the man's receding shouts, of forest deep with miles of birdsong, bats' squeaks, and insects' chatter. The air was a thick sea of smells, too. Earth, and tree, blooms, carrion, and days of trails from creatures' passing. She swivelled her head as she ran, the breeze on her whiskers guiding her nose into the odours on the wind. Smoke. People. Food. She trotted faster. A familiar glade opened off the road. She slowed. Buildings. Someone singing quietly in one of them. Paisley stalked closer, low, and edged open a door with her nose to enter a dark place. She crept in, smelling what she wanted. She lunged, things exploding with screeches all around, and fled back to the trees with the savour of blood in her mouth. When the distance seemed safe she set the thing down to better rip out mouthfuls of feathers, spit them aside, and gulp down warm bites of the chicken's flesh.

People at the house were shouting now. Thunder boomed, and echoed. Only cracked, sharp bones were left, so she abandoned the bird. Home. She wanted to go home now. The plants nearby had been crushed by feet, a path of sharp green smells simple to find, and in it her own scent, growing weaker. She followed the fading trail until the land opened onto a broad field sloping to a house, one that drew her. She started down the hill, following the cover of a hedge. A loud crack, not thunder, broke her stride, then she loped faster, towards it. Familiar scents, too. Sour vegetables. Sardines. Lovely ham. People. People she knew. One… she didn't. And smoke. Wrong smoke. Only one light burned, upstairs. There was a clicking under the apple tree, and Paisley turned, moving towards it. Someone inside the house came to the window and looked down at the tree. The boy was silhouetted before a lamp. Elliott… Paisley bounded towards the tree, where a man in shadow braced a long gun against a branch, aiming for the window. She sprang, snarling, her teeth tearing into a throat as the gun exploded in her ears.

Chapter Nine

"...AND SAVAGE FACES, AT THE CLANKING HOUR,
SEEN THROUGH THE STEAM AND VAPOURS OF HIS
DUDGEON..."

IN FLEEING TO his room that night, Elliott retreated into what could easily be described as a funk. Easily, but not quite accurately. *Dudgeon* would have been closer to his feelings. Dr Maddox's encouraging suggestion of inviting Paisley out to lunch had offered a smidgeon of hope, but it was a pretty small smidgeon, and the seriousness of his problems was starting to weigh on him as his concussion-induced flippancy wore off.

He had held the belief, up until a few days ago, that the world generally made some kind of sense most of the time. Even his vigilante-like pursuit of Oswald Slack, cad, formerly of Spohrville, Nova Scotia, and also known as Professor Strange, had begun to seem like a normal pastime for a young gentleman. Now... topsy-turvy was the only word for it. If that was a word, and not a phrase. He would consult Paisley at the next opportunity; she probably had a dictionary about her person. Now... what kind of world was it, where fellows needed to own a submarine vessel, and had to shoot young ladies in order to win their affections? A dashed rummy sort of world, that's what kind it was.

He commiserated with Sniggler over a tin of sardines that had been charitably slipped to Elliott by the maid, Mary, — a nice girl even if she was cockney, and prone to things like calling the stairs the "apples and pairs". Lured out of England by Paisley's aunt, she'd been, she told Elliott, less than thrilled to discover on her arrival in the New World that her duties included the *tasks* of everyone from scullery to lady's maid, but not the *wages*. Worst of all, Baddeck lacked some of the metropolitan attractions of London.

Elliott dangled a sardine for Sniggler to nibble. Perhaps if he and the maid pretended to be romantically entangled, it might make Paisley jealous? No. Madness lay waiting on the wayside of that course. And further embarrassment. In any case, Elliott didn't feel equal to the chore of simulating a lovesick swain's antics. Merely contemplating it was depressing. There was no alternative. He would just have to age ten years, become dashing, and obtain a submarine boat. But he drew the line at shooting Paisley. Even when it was for love, some things were beyond the pale.

He turned the lamp wick up for more light and served up another fish. The creak and shuffle of the household going to bed had died away some time earlier, with the approaching thunder taking their place. Sniggler's nerves were on edge from the electricity in the air, so Elliott fed her one more calming dose of sardine. With Paisley's aunt dead set against cats, it was lucky the maid, at least, liked them. Nevertheless, Sniggler could hardly stay in the room all summer long. Once he was sure that everyone was harmlessly tucked into bed, they could sneak down and get Sniggler installed in a comfortable wood shed, with running mice and all the conveniences. A few more minutes and everyone would be asleep. Unless the thunder was keeping Miss Hayward and the guests awake. To give them time to nod off, Elliott set up the framed photograph Strange had taken last year in Spohrville, of Elliott crowning Paisley and Denis at the Eel Fair, and dug out some colour-tinted postcards he'd bought in Halifax to sort through and decide which to send to whom. The train station, in all its Second Empire glory... Thomas, that one. The view of the Citadel fortress... The DeLoups, in Spohrville; Mr DeLoup liked fortifications. The view of ships in Halifax harbour... hmm. Elliott tapped his second-best fountain pen against his teeth, until he noticed Sniggler, fishless now, eyeing the instrument. He stopped, recalling the blue nose incident. It wouldn't do to appear at breakfast with blue lips from another cat-versus-pen attack. People would talk. More.

His parents for the harbour scene, he decided, bracing himself for the real challenge: the composition of an account of his vacation so far that was suitably harmless. A problem of this complexity really needed the support of tea, but the samovar, gleaming like gold in the lamplight, was if anything even more complicated than his life. Not a thing to wrestle with at this time of night. It was another of life's countless cruel paradoxes that one probably needed a strong cup of tea in order to face operating the samovar.

He wrote his address on the card. Sniggler washed her whiskers. Elliott found a stamp in his suitcase and carefully stuck the Queen on right way up, as he'd heard that it was treasonous to glue her to letters upside down. He tapped the pen on his teeth again, then quickly stopped himself.

"Dear P & M," he wrote.

The train was most stimulating. That was true enough. *Aboard, I made the acquaintance of the Justice Minister of the Dominion. He is also visiting Baddeck. I am staying next door to A. G. Bell's house. He is in a hotel due to the house being on stilts. Conditions are salubrious, and I am eating plenty of vegetables...*

He smeared the ink when a crack of thunder sounded hard by. Behind, beyond the lamplight, a little plaster crumbled from the wall into the shadows. Elliott hoped Paisley's aunt had had the sense to install lightning rods on the house. It had almost felt as though something whizzed through the room. He'd heard of eccentric forms of lightning, ones that travelled down chimneys, or slipped though keyholes, and drifted about looking for people to electrocute, but... surely they glowed? Lightning was supposed to be... well, light. Or bright, anyway. Sniggler, he noticed, was sensibly out of sight under the bed. Being an animal, she lacked mankind's superior obliviousness to danger. To be on the safe side, and for the sake of Sniggler's delicate constitution, Elliott got up to shut the window. Swollen with humidity, it was as bad as the front door, so much so that he had to pound on the thing to move it an inch. Another 'crack' sounded over the rumbling thunder, and this time Elliott thought he saw a flash. Being below, it must have been, what, a reflexion? Or a firefly? More flashes lit the sky this time, and booms punctuated the steady patter of the rain.

It had all looked so straightforward in Kingston. A pleasant holiday on the lakes with Paisley. Picnics. Boating. Long afternoons picking wild berries and strolling in the sun. And by the end... not betrothal, exactly. Yet. They were still young. An understanding of some sort?

Not assassins. Definitely not Germans with motorwagons and undersea boats. Elliott frowned at the turbulent night and ground his fists into the pockets of his bathrobe. He felt very disappointed in the world for its failure to live up to his expectations.

"Elliott?" said someone, so softly that for a blood-curdling moment he thought a disembodied spirit of fate had arrived to apologize for all of the recent inconveniences. When it spoke his name again he placed the voice outside, beneath his window.

"Help," begged the voice. And the petrifying sensation seized him again as he recognized the voice as Paisley's.

"What's the matter?" said Elliott, leaning out into the dark. He could see nothing but the occasional glimmer in the clouds.

"Don't wake anyone," Paisley pleaded in a hoarse whisper, "just come down. Hurry."

He went, faster than secrecy would have recommended, but his stockinged feet hardly made a sound speeding down the stairs. He took the kitchen door, nearest to his room, and stepped uncertainly into the wet yard, the rain the only thing he could detect in the overcast night. He headed for the sole window showing a lamp, his own.

"Paisley?" he whispered. "Where are you?"

"Here."

He nearly sprang away when a cold, wet hand grabbed his from out of the dark. It was… below. It pulled him to his knees, and he understood that Paisley was kneeling on the grass, shaking like her voice.

"Elliott, help me, I don't know…"

She threw her arms around his neck and held him with a drowner's grip. His mind reeled like a drunkard. Trying to comfort her in her sobbing and trembling, it took an age for his brain to register what his hands were telling it, that they were clasped around bare wet skin. And before the meaning of this could sink in, a bolt of lightning blazed in the clouds for an instant, revealing Paisley's body — in the second before the blackness closed over again — to be dripping with blood.

Chapter Ten
A BREAKFAST, INTERRUPTED

THERE ARE TIMES when one longs to forget the past, and times when one is desperate to remember; breakfast was a little of both for Paisley. Over her bowl of grey, unsweetened porridge, she felt there was something to be said for each approach. Down the table, Elliott kept looking up with a panicked smile from prodding his own porridge. Paisley hurriedly dropped her eyes back into her gooey oatmeal. It was made all the more unsatisfying in contrast with Mary's recent baking; the mouth-watering aroma of apple pie lingered in the kitchen like a delicious fog. Presumably Lady Beauchamp, in her silliness, did not realize that pie crusts were made with lard. Even if they were old apples from last year, with all of that cinnamon, and cloves… As soon as breakfast broke up and everyone was going about his or her business, she would descend on the pies as Byron described the Assyrians,

The young Paisley came down like the wolf on the fold,
And the pastries were gleaming in purple and gold.

Perhaps not purple, unless Mary had thrown in some dried blueberries. Somehow, she would have to return Elliott's bathrobe. Of how she'd found herself outside in the rain the night before, in a state of… well… *déshabillé*… Paisley had no recollection. The last that she remembered was meeting that man about the note, McKelvie, and something about Sir Walter Scott. None of it made much sense. It was like trying to summon up an especially strange dream.

"Does everyone have a spoon? I do hope there are enough for everyone," said Aunt Claudia. She studied each guest with a faint air of accusation. "I can't think where the others can have gone."

Lacking Dr Maddox today to lend an air of symmetry to the seating, Elliott was now a bit of flotsam in a pool of aunts and ladies, and was looking fittingly adrift. Thanks to the thunder, perhaps, he'd been able to get Paisley to her room without raising the household from their beds. Paisley had lain alone in the dark for hours, bewildered and aching all over. Whatever had occurred, it had taken away her appetite. After last night's vegetable repast, she remembered being pretty peckish. The shock of some event must have suppressed her hunger. Unless it was the chicken.

Paisley choked on a spoonful of porridge. A hen. She remembered killing a hen and eating it, raw.

The other breakfasters stopped clinking their spoons until Paisley chased the coughing away with tea. Thank heaven tea was a vegetable, as long as it contained no milk. Luckily, it didn't require a spoon that way, as there weren't any teaspoons left.

That hen. A nightmare, surely. A dog eating a bird. The smell of blood... the crack of bones...

There was a scream, muffled, from... outdoors. A *real* scream, not dream or memory. Not the scream of a maid seeing a spider. Paisley's skin told her it was much, much worse. Again breakfast was suspended, and silent glances were sent around the table like a game of pass the parcel. A parcel they were all afraid to unwrap.

Thumps of doors, raised voices, and urgent footsteps approached. At the dining room door, Lady Beauchamp's maid appeared, flushed, in a state of excitement.

"Yes, Alison?" asked Aunt Claudia.

"It's Mary, Ma'am. She was hanging the laundry..."

"Yes?"

"She says... she says she's found *a body*."

"A body."

"Yes, Ma'am. Under the apple tree. She's rather upset."

"You have seen this body."

"No, Ma'am. I came straight here."

Aunt Claudia pushed her chair back and rose.

"I will investigate. Please," she said to the table, "continue with your breakfasts."

No-one did. Paisley played with her empty teacup in a state of dread, rolling it over and over between her palms. A body? What could it mean? Mary. Did she see some... *fowl* murder... and think a bit of animal blood was a crime?

Steps approached. Aunt Claudia entered, shut the door behind her, and silently surveyed the room, pale, her hands clenched. They all waited for her to speak.

"A person has been killed."

"Oh, no," said Paisley, aloud without meaning to.

Her aunt grew more certain, and emphatic.

"You will all remain in the house until... assistance is summoned. The scene is too shocking. The... person... has been terribly mutilated by some creature."

Paisley's hands were full of shattered china. She dropped the shards, hardly understanding she'd crushed them. She stood, shaking, backing away from the bits.

"An... animal?" she said

"Yes. Only a bear, or a wolf, could have done... what was done to the body."

No. no... Paisley backed against the china cabinet for support, feeling sick.

Her aunt looked at her in particular. There seemed to be pity in her face.

"The person must have been hunting. There was a rifle near the body."

The room grew black. "Adelmo," mumbled Paisley, as she slid down the cabinet and into unconsciousness.

SMALL COLD THINGS were crawling over Paisley's face. She sat up with a shout. The doctor, the one who had seen to her leg, was standing over her beside the chesterfield, and was flicking droplets of cold water onto her forehead.

"There you are," said the doctor. "Just as effective as smelling salts in cases of fainting or hysteria."

"Cheaper, too," said Elliott, who, Paisley now noticed, was kneeling by her head with a glass phial in his hand.

"Now, if you're quite well Miss DeLoup, I must attend to a less pleasant matter." He nodded and departed. Less pleasant... he meant the body. The dead body.

"Oh, Elliott," Paisley scarcely whispered.

Elliott frowned, and then laughed a quick, mirthless laugh. "*He's* all right."

Paisley sat up like a shot. "What? He's only injured?"

"That fellow in the yard, you mean? No, he's *dead*. His head is practically... What I mean is that your... German... is safe and sound. He rode by on that machine of his, a few minutes ago."

Paisley fell back onto the pillows with a thump. It was all too much to take in. The relief swept through her like a drug, waking her from a numb sleep. He was alive.

"But wait," she said, the horror coursing back through her veins. "Who did I... Elliott, I killed *someone!*"

Elliott waved anxiously for silence. "No-one thinks that," he whispered. Something in the way he said it, though, told her that he was the exception. "Can you get up? You need to see something."

He steadied her with an arm about her waist on the ascent of the stairs, much as he had the previous night. Unlike that night, muted sobs were now coming from the servants' room over the back stairs, but Elliott led them away from that direction, heading instead for his own room. Once inside, he eased the door shut. Paisley continued to the window. It drew her irresistibly, like a cliff edge.

"No," said Elliott hurriedly, "not *that*."

But she was already gazing down at the apple tree, pink-white with blossoms, where a little cluster of people stood about a sheet-covered shape, the doctor lifting up one corner. Something that had been a man lay underneath. Had been one, until Paisley met him.

"This," said Elliott, gently taking Paisley's elbow and guiding her away from the window to the rear wall of the room. He pointed mutely at the wall. The plaster was in poor condition.

"I don't think," said Paisley, her voice growing shaky again, "under the present circumstances, that that aunt will be overly upset if you've damaged the wall." She'd killed someone. She must have. She must have…changed. Become a beast. A beast that murders. Her hand went to her mouth, only just stifling a moan. These teeth tore into his throat… these lips, red with his blood. She remembered now, the taste…

Elliott had produced some string from somewhere, and had tacked one end of it to the window ledge. Paisley's own private misery receded now before the inexplicable. She watched him stretch the string across the room to the crumbling wall, where he fixed the other end with a tack. He then repeated the bizarre procedure, joining another spot on the window to a deep hole gouged into the door post. With the room rigged out like a ship's mast, Elliott grew pensive and carefully placed himself between the strings, close to the first one, which ran past his ear.

"This one," he said, indicating the nearest string, "missed me by an inch. And the other…" Elliott dug into his pocket and showed Paisley a grey blob of lead. "The other bullet would certainly have gone through my skull if it hadn't been for what you did."

The gun. She remembered now. She remembered it all.

O

Chapter Eleven
Young Lochinvar is Out to Lunch

THE RATIONALIZATION OF having protected him had calmed Paisley's conscience, Elliott noticed as they walked towards town. The sky was fine and clear that morning, with a strong wind off the lake, promising a pleasant June day, and for Paisley at least it seemed that thoughts of bodies and murder had been left behind at her aunt's house. They were still troubling Elliott, though. Since it seemed that he was the target of Strange's anger, and the bullets of his assassins, Elliott's overtaxed brain was inserting sharpshooters behind every tree and hedge along their route, each one drawing a bead on Elliott's head. It was making his scalp itch in anticipation.

"There'll be an inquest, I suppose," he said.

"Hmm," agreed Paisley, starting to hum some tune.

The doctor had told Elliott that the corpse hadn't looked like anyone local. There were a lot of people from away lately, visiting…

"We won't be called as witnesses," Elliott guessed. His father had given medical opinions at a few such proceedings. Inquests for wild animal attacks tended to be perfunctory. "They'll… be looking for the animal," he added, with a sidelong glance. Surely she knew that he'd pieced together some notion of her unusual connection with wolves. Or did she not truly trust him? It was a thought that only magnified the gloom of the situation.

Then it came — what he'd feared — the report of a gun from somewhere behind them. In the blink of an eye, hardly thinking, Elliott leapt. He flew into Paisley, knocking her off her feet and into the road gravel. Lying over her, he tensed, almost feeling the impact of the bullet on his flesh through sheer fevered imagination. Paisley was trembling. She looked up at him, her eyebrows arched above her smoked glasses.

"That," she said, "was Adelmo's motorwagon. It makes loud bangs sometimes," she said, her trembling emerging as laughter.

"I thought…"

Paisley tipped her glasses up onto her forehead. "Do you see anything abnormal about my eyes?"

Elliott gulped. Lying atop girls on the public highways was even more improper than lying on tombstones. Or on club membership applications. "I, uh…" Her eyes. They were big, and brown, and looking into his. "They're… they're *lovely*."

Paisley's eyebrows rose a little higher.

"I, I mean," stuttered Elliott, trying to horsewhip his mind into motion. He stared harder, more clinically. Irises… golden brown… mesmerizing… Lashes… long. Pupils… dilated… and…

"The *plica semilunaris* looks, ah, a little larger than normal."

Paisley did something that was probably a nod, or as close to it as she could manage with her head on the ground. "Thank you. Perhaps we should get to our feet. I hear Adelmo's motorwagon approaching."

Elliott scrambled up and offered Paisley his hand. They tried, rather ineffectually, to brush off the damp earth of the road, Paisley clinking a good deal as she did so. She wasn't, Elliott hoped, planning to pay for her own luncheon with all of that change. Surely he could at least buy her a meal.

The German puttered up the road on his machine while Elliott's thoughts were flitting back to the summer of '86. Silver. Paisley had made some casual remark then, about werewolf legends being confused. Silver, she'd claimed, was not deadly but… what? A sedative, soporific, an intoxicant? Like catnip? That reminded him to check on Sniggler, something he'd forgotten in all of the morning's other excitement. But Paisley… was she lugging around a load of coins to settle her nerves? And did that mean he'd get to pay the restaurant bill?

The motorwagon drew to a halt beside them, the German shoving levers and switches to brake the thing. Paisley greeted him with a burst of oration.

"O, young Lochinvar is come out of the west,
Through all the wide border his steed is the best!"

During the shutting-off of the machine, Elliott scrutinized the driver, the vehicle, and the road. "That's not the west," he said. "It's north-east."

Paisley sighed.

Elliott recognized the poem, though, and was none too pleased to be relegated to the role of "the young craven bridegroom… dangling his bonnet and plume," while the girl he's supposed to marry rides away with the dashing Lochinvar. It was just the sort of unexpected turn of events calculated to give a young bridegroom the pip. Not, Elliott was forced to admit, that he was engaged to Paisley. Nevertheless…

The German pulled off his hat and a ridiculous pair of goggles. "Please," he asked Elliott, his face contorted into something between confusion and annoyance, "why were you, just now, lying in ze street atop Paisley?"

This, Elliott felt, was a question too impertinent to dignify with an answer. In any case, it was too mortifying.

Paisley laughed again. "He thought that the noise of your motorwagon was a gunshot."

To Elliott's relief, this reminder of the recent "accident" discomfited the German, who seemed willing to let the subject drop.

Now, if there's one thing more dispiriting for a young would-be bridegroom than having a Lochinvar ride off with his would-be bride, it's having to get a lift from them as they ride off together. Not that he could blame Paisley for accepting the offer of a ride. She *had* been shot in the leg only the other day. Which made her being up and about already even less normal than her *pica semilunaris*. Though really, if she could grow fur and a tail, there wasn't so much to wonder at in a rapidly healing leg. But as far as the ride was concerned, it was that or trudge sulkily in their dust. So, ignoring the fact that he obviously wasn't included in the offer, he hopped aboard anyway.

"A bit cramped," he observed, squeezing onto the bench beside Paisley.

The German replaced his hat and goggles. "It is not intended," he said, a little coldly, "for three."

It wasn't that the machine was noisy and wobbly — having been raised on a diet of futurism, Elliott could adapt his mind to its mechanicalness, certainly more easily than his stomach could adapt. It was the lack of horses. He'd never realized how comforting it was to have a huge beast or two plodding along in front. Without them, a carriage seemed to careen along like an out of control locomotive, with the ground racing past his feet and nothing between him and a crash.

Apart from Adelmo mentioning the severity of the thunderstorm and his discovery of a large scorch on his submarine boat where he thought lightning had struck, the conversation tended towards the stilted side, as was to be expected when riding a sort of berserk mangle on wheels. The peace, if you could call it that, suited Elliott. He didn't think he could stand much more poetry. And what was this German going to reveal that he owned next? An airship? A moon-cannon? Any normal suitor Elliott might have felt able to compete with on fair terms. He would have preferred them to be ugly, poor, and dull, but that would have been asking rather a lot. Instead, the fellow was exotic, rich, older, and — Elliott was forced to admit after a withering look towards the German — not entirely unsightly. Fate, Elliott had heard it said, was a wheel that would carry you up one minute only to plummet you down the next. Even the thought of whirling wheels made Elliott feel unwell. He put a hand to his head to steady the throbbing. Perhaps for some people it was a wheel. For Elliott, fate was more complicated. More like a carousel. It bobbed him up and down continuously on a silly toy horse, and spun him 'round until he got sick and fell off.

Even the seating arrangements on the motorwagon were a dilemma. On his right side a blurry void, nastily similar to the one he had been dangled over on his train trip. Any jolt threatened to fling him off the bench and under the wheels of the infernal contraption. On his left sat Paisley. Under ordinary circumstances, Elliott would have felt more inclined to lean on Paisley than be killed by falling off a speeding motorwagon. Under these circumstances, however, moving over only pressed her closer to the German. It was one of the great conundrums, as hopeless as anything dreamt up by the ancient gods to vex Greeks they didn't like.

All things considered, Elliott felt he would have been better off staying in bed, where anyone with concussion and contusions and an ounce of sense should have stayed. Certainly his plans to take Paisley to lunch were coming a cropper. Then he remembered the bullet holes in his bedroom walls. Not a restful prospect for an invalid with nerves in a delicate condition. And there were the Brussels sprouts to factor into the equation.

"Good heavens!" interrupted Paisley. "It's Denis."

"Denis?" said Elliott, coming out of his brooding.

"Denis... Ludlow. Look."

They had reached Baddeck now, the area about the harbour, and were attracting considerable attention from everyone they passed. Horses shied. People stared. Children wept. Sitting at the front of the machine was not only precarious, it was conspicuous. At least the public were reacting to the motorwagon rather than his face, for a change.

Among the onlookers, slouching against a wharf-post, was Denis.

"So it is." Elliott waved. Denis curtly returned the courtesy with a couple of fingers.

"Stop!" instructed Paisley. "Please stop here, Adelmo."

With a flurry of mechanical manipulations, the German succeeded in bringing them to a halt a few wagon-lengths past Denis. He laboriously reversed until they were side by side.

"Morning," said Denis, his eyes going like paintbrushes all over the machine. Denis was looking sunburnt and ruddy with good health, for a change. He'd looked almost consumptive the summer before.

"Denis," exclaimed Paisley, "where have you been? We though you'd gone off on a vendetta."

"You didn't reply to my letters," said Elliott.

"Not much of a letter writer," said Denis. "This yours?" He indicated the motorwagon.

"This," said Paisley, introducing the German, "is Burggraf von Hasselberg. The motorwagon is his."

"Hmm." Denis frowned and nodded thoughtfully, as though deciding whether the vehicle was an acceptable specimen of engine-driven carriage, given his wide experience in such things.

"It is ze first one in zis country," commented the German.

"Nice," said Denis.

"But," added the German, "I must continue. I am to be meeting some persons for luncheon. Would you," he asked Paisley, "like to remain here and re-acquaint with your friend?"

"That fellow courting you?" Denis asked Paisley, after the German had driven off towing Paisley's eyes behind him.

"That's none of your business. Now tell us what you've been up to."

"Sailin', mostly," he said, hooking a thumb over his shoulder to a small black schooner docked behind him.

"So, you got hired to work on that boat all this time?" asked Elliott.

"Ship," corrected Denis, who invited them to inspect it. "And no, I hired them." There were a couple of hands on the deck. "I own her." With a little flourish, he presented the escutcheon bearing the name on the stern. "I was thinking of callin' her *Moonraker*, but settled on *The Avenger* instead." A bronze swivel-gun of an earlier era was mounted above the escutcheon — a gift from Paisley's parents' antique arsenal of 18th century weapons.

Once Paisley and Elliott had exhausted their astonishment and outrage at Denis' profligacy in buying his own ship with money meant for revenge against Strange, Denis started to explain.

"How much of that cash I took from Strange do you two have left?"

Elliott ran over the list of rewards posted for information, the telegrams sent, and other expenses. Then the extravagant tips he'd paid out, and the first class rail tickets. His new suit. Salmon for Sniggler, and so on. Paisley seemed to be performing a similar tally.

"Most of it," said Elliott. Paisley nodded.

"Well," said Denis, "I've doubled mine. But what are we standing here for? Let's eat. Anything but ship's biscuits, salt fish, or salt beef. Between the salt and the pipe smoke, I'm just about kippered."

Denis had, he told them on the way to the Telegraph Inn, been using his and his father's shipbuilding savvy to buy and sell vessels up and down the coast from Cape Breton to New England, running cargoes between times.

"Is that what brings you here?" asked Paisley.

Denis stuck a short pipe in his mouth, and lit it with ostentatious casualness.

"I knew you two were here, of course. I do read letters. But I've a cargo too. No sense wasting a trip. Business-wise, I mean," he added, when the others looked slightly slighted. "They better hurry up and finish that ship railway across Chignecto. It takes ages to get here from the Bay of Fundy."

"This cargo," asked Elliott. "It's not eels, is it?"

"'Course not. It's *lemons*."

Elliott and Paisley found a shipload of lemons a peculiar thing to bring to Baddeck, a feeling given eloquent voice by their faces.

"Mostly lemons," said Denis. "Folks always want lots of lemonade at fairs, and jubilees, and elections, and that."

Tiring of lemons, Paisley breathlessly related to Denis everything she knew about submarine vessels, especially the one her German acquaintance had left blocking Baddeck bay. She was still burbling about them as they mounted the steps and approached the desk inside, where the hotelier surveyed them with a jaundiced eye. Not *literally* jaundiced, of course, or Elliott would have felt compelled to advise him about the state of his liver.

"We're here for dinner," announced Denis. "Where's it served?"

The man across the desk didn't seem to think much of Denis' collarless shirt, much less his manners. Neither was he impressed when he examined Elliott's face, or the road dust all over Paisley.

"I'm afraid we're rather full up today. There are no tables available."

Denis withdrew his pipe. "Now, now. Don't be afraid. We got a reservation."

"Do you."

Elliott was asking himself the same question.

"Yeah," said Denis.

"In whose name is this... reservation?"

Denis rummaged in his pocket. "The Marquess of Lorne," he said, and flattened a crumpled banknote on the counter. It was a four-dollar bill with the former Governor-General's moustachioed face on it.

The hotelier put a pince-nez onto his nose and inspected the note, front and back. "We may have one table," he conceded.

The hotelier had been almost truthful when he'd claimed there were no tables left; they were ushered into one of the few empty ones, the diners being packed together like sprats in a tin. Business was so brisk that it looked as if Baddeck's population had gotten wind of Lady Beauchamp's militant vegetarianism and were out for a last cutlet or omelette before she stormed the butcher shops, overturning the tables of meat and smashing all the eggs, just in case anyone socially noteworthy had been transmigrated into a chicken.

Awaiting their beefsteaks, they made do with bread and butter while catching up with Denis' recent adventures on the high seas, the chatter of the neighbouring diners loud enough to allay fears of eavesdropping. Denis, who'd been playing with his pipe, tapped the ashes onto his bread plate and stowed the pipe away in his pea-coat.

"So you're really kipping next door to Alexander Graham Bell?" he asked, sounding mildly impressed.

"Next to his house," said Paisley. "It's being re-built. Bell is staying here at the inn while he's in town." She turned away, surveying the host of diners. "He doesn't seem to be lunching right now. There's Adelmo, though, with that Captain Rawlins. And there is Doctor Maddox, not far from Adelmo's table."

"Bell's not," Elliott asked Paisley covertly, "you know, one of *you*, is he?"

Paisley swivelled back to the table to give him a guarded look. "What on earth do you mean? A relation? He told me he was connected to the DeWolfes of Wolfville, but whether they're related to the DeLoups... who knows? He's an avid genealogist. He could tell you."

A genealogist, yes, but what else was Bell? An inventor and eccentric, or a werewolf, like... "It's just that I saw him out on that headland, Red Head is it called? He was eating lunch with no clothes on."

"Really. And this made you suspect he was one of my relatives?" said Paisley, querulously, before getting Elliott's meaning. "Oh."

Denis leant forward, elbows on the table. "Just what have I been missing?"

"Nothing," Paisley quickly assured him. "In any case, it's Elliott we should be concerned about. He has been nearly killed several times."

"Hows about we hire somebody of our own," suggested Denis, when the steak-bearing waiter had come and gone, "to introduce Mr Strange to his maker?"

"We're *not* hiring assassins, and that's that," said Elliott.

Denis shrugged and started sawing into his beef. "Not like the law's do-ing much."

"I know. So far the courts have been useless. But I met the Minister of Justice — Mr Thompson — on the train, and he believed me about Strange. He'll set things in motion, just watch."

"We'll see," said Denis, around a mouthful of steak.

Lunch attracted Elliott's attention too, until he noticed that Paisley hadn't begun on her own food yet. "Not hungry, Paisley?"

She seemed to be thinking, her head tilted and gaze directed at an unin-spiring bit of plasterwork on the wall, as though she'd spotted a fly and was considering a complaint to the management.

"I'm trying to hear what Adelmo is saying to Captain Rawlins," she said, tipping her head towards the far corner where the two men were in conference. Next door to their table sat Dr Maddox, very obviously hoping to give the impression, behind his newspaper, that he wasn't also listening to the men's conversation. "Captain Rawlins," continued Paisley, "said that he truly has no idea how his underwater engine works — the one he is selling for the submarine boat. Apparently his cousin, or someone, made it. There is only the one. No plans. Adelmo is hoping that once the Captain sells it to the Wellborn Trust, they will be able to work out the principle of its operation by taking it apart and studying it, whereupon they will be able to make copies to use in future vessels."

Elliott had already heard more than enough about German devices for one day. Surely the fact that he might be murdered at any moment was of more immediate concern than the inner workings of submarine propulsion systems. He was darned, though, if *he* were going to be the one to point this obvious fact out to Paisley.

"Why not telegraph that cove in New York," suggested Denis. "What's his name? Gibson. Get him up here to keep you alive. He's a constable, or a marshal, or something."

"That's right. Waiter?" called Elliott, grateful to have the derailed conversation placed back on track, and summoning the man for a reply-paid telegraph form to fill out.

STRANGE DANGER COME SOONEST EXPENSES PAID.

The appearance of the form brought Paisley out of her latest eavesdropping trance. "That," she said, "was an extraordinary cablegram that Lady Beauchamp received."

Denis raised his eyebrows interrogatively.

"It made even less sense," Paisley went on, "than most telegrams. Let me see... it ran, AT CHRYSOPOEIA REVELATIONS JOB CALIGULA DIES. What can her grandfather have possibly meant by it?"

"Likely he's potty," said Elliott, tipping back the last of his raspberry vinegar cordial. "Look at Lady Beauchamp."

"True..."

"Sounds Biblical," Denis proposed. "Where's Chrysopoeia?"

Everyone agreed that the place was a mystery, if it existed at all.

"What," mused Paisley, "would Auguste Dupin conclude from the evidence, after applying his skills in ratiocination?"

Elliott didn't know what answer the French detective would come to, nor did he plan to ask what "ratiocination" meant. It was once of those beastly-sounding words that ought not to exist, like "isthmus".

"He might conclude that it was none of our business."

Paisley fondled her silver-plated spoon with palpable disappointment. Then something seemed to strike her — something besides the spoon, with which she was now tapping her temple.

"There was a saint named John Chrysostom," she said, tempting Elliott to comment that there probably still was, unless he'd been de-sainted. When he had decided not to, she elaborated. "Chrysostum means 'golden mouthed'. It was on account of his way with words, you see. So, 'chryso' is Greek for 'gold'."

"A golden city?" offered Denis.

There was a place in South Africa that was having a gold rush. What was it called... Witwatersrand? Maybe that was the place. Elliott couldn't see how it would be connected to anything going on in Baddeck. All this talk of Greek, though, *that* struck a faint chord. He just couldn't think why exactly. Something scientific. Cassiopeia, the constellation? No. More medical. Pharmacopoeia. Meaning "drug making". It had stuck in his mind as odd, since a pharmacopoeia is a book full of drug information, rather like a cornucopia being a horn full of... plenty. But "poeia" must be different from "pia". Or "copia".

"It means gold-making," he guessed.

Denis rubbed his fingers together with theatrical avarice. "That's what I'm doing," he boasted, "turning lemons into *gold.*"

"Do you suppose the grandfather is an alchemist?" wondered Paisley.

Elliott hoped not. The world was weird enough without getting involved in alchemy and magic as well.

"The Golden Jubilee, maybe?" said Denis. "That's sort of making a thing golden. The Queen's reign, I mean, with a golden anniversary."

Paisley dropped her spoon, the one she hadn't seemed very satisfied with anyhow. "Yes! That must be it: At the Golden Jubilee... Revelations, Job, and whatnot. Still not very lucid, but it's a start."

The waiter having returned to offer desserts, Elliott ordered — on top of tea and pudding for three — a Bible.

"Excuse me?"

"A Bible, man," said Denis, "you know what a Bible is? Not a heathen, are you?"

When the man, a little less flustered, came back bearing the prescribed volume, Elliott turned to the Book of Revelation. It had always been one of the more perplexing and alarming ones, and was no less so now. He skimmed through, trying to find any relevant parts. "Breaking seals... riders of the Apocalypse... eating books... seas turned to blood... lake of fire... I don't know. Apart from some aquatic connections, it doesn't seem to have much to do with our present circumstances, unless Lady Beauchamp is planning to bring about the end of the world." He handed the Bible to Paisley for a second opinion.

"Then again," said Paisley, "REVELATIONS could mean something is going to be revealed at the Jubilee. Let's try the Book of Job."

Elliott concurred. He could definitely sympathise with Job.

"Unless," cautioned Denis, "'Job' means 'job', as in work."

Paisley made a face. "I hardly think even one of Lady Beauchamp's relations would be mad enough to send a coded cablegram with a hidden message informing her that an opportunity for employment would be revealed on the day of the Jubilee. Apart from anything else, I doubt very much whether she works." She opened to the Book of Job.

"Let's see… There was a man in the land of Uz, whose name was Job… he had lots of property… becomes the object of a bet between God and Satan… oh! It's going to take forever to hunt through all forty-two chapters of Job."

On second thoughts, poring through the entire trials of Job was not something Elliott found more enticing than his plate of clootie dumpling, much as he and Job might have had to chat about by way of comparing notes. He picked away at the pudding, considering alternate approaches. In crossword puzzles, it was often helpful to move on to the next clue when the current one proved intractable.

"How about the CALIGULA DIES part? Caligula is an Emperor, and 'dies' is, what, Latin for 'days'?"

"Or 'dies', as in 'drop dead'," said Paisley.

"Either way," said Elliott, "it might be a number. Caligula Day… well, I can't believe anybody ever proclaimed a holiday to honour Caligula, unless it was to celebrate the day he died, so that's out. But he did die, on some day, and month, and year. That might give the part of the Book of Job that he meant."

Elliott looked hopefully first to Paisley, then Denis, but neither of them had any idea of when Caligula died, aside from "a long time ago", which was lacking in numerical precision. Paisley suggested that, as Caligula was a nickname meaning "little boots" in Latin, that the telegram might mean that someone was going to have a baby on or about the Jubilee, but this also seemed somewhat far-fetched.

"Someone must know when he died," said Paisley, scanning their fellow diners. She smiled winsomely at a plump, elderly lady at the next table who was eating a jam tart with a young man who must have been her son or nephew. "Pardon me for intruding. We are doing a little Biblical study, and need to know the date on which the Roman Emperor Caligula died. You wouldn't happen to know by any chance, would you?"

The woman considered, but both she and the young man said that they didn't have the fact at their finger tips. "I am sorry, dear," said the lady. "What about Mr Campbell, there? Just lean over and ask him, would you, James?" she requested of the young man, before beaming benevolently on Elliott and his companions. "So nice to have young people taking an interest in things." James agreed that it was jolly industrious of them to pursue their studies over luncheon. "Good for the brain."

Mr Campbell, it seemed, was no better versed in the lives of Roman maniacs than the pair at the neighbouring table, so that gentleman passed the query on to the next diners. Elliott tried to renew his acquaintance with his pudding, but the venomous stare of a severe-looking middle-aged woman at another table was putting him off dessert as effectively as a dose of syrup of ipecac. Paisley caught sight of the sour onlooker and whispered to Elliott.

"That's Miss Rivers, the *Antilibrarian* whom I mentioned."

Already in possession of a surfeit of enemies, Elliott wiggled his fingers in a friendly wave at Miss Rivers, to which she reacted as though he'd done something positively indecent. He smiled. It wouldn't do make an enemy of a librarian. The way things were going, they might turn out to have mysterious powers. Bibliomancy, perhaps. Moreover, she might know the date when Emperor Little Boots died.

"Excuse me, Miss Rivers, but would you happen to know the date on which the Roman Emperor Caligula died?" When she shrank back into her chair, Elliott added "I believe 'Gaius' was his real name. Caligula was only a nickname, meaning 'little boots'..." he trailed off. Miss Rivers was looking aghast. He wondered if it was his differently-coloured eyes that were putting her off. Some people found them disconcerting. "It's all right, Miss Rivers. My eyes are supposed to be like that. It's called *heterochromia iridum*."

Miss Rivers spilt her coffee. She mumbled. "Not happening. It cannot be happening," she said, to her now empty coffee cup. "It is not realistic," she muttered, lecturing her cup, "for a boy of his age to be using such an advanced vocabulary. I must be dreaming. Yes, a dream." She cheered up considerably at this realization. When she caught sight of Elliott again, the mood evaporated. "Or a play. An unrealistic play." Miss Rivers glared at Elliott, and then at the other diners. "Boo!" she said, as if one of the actors had fumbled his lines. "Hiss!"

The other patrons shook their heads sadly, trying to pretend Miss Rivers wasn't there. No doubt there was a wicker cage awaiting her in a bedlam someplace.

Meanwhile, the Caligula query had been propagating along a leisurely route through the dining room until reaching, quite on the opposite shore,

Dr Maddox, whom Elliott could even now see, receiving the question from a helpful man who gestured back towards the source of the conundrum. Dr Maddox stared over the intervening customers as if trying to ascertain whether he had been the target of a comic pleasantry too obscure to penetrate. He communicated something in the nature of a negative to his questioner, who then, to Maddox's unmistakable frustration, egged him on to keep the query moving to the next table. Hasselberg's table. After casting an inscrutable look at Elliott, he laid aside his newspaper shield and posed the question to the German. There was a moment of argument before Captain Rawlins replied to Maddox, who passed intelligence to his questioner, and so on back along the chain until finally James, at the next table, told Paisley that he was pleased to report that the Emperor Caligula shuffled off this moral coil — if being stabbed thirty times could be considered shuffling — in the Year of Our Lord 41.

"Thank you *so* much," said Paisley. "How helpful everyone has been." Turning back to the Good Book, she flipped through to Job again. "All right, so we have 'At the Jubilee revelations, Job 41', which is…" She stared at the page, reading it through.

"What?" asked Denis. "What's it say?"

Paisley looked up from the page, then over her shoulder towards the German and Captain Rawlins, and back to the Bible.

"Canst thou draw out leviathan with an hook? or his tongue with a cord which thou lettest down? Canst thou put an hook into his nose? or bore his jaw through with a thorn? Will he make many supplications unto thee? will he speak soft words unto thee? Will he make a covenant with thee? wilt thou take him for a servant for ever? Wilt thou play with him as with a bird? or wilt thou bind him for thy maidens? Shall the companions make a banquet of him? shall they part him among the merchants?"

She passed the Bible to Elliott. "The leviathan is the submarine boat. There will be a revelation about it on the Jubilee, and Lady Beauchamp is here to either prevent the announcement, obtain the machine, or else destroy it."

Chapter Twelve
SPOOKS ON STILTS

IN MANY WAYS a woodshed was not the best place in which to conspire with confederates. The furniture, such as it was, was uncomfortable and full of spiders. Aside from a single bull's-eye lantern, the lighting, particularly at night-time — as it was now — was limited, and refreshments virtually non-existent. Unless, that is, one were a cat and one enjoyed mice; Sniggler's solid frame was certainly showing no want of feeding. As a good trencher-cat she was loath to waste anything tasty, and tucked heartily into the waxed-paper bundle of miscellaneous chicken giblets that Elliott had procured from a butcher in town. The spectacle of Sniggler devouring that slurry of viscera did little to improve the atmosphere of the woodshed, even if it did lend the proceedings a certain ghoulish ambiance. However, with Aunt Claudia's house bursting with suffragists, the woodshed was the best that Paisley, Elliott, and Denis could do. At least Denis had had the foresight to come provisioned with bottles of ginger beer, even if Paisley wasn't sure how to get into them. There was no stopper.

"It's a Codd-neck bottle," said Denis, setting his pipe between his teeth while he pushed on what looked like a marble lodged in the mouth of the bottle. It hissed, distracting Sniggler.

Elliott poked his bottle. "There isn't any *cod* in it, is there?" he asked, always suspicious of fish, especially where Denis was concerned.

Paisley became aware that she was playing with a teaspoon and furtively stowed it away inside her stocking with the others. Killing that man last night… it hardly seemed real now. It had saved Elliott, that was all that mattered. Knowing she'd *had* to do it eased the strain. That, and the silver. Last night had crossed a line that could never be re-crossed, or undone. Or forgotten. She could only push the memory aside for a little while. There was too much else for one mind to hold right now.

Adelmo was another matter. With the town openly chattering about ferocious wolves running loose, and Aunt Claudia's guests scheming over the submarine boat, the chances of building a relationship with Adelmo were slim. If only Elliott had never found out about her, they might have had a chance... She touched her silver locket. It was so much simpler for Mama to accept Papa's condition. Women *expected* men to be hairy and brutish to some extent, but the fair sex were supposed to be mild and delicate, not savage beasts who dismembered their adversaries in a gory frenzy. Slanderous gossip was the limit of the genteel lady's arsenal. That, and cutting people socially. Cutting them with long fangs was not at all the thing.

She worked out how to open her bottle of ginger beer, releasing a hiss as the marble dropped into the goitreously distended neck.

"Put that thing out, would you," she said, referring to Denis's pipe. "We have enough problems without burning down the woodshed as well."

Elliott nodded feelingly at the mention of troubles. "It's bad enough being assassinated all the time."

"Seems to me," said Denis, chewing on his now-dead pipe, "it's about time we did something about Strange. Before he does us."

"Well, we have been trying," said Paisley. She herself had drawn the "wanted" posters of Strange, the ones Gibson, the U.S. Marshal — or former U.S. Marshal — was supposed to have posted in New York. "It's not as if we can hunt all over the world for him ourselves."

"We got the cash," countered Denis. He took a swig of his ginger beer.

"Look," said Elliott, "you may get to swan about the seas on your very own ship, but I'm pretty certain *our* parents would object to us leaving home indefinitely on a globe-trotting vendetta."

Denis shrugged. "You swore he'd be brung to justice. I'd've thought you'd want that as much as anybody. Seein' as he's tryin' to kill you. How'd you survive, anyway? They miss?"

A miss had something to do with it. A certain Miss Paisley.

"Mr Thompson did for the first one. Punched him right off the train," said Elliott.

Denis looked questioningly at the name. "You remember — the Dominion Minister of Justice," Elliott reminded Denis.

"Well, I'm glad *someone* met justice," said Denis. "And the other one?"

Elliott glanced at Paisley. "He, uh, met with an accident."

A strong breeze was coming in from the lake. Paisley looked out the rattling window into the dark yard. There wasn't much to see.

Denis tapped his teeth with his pipe. "What I heard 'round town was that he'd had his head bit nearly clean off."

"Elliott," said Paisley, still watching the blackness, "would you please move Sniggler's snack outside?"

When Elliott returned, Denis was still awaiting an answer.

"Well," said Elliott, "people seem to think it was a wolf. Or something. If you don't mind, we'd just like to leave it at that, for now."

"Oh....kay," said Denis. "Question is, how do we get him? The law's no good. Tried that. They'd just laugh at us again if we started on again about sleepwalkers, and Strange, and mushroom spores and that."

Paisley had no suggestions, temporizing with a drink of ginger beer instead. Seeing Adelmo with Captain Rawlins discussing the Wellborn Trust... it was hard to know what to think. Perhaps Strange *was* a loose cannon, with nothing to do with the Wellborn Trust any more. They were a charity, after all. Some kind of charity. Strange must have been acting without their knowledge in Spohrville.

"Mr Thompson is looking into it," said Elliott. "He believes me. At least, he believes someone tried to kill me. He's working on it."

Denis set down his bottle and folded his arms. "Lay a trap, that's what I say."

"And if we catch him?" asked Paisley.

Denis cut his flattened hand across his throat and clucked his tongue. "Self defence."

"Have you ever killed anyone before?" asked Paisley.

"Not yet."

"Then don't treat it so lightly." *He jests at scars that never felt a wound.*

Elliott cleared his throat. "They're not the same. Planning to kill someone, I mean, and doing it to stop them from committing murder. It's..." Elliott's gaze fell on Paisley, and then slid past her, out the window. "I thought Bell's house was empty."

Paisley followed his line of sight. "It is." The house was as dark as the sky. And it was only half finished. No-one would be there at night. "There was some talk of ghosts. The last builder was scared off. He wouldn't set foot in the place. He said there'd been..."

Lights. There was one now, faint, moving inside, just visible through an upstairs window. Or, was it the ground floor? It was hard to know, when people propped up a house on stilts to add another storey. No, it was near the roof. The corner room.

"There is someone in there," said Elliott.

Denis loomed over his shoulder. "Or some *thing*."

"Right," said Elliott. "Ghost or whatever, I'm not waiting to see if it takes a shot at me. Shall we?"

Paisley nodded. Denis pulled the axe out of the chopping block. Elliott hooded the lantern. They eased silently though the woodshed door and trotted towards the Bells' house, their footfalls in the damp grass quieter by far than the voice of Mrs Leonowens, pouring out of Aunt Claudia's house in waves of sternly-worded organization. They hopped the hedge, the dim glimmer still appearing and disappearing in one of Bell's windows. At the front door, they had to pause. The only way in was by some scaffolding with a plank extended to the gap where the front door had been, now about eight feet off the ground. A ladder took them up level with the door.

"I'll have to use the lantern," whispered Elliott.

From within, there came faint noises, like things moving through leaves. Scraping wood.

"Shine it over the plank," suggested Paisley, barely aloud. "Denis, you go first. Then I will. Then Elliott. Go upstairs and make for the last room on the left side of the hall. I think that's where the light was." Paisley paused, picturing what might follow. She looked from Elliott to Denis. "On second thought, once we're inside, hood the lantern and follow me. I've been here before. And I can... see pretty well in the dark." And hear the faintest sound.

When they'd crossed the plank, a little unsteadily in the wind, Paisley took Elliott's hand. For a moment he looked blankly at it, and at Paisley. "I'll guide you," whispered Paisley. Seeming a little confused, Elliott lifted the lantern, inclining his head towards it. Getting the idea, Paisley mimed that Denis should put his hand on Elliott's shoulder before shutting the window of the lantern to cast them into darkness.

There wasn't much light in the house, that was certain. Paisley could only barely make out anything, provided she didn't look straight at it. What the others could see... was probably nothing at all. She stepped carefully along the main hall with an arm outstretched in case the Bells hadn't sensibly removed all of their hall furniture before elevating their position in the world. There had better not be a gale before the renovations were done, that's all she could say; all houses move a bit in the wind, but this one... at least it was creaking enough to hide the occasional squeak of the floorboards. She was setting her foot down softly to avoid just such a disturbance when it failed to reach the floor. Only by pulling hard on Elliott did she manage to stop herself pitching in to the hole. The others piled into her as she teetered on the edge on the dark cavity she'd mistaken for a rug.

"There's a gap in the floor. Be careful," she advised. Elliott sighed. They set out again to edge around the hole.

The stairs were the next obstacle. They did creak, rather a lot, but by going at a snail's pace and trying to avoid getting into a regular walking rhythm, Paisley was pretty sure that the groans of the wood were lost in the house's other noises. An occasional flash of light across the ceiling above the stairs, and the continued rustlings up there, suggested that whatever was going on hadn't been interrupted by their arrival yet.

Elliott, momentarily losing his balance in the dark, bumped into Paisley and squeezed her fingers. Like last summer. That was what had been at the back of her mind since they'd set off in the dark. That was the last time she'd... well... held Elliott's hand. It had only been a séance, of course. There certainly wasn't anything more than that in it. There couldn't be, really. Who could fancy a girl he thought was some kind of monster. It wasn't ladylike, turning into a beast that... did things. It didn't seem the sort of thing fellows looked for in a girl. Elliott had been good about it, really. Hardly displaying any horror at all. It was just a shame he knew. If only... if only he were a little taller. And older. And didn't know. And... there suddenly wasn't a next step. With a squeak of her own, Paisley flailed her arm about and fell onto the landing. Elliott fell on top of her. From the weight, she suspected Denis had fallen on top of Elliott.

"Ow! Ow Ow," muttered Elliott. There was a slight clank. "Hot," he said, and by the singing smell he must have meant the lantern. She heard the smack of burnt fingers being popped into a mouth.

It's no simple task for three people to untangle themselves quietly in the dark, on a flight of stairs. Not when one of them is holding an axe, the second a hot lantern, and the third is feeling foolish. It only makes matters worse when some rogue — probably a hired assassin — is down the hall, ready to murder them all at the slightest sound. The fact that they succeeded, Paisley attributed to the dexterity she'd acquired from dancing lessons. It certainly owed nothing to propriety or etiquette. She could hardly guess how the others managed. She'd heard sailors had to be pretty quick on their feet. Whatever the reason, they set out again along the upstairs hall having suffered merely a few bruises, which in Elliott's case could hardly make much difference.

The end door was ajar. Weak candlelight leaked out, casting a pale patch in the hall. Coming even with the door frame, Paisley paused, hearing more rustlings within. The question of what to do next presented itself. The boys shuffled to a halt behind her. They could rush in... Now, almost too late, it occurred to Paisley that the light could easily be Dr Bell, come to get something from his study. Should they leap upon him out of the night without warning, the shock might kill him. She edged closer to the door and slid one eye past the frame. Chairs. Carpets. Bookcases. Desk... and someone. A man, bent over a drawer. Not Bell. An intruder. Paisley withdrew her eye. It was time for the axe.

In the dim light she nodded to the others and pointed to Denis, sweeping her hand to the door to tell him to rush in first.

Denis nodded back and launched himself past, through the door, Paisley and Elliott in pursuit.

"Thief!" shouted Denis, the axe raised as he skidded to a halt before the desk. The man, still seated, rocketed back from the drawer into the wall behind, mouth agape with surprise. He had a long curling moustache.

"Don't move!" warned Denis.

The man didn't. He stared. Paisley wasn't sure what to do next. The moustachioed villain, seemingly with tremendous effort, dragged his gaze off Denis and looked, if anything, more bemused by his other assailants. A tug on her fingers reminded Paisley that she was still holding Elliott's hand. With a tinge of embarrassment, she let go. At least they'd confused the thief by confronting him with the strange tableau vivant of what looked like a pair of sweethearts accompanied by an axe-wielding maniac. It was a good tactic to surprise the enemy. That's what Paisley's Papa always said.

"You!" said Elliott.

"You!" replied the man.

"What!?" said Paisley.

"Him," explained Elliott. "We met. On the train. But," Elliott told the man, "I didn't have you down as a common house-breaker."

"I am not a thief," claimed the fellow, relaxing slightly, but still watching Denis warily.

"Then what are you doing here?" asked Elliott.

The man tilted his chair back down onto all four legs. "That is my business, not yours, young man," he said, a little pompously. He had an accent. French.

"It'll be the police's business," warned Denis. "Fetch the constable, Paisley."

The man made as if to stand, but desisted when Denis hefted the axe meaningfully. "Wait. It is only to get some papers for Dr Bell that I am here. There is no need for the police."

"Get Bell, then," suggested Denis, in lieu of the constable. "We'll ask him."

The man shrugged, as if it was on their heads if they annoyed Bell. Paisley turned to seek her neighbour when a crash made her wheel back around. There was a melee on the floor by the desk now, the man having dived over it into Denis, flinging the axe away. The candle teetered atop a pile of papers, giving Paisley an instant of fire-panic before it tipped to the floor amid the scuffle and plunged them all into a noisy darkness until Elliott remembered to open the shutters of his lantern. He and Paisley sprang upon the wrestling pair, where the man was desperately trying to get free of Denis.

Elliott set down the lantern and grabbed the thief's collar. Paisley took hold of one of his arms, twisting it round, kneeling on the small of his back in exactly the way she'd found most effective for conquering teasing cousins.

The man yelped and squirmed, unable to extricate himself. Denis jerked away from him and seized his feet.

"Now," said Elliott, panting from the exertion, "Who are you? What are you doing here?"

Their prisoner struggled a little more, then went limp, breathing heavily himself. "Summon your constable. I have stolen nothing."

"Are you with the Wellborn Trust?" demanded Elliott.

The man twitched his head around to look at them before resuming his contemplation of the floorboards. "What is that?"

Denis bundled the man's legs together under one arm like a bunch of kindling. "Lift him." Elliott and Paisley each took an arm.

The man groaned. "What is the meaning of this?"

They heaved him off the floor. He was not a large man, no taller than Elliott, and lightly built. They easily lugged him into the hall, as directed by Denis. At the head of the dimly-lit staircase, Denis halted.

"Over you go, my friend," he said, leaning his weight on their captive's feet, forcing Elliott and Paisley to release his arms or be pulled over the brink. Elliott protested, and so did the man. Vigorously.

"Don't kick," warned Denis, "or I might have to let go."

Elliott ran back to the study, returning in a moment with the lantern.

The inverted man clutched desperately at the banister rungs to stop from swinging. Denis had him gripped tightly at the feet. A very red, moustachioed face swung past the banister like a condemned prisoner behind bars.

"Are you listening?" asked Denis, rattling the bars with his toe.

"Yes," said the man, in a strained croak.

"Good. I'm going to ask you a few questions. And you're going to tell me the truth. And quick. I dunno how long I can hold you like this." Denis' arms quivered in testimony to the urgency.

"You are correct! I am a thief! Only a thief! I confess!"

"I don't think so," said Denis.

Paisley squatted to look the man in his upside-down face. "A man tried to kill Elliott on the train. That man met with an accident. So did the man who tried to kill Elliott last night. We mean to know what you're really doing here, or there may be another accident."

The man's eyes bulged distastefully. From his waistcoat pocket his watch slipped out, the chain lengthening until the fob pulled loose and both plummeted past his face and into the depths. A faint delayed crash announced its destruction below.

"It's a long way to the ground," observed Paisley.

"Yes! I will tell you, please, let me down."

"Tell us now," said Denis, "or I let you down farther'n you'd like." He released one foot.

"Please! I will tell you! I am from the *Deuxième Bureau*, I investigate the Wellborn Trust, it is true!"

Elliott squatted beside Paisley to look at the panicking man. "What is the *Deuxième Bureau*?"

"Military intelligence. Submarine boats. It is for the Wellborn Trust that I am here, I swear it!"

"Reel him in," said Elliott. Denis hauled the spy back over the banister and let his drop to the floor, where the man tried to regain his composure by patting his moustache back into shape. "That was a very nice watch," he complained. The congestion of blood began to drain from his face.

"Why?" asked Elliott. "Why are you interested in them?"

The spy frowned, as if he might resist again, but merely shrugged. "France has had one war with the German Empire. We shall have more. For Germany to have a naval weapon that we do not is... unacceptable."

"But it's only a little ship," said Paisley. "And it's bound for Africa. To stop slavers."

"Miss, do you know what a torpedo is? That little boat could sink a battleship. It could render our fleets useless. It could start another war. A great war, perhaps. Do not deceive yourself that a weapon may be used only for good. A country with such a weapon is not a charity. If they do not have a warlike purpose for it... they will devise one."

The man started to get up, paused to await permission, then rose. He brushed down his rumpled suit. "Please believe me that my government has no interest in any of you coming to harm."

"And," said Paisley, "we have no intention of letting our country's interests be harmed by foreign spies."

"Ask yourself, young lady, whether the British Empire, the greatest naval power in the world, will benefit from Germany possessing a weapon that causes the British Admiralty to become as obsolete as the sailing ship. Perhaps your interests are not so far from those of France. Miss, gentlemen, with your leave, I will bid you a very good night."

While they considered this, the Frenchman nodded and descended the stairs carefully in the dark. He'd left them with much to ponder.

Paisley leant over the banister. "Mind the hole!" she shouted. A much wilder shout came in reply, cut off abruptly with a thump.

Chapter Thirteen
NOWHERE TO HYDE

THE FOLLOWING MORNING Elliott found himself, after the questionable fortification of another breakfast of porridge, longing for a bit of that peace and quiet he'd expected to find on his holiday. It was an expectation that had, unlike Elliott, not survived the first attempt on his life, back on the Halifax Express.

With the ladies of the house occupied in their political machinations, Elliott perused Miss Hayward's library, as he'd been invited to do, to find a distraction for the day. He dipped into various innocuous-sounding books on history and politics without finding them diverting enough, eventually choosing a slim new volume entitled *Strange Case of Dr Jekyll and Mr Hyde* as being just what was needed: something bizarre and unlikely enough to seem credible and engaging when placed beside the events of his own life. Most of the critics in Canada had either ignored or sneered at it, so it had to be pretty good.

He settled into one of the armchairs of the library, only to find that the shouts and arguments and urgent footsteps upstairs distracted too much from his reading, and so he headed for the front porch to put even more distance between himself and the hurly-burly of the suffragist movement. Reaching the front door, he discerned a looming shadow outside, one that gave him a tense moment of dread until he was able to convince himself that assassins most likely didn't call at the front doors of their victims' domiciles. Particularly not in the Maritimes, where in most houses people rarely used the front door for anything at all, apart from keeping draughts out. Possibly the killers had heard of Miss Hayward's cosmopolitan attitudes, and assumed she disdained such parochial customs. He reached for the knob, and then stopped. *Probably* assassins wouldn't use the front door. But if not, what was this fellow doing standing there, definitely looming, and definitely not ringing the bell. Generally people rang the bell if they found themselves confronted by a door. Unless they were violent criminals. Not that Elliott was completely certain what violent criminals did when they came round for a visit, despite his ever broadening experience with that class of person. For the sake of prudence, he went to the window beside the door and shifted aside the curtain. There was a mountain of man deposited on the doorstep, a large bundle in its arms, topped by an unruly red beard and wild, darting eyes. The eyes careened about until they landed on Elliott, causing the mountain to reel like an earthquake had hit it. They looked back down the driveway as if planning to make a run for it, with or without the rest of the body.

Elliott smiled, nervously. So did the man. Elliott decided to try opening the door.

After a while, he called through the door, "It sticks a bit. Would you mind giving it a shove?"

He was able to dodge aside as the door burst inward.

"Thank you," said Elliott. "Are you, ah, looking for someone?" From the bundle and the furtive attitude, Elliott had concluded that he was dealing with a hobo, or a peddler.

"It's… it's aboot the lassie. These," said the man, pushing his bundle across the threshold to Elliott, "are her *things*."

"Yes?" Elliott glanced at the bundle. It looked like what Paisley had been wearing a couple of days ago, the day she…

"Mrs McKelvie does… you know. Laundry," said the man.

"Really?" Elliott looked again at the bundle. "She washes shoes, too, does she?"

"Yes. No. What?"

"And you are…"

"Mungo," said the man, who produced a handkerchief and began mopping his brow. His eyes were starting to wander again.

"Right," said Elliott. Elliott looked over his own shoulder, hoping that the discussion had attracted someone else to deal with whatever was happening.

The mopping settled the man enough for him to further *un*settle Elliott by dropping a heavy hand, complete with sweaty hanky, onto his shoulder.

"It's me ain fault. If there's to be a reckonin, let it fall on me, and not the puir wee lass."

"Reckoning…?"

Mungo, if that was his name and not his way of describing his state of mind, leant down to whisper huskily at Elliott with breath that smelt of kippers and boiled tea. "For the killin, Sunday nicht. Twas no the lassie's fault. She was no in her richt mind. My doin. All of it."

Finally, they were getting someplace. As was usual for Elliott, it was someplace that wasn't very nice. He unburdened himself of Paisley's apparel and coaxed Mungo back onto the porch, shutting the door again so their undertones wouldn't be overheard.

"You mean the man killed by the... wolf."

"Aye. My carelessness did it, killed a man. Mrs McKelvie's beside herself."

"Take heart, then. The dead man was trying to murder me. Paisley only did him in to save my life."

"Murder you?" said Mungo, in a mixture of astonishment and relief.

Elliott dropped into a wicker chair. "Put two bullets right through my window. The last one would have been through me, but for Paisley. So don't worry yourself. They say it was a wolf that killed him, and that's as far as it need go. If you hadn't... done whatever it was to change Paisley... it would be me they're holding an inquest over, not that would-be killer. Thank you."

Mungo scratched his beard. "But why?"

"It's complicated. Paisley and I have enemies. Dangerous enemies. This isn't the first time they've tried."

Shaking his big head, Mungo blew out his fishy breath. "Phew! Well, you've taken a load off my mind, lad. If there's e'er anythin A can do tae help you and the lass in your problems, jus say the word!"

There was only one thing Elliott could think of at the moment, so he stood to thank Mungo again and shake his hand, adding that if Mungo were to see any suspicious strangers, particularly one calling himself Strange, or Slack, or bearing Strange's description, then Elliott would be most grateful to hear of it. When Mungo had wandered off, slightly dazed, across the yard towards the woods, Elliott returned to his chair again to open his book.

Not at all aided by the continual racket of renovation next door in the Bells' house, Elliott became more and more engrossed in Stevenson's latest tale, all the more so because of a niggling feeling that there was something familiar about it. That double life of man and monster. He was pretty well absorbed in the story when footsteps on the path summoned him back to the world. Looking over the book, he perceived a familiar Irish face under a familiar derby hat.

"Morning, Elliott," said Garrity, Elliott's erstwhile cabdriver. "You're looking better. Not so sozzled as last time I laid eyes on you. How's that girl you're sweet on? What was her name? Parsley?"

Elliott sank low in the wicker chair before realizing that hiding would do no good. He grimaced, and waved a little desperately. "Shh!" With any luck, Paisley would be out of earshot at the other end of the house. "Garrity, what are you doing here? Don't tell me someone hired your cab all the way from Halifax to Baddeck..."

Garrity removed his hat and fanned his face with it. "I'm here to see the girl's aunt, actually. Miss Hayward. Did I forget to mention that I write for the papers? Part-time. You'd be surprised at the news you can pick up in cab." Garrity handed over a calling card.

Mr James Garrity, Journalist
The Daily Muse
Halifax, Nova Scotia

"Ah," said Elliott. "About the..."

"The election. Women's suffrage, and all that. You said she was active in that sort of thing. No-one much cared to cover a by-election in the back-and-beyond, but I thought the votes-for-women angle might make for a good story."

"Oh." About the... dead body in the yard, Elliott had been about to say. Having city papers asking questions would have been awkward. It was bad enough to have the local paper sending people around. Elliott stuffed *Jekyll & Hyde* behind his back, so as not to give Garrity any ideas. "She's inside. I expect she'll be happy to give you a..." A lecture? A harangue? "...an interview. By the way, how's Starko?"

"The Russian? I believe he's in port for a spell yet. Say, it looks like you've another visitor."

Sure enough, Dr Maddox was approaching with a thoughtful expression and a pipe. Elliott supposed the pensiveness was due to the news of the recent gruesome death. Elliott was uneasy himself, of course, but nearly being murdered by a fellow has a tendency to blunt one's concern for the assassin's wellbeing. Elliott's mind had been dwelling more on the French spy than on the nameless corpse. The spy had survived his little tumble all right, with a few sprains and scrapes. And some mild mortification; wherever the Frenchman's lost watch had gone, at least it had his lost dignity to keep it company. Arriving at the porch, Maddox extracted his pipe. "Elliott," he said.

"Dr Maddox, isn't it?" said Garrity. "I, uh..." Garrity glanced at Elliott, barely suppressing a grin, "attended your recent lecture in Halifax. James Garrity."

The two men shook hands. From somewhere upstairs, Mrs Leonowens called out.

"Miss Hayward? Miss Hayward? Will you come to the cellar and examine these election posters of your niece's? They simply *won't* do."

The front door knob rattled. It creaked, popping open a crack. Paisley's aunt edged out, wearing a hunted, faraway look, like a fox who has just panted up a hill with a hooting troop of half-witted aristocrats on her heels, only to find a mob of hounds on the other side.

"Miss Hayward," said Maddox, "if there is anything I can do to assist you, you need only ask."

"With Mrs Leonowens?"

"I have examined the body," continued Maddox, "with the permission of the authorities of course — and the conclusion, of there having been an animal attack, seems undeniable. Still..."

"The garden," she said, laying a hand on Mr Maddox's arm. "You must have a look at my garden."

She urgently ushered Maddox back down the front steps and around the house, with Elliott and Garrity trailing along behind, Elliott feeling vaguely faithless for leaving poor Paisley inside at the mercy of Mrs Leonowens, whom even now he could hear descending. Having seen the garden already, Elliott was not anxious to have all of the diminutive carrots and marjorams and roses itemized yet again. Something hesitant about Maddox's agreement with the animal attack conclusion, though, made him wish to hear more of the man's mind.

Garrity delayed Elliott by an herb bed. "What's this body Dr Maddox is talking about?"

"Oh, just a body that turned up under an apple tree. Nothing to be concerned about. A wild animal attack," Elliott added hurriedly, as Garrity produced a notepad and pencil from his pocket. "You know the country. Full of nasty, dangerous creatures. You should get back to Halifax, where it's safe. Hadn't we better be catching up?" He set off to rejoin Dr Maddox and Miss Hayward, pursued by Garrity, chewing his pencil.

"... some unusual features in the dentition of the attacker, as indicated by the bite marks," Maddox was saying as Elliott reached them. "A mixture of the dental characteristics of the carnivore and the omnivore. If I didn't know better, I would almost be inclined to think the bites were made by some type of huge raccoon, or werewolf."

Garrity nudged Elliott with an elbow. "Ha! That's just like your girlfr..."

"Speaking of raccoons," said Elliott, a little too loudly, "aren't they quite troublesome to gardeners?"

Paisley's aunt looked pained at the mention of them. "Not as destructive as cats, of course. Cats commit *infamies* in the herb beds. But look at these cucumber frames." She pointed out some glass boxes with plants inside. "The raccoons are constantly interfering with them. And then there are the hurricanes that come through in late summer."

Relieved at the redirection of the conversation, Elliott helped push it along its new course. "And hurricanes have several times the destructive power of raccoons," he pointed out helpfully.

Miss Hayward studied him for a moment. "Elliott, are you truly, as Paisley claims, considering a career in the sciences?"

"That's right."

Miss Hayward shook her head sadly. She became even more forlorn when she pointed out the catnip. "Look at it," she dared them. It was not an inspiring sight. All that remained of the plant were a few broken stumps covered in fur, with a pathetically withered leaf or two. The fur bore a certain resemblance to Sniggler's fur. "I would have given you some catnip tea for your headaches and megrims, Elliott, but as you can see..."

It was a shame, as Elliott felt another headache coming on, and not only due to his concussion. There was a tail moving jauntily though the rhubarb in a line for the catnip.

"Miss Hayward, ah, this..." Elliott pointed to Garrity.

"Yes, who exactly are you, sir?"

With Miss Hayward launching into an interrogation of Garrity, Elliott proceeded in a businesslike and unsuspicious manner in the opposite direction, plunging an arm into the rhubarb to extract Sniggler as he passed.

"No more catnip for you," he whispered. "You've taken the pledge."

Rounding the corner of the house, he found the cellar doors fortuitously open, and descended into the evil-smelling gloom. This was where the acid baths for the etching were kept.

"What do *you* think of these posters?" said Paisley's voice in the dark, causing Elliott to drop Sniggler in surprise.

"Posters?" He squinted. His eyes hadn't adjusted yet. Paisley shone a carbide lamp dazzlingly over a sheet of paper with a picture of Britannia on it, and something to do with votes. Voices drifted down into the dank cellar from the garden while Elliott examined the art.

"...of course," Dr Maddox was saying, "a wolf may sometimes kill to protect its mate..."

Elliott concentrated on the poster. "It's, ah..." he said, avoiding Paisley's eye, "um, skilfully done. You're quite good at etching."

Paisley cleared her throat. "Mrs Leonowens says it isn't any good."

"Mrs Leonowens is an irksome old baggage."

"Indeed?" said Mrs Leonowens, stepping out of the shadows.

"I think," said Elliott, holding his aching head in his hands, "I'm going to go and lie down somewhere."

Rest. That's what was needed after a concussion. There wasn't any other treatment, after all, and if he wandered around dimly-lit cellars feeling dizzy, it would probably just end in another head injury. Elliott took the inside stairs back up into the house, removed his shoes, and kept plodding as softly as possible around to the main stairs and up to his bedroom, to avoid jarring the delicate tissues of his brain. With any luck, everyone would be busy outside or in the cellar for a while, and there'd be enough peace to let him nap until the nausea went away and he could enjoy lunch. Or sneak into town again for lunch at the Telegraph Inn. Sniggler would be happily occupied for the balance of the morning, eating all of the rodents in the cellar.

Elliott was passing Lady Beauchamp's room when he noticed the door was ajar, and Lady Beauchamp was standing, facing away, fiddling with something in her hand. Despite his feelings on mandatory vegetarianism, he was about to wish her a good morning when it struck him that she was acting very oddly. Perhaps it was a new exercising fad, like Indian clubs. She was shifting from foot to foot and pointing one arm while keeping the other behind her back. She whirled around, arm extended, pointing a revolver at him. Elliott shouted. Lady Beauchamp fired.

Chapter Fourteen
DARK WATERS

"I ONLY WANTED A holiday," muttered Elliott, stretched in a bewildered sprawl on the chaise longue in the front room, where all and sundry were gathered around as if waiting on his last words in hopes of a legacy. Paisley could recognize on his face the long-suffering expression Elliott always wore when someone had been trying to kill him.

"Give him some brandy," suggested Aunt Claudia. The bystanders, including Garrity and Maddox, made approving noises.

Elliott shrugged off a blanket that some concerned party had thrown around his shoulders. "No spirits," he insisted. "I'm quite all right."

"I'll get some cocoa," suggested Paisley. The maid, Mary, who was also among the audience, said she would fetch it, and left for the kitchen. From upstairs, there were distant sounds of glass being swept into a tin dustpan.

Paisley turned a disapproving frown on Lady Beauchamp, who was taking in the consequences of her irresponsible gun-play with — as was her wont — an almost idiotic expression of aloofness. If the woman's nonsense delayed Paisley's excursion to the submarine boat, she would be quite put out...

"It was lucky you were aiming at the mirror," said Paisley, disregarding superstition, "rather than the real Elliott. But why on earth were you playing with that revolver?"

Paisley briefly entertained, and dismissed, the possibility that Lady Beauchamp might be yet another of Professor Strange's seemingly inexhaustible legion of accomplices. Really, the woman was altogether too unlikely, not to mention too inept, for the rôle. It was appearing more and more likely that Elliott's theory about her was correct: that Lady Beauchamp's singular meat-free diet was denying her certain essential elements vital for the maintenance of mental equilibrium. It was well past time to enact Plan H (for "hepatic"). To wit, the concealment of small quantities of cooked beef liver in Lady Beauchamp's meals, to forestall her descent into utter insanity. If questioned, they could plausibly claim that the liver was actually wild mushrooms, a subject on which Paisley had considerable expertise.

"One was hardly *playing*, my dear girl," said Lady Beauchamp. "One merely wished to be prepared against a return of that savage beast that lately despatched a man beneath our very windows."

"Beast!" exclaimed Elliott. "Lady Beauchamp, you…" He fell silent, appearing worried by the signs of interest from the two gentlemen present. "Lady Beauchamp, would you oblige me with a private word in the library?"

The mad gunwoman nodded, and reluctantly preceded Elliott to the next room, Elliott stiffly avoiding anyone's eye on his way out.

Aunt Claudia tapped her foot. "There are far too many firearms about these days. This is Baddeck, for heaven's sake, not Buffalo Bill's wild west. It would be a safer world if mankind would only confine itself to decent weapons. Parasols, letters to the editor, and so on."

"How's 'Beechum' spelt?" asked Garrity, producing his notepad again.

Paisley withdrew from the general conversation, her attention drifting instead to the other one in the library, received, imperfectly, by her oversensitive ears. Sometimes a curse, at other times a boon, her heightened senses were forever tempting her to unseemly curiosity. Through the wall, there was a pleading note in Elliott's voice. She leant closer.

"…to promise me you will not shoot any animals…"

For Sniggler's sake, Paisley hoped Elliott would succeed in curbing Lady Beauchamp's bloodlust, which, now that Paisley thought about it, was rather difficult to reconcile with the woman's vegetarian ideals. It had to be a deranged mind.

Oh. He means me.

Not that Paisley had any intention of going through that awful and indelicate metamorphosis again. Even thinking of it gave her a frisson of goosebumps. The strange sensations. The horror of having her mind slip away, to be replaced by… what? And *had* it been horrible? That was even more worrying. There had been a comfort to it, like slipping into sleep. Or into her real self. No politeness. No rules. Only action. Bloody action…

"… I assure you, Master Graven…" Lady Beauchamp was complaining now, in her haughty way. Paisley yawned to lend verisimilitude to her weary leaning, and pressed her ear harder against the wallpaper. No-one noticed. Her aunt was still holding the room spellbound with her itemization of the manifold ills of modern society. The maid arrived with the cocoa; she must have had the stove going for something already. Paisley took it and sipped pensively, at an angle of thirty degrees from vertical.

"…care if you're if you're the Empress of Abyssinia, I'm telling you that if you point that pistol at any wolves, you'll regret it."

"…propose to do?"

"…my friend, the Minister of Justice, to charge you with attempting murder this afternoon and…"

"…ishness. You would rather see me killed than some wolf, I suppose."

"Yes! And I'll be the one doing the killing if you start shooting at any wolves in this town!"

Paisley started, almost spilling her cup as a door slammed and Elliott re-appeared in the front room, red in the face. She felt her own cheeks getting warm from eavesdropping. Elliott… had just threatened to kill Lady Beauchamp. For her.

"Um," said Paisley, "here's your cocoa."

Elliott looked into the half-empty cup. His temper seemed to run off its rails and hiss to a halt. "Thanks."

"That will be Adelmo," said Paisley, when they were interrupted by the door bell. She lowered her voice to a whisper. "You won't tell him, will you? About my little *problem*?"

"Problem? You mean turning into an animal and ripping out people's throats?"

Inwardly, Paisley slumped. How could anyone love a monster?

IT WAS ALL becoming a bit much. People turning into *things*. People trying to kill Elliott. Elliott threatening to kill Lady Beauchamp. Spies in the night. Cupid firing rifle bullets. Spoons. Paisley watched Adelmo working on his motorwagon, feeling that a pleasant summer swim had led her unexpectedly into a whirlpool of intrigue, a whirlpool spiralling down, and down, to a submarine craft. Somehow, Aunt Claudia must be to blame for it all. It was her invitation that had led Paisley here in the first place.

As Adelmo cranked the motorwagon to take them up Baddeck Bay to the *Paradoxo* again, for a look inside this time, a weird wailing floated down from somewhere in the wooded hills behind the house like the lamenting of damned souls.

Adelmo paused in his winding to cock an ear. "Is that von of your local fowl? Or perhaps some poor animal in distress?"

"It's a creature called a Scotch Windbag." Hearing the screams and howls made Paisley realize that there was a good deal of truth in what Mrs McKelvie told her husband the other day: 'Ye may lairn a great many things from books, Mungo, but the bagpipes is nay one 'o them.'

"They are an industrious, resolute people, the Scots," said Adelmo, once they were on the road, the attempts at highland tunes drowned out by the roaring engine, "and fine engineers. It surprises me that the English were able to conquer them."

"Oh, they didn't. It was the other way around. The Scots run most of the empire, you know." That was almost true. They were in New Scotland, after all. The Scots had spread out like a miasma of whisky vapours, filling every stratum of society from Parliament to the boiler room. They were even next door, inventing telephones, and in the woods tutoring the werebeasties. At least there'd be no more of *that*. Paisley had enough to worry about without finding herself unexpectedly running wild on all fours, covered in fur, human blood dripping from her lips, *thank you very much, Mr McKelvie*. People in Baddeck were open-minded, but open-mindedness only goes so far, and appearances still counted for something in this world.

Only the one road ran along Baddeck Bay, so their drive was largely a repeat performance of their trip the other day, except that the neighbours were now stoically pretending to be less amazed by the motorwagon. The local mongrels suffered from no such well-bred restraint. One followed, playfully woofing and gnarling, as far as the shore, where it chewed the tires and bounced excitedly until it sniffed Paisley. It ran off homeward, whining. Adelmo waved cheerily at the departing hound.

There was a definite jauntiness to Adelmo today. He'd even stuck a red rose in his button hole. The bloom had given Paisley a jolt when she first spotted it, reminding her as it did of the rose Madam Defarge had worn in *A Tale of Two Cities*, to warn her fellow conspirators of the danger of spies. But Adelmo's face told all there was to tell about that; it was a sunny wheat-field of a face, and not just because the wind was making his corn-coloured hair stick up. There were no dark secrets there. No black forests full of lurking evil in that landscape. He was open country, all the way to the horizon.

What had looked insignificant from the shore was a brooding bulk as they half rowed, half blew towards it on a northerly breeze, through the wind-whipped waves. The submarine vessel lurked just under the sunlit world, black and sleek as a great iron porpoise waiting to dive. Only the hatch and a strip along its spine broke the surface, hinting at the body that lay below. Paisley almost expected it to yield like flesh when she touched its skin. Instead, the hull was hard and cold, nubbly, with rivets in place of a whale's barnacles. Ever since learning of the thing's existence, she had wanted to have a closer look at the submarine boat. It had seemed so fantastical and thrilling before, in her imagination. Knowing that it was the centre of an international scheme of potentially catastrophic consequences had put a somewhat different complexion on the machine.

At least, if the spy were to be believed. It could well be best not to believe everything that spies said. Particularly other people's spies. But there was Lady Beauchamp's telegram, too.

Paisley tasted the brackish spray from the lake on her lips, bringing back unwelcome salty, and sanguine, memories. "All that iron," she said, as Adelmo, stepping aboard the sub to tie up the dinghy, lifted her onto the deck. She had enough metal secreted about her own person to make her nervous of slipping into the lake, where the silver would drag her to the bottom long before Adelmo could even remove his shoes to dive in to the rescue. "It's a wonder it doesn't sink."

And he was off with a sparkle in his eyes, telling her everything about buoyancy, and displaced water, and even launching into the old tale about Archimedes, before deciding that the Greek's discovery was an indelicate anecdote.

"It's all right," Paisley assured him. "I take baths too."

On the opposite side of the small, square hatch that presumably led inside, Adelmo dodged the vexed subject of baths by fishing something out of his jacket pocket.

"Perhaps, my dear Paisley, you would do me the honour?" His hand opened, revealing a long brass key. It was inscribed *Paradoxo*. He flipped open a tiny rubber-sealed door in the hatch that hid a keyhole. When she'd turned the key in the lock and offered it back, Adelmo smiled, waving it away. "A memento. Of your visit. Did you not tell me that one of your ancestors was a commander of a castle, a *châtelain*? Would you be my *châtelaine*, and keep my keys?"

Paisley mulled over the significance of this during her descent of the ladder leading below the waves, down into the silent steel cavern. She hoped she hadn't exaggerated her place in society to Adelmo when she'd said that her father was a mayor, and they lived in a château. It was more or less true, and sounded so much better than admitting that her father also ran a store where she was a clerk, selling bootlaces and peppermints by the penny.

Only a little pale blue light leaked in through a small porthole, filled with a thick block of glass. When she reached the bottom, she could make out little of the surroundings until Adelmo, above on the ladder, swung the hatch back into place over his head and secured it, then flicked a switch to flood the narrow corridor with electric light. Every surface was festooned with dials, and pipes, and valves.

"I bought a quantity of incandescent lamps from a couple of gentlemen in Toronto, named Evans and Woodward, but zey are not making zem any more. I must order some more from the Edison & Swan Company in London." He tapped a flickering bulb with his fingernail. "These one's keep burning out."

A drip from the ceiling landed on Paisley's head. She was making a brave effort not to be disappointed by the insides of the vessel. It was not quite up to the standards of Nemo's *Nautilus*. The damp and the fizzing light bulbs were par for the course with new inventions, she supposed, but there was a depressing lack of luxury in it. No furniture to speak of, except for a few metal stools. No wood panelling. Or wallpaper. Or carpets. In fact, it was not so much like the *Nautilus* as like being inside a locomotive boiler, if someone had been deranged enough to install all of the gauges and controls on the inside. That was the trouble with wild scientific romances like Verne's — they made real inventions so disappointing. Novelists have a great deal to answer for in this life.

Adelmo was waiting expectantly. She needed to say something.

"I suppose there's still some work to do on it?"

"*Ja*, sure, the engine has yet to be installed. That will be a task for Captain Rawlins. Because of this, the *Paradoxo* was towed here."

Perhaps décor wasn't of the essence. The *Paradoxo* wasn't intended for 20,000 league voyages in style and comfort, after all.

"So, we won't be able to cruise about the lake a bit?"

Adelmo looked crestfallen. "Well, no. Not cruise. I am sorry. Not until ze engine is fitted." Paisley immediately regretted mentioning it. Then he perked up slightly.

"We could... dive. If you would like that..."

"Very much."

It seemed to please Adelmo to be able to make the craft do *something*. He consulted some of the dials and, satisfied with whatever he divined from them, pulled on a pair of stiff levers. The ship shuddered, rumbling. Bubbles flowed past the widow.

"I am letting water into the ballast tanks, to lower our buoyancy," explained Adelmo, who had removed his jacket (and the rose, giving it to Paisley) and was rolling up his sleeves, transforming him from a minor nobleman on holiday into the confident shipbuilder who had laboured over the *Paradoxo* in the shipyards of Kiel. Here, in his machine, his pride shone like the polished brass of the instruments. Paisley basked in it, wondering what he'd look like in a trim blue nautical uniform, with gold braid, and a sword. Well, perhaps not a sword. Space was at a premium down here, and a sword would make turning around a perilous manoeuvre.

The dive was accompanied by a slight sinking sensation that sent Paisley's hand reaching for a steadying pipe. Her ears popped. She went cautiously to the porthole to see what could be seen in the murky depths. Tentacles, perhaps. Tennyson came to mind.

> *Far, far beneath in the abysmal sea,*
> *His ancient, dreamless, uninvaded sleep*
> *The Kraken sleepeth: faintest sunlights flee*

But then, probably krakens found the lake too shallow. In all likelihood, she was the only monster under the lake at the moment. She, and the sinister forces that lurked about the *Paradoxo* like kelpies, waiting to lure humans to their doom.

"How long will it be before the *Paradoxo* can cruise about under its own power?" asked Paisley, wiping steam from the porthole glass and shading the dim view with both hands.

"I hope we will very soon be able to go motoring on the lakes together. Perhaps in a fortnight. Captain Rawlins says his engine will not take long to install. A most ingenious device! So compact! So advanced!"

Paisley sniffed the rose. "Is it a steam engine? Or, like the motorwagon engine?" Not the latter, please. She was willing to sacrifice comfort to go for a lake cruise with Adelmo, but being cooped up in a clammy boiler with a deafening, suffocating engine would rather spoil the trip.

"It is an electric engine. And silent. And it has no moving parts what-soever!" said Adelmo, flinging out his arms so excitedly that he barked his knuckles on the hull.

"What use is an engine with no moving parts?"

"Ah!" said Adelmo, grinning and kneading his hands, "It works by a struggle of electric and magnetic currents, pushing the sea water, and driving the vessel forward!"

Well, that was something, anyway. A silent engine might not be so bad. Paisley glanced at the dial beside Adelmo. *18 metres / 10 fathoms*. The steel plates of the hull were groaning and ticking occasionally as they dropped. "Will we be able to travel far?"

"Several hundred kilometres, I hope, before charging the electric cells."

Enough to cruise the lake, certainly. It was the sort of information Paisley suspected the French spy would give his waxed moustaches for. In fact, as she satisfied her curiosity with further questions, it became clear that Adelmo was eager to tell her absolutely everything about the *Paradoxo*, from how long it took him to build it, to how many torpedoes it could carry. A certain uneasiness stole over her, as though she herself were spying on Adelmo. Which she was... Along with Elliott, she was still gathering infor-mation about the Wellborn Trust, only Adelmo had no idea. He just though she was interested in his *opus magnum*. Which she was, too. But it was... complicated. It wasn't Adelmo, after all, who was doing anything wrong. If anyone was doing anything wrong.

Now Adelmo's beaming seemed to be exposing her as the duplicitous sneak she really was. No more espionage questions. The *Paradoxo* rocked gently as they settled onto the lake bed.

"Is there a kitchen aboard?" asked Paisley. That seemed an innocent enough question.

"*Ja*, ve shall be vell stocked with provisions. I have acquired a large supply of Johnston's Fluid Beef. Nourishing. Long lasting."

"Johnston's Fluid..."

"...Beef. Mr Johnston received an order for one million tins of beef for the French army, you see. The French lost the war with Prussia, the war which saw the end of the French Empire and the creation of the German."

"So when the French lost he turned the million tins of meat into this... fluid beef?"

"No, no. The French bought the beef afterwards. They thought a lack of food was to blame for their military failures. Johnston made his *fluid* beef out of, well, not exactly beef. The other parts of ze cattle. Ze parts zat did not go into ze tins." Adelmo rummaged in a crate and withdrew a small bottle which he handed over. It was filled with something tarry, like pitch, or black treacle.

"I see," said Paisley, peering into the jar. These were dark waters, indeed.

Chapter Fifteen
TALKS AT THE TELEGRAPH

ARRIVING AT THE Telegraph Inn dining room for luncheon — alone, since Paisley was busy with her aunt's political machinations, and Denis was on the dock doing a brisk business in lemons — Elliott cast his eye over the tables for anyone he knew, or who had a bloodthirsty look about him. So far he'd only seen strange faces, mostly glowing with the electricity of jubilees and by-elections. Baddeck was decked out with notices for rallies and speeches, and everyone was moving with mysterious purpose, discussing the great issues of the day. Temperance. The future of the Dominion. Fish. Women's suffrage. Patronage jobs. The county simmered with the sort of excitement that usually only precedes circuses, or public hangings.

He was heading to a table-for-one when he spotted a familiar nose, one bent rather far from true. Its owner was similarly bent — sullenly, over a coffee cup — in what Elliott easily diagnosed as despond.

"Gibson?" said Elliott, changing course to the man's table. The American had a few more grey hairs than when Elliott had seen him last, the previous year, and wasn't very clean shaven. "So you've arrived."

The delayed look of shock that Elliott got from everyone who saw his bruised face, even now that it was fading to green, was so common that he hardly noticed when Wallace Gibson performed it.

"Gar," said Gibson, "you're the worse for wear. You look like you've been through the wars, young Graven."

Elliott gave a wry smile. That was how he felt, too.

In lieu of conversation, Gibson stirred his coffee while Elliott tried to catch the waiter's eye, as a customer rather than as a hideous spectacle. Before he did, Gibson forced out what was only too obviously on his mind.

"I guess you know I've been sacked from the U.S. Marshal Service."

Elliott did, from the exchange of telegrams with the New York office, but not the reason. Gibson's gaze dropped into his coffee, his voice descending with it.

"Light fingers. Watches. Clocks. Couldn't stop myself. It's what that b—, that blasted Strange, or Slack, or whatever he calls himself now, did to me. Those spores of his. That *laboratory*," he said, in the way Elliott might have said *torture chamber*. "I'll never be a lawman again, not now. Lucky I didn't end up behind bars." Gibson laughed bitterly, clearly not feeling so lucky. Elliott fiddled with his cutlery, hardly feeling any more sanguine himself.

"I hate to take your money, Graven. This hunt for Strange, it's just been a dead end. No trace." Gibson looked up from his cup. "Don't suppose you've had any luck?"

"A dead end is just about what I came to, actually."

"Eh?"

"This past week I've been, let's see, nearly blown up by a suitcase full of dynamite, beaten half to death by someone who tried to throw me off a train, and shot at through my bedroom window."

Gibson set down his cup to stare at Elliott.

"Oh, and a crazy English lady took a shot at me with a revolver. But that wasn't related to Strange. I think."

"Jeepers. Are you serious?"

"I am."

Tea and biscuits arrived. Elliott waited for the waiter to leave before going on. Gibson seemed lost in thought.

"Look," said Elliott, "I'm sorry about your losing your job, but we still need your help on this case. If we don't find Strange soon..." Elliott checked that no-one was eavesdropping. "...I don't know how many more bullets I can dodge."

"Right." Gibson nodded, as much in drowsiness as assent. "I don't know how much I can do. I did bring my files, if you think they're worth looking over."

"Maybe you'd better get some rest," suggested Elliott.

"Yeah. I'm all in. It was a long trip."

Elliott cut short Gibson's rummaging for his wallet with an offer to pay the bill, which Gibson accepted without meeting Elliott's gaze. "Room twelve," he said, turning as he left, "when you want to see the files."

Poor Gibson. Perhaps once he got some sleep the investigation would take his mind off his troubles for a while. Justice might be an antidote to misery, if only they could pick up Strange's trail somehow. When it was all over, Elliott resolved, he'd goad Gibson into travelling to Kingston to see Dr Graven. His father had learnt a thing or two about Strange's methods. There was a chance that his efforts to cure Mrs Graven might help Gibson too.

Elliott addressed the waiter as he was passing the table again. "Do any of the rooms in this hotel have clocks?"

"I don't believe so, no."

At least Gibson would be spared that temptation.

"Elliott?" came a voice from behind, disturbing Elliott's meditations on his biscuit crumbs. It was Mr Thompson.

"Sir, hello. Will you join me?"

The Minister settled his heavy, if short, frame at the opposite end of the table. "I'm just back from a jaunt up north. One speech after another, and the requests — nay, *demands* — for patronage positions! I've only just had the chance to get back to your problem. It's a slimy business."

Elliott wondered which part of the business Mr Thompson was referring to, the eels, or Strange. "Yes, that summer in Spohrville was pretty unpleasant for everyone."

"I was referring to politics. The sooner I'm out of it and back on the Supreme Court bench the better. Politics is going to be the end of me if I spend much longer in this muck of corruption and hypocrisy."

"I think this affair may be the end of *me*. I only wanted a holiday…" It had been quite a nice one, too, up until the bombings and beatings.

"I know how you feel, Elliott," sighed Thompson.

"Someone is trying to kill you too?"

"No, no. I mean about the holiday. For instance, in the next few weeks my son will be returning home, my wife will be having her birthday, and our wedding anniversary is coming up, but here I am in Victoria County for somebody else's by-election. Each time I try to go home, or do anything with my family, there is always a crisis, or scandal, or rebellion, or by-election, or that ass Sir Charles Tupper does something, and off I am again to fix it."

"Gosh."

"Well, we have to keep the country running, eh?"

"Yes, sir. Thank you for taking time out to kill that man the other day."

"Please stop describing it that way, Elliott. Particularly in the middle of a restaurant. And an election."

That was something Elliott had meant to ask about, but what with murderers and Germans and whatnot, he'd never found the time. "Why *is* there any election, sir? Didn't we have one only a few months ago?"

"Ah, you see this is a by-election. It's only in Victoria county. The seat is empty since the incumbent, Campbell, went up to his great reward."

"Oh. I'm sorry. Was he very old?"

"I mean he went to the Upper Chamber. He was appointed to the Senate."

The waiter returned to take Mr Thompson's order with rather too much deference, almost as if he too were hoping to be awarded a plum civil service job. Thompson rattled off some dishes, and it soon became clear how he'd grown so stout. The Minister started with oyster soup, followed by cutlets, vegetables, claret, Charlotte Russe, cheese, then finally fruit. It gave them plenty of time to chat as he worked through the courses, starting with everything Elliott knew about the submarine boat, and the chat was rather cathartic for Elliott after trying for so long to make officialdom believe what had occurred in Spohrville.

"The magistrate," said Thompson, between mouthfuls, "Donaldson. No head for the law. No experience. I believe he was a fishmonger before getting himself appointed a J.P. Justice of the Peace, I mean. Now *that* must have been one of these infernal patronage appointments. I do not doubt someone in government owed him a favour, or was his relative, or both. I do not like to interfere with the magistracy, but in this case... I have reviewed his record. It is a shameful litany of nepotism and incompetence. Too early to say if he simply did not credit the charges against your man, Strange, or if he was being paid to look the other way. Either way, I will see that he is removed."

Elliott nodded. So that was why there'd never been any legal action against Strange. Granted, Strange was long flown, probably from the country.

"Is there anything you can do about Strange himself?"

Thompson set down his glass of claret. "I have issued a warrant for his arrest. If half of what I have heard about the man is true, he will have no end of charges to answer. Murder. Piracy. Slavery. Fraud. Kidnapping. Unlawful confinement. Administering a noxious substance. I am not even certain what to call some of the things he is accused of. Who has ever heard of using electricity, or fungal spores, to eradicate a person's free will? There may be a precedent — mesmerism, perhaps — but some of these offences may turn into cases of first impression that set new precedents. Common law is wonderfully flexible. A jumble, though. Wants codification."

Elliott opened up his teapot. He'd drunk it all. "You might wish to speak to Wallace Gibson. He's a... former U.S. Marshal investigating Strange privately, on our behalf. He knows Strange's history in the United States and South America. Strange has a lot of crimes in his past."

"Yes. Yes, I would like to meet Gibson. Though the courts here cannot charge Strange with acts committed outside the country. Except for piracy. I would prefer to see proceedings carried out in our courts, rather than take our chances with extradition. Assuming Strange is arrested here."

Six of one, half a dozen of the other, was how Elliott felt about the matter. As long as Strange was in a soundly-constructed cell, he didn't care which government was supplying room and board. Or rope and gibbet.

Scraping up the last of his Charlotte Russe, Thompson added "There haven't been any further incidents, have there? Of violence?"

It would be hard to explain. A mad Englishwoman who played with revolvers. A German who shot Paisley by accident. An assassin who was only prevented from killing Elliott by Paisley biting out his throat while she was a wolf. Thompson was looking so pleasantly sedated by his heavy meal. It would be a shame to have to tell him the sorts of things that would act on a highly-trained legal mind like sand in an engine, or alders in a woodstove.

"Ah," said Elliott, "nothing that presents any immediate danger."

Thompson, no doubt used to perfidious double-talk in witness boxes and on the hustings, tapped his empty dessert bowl with his spoon, eyeing Elliott judiciously. "Well, to be on the safe side, perhaps I should bring in some Dominion Police for your protection. Though that will take time. Better yet, appoint a couple of special constables here. I wish I knew the place better…"

Special constables. Elliott didn't like the idea of having strangers chasing around after him for his protection. They might interfere when he needed to do things that were strange, or illegal. Someone familiar, though…"

"There's Mr McKelvie. He's local." Not the Irish reporter. Whatever happened would be in the papers the following day. "And there's Dr Maddox. I'm sure he's a reliable gentleman."

O

Chapter Sixteen
OF THE MANY USES OF SPOONS

RESENTMENT WAS GROWING in Paisley for her aunt's interrogations, which had been going on since before they even set foot in the open carriage that Mrs Leonowens had cajoled from the mayor, one meant for the dignitaries to ride in at the upcoming jubilee festivities.

"You say the engine is not yet installed in the vessel?" asked Aunt Claudia.

"Not yet," said Paisley. She tried to convey her indifference to submarine boats by watching through her smoked glasses the clouds scudding overhead — the only way she could enjoy a scene so bright. With luck, a gust of wind would blow up and carry off their stacks of laboriously-printed political posters before the carriage reached Baddeck, sparing her the even more tedious task of posting them all over town. Alison, beside her, seemed like-minded. On the facing bench of the carriage, Mrs Leonowens was studying some papers next to Aunt Claudia, while Lady Beauchamp played with a deck of Tarot cards.

"Presumably," pursued Aunt Claudia, "they will be built in German shipyards?"

Paisley's non-committal noise of response induced Mrs Leonowens to briefly set aside her agendas and issue a rebuke. "Do speak up, Miss DeLoup, when your aunt asks you a question. It is unladylike to grunt and grumble. And do remove those glasses, child. They are so unbecoming. They make you look blind."

"Oh, I *am* sorry," said Paisley, ignoring the advice regarding the spectacles. "Shall I, Aunt Claudia, ask Herr Hasselberg on the next occasion I see him, to lend me all of the submarine boat's blueprints and plans for you to peruse?"

Lady Beauchamp's head bobbed up from her cards. "How thoughtful, Paisley! That would be most…" she said, cut short when Aunt Claudia accidentally brought the iron cap of her *Peabody's Patented Parasol* down on Lady Beauchamp's toe.

"Kindly do not be facetious, Miss DeLoup," complained Mrs Leonowens.

Aunt Claudia, after apologizing to Lady Beauchamp for her clumsiness, tossed the topic aside. "Never mind, Paisley. We shall be passing the inn in a few moments. I shall call upon Herr Hasselberg. He can assuage my concerns for your safety during your visits to his machine. Technical specifications are so re-assuring."

Mrs Leonowens consulted one of her lists. "Oh, no, Miss Hayward. I have arranged a meeting for you with the local clergy."

"Afterwards, then."

"After the clergy," said Mrs Leonowens, resorting to her list again, "is your address to the Women's Temperance Association."

Lady Beauchamp plucked a card from her deck. She made a portentous face and flipped it for Paisley and Alison to see. It showed a woman pouring liquid between two goblets with the caption *Temperance*. Alison heaved a bleak sigh.

"And then," said Mrs Leonowens, as Aunt Claudia was about to speak, "a meeting with the Orange Order. Later, you will be dining at the mayor's. You needn't concern yourself with scheduling your time. I have taken care of everything through until polling day."

"I see," said Aunt Claudia, taking a firmer grip on her parasol.

Lady Beauchamp fanned out her fistful of cards, plucked one at random, and displayed satisfaction at the choice. "Never fear, Claudia. It will be my pleasure to…"

"Lady Beauchamp," said Mrs Leonowens, passing over a page, "here is your agenda for the coming days. "As you see, I have arranged a full schedule for you also."

Momentarily dismayed, Lady Beauchamp twitched an eyebrow mischievously, flipping another card over and displaying it to Paisley. *The Fool.* "I am sure it would be such a comfort for you, Claudia," she said, "to be able to undertake your labours untroubled by that inscrutable mystery, the disappearance of your spoons."

She knows, thought Paisley, squirming in her seat. *She's a witch. She must be.* Oh, the shame, the ignominy! They would certainly search her, and find secreted about her person enough silver spoons for a tea & sherbet garden party. What could she look forward to but being sent home in disgrace, never ever again to show her face to Adelmo. Or Elliott. Any moment, Paisley expected to swoon from the sheer, dreadful, awfulness of discovery, and was crestfallen at her body's mulish refusal to be frail and vaporous. She was deliberating on whether or not to hurl herself to the floor of the carriage in a mock fit when Aunt Claudia broke her concentration.

"Indeed, it is a most baffling situation. Why, for instance, only spoons? Surely the forks are as valuable."

They were, but they were also too prickly for pockets and stockings, a fact Paisley barely kept herself from blurting out. Was it possible that the sheer number of spoons was unsettling her reason? Had she passed some natural limit of endurance, beyond which the mind could withstand no more spoons? In this great age, when heroes were testing the boundaries of experience, with balloonists and mountaineers scaling the heights, and submariners plumbing the depths, it looked as if it would be her destiny to discover the number of anxiety-reducing silver spoons a girl of sixteen, with one-sixteenth werewolf ancestry, could carry about before losing her senses, or the respect of her fellows. The DeLoup Limit would be a nice name for it.

"Do not, if you please," complained Mrs Leonowens, "snicker like that, Miss DeLoup."

"And such a recent problem," said Lady Beauchamp, shuffling her cards. "Why, it is only since Sunday that we noticed the lamentable decline of the cutlery. I remember particularly, for that was the day Mrs Leonowens arrived."

Mrs Leonowens nodded in acknowledgement of this fact. Then the blood rose in her face, right up to her greying hair. "You are not suggesting...!"

"Perish the thought, Mrs Leonowens," said Aunt Claudia. "Naturally, one understands that some among us suffer from ungovernable urges through no fault of their own, and are to be pitied, not censured."

So piqued was the king of Siam's former tutor that she even set aside all of her lists and timetables. "It is outrageous! If anyone took your spoons it was undoubtedly that horrible Graven boy. He is incorrigible!"

"How dare you," said Paisley, so livid from this impugning of Elliott's reputation that she quite forgot her own guilt for the moment. "Elliott would never do such a thing!"

"Quite," said Lady Beauchamp soothingly, "quite. Alison has already searched his room, so it cannot have been him."

Paisley turned to the girl beside her to confirm this latest outrage. While Alison wore a rather pained expression, she didn't volunteer to verify or deny the accusation.

"A cousin of mine," said Lady Beauchamp, pouring more oil onto what was either troubled waters or a fire, "was inordinately fond of boots. The servants had to keep them under lock and key or else he would whisk them away before one knew what was happening."

"What did he do with them all?" asked Paisley, over Mrs Leonowen's puffing and spluttering indignation. The boots suggested the existence of unplumbed depths of lunacy in Lady Beauchamp's family, of which this latest example was only the surface. No doubt an unfathomable slough of depravity lay below.

"I daresay he polished them, and admired them — rather as one might do with spoons," she added in a gentle aside to Mrs Leonowens. "They took him away, eventually, when the gardener found him eating the philadelphus bushes. He thought he was a caterpillar, you see."

"So," said Aunt Claudia, not very logically to Paisley's thinking, "there is nothing at all to be ashamed of, Mrs Leonowens. The subject need never be mentioned again. We hardly need stir our tea in any case, what with Lady Beauchamp's objections to milk, and sugar."

"Return me to the house at once," demanded Mrs Leonowens of the driver. "I am leaving. *Immediately!*"

"Oh, my," said Aunt Claudia. "Just let us out here."

Lady Beauchamp waved her deck of cards sadly at the wooden and purpled figure of the departing Mrs Leonowens before re-examining the schedule of events she was meant to attend, and letting it flutter away onto the street outside the town hall. "We shan't be needing this, then."

"It is too bad, it really is," lamented Aunt Claudia. "There is nothing for it but to go about our own plans. You and Alison run along and post those suffrage advertisements, Paisley. Lady Beauchamp and I have some persons whom we need to visit."

So saying, the two ladies set off towards the inn, bearing up well under the strain of losing Mrs Leonowens, Aunt Claudia so far forgetting the tragedy of it as to give her parasol a twirl.

Alison had the bundle of posters under one arm, and the fatalistic expression of a girl who has encountered no more than she expected. She drank in the neighbourhood.

"I don't suppose," said Paisley, "that you would know anything about the rather bomb-like so-called lightning strike that scarred the hull of the *Paradoxo*?"

"I really couldn't say," said Alison, dividing the sheaf of posters into two stacks and passing one to Paisley along with some pins. "I don't suppose you know anything of that wolf attack on Sunday night?"

"I really couldn't say either."

"Very well," said Alison. "I'll take the west side of the town. You can take the east."

Chapter Seventeen
CELEBRATING 129 YEARS OF NOVA SCOTIAN DEMOCRACY
OR
ELLIOTT ELECTS TO CAMPAIGN

THE GRAND CAMPAIGNING Saturday prior to the by-election arrived with outstanding clemency on all sides, the sun lending the shiretown a wholesome, hygienic gleam that appealed to Elliott's modern medical sensibilities. The clouds, to the optimistic, were more decorative than threatening. All was well.

This air of good spirits on the part of the atmosphere had spread down to the earthbound citizens of Baddeck like fumes from a steam-sterilizer, mellowing and subduing — at least temporarily — their germs of ill will. Catholic and Protestant had each forgotten that the other would be condemned to everlasting fire for their perverse heresies. Likewise the Liberals and Conservatives. So close was the election, now, that they could almost feel the fistfuls of cash they'd receive when their candidate was duly elected to patronage. Or rather, to *Parliament*. It was not unlike race day, just before the horses run, with the feverish bettors lined up along the track clutching their one-way tickets to wealth. In this case, ballots.

Elliott Graven, one of the few in Victoria County who had failed to join wholeheartedly in this democratic tide of avarice and bonhomie, had emerged newly shaven from the barber shop at around ten o'clock feeling bucked up by the process, which still had an invigorating grown-up novelty to it. Aside from the pleasantly bracing sensation of soap, razors, hot towels, and embrocations that lingered on his freshly-shorn cheeks, the main ointment in the flies from Elliott's point of view was that it seemed like whole days had past since anyone had tried to murder him — reason enough for the most cynical to kindle a spark of *joie de vivre*.

Even the lone prisoner of Baddeck's quaint old gaol bade him a good morning as Elliott passed the barred window.

"Is it?" asked Elliott, who felt that, despite every sign to the contrary, he would still like to have someone's re-assurance that all of this niceness didn't betoken imminent disaster.

"I mean, I wish you a good day," said the young man, who after another look at Elliott added, "Not from around here, are you."

Elliott, after noting with satisfaction that he was far better shaven than this slovenly criminal, explained that he was only visiting, and didn't anticipate the need to visit the local gaol during his stay.

"Oh, you really should. It's nice. Look at that hipped roof."

Elliott did. The roof was shingled on four sides, and capped the single-storey walls of roughly-shaped brown stone quite pleasingly. Two chimneys stuck out of the roof, and two gabled dormers.

"Charming," admitted Elliott. "If I find myself in need of incarceration while staying in Baddeck, I shall be sure to consider your fine facility."

"Do — tell 'em I recommended it."

Once he had said goodbye to the architecture-appreciating prisoner, formerly of Her Majesty's Customs Service (which was what the man claimed his job used to be), Elliott set his feet clumping along the sunny byways of Baddeck again, the balmy day belatedly performed its miracles on Elliott, as it already had on so many greater and lesser souls in the neighbourhood. He heard the merry clinking of the crates marked "LEMONS" being trundled away from the dock in a wagon; he heard more distant noises, and to his surprise didn't groan or duck for cover. Somewhere in town — if it wasn't just his ears ringing from his recent bashing on the head — a band was honking out a slightly off-time rendition of "The Maple Leaf Forever". Thither Elliott turned his steps, towards the cheerful patriotic hullabaloo that was almost certainly the centre of the day's electioneering activities, where Paisley, her aunt, and Mr Thompson would be gathering.

En route to the tubas and flugelhorns, Elliott mused on the significance of the uniform being worn by the small, beetle-browed creature blocking the sidewalk a little further down the street. He had guessed, and dismissed in quick succession, postman, railway conductor, ship's steward, hotel porter, Salvation Army officer, and customs inspector, by the time he was getting close enough to start thinking instead of stepping out into the street to avoid the fellow before he asked for money. Elliott was about to act on this shrewd notion when his meditations were disturbed by the oddly uniformed man suddenly shouting hello, as heartily as a crook at a carnival.

He's going to kill me.

Elliott kept walking. It would be too degrading to run off in a panic. He took a quick look over his shoulder, but couldn't spy any accomplices. Best to brass it out.

"You, my good lad!" shouted the man. "Do you wish to destroy yourself, body and soul, with the evils of liquor?"

Elliott looked about again, hoping that it was someone else whom the man was addressing. It was sounding less like an ambush, more like some new advertising campaign for rum. However, it really did appear that Elliott was the target.

"No, thank you," said Elliott, as he drew up to the man. "Not today."

The man beamed. "Good lad! I'll wager the villain that knocked your face about like that was a drinker, and a vile one, too!"

"Very possibly. Though I believe he stopped, quite suddenly. In the middle of a train journey." Hitting the ground at fifty miles per hour could be a very sobering experience, Elliott supposed.

"Brother Cripton," said the man, shaking Elliott's hand and apparently introducing himself. "A fine lad like you, with a clean record of teetotalism, ought to join our cause: the Sons of Temperance! Will you take the pledge, and swear off utterly the demon liquor?"

Elliott considered the pros and cons of this. "All right," he said.

"Good lad!" said the teetotaller, who produced a red ribbon and tied it around Elliott's arm. "That's two dollars, to join the Cadets of Temperance."

"*Two dollars?*" Already Elliott felt himself backsliding away from the lofty sphere of red ribbons, into mere solitary abstinence. He edged out into the street. "I'm only visiting, really…"

Brother Cripton, however, had not risen to his rank by being a man who lost souls to the evils of drink over a paltry sum like two dollars. "I'll tell you what, as you're a guest in town — why don't you try us for a week. That's six cents."

Elliott eyed his arm before deciding. Brother Cripton witnessed the hesitation.

"And you can keep the ribbon," added Brother Cripton.

The bargain struck, Elliott left again in pursuit of the band, six cents poorer, but countless cents richer in spirit, no doubt, if not in *spirits*.

Now, if cross-examined on the subject, Elliott would have been forced to admit that he found public gatherings to be beastly nuisances that ought to be forbidden by law, and who could blame him? At the Fair in Spohrville the previous summer, he had been subjected to eel whipping, theft, and lukewarm tea, any one of which is practically guaranteed to put a fellow in the stay-at-home frame of mind. It should be no surprise, then, that the festive scene in Baddeck on Saturday, June the eleventh, 1887, did not entirely meet with his whole-hearted approval. The fact that things had not yet gotten into full swing was more of a source of dread than disappointment

— who knew what was yet to come? The band, taking a break, had dispersed to the several refreshment tables — which were well supplied with lemons, Elliott noted; Denis had not been talking through his hat when it came to the appetite for lemonade at these affairs. The speeches — another reason do avoid rallies — had begun while the euphonium-players and their colleagues were slaking their thirsts. The woman who had replaced the musicians on stage, as the latest variety act to warm up the audience before the main political entertainment, was haranguing a rapt crowd on some subject that seemed to relate to *Progress*.

Since Elliott was for the most part in favour of progress — so long as it didn't involve dynamite, or eels, or rampaging armies of demented sleep-walkers — he slipped into an empty chair at the back, from where he could conveniently escape if things took a sinister turn.

Usually in these situations Elliott found that he ended up installed beside one of a limited variety of people. Often it was someone deaf, who would keep asking him what had just been said. Equally likely was someone whose cough not only distracted from the show but also suggested a communicable disease. On rare occasions it would be someone like Starko, who snored. This time, Elliott noted with sadness, the neighbour-*du-jour* was a small boy of about five years, eating a candy apple, which was arguably worse than all of the others put together. Elliott nodded civilly. He hoped the apple wouldn't attract wasps. The boy, covered in sticky red goo from his eyes downward, nodded back.

"I'm Weginald," he announced.

"Oh, yes?"

"Weginald Wuggles-Gates."

"Jolly good. I'm Elliott Graven."

With the introductions completed, the two lapsed back into silent appreciation of the speech being delivered by the lady, whom Elliott now recognized as Mrs Sowerby, the woman connected with the Wellborn Trust. He paid her more attention, hoping that she might let something useful slip out during the talk — like the current address of Oswald Slack, aka Professor Strange.

It didn't take too long to pick up the tenor of the speech, the gist of it being that civilization, for all of its benefits, had one chief flaw. Had anyone asked him, Elliott would have said that this flaw was blond German blighters messing about with submarine boats, but Mrs Sowerby had her own ideas; she claimed that peace, plenty, progress, Pasteurization, and the other P words were all very fine, but they were rendering the world soft and weak. Without the pressures of struggle, disease, competition and war, mankind was degenerating, regressing. Pitching the idea to her rural audience, she went on to make several agricultural analogies about livestock, and how immigration was blending the races; former slaves were proliferating, with the weak or substandard being allowed to live and to breed inferior stock.

On his left, Elliott saw Weginald, or Reginald, pout at and then lower his sticky apple like a sceptred sovereign preparing to pronounce upon some great matter of international import. Reginald's gaze then turned solemnly upon Elliott.

"I wone be a bweeder of infeeweeyor stock," he announced.

"Don't worry," Elliott assured him, "I don't think there's much danger of that."

The solution to the dismal spiral of man into subhumanity was, according to Mrs Sowerby, the establishment of programmes to encourage the better sort of people to have large families, and to prevent everyone else from doing so. It sounded familiar to Elliott, who had only last year heard "Professor" Strange in Spohrville spouting the same sort of smug piffle. Even if Strange was no longer a member of this Wellborn Trust, whoever they were, the whole lot of them sounded like a load of conceited hucksters.

Mrs Sowerby received the polite applause of the audience as if it were only her due for such an uplifting performance. She asked if there were any questions. There were a few murmurs, but no takers. Elliott stood up.

"Yes, the young man at the back. What is your question?" asked Mrs Sowerby.

"Do I understand you correctly, ma'am, that your eugenics movement believes that those who carry serious inherited diseases should be prevented from passing them on, through laws forbidding them from having children?"

"That is correct."

"Would anyone be exempt from these laws?"

"Naturally, the laws would have to apply to the whole population, to ensure that no defects were passed to the next generation."

Elliott nodded. Mrs Sowerby surveyed the audience for any other questions.

"If there are no further…" she began.

Elliott cleared his throat. "It's just," he said, many in the audience craning around now to listen in a way that reminded Elliott unnervingly of the lecture hall in Halifax. "It's just that our sovereign — you know, Her Majesty Queen Victoria — might be somewhat put out if a law were passed forbidding the royal family from having children. In fact, that sounds almost treasonous, we being subjects of the monarchy and all."

Mrs Sowerby glared in exasperation..

"What on earth are you talking about, young man?"

Everyone had turned to look now, the sea of hats becoming a tide of incoming gazes.

"Well, I mean Her Majesty's son, the late Prince Leopold. We were all very saddened, of course, to learn a few years ago that he had died."

There were a few grave nods from men and women seated nearby.

"Died of haemophilia," said Elliott. "A fatal disease he inherited from his mother. If the sort of laws you propose existed, then the Queen would have been forbidden from having any children. It just doesn't seem very loyal, especially a few days before Her Majesty's golden jubilee, to debate the passing of laws that would treat our beloved Queen as though she were a... a cow that can't be bred because of a defect, does it, Mrs Sowerby?"

Elliott waited to give Mrs Sowerby the opportunity to reply to this rhetorical question. The silence was filled with a few shocked intakes of breath. Someone said "Here, here!" and Mrs Sowerby descended wrathfully from the podium, signalling the conclusion of the presentation, some few spectators giving Elliott encouraging words before they departed for refreshments. Notably absent from this category was Paisley's aunt, who was seasonally attired in a white dress and a straw hat bearing a band with the slogan "Votes for Women".

"You might have criticized Mrs Sowerby's theories more tactfully, Elliott."

"I might have, yes," Elliott agreed. The admission failed to placate Paisley's aunt, who appeared under some strain when she attempted to smile at the approach of Mrs Sowerby. The Wellborn lady, on her arrival, regarded Elliott as if he were something even less appealing than a sticky Weginald Wuggles-Gates.

"Miss Hayward," she said, "I regret that I will not be able to attend your suffrage talk. Something," and she looked witheringly at Elliott for some reason, "has made me feel unwell. I shall be returning to my hotel."

"Did you have too much lemonade, Mrs Sowerby?" asked Elliott. She did look rather sour.

"Young man, have you always been so disrespectful towards your elders and betters?"

Elliott thought a moment, and rubbed his smooth chin. "No, ma'am. Up until quite recently I was only that way towards my betters." He shook his head, sadly, in acknowledgement of his declining behaviour. "Then I starting being disrespectful towards people like you, too."

Watching Mrs Sowerby stamping away left Elliott with the impression that she had a personal grudge against the grass. It left the grass with that impression, too. Paisley's aunt watched the departing eugenicist.

"You have a positive talent, Elliott, for making enemies. I was attempting to cultivate Mrs Sowerby's acquaintance..."

"Sorry, Miss Hayward."

"Never mind, Elliott. Since you're here, you had might as well help us set up."

As this consisted of stringing a few banners, and arranging some chairs on the stage, it was quickly accomplished. A table with the inevitable lemonade had already been laid out. Paisley, Mr Thompson, Lady Beauchamp, and Alison gathered on the stage and settled into their chairs.

"Thank you, Elliott," said Paisley's aunt, her arms full of beribboned and besloganned straw hats. A hand emerged from the hat heap and gestured. "If you would like to join the audience, we will get started."

Elliott had mentally reserved a chair next to Paisley on the stage, and said he thought he'd be sitting on stage too.

"Oh, that's for our supporters, Elliott. I don't expect you to support the cause, you know. Being a young man, and all."

"Mr Thompson is up there."

"Yes, Elliott, but he's important."

"Really, I do support votes for women." Which was more or less true. When it occurred to him to think about politics at all, it didn't seem to make any sense to have so many convoluted rules about who could or could not vote. Good luck to them, that was Elliott's feeling on the matter. And if Paisley was going to get involved, then he was dashed well going to also.

"Now, Elliott," she said, dropping several hats, "you don't have to pretend to support us out of politeness."

"No ma'am, I'd never be polite about politics." He stooped to help pick up the hats, found one more or less his size, and stuffed his head into it. "Shall we?" he asked, extending a hand to the stage.

"Very well, Elliott," she conceded. He went to the seat between Paisley and Mr Thompson and waited for the crowd to gather, not recognizing any of them except for the reporter, Garrity, who was looking even more than usually sardonic under his bowler. He was staring at the ground between frantic scribbling in a notebook, as if he were trying to remember a conversation he'd heard in order to jot it down just so.

Paisley was speaking to Lady Beauchamp, on her right. "Was Mrs Leonowens *very* angry?"

"Do you know, Paisley, I think she was. She kept saying that she had never been so insulted in all her life — a claim which I, in all fairness to her, find difficult to believe — and saying a good deal about spoons and the morals of your Aunt's household. A pity that she did not stay to enjoy the fruits of her handiwork, after organizing the banners, hats, and so on. The woman has a superb talent for it. One hardly knows how in need of organizing one is until one meets Mrs Leonowens."

"Oh, those spoons…" said Paisley. "Oh, dear."

On Elliott's left, Mr Thompson finished eating his bag of cocoanut cara-mels and turned to address him. "That was a nice bit of debating with Mrs Sowerby," he said, brushing away the crumbs that had drifted like snow all over his broad expanse of waistcoat and his blue Conservative rosette. "Never liked that woman. Pompous. No respect for human dignity."

"No, sir. I think their whole organization is like that."

"Well, it's good to have you on our side. Or," he indicated Elliott's red armband, "have you turned Liberal?"

"I thought *you* were a Liberal, sir."

"What? No. In the last election I stood as a Liberal-Conservative."

"Is that somewhere in between?"

"No, it is simply the old name for the Conservative Party. Some of us still call ourselves Liberal-Conservatives, but we're all Tories."

Elliott supposed that made about as much sense as anything else in poli-tics. "About the armband, sir. That's from the Cadets of Temperance."

"Ah. I was in the Cadets as a boy. That character. What's his name. Cripton? He's a Liberal, you know. Fell out with the Orange Order, for some reason. The Order are Conservatives, of course — more's the pity. They're an embarrassment. Their bigotry has no place in our party, or in the country if it comes to that. And I don't say that just because I'm a Catholic. I abomi-nated that lot when I was a Methodist, and so did my father. Whenever they start their anti-Catholic foolishness, the party always calls me in to patch up the hurt feelings of the Catholics who've been insulted. I wish they would start their own Orange Order party, and then we could all ignore and mar-ginalize them as the dogmatic crackpots they are."

Politics was even more fraught with complications than Elliott had im-agined. "Do you expect to win the by-election?"

"Our man — Borden — is all right. The other fellow… well, judge for yourself when you hear him speak. I'm mainly concerned about this sub-marine business. If it gets out that the British have been playing Imperial politics in Canada over the heads of the Dominion government, it could inflame anti-British sentiment, sentiment that the Liberals would exploit. Some in their party are calling for independence. What they call *independ-ence* is the first step to our annexation to the United States of America. We believe some of them have been supported by an annexationist faction south of the border."

Worse and worse. Elliott found it hard enough trying to stay alive, with-out getting mixed up in all of this statecraft. But it was all knotted together too tightly to get out of, now that he was involved.

After some introductory remarks by Paisley's aunt on the nature of the

Cause — bringing up, Elliott noticed, the subject of the Queen again — Mr Thompson spoke for a few minutes, concluding his comments with the anticipation of changes in the electoral laws.

"We look forward to it," said Thompson, "as one of the aims which are to be accomplished in the public life of Canada, because the Conservative party believes that the influence of women in the politics of the country is always for good. I think, therefore, that there is a probability of the franchise being extended to the women on the same property qualifications as men."

There was general applause, marred by a few hecklers. One of these, broad-shouldered, an Orangeman to judge by his orange ribbon, persisted even after Thompson had taken his seat.

"Papists and pansies!" shouted the Orangeman, to a scattering of boos and cheers.

"Pansies?" said Elliott, eyes narrowing.

"Ignore them," suggested Thompson. "Politics always attracts some slime."

The heckler persisted. "Or is that one beside the Catholic a girl dressed up as a boy? Give 'em the vote, and they'll all be wearing trousers next!"

Amid some public laughter, Elliott stood up.

"Elliott..." cautioned Thompson.

"I'm only going to be civil," said Elliott, through gritted teeth. There was more nervous tittering as he dismounted the stage, went to the adjacent table, and filled a large glass with lemonade. He turned to the audience, watching expectantly from their chairs as if waiting for Elliott to do a conjuring trick.

"Who was it who made the remarks about Catholics, and... so on?"

The audience went quiet. "Of course, if you're afraid to come forward..." Elliott added, wishing he had his father's sword-cane rather than just a glass of lemonade. A muscular figure rose from a chair in the third row. It threaded through the audience to approach Elliott, glancing at friends to leer contemptuously as he did.

"You the Pope's handmaid? So, what're you gonna do?" asked the Orangeman, halted akimbo before Elliott, who had to look up to meet his eyes.

"Ask you nicely to apologize, and offer you a glass of lemonade."

The Orangeman laughed. "Apologize? Ha. But I'll have a drink, all right, as long as it ain't none of your communion wine." He reached for the glass. Elliott threw the lemonade in his face. Eyes pinched up and squinting, the man roared and swung at Elliott, who dodged easily. Elliott punched the wind out of the man with his right fist, doubling him up, and instantly brought his left around to the man's now-lowered jaw. The heckler crumpled to his knees, then toppled face-first onto the turf. Elliott wiped the lemonade off his numb knuckles, settled his suffragist hat back onto his head, and re-mounted the stage amid silent stares. From one of the Sons of Temperance in the crowd there was a lively "Hooray!", taken up by some of his fellows. Paisley, her aunt, and the others clapped in dignified approval as Elliott took his chair again. All except for Thompson.

"In future, Elliott," said the Minister of Justice in an undertone, "I would appreciate it if you would resist the impulse to beat men insensible at public gatherings."

"Sorry, sir."

"You can see that it might be awkward for me."

"Yes, sir."

"As the chief officer of the Dominion charged with maintenance of the Queen's Peace…"

"Yes, sir."

"… to have one of my companions brutally assault a member of the public, in front of me, as I am attempting to convince the public to vote for my party in a by-election."

Elliott could see his point. "Sorry, sir. I learnt that right-left combination from you, sir."

"Please don't tell anyone that, Elliott."

"And I was provoked."

"There is that."

"Don't you think, sir, that the slight to my manhood, before all of these witnesses, was a more grievous injury than a glass of lemonade in the face?"

"Don't think that I didn't notice you blinding him with lemon juice before engaging in fisticuffs."

"He's very big, sir. And he swung first."

By now, some other Orangemen were carrying their fallen comrade from the field.

"Have you ever considered, Elliott, entering the legal profession?"

Elliott gazed thoughtfully into the rustling maples beside the stage. "Do you think I would have a talent for the law?"

"Forget I mentioned it, Elliott."

"I'm sure a jury from that crowd wouldn't convict me of assault. They mostly looked impressed."

"Yes, they seem to feel you acquitted yourself quite nicely."

A BRIEF INTERMISSION gave everyone an opportunity to wet their whistles, the better to concentrate on the Liberal candidate, Mr Ogilvie. When they reconvened, Elliott detected a significant lessening of that public-spirited good will he had noted earlier. Not that spirits were not high; his new comrades, the Cadets of Temperance — perhaps buoyed up with Elliott's thrilling triumph over the Orange Order — were in an excited state. Several slapped him on the back, and shared their favourite episodes from the duel, faces flushed with vicarious bravery. Or something. But there were divisions in the many-headed monster that was the public, grave divisions of partisanship. Elliott could tell by the friendly way in which two Orangemen inquired about Elliott's height, one commenting to the other that it must be Elliott's lucky day, as there just happened to be a coffin on display at the undertaker's that was a perfect fit. Which was why Elliott greeted Garrity, the non-partisan journalist, with something of the relief a refugee feels when, fleeing the war zone, he spots the border post of a neutral power.

"Let me shake that hand of yours," said Garrity.

"It's a bit sore."

"Never mind then. You've got my thanks, though. Two articles you've given me already: *Patriotic Lad Debunks Eugenicist*, and *Orange Disorder Put Down*. To think, when I got here I was afraid it might be boring!"

"I like things to be boring..." The way it was going, his enemies were going to have to draw lots to see who got to kill him. Already he'd lost count of the people with grudges against him.

Garrity cut short Elliott's reflections on the virtues of tedium by jabbing his pencil at the pudgy man in side whiskers and a plug hat who had mounted the stage.

"Shh, you'll want to hear this," said Garrity.

Ogilvie didn't look like much of a rabble-rouser. More like a butcher who was too fond of his sausages.

"A dazzling orator, is he?"

Garrity's pencil was quivering in anticipation over his notebook.

"One of my fellow gentlemen of the Fourth Estate told me that listening to Ogilvie was like viewing the English language through a kaleidoscope. I've got to get a few quotes down. The man mixes his metaphors like a baker stirring up sugar and eggs, only Ogilvie's cake is always half-baked, and falls flat."

Enlivened by Elliott's earlier performances, the audience chattered, reluctant to hush. Ogilvie's campaign chairman, or flunky, or whoever he was, called for quiet, waving an arm like someone hailing a cab. Elliott expected Garrity to jump up at any moment and offer him a ride. Ogilvie, a man of enterprise, a man of importance, a man of business (all according to his crony), rose to address the people.

"Ladies and gentlemen of Victoria County, I stand before you on the brink of my seat in Parliament, as our country sits poised to literally take flight into the groundwork of a new sea change: from prosperity to free trade, that is what our party stands for!"

"Good stuff, isn't it," said Garrity, his hand scribbling like he had the palsy.

Elliott was reserving judgement, as he couldn't yet understand what Ogilvie was trying to say. He concentrated harder.

"The Premier of the Dominion, Sir John Macdonald, may have believed that in calling this by-election he would catch our party unprepared to stand in this riding, but I say that we were sitting ready for the moment the curtain dropped!"

Over the applause of the Liberals, and the hoots of the Orangemen, Elliott asked Garrity what on earth it all meant.

"He's muddling *the curtain rises*, as in the start of the show, with *the writ drops*, which means when a writ of election launches the campaign."

The candidate raised a hand for silence, or in appreciation for his supporters' acclaim. His face took on an even graver expression. "When the guillotine time comes, we must rise to the occasion!"

Elliott resorted to his political interpreter. Garrity shrugged, and kept writing.

"Our party," continued Ogilvie, "has always steered its own course through the ship of state and when, like the Ancient Mariner, our captain, The Honourable Edward Blake..."

Here Ogilvie's campaign worker cued him with a hoarse whisper. "He resigned!"

"...when our leader, whoever he may be, takes the helm of state and wears it with his customary dignity, we shall stay the course and steer by the constellations of a bright and sunny future! Now, some in Mr Macdonald's party accuse us of disloyalty for our policy of free trade and independence..."

"Boos", and shouts of "shame" rose from outraged Liberals.

"You have heard all of our arguments on the subject before, but now allow me to resort to reason. Britain is our mother, but like any child we must hatch from our mother's wing and rise like a phoenix to build a house of our own! Our party is resolved to build that new house, then build for it a strong foundation, and to set it ablaze with a passion for independence!"

Howls, pro and con, along with a few laughs, greeted this proclamation.

"I may," said Elliott, "still be suffering concussion, but I couldn't follow any of that."

"I usually paraphrase to some extent," said Garrity. "Here's how I'll summarise for the Tory papers: 'Mr Ogilvie explained his party's policy of separation from the Empire, using a classical allusion to convey that the independence sought by his fellow Liberals would be a conflagration that would destroy both Britain and Canada."

Elliott remained confused.

"It's not my fault," said Garrity, "that he can't say what he means. By the way," he whispered, grinning, "don't drink any lemonade at the Orangemen's table." He aimed his pencil towards a punchbowl at the harbour side of the stage. Elliott followed the line.

"That? That's the Sons of Temperance table."

"No, that's..." Garrity shifted to look at a table at the other end of the park. Usually ruddy of complexion, he grew suddenly pasty. Elliott reassured him.

"I know it is, because I saw Brother Cripton having a sustaining ladle or two before this speech." And Brother Cripton was now in the audience, cheering lustily, looking much more in the pink than Garrity.

"Oh, cheeses," said Garrity.

"What?"

"I poured three quarts of rum into that punch bowl."

They were still staring at one another, trying to come to grips with the significance of this latest development, when the first egg flew, catching Mr Ogilvie in the top hat. The audience erupted like a church congregation discovering it has been sharing its ceiling with a shoddily-attached hornets' nest. Chairs tipped over. Women screamed. Cadets of Temperance seemed to launch themselves through the air. Orangemen tackled Liberals. Elliott and Garrity, by unspoken agreement, sought the nearest escape route. Once they had secured a position outside the range of eggs, apples, Temperancers, and other projectiles, they were joined by Mungo McKelvie, who looked on the riot with detached interest, as though it were all part of the natural process of selecting the right candidate for Parliament. He was singing a little song to himself, the words of which sounded somehow incorrect to Elliott.

> *"Scots wha' ha' on haggis fed*
> *Steal a goose and go to bed*
> *Tum te tum te tum te ted*
> *Glorious victory!"*

"Are you Liberal or Conservative, Mr McKelvie?" asked Elliott.

"A'm a whisky man, meself," said McKelvie. "That is, a Tory."

A thought occurred to Elliott. "Shouldn't you be doing something? You're a Special Constable, now."

"Aye, that's richt," said McKelvie, brightening up. He rolled his sleeves to the elbows and waded into the melee.

"Well," said Garrity, "that's story number three: *Grit's Rambling Speech*

Incites Riot. Or maybe *Imbroglio by the Bras d'Or*."

"It's pronounced 'bruh-dor', not 'brass door'."

"Is it? Anyhow, I'm off to telegraph my stories to the paper." He looked again from the Temperance punch bowl to the Orange Order punch bowl. "I think I've done enough for one day. Let me know how it all turns out."

Alone now, Elliott circled the scene, considering flight to somewhere more civilized, like a pig sty, or the *Admiral Shovell*. Even Mr Thompson was dismayed, and being a politician he had to be used to this sort of thing by now. But he was watching from the sidelines in a dented top hat, shaking his head, muttering, "Drunkenness. Cursing. Brawling. It's like Question Period in the House of Commons..."

From among the non-combatants streaming out of the battlefield, Paisley appeared, a little disarrayed, with mussed hair and sunglasses askew. She settled them back into place.

"Papa's election as Reeve of Spohrville wasn't like this," she said.

"Why don't we move off a little farther?" suggested Elliott, struggling out of his red armband. Six cents or no six cents, he was through with temperance.

They withdrew towards a location Paisley suggested as more defensible — a partly-finished observation platform being built for the Jubilee fireworks in a week or so — and mounted the wooden steps to watch for the appearance of any other survivors.

"Have you learnt anything more about the connexion between the Wellborns and the submarine vessel?" asked Elliott.

"Yes. I think Aunt Claudia is more interested in them than in politics. And if that's democracy down there," she said, looking towards the turbulent mob, "why would she want any part of it? It looks pretty sordid to me. She may be able to help now that Mrs Leonowens has stormed off, leaving us to organize ourselves."

"She's really gone?" That, at least, was good news. "But what was all that about spoons?"

"Look — there's Aunt Claudia." Paisley turned, and Elliott joined her, still wondering about spoons, as she headed for the stairs. But a man was ascending them. He had a big, black moustache, and didn't look very happy about it. No orange ribbon. Though it could have gotten pulled off in the fighting.

"Excuse us," said Paisley, stepping back from the head of the stairs. The man reached the top.

"Elliott Graven?" he said.

Elliott had a sinking feeling. "Yes..."

"This is from Professor Strange." A long bowie knife flashed out of the man's pocket, towards Elliott's heart. He lunged back into Paisley and tripped, looking up just as the blade shot past his face and into Paisley's chest. They all froze in place. There was a great gash in Paisley's dress. A silver soup spoon dropped out of the hole, onto the deck.

Elliott grabbed the man's forearm with both hands and wrenched. Paisley bit him. Still hollering after he'd dropped the knife, the man backed away, stumbled, and took all twenty steps in a sprawling, tumbling fall. He didn't get up.

Chapter Eighteen
THE FRENCH TRAP

IS HE DEAD?" asked Paisley as they crouched over the body. She raised her dark glasses for a better look. The man didn't appear to be breathing.

Elliott felt the twisted neck for a pulse. "Yes."

Perhaps it was the pacifying proximity of all the silver she was wearing — the silver that had just kept six inches of steel from going through her heart — but this latest body didn't upset Paisley as much as the last one had. Either that, or she was growing accustomed to corpses as merely another of the unpleasant features of summer, like mosquitoes and sunburn.

"You'd better go and fetch someone," said Elliott, as he rifled through the assassin's pockets, pulling out and examining coins, keys, and other objects. "The constable, or the coroner. Or Mr Thompson."

"Check his clothes for tailor's labels," suggested Paisley, as she turned to go. That seemed the sort of thing investigators like Auguste Dupin would look for. A letter addressed to "Mr John Smith, Assassin, 23 High Street" would also be handy.

Crossing the park, Paisley found that the riot precipitated by Mr Ogilvie's speech had given way to ordinary politics again, with something like order restored. Mr Thompson and his party's candidate for the riding were now on the stage before the audience, and as the speeches were resuming she didn't like to interrupt merely to announce a body. Awkward questions might be asked. She searched the crowd for any sign of someone else with authority who might be able to slip quietly away from the event, while Mr Thompson, sweating under his injured top hat, addressed them.

"You have heard the policies of Mr Ogilvie's party. If, as we expect, Mr Laurier is to be the next leader of that party, then we well know what his goal is will be: the commercial union of the Dominion of Canada and the United States of America."

Wilfrid Laurier, mused Paisley. Mr Thompson had mentioned

another bothersome thing about Mr Laurier, besides his determination to trade Canadian sovereignty for filthy foreign lucre. Laurier also borrowed all of the best new books from the library of Parliament, before anyone else had a chance to read them. Thompson had had to wait for aeons before he'd got the chance to read Stevenson's *Kidnapped* and *Strange Case of Dr Jekyll and Mr Hyde*. Paisley had always suspected politicians of duplicity and graft, but really — the way some of them carried on was shocking. This insidious book-hogging habit of Mr Laurier's made Paisley strongly inclined to vote against his party, assuming that she ever received the franchise.

"Too often," said Thompson, "those who cry out for independence from Britain mean only to make us a dependency of the United States. Scant years after we forged one great, united Dominion from a diverse collection of colonies, they would have us become the colony of another power — in the name of independence!

"To those proponents of commercial union with, or outright annexation to, our southern neighbour — those who tell us of the advantages to business and trade — I ask them this: How much profit is their loyalty worth? What is the price on our independence? So long as Sir John Macdonald is Premier, I promise you, the Dominion of Canada shall not be for sale!

"And to the Carnegies, the Astors, the Roosevelts, and the Cabot Lodges, whose wealth is being employed to effect continental union, I say this: the Dominion of Canada shall not be bought by your gold!"

As Mr Thompson seemed ready to continue in this vein for some time, and she couldn't see anyone useful in the audience, Paisley headed back to the observation platform, humming one of the airs from that infernal nonsense *Pinafore*.

> *"Oh, god of love, and god of reason, say,*
> *Which of you twain shall my poor heart obey, my heart obey,*
> *Which shall my heart, my heart obey!"*

sang Paisley, from "The hours creep on apace".

Not surprisingly, when she returned the body was still there, lying in much the same abandoned attitude — one arm pointing pointlessly towards nothing in particular. Elliott had scattered the contents of the fellow's pockets about the grass, but Elliott... Paisley looked around. Elliott wasn't there. She sniffed. Only a trace of his scent. And the corpse's. Tobacco. The distant lemonade. And another scent that seemed familiar.

Now that she'd stopped humming and singing — and sniffing — she was aware of a faint scratching under the half-finished platform. Stepping into the shadows between the supports, she could make out a person lurking, light glinting off a blade — the same big blade that had come so close to killing Elliott, then herself.

"Oh, not *again*. You there. I've had about enough of this for one day!"

The villainous form moved out from behind a beam.

"Sorry, miss. Really, I don't have any more to deliver." It was George, the telegram boy.

"Oh. It's you, George. What are you doing with that knife?"

"Nothing." His hand went behind his back. Paisley marched over to him. Seeing the look on her face, he stepped back, giving Paisley a clear view of the beam he'd been carving. It said *George & Mary*. Paisley was impressed. Not many boys George's age could whittle such a graceful ampersand.

"Well," said Paisley, "never mind. But, you shouldn't be playing with that knife. It's evidence."

"Of what?" said George, growing interested.

Paisley leant closer, widening her eyes melodramatically. "Of... *Murrrdurrr*..."

"Go on."

"Honestly, George, do you mean you're so love-struck with Aunt Claudia's maid that you didn't even notice the dead body?"

"Which body?"

Paisley sighed. "Right there," she said, aiming a finger at it. Had *everyone* become apathetic about corpses?

"Him? You mean he's *dead*?"

"What did you think, that he was napping?"

"I... I mean, the fight earlier. I though he'd gotten bonked on the conk or something and was laid out there 'til he came round. Dead?"

Paisley nodded. "He tried to kill Elliott with that very knife you're holding. He almost killed me," she added, pointing out the gash in her dress. "Then he... fell down the stairs and broke his neck," which sounded like a bit of a let-down after the homicidal attack. "But don't go around telling everyone all that," she added, feeling certain formless doubts about the wisdom of sharing all her secrets with George.

"Cor!" said George.

"George, don't tell me you've started speaking cockney, like Mary."

"Sure. She's lonely for London, so I'm trying to make her feel at home. Say, can I have a butcher's at the body?"

"A *what?*"

"*Butchers* means a *look*. From *butcher's hook*."

"Oh, all right."

"Cor," said George again, when they reached the body.

"You don't recognize him, I suppose?" asked Paisley.

George examined the face, trying to act nonchalant about it. "Nope."

"What I would like to know," said Paisley, "is where Elliott went. It's not like him to get distracted."

"He went off with someone."

"Oh?" Paisley's mind sharpened a little. The feeling that she had grown used to recently, of wanting to skip through fields of flowers singing "la, la-la, la-la", was not her normal self at all, and was now seeming an impediment to the rational investigation of serious problems. She made an effort to focus her mind; something wasn't right. "With whom did he leave?" Even grammar was an effort.

"Some other stranger. He sent a telegram once. About a week ago. On a Friday. He was in every day checking for messages."

A week ago. Friday. Paisley tried to think, but her brain seemed to have turned to porridge. "Turn around for a moment, please, George."

The boy hesitated, then did as he was bid. Paisley hurriedly rummaged into the various loops and pockets inside her dress and divested herself of a fistful of sterling teaspoons. That was some of them, anyway. "You can turn around now." She thrust the spoons at George, who took them, his mouth a little agape. "Keep these for me, please." That was better. Like coming out of a doze. Except for the tension. And the fear.

"Friday," muttered Paisley. George nodded. Friday. Eight days ago. Elliott was getting on a train. The train that was almost bombed. "I don't suppose you know where the telegram went?"

"Sure. He'd got one from Kingston that morning. Came in, read that one, and sent one straight away to Montreal."

So. Someone wired whoever was just here that Elliott was leaving Kingston. That person sent a message to Montreal. Where someone boarded the train with a bomb.

"George," said Paisley, her stomach suddenly going all cold, "where did they go?"

He pointed towards town. "That way."

Paisley couldn't see them. They must have disappeared amongst the houses and shops of Baddeck.

"Where does he live?"

"Don't know. He always *came in* to check for telegrams. I never delivered any."

"George, Elliott is in danger." Again. "Very great danger. I need you to tell Mr Thompson," she said, looking back to where the political rally was yet underway. "Interrupt the speeches if you have to. Tell him Elliott must be found at once."

And Paisley was off, running in the direction George had indicated as the route Elliott and the other man had taken. There might be time to catch up, to see where they were going.

She overtook various people limping home after receiving their full dose of politics. Monsieur Percheron, the French spy, who was leaning on one of the two wheels of a horse-drawn trap, looked up in annoyance from sponging egg off his boots. He watched her approach, shaking his head, no doubt assuming that she too was fleeing, in terror.

"*Quel manifestation extraordinaire!*" he said.

Paisley puffed to a halt. "Monsieur Percheron. Is this your trap?"

"This? Yes, I have hired it."

"Please — will you take me into town? As fast as you can! Someone's life — my friend Elliott's — may depend upon it!"

Monsieur Percheron went up greatly in Paisley's esteem when he instantly forgot his boots and gave her a hand up onto the seat of the trap, sprang up himself, and set off at a brisk turn of speed. Paisley guided him roughly along the direction she thought Elliott went, urging Monsieur Percheron to go faster, and leaning forward anxiously in her seat; she could afford the five dollar fine for furious driving.

There was no sign of Elliott. Not in the centre of Baddeck. Not on any of the streets they followed out of town. He'd disappeared.

Monsieur Percheron slowed. "Where now?"

Paisley felt ready to run off in every direction at once. If only she hadn't been so… stupefied, she might have been able to think sooner. She'd lost the scent. Or…

"Please, would you take me to Crescent Grove? My aunt's house? As quickly as possible!"

Monsieur Percheron adjusted his pince-nez, nodded, and urged the horse to speed up along the road out of town.

"Thank you," said Paisley. "If you would be so kind, when we arrive I need for you to wait at the house. After a quarter of an hour, I will send a… a large dog to you. I need you to take the dog back to the place where the rally was held. Would you please do that for me?"

If the spy found anything unusual about the request, he made no sign of it.

"I will," he said. "What is your dog's name?"

"Paisley. The same as my name."

"I see." Monsieur Percheron was edging them up to near harness-racing speed now. "The dog — she will track your friend?"

"Yes. I hope so."

"This has to do with… our problem?"

The submarine craft, he meant. "I don't know. Perhaps. I am concerned about finding Elliott at the moment."

"He was very outspoken earlier. About the Wellborn Trust woman's — Madame Sowerby's — opinions."

"Yes. He was." Much to Aunt Claudia's annoyance. Why was she cultivating that awful woman, anyway? Was she helping Lady Beauchamp obtain or sabotage the submarine boat? Aunt Claudia was certainly interested in it. They must be working together.

"It occurred to me," said Percheron, "when your friend was speaking with Madame Sowerby, that the public were not very well disposed towards her afterwards. If you knew when they were to announce their plan, and were to reveal something before then, something that would call into question the reputation or motives of the Wellborn Trust...?"

"We know when their announcement is to happen. On the Jubilee."

"Ah."

He hadn't know that. "I am not yet convinced," said Paisley, "that there is any great danger in their plan, Monsieur Percheron. The German Crown Prince, Frederick William, is a great friend of the British Empire. I cannot believe that he would make war with us."

Monsieur Percheron shrugged. "It could be so. But, mademoiselle, not everyone in Germany is your friend. Do you know logic? Aristotle? Consider the syllogism: all kings are men; all men are mortal; therefore all kings are mortal."

This seemed pedantic to Paisley. "The prince is only in his fifties. He could reign for a long time. The Queen has. It's her fiftieth jubilee next week."

Percheron found a newspaper beside him and passed it to Paisley. It was folded to the *News from Europe* page. Paisley glanced at it.

"Five hundred thousand eels travelled to Budapest by rail?" read Paisley. That didn't sound like a world-shaking *casus belli*. Not unless one was in Budapest and didn't like eels.

"The other," said Percheron.

Paisley looked again. Various minor news. Ah. *Crown Prince's Serious Illness*. A growth in the prince's throat. Doctors divided as to whether or not it is cancer. Operation needed. Crown Prince confident of the ability of Dr Mackenzie. Uncertain whether Crown Prince will be able to attend the Jubilee in London.

"You see?" said Percheron.

Grim news. "But their son. William. Surely..."

"The young prince is educated by Bismarck and the Prussians, not by his English mother."

"But what can we reveal about the Wellborn Trust? We don't know anything."

"I was speaking with your employee, Mr Gibson, formerly of the United States Marshal Service. He tells me that he has very extensive files on everything related to the Wellborn Trust. I would suggest looking there. Some of the members have been very outspoken on matters of eugenics. They have voiced opinions amongst themselves, opinions which the world in general would consider repugnant, and which the Wellborn Trust might not wish to have publicly associated with their current project."

"I will consider it," said Paisley. "After I have found Elliott."

"Of course."

They were turning up the drive to *The Hypatium* now.

"I do hope the campaigning is over by the time we... I mean you, return."

"Your elections are very exciting, I will give you that. But I prefer our French elections."

"As my father says — taking liberties with Clausewitz — 'Politics is merely the continuation of war by other means.' I hope it has not soured your visit to our country, Monsieur."

"No, no, mademoiselle. In fact, it is worth the travel simply to use your wonderful *papier buvard* whenever I write my reports. What do you name it in English? Plotting paper?"

"Blotting," corrected Paisley, getting ready to jump to the ground as they rolled to a halt.

"Ah. Blotting paper. At the *Deuxième Bureau*, they give us only sand to blot our letters. *Mon Dieu!*"

Paisley leapt from the trap, and in another moment Monsieur Percheron also dismounted.

"I shall await your *dog*, mademoiselle."

"*Vous êtes très gentil et honorable, monsieur,*" said Paisley. "*Merci infiniment de toute votre aide.*" Then she took off at a run up the hedge row to the woods, and the path to the McKelvie's house.

When she'd reached the clearing with the cabin, she sprinted the last few yards to lean heavily on the doorframe, panting for breath, before pounding on the door. It was answered almost at once by Mrs McKelvie. In a second, her face went from welcome to worry.

"Is it Mungo? Wha's happened?"

"He... he's not here? It's... Elliott. He's... in trouble. I... have to *change*."

"Ach, but he's no here, dear," said Mrs McKelvie. "But come in, come in!"

Mrs McKelvie said Mungo hadn't been back since he left in the morning.

She couldn't say when he'd arrive. "Hoots! Just when you need the man, and he's off somewhere, up to nonsense!"

Paisley, reviving after a cup of water, got to the nub of the issue. "The elixir. The drink. Whatever it is. I need it, now."

"Ah! It's here in the cupboard!" She opened one door, then another, and brought out a big stoneware jug. "Here is it. Mind you tak it careful, dear. It's strong stuff."

Paisley pulled the cork and sniffed to make sure it wasn't whisky. It wasn't. "But how much?" she asked.

"Depends on the moon."

Right. Well past Full. Four times the last dose then, to be on the safe side? She hefted the jug and gulped down four swallows. Then four more, just to be sure. Already feeling odd, she passed the jug back to Mrs McKelvie, thanked her, and ran out the door, pulling off her dress as she went, leaving a trail of garments over the clearing and along the wooded path until only her silver locket was left. She kept it round her neck, in case it might help, and keep her from losing all control.

Chapter Nineteen
FORGIVE THINE ENEMIES

PAISLEY'S PARTING SUGGESTION had some merit to it, so Elliott tried to examine the corpse's jacket for tailor's labels without disturbing the body too much. Paying attention to little else, he was startled to be greeted from behind.

"Elliott. Elliott Graven. Mah, but it's been awhile, hasn't it, mah boy?"

That voice. It was... him. He had a short, white beard now, and a grey suit instead of white. But it was Professor Strange. Elliott sucked in a breath to shout for help.

"*Do* sound the ol hue an' cry, why don't ya, Elliott? Might call back that DeLoup girl, an' we *all* could get re-acquainted, like," purred Strange, lifting his hand just enough from his pocket to reveal the handle and hammer of a revolver. "This one really *is* loaded, mah boy."

Strange twitched his head towards town, giving Elliott a hint he had to follow. They set off, Strange hanging a little behind to keep Elliott covered with the pistol; Elliott wished his companion were hanging somewhere else.

"Y'all've been a real nuisance to me, Elliott. Especially you."

Now Elliott was remembering how insufferably self-absorbed Strange was, the first shock of seeing him fading. "You expect me to apologize for preventing you from enthralling my mother, killing my father, and enslaving a whole town?"

Strange seemed hardly to be listening. "It was all goin' so well, Elliott. Til you an' your papa turned up."

"You're a swine, Strange."

Strange chuckled. "This li'l piggy has a pistol in his hand, and don't ya forget it, boy."

They were soon past a stand of pines, and a workshop, out of sight of the election rally, heading for a horse and trap.

"Ah must thank ya for one thing, Elliott. Bah getting' rid o' all those useless buffoons Ah sent after ya, ya saved me a few dollars. Pay on success, that's mah way. Seems if ya need somethin' done, ya have to do it your own self. Though that face o' yours does look a little the worse for wear. Up ya go, Graven," said Strange when they reached the trap. Strange joined him, carefully hoisting himself onto the carriage with one hand, the other on his gun. He jerked his chin at the reins. "You drive, Elliott."

Strange directed him out of town, away from the lake, along a gradually rising mud road that was new to Elliott, like most of the area around Baddeck. It was quickly engulfed in forest, with no view of the lake or town, and in a few minutes Elliott hardly knew where he was or which way the road was leading. Strange hummed, without much of his old ebullience. Grimly, Elliott thought, like someone filling the hours before it was time to do something dreadful. In fact, Strange's banter had lost most of the rosiness it had ever had. He was angry. He'd been angry for a long time. And when he said "if ya need somethin' done, ya have to do it your own self", he wasn't talking about finding Elliott. He was talking about killing him. Elliott considered tackling him off the trap, but Strange wasn't dropping his guard, or his gun. He was watching. Elliott forced himself to take a deep breath. At least Paisley was safe.

At length they came to the drive of a remote farmhouse with peeling paint, long grass, and apple trees with last year's windfalls still under them — the look of a place abandoned for a few years. Bushes grew almost up to the house, and the barn was missing boards. Elliott had to check himself from taunting Strange about his decline in fortune; he didn't want to die any sooner than he had to. Strange pointed to one side of the house. Elliott halted them there.

"Get down," said Strange.

Climbing down, Elliott was able to take another look at him. There had been something unsettling, something different about Strange. Now he saw what it was. The stare. Strange's pale blue eyes seemed to be looking past Elliott, past the world. Perhaps he'd gone senile, or a little mad. Elliott wasn't sure if he was more or less dangerous because of it.

Strange followed him, ordering him to walk slowly to the front door.

"A word of advice, Strange?"

"What is it?"

"If you want to fit in down here in the Maritimes, you have to go to the back door. No-one uses their front doors, except for..."

"For what?"

For funerals, Elliott was going to say. "Never mind. There aren't any neighbours to notice."

Strange grunted. "Go on," he said.

Elliott was reaching for the doorknob, considering the merits of rushing in and locking himself inside, when the mass of lilac bushes nearby rustled. Wind? There was none. It was still as... the grave, he thought, trying to think of something else. They rustled again. Leaves and sticks exploded at Elliott and Strange as a large thing, a wolf, shot from the lilacs, landing only a few yards away, growling, bristling. Elliott spun towards Strange. The wolf crouched to spring again. Strange fired.

A thin yap came from the wolf as it jerked back and fell to the grass, feet juddering, then going still. Elliott was beside it in a second, kneeling, taking its head onto his lap. Hot tears rose in his eyes; he blinked them away, trying to see the blood.

A long wound cut across the wolf's head; part of her ear was missing.

"Get away from it," ordered Strange. "I'll put the thing out o' it's misery."

"Shut up! You'll leave her alone, or I swear, Strange, I'll kill you, even if you shoot me, I'll kill you before I die!"

Strange took a step back. Either he was startled, or he didn't care about the wolf one way or another, not enough to take the risk. Gently testing the wound with his finger tips, Elliott searched for signs of a skull fracture. The skull felt intact. He took a clean handkerchief and pressed it over the gash to staunch the blood. There wasn't much he could do about the ear. Maybe she'd be all right. If only he could convince Strange to leave the wolf outside, she might have a chance to wake up and escape, and bring help.

Probably this would be the last time he'd ever see Paisley.

Elliott shifted slightly. Bending low, he kissed the wolf on the muzzle, between her eyes. Maybe she'd be happy with that German. He didn't seem like such a bad fellow, not really.

The wolf trembled, and moved. Or... not moved. Changed. Fur shortened. Legs... face...grew and reshaped, muzzle shrinking, shoulders forming, skin appearing...

"Oh," said Strange, somewhere behind Elliott, "my..."

"Good Lord!" exclaimed Elliott, lurching back.

The wolf had become human. Elliott had known it must be possible, but he'd never anticipated this; it had become Mungo McKelvie. Elliott watched, dumbfounded.

Then he dragged the back of his sleeve across his lips and shuddered. McKelvie was here. So... Paisley was safe.

"How interestin'," said Strange. "How very... interestin'. You. Graven. Carry it inside."

Carrying McKelvie was easier said than done. Elliott did the next best thing by dragging him slowly into the house. It was a sparely furnished place, mostly bare. Floorboards were warped. Ceilings were stained with leaks. Strange directed him into a parlour, or what would have been one in a normal house. This one held only some packing cases, a couple of chairs and a table with some luggage. Something about one of the chairs looked...

"Tie 'im up," said Strange. "Hands and feet. Here." He tossed Elliott some twine.

Elliott used the loosest knots he thought he could get away with. McKelvie didn't seem too badly injured, just knocked out. He might have a chance to break free later.

"Is he bound?" said Strange, behind Elliott.

"Yes, he — " A sharp blow struck Elliott on the back of the head. He staggered, then fell, into starry darkness.

PAIN. THROBBING PAIN woke Elliott. His head hurt in several places. Strange must have clubbed him with the pistol butt. Falling would have supplied the rest of the aches.

Didn't Strange know that people with concussions had to avoid further head injuries? Trying to rub his sore head, Elliott found he couldn't move his arms. Or legs. Or head. He was strapped into a chair. He dimly remembered seeing something disturbing about one of the chairs.

At the other end of the room Strange was dabbing blood from McKelvie — the wound, Elliott noted, had changed shape along with the man, running up the forehead, then curving down to his ear in a trajectory impossible for any but a magic bullet — and smearing it onto a microscope slide. Strange noticed Elliott's struggles with the chair.

"Back with us again, are ya, boy?"

"Unfortunately."

"Ha. What do ya know about this fella?"

"Nothing much. He has a Scotch accent, and is a Special Constable."

"Is he, now? A *very* special constable, Ah'd say. Ah been collectin' specimens for a donkey's years, an' never seen anythin' like what that fella did." Setting down the slide, Strange folded his arms and contemplated McKelvie. "Ah wonder what'd happen if Ah took a pint o' his blood an' ran it into mah own arm. Would Ah be able to change like that?"

Blood transfusions were a dangerous business. Sometimes they saved a life. Often they killed the person getting the blood.

"Why don't you give it a try?" suggested Elliott, woozily. That second crack on the cranium was definitely not what the doctor ordered.

Strange smiled. "Or, Ah could pipe some into you, Graven." Strange came over to the chair. "But Ah wouldn't do that. Might kill ya."

"Isn't that what you've been trying to do for the past week or so?"

"True. True." Strange nodded. Elliott immediately regretted raising the question. Keeping Strange talking might be the only way to stay alive, something Elliott was inclined to strive for, not least of all because he didn't want as his last act on earth the accidental kissing of Mungo McKelvie.

"I suppose," said Elliott, hastening to come up with some sort of diversionary conversation, "that you want to know how much I've learnt about the submarine boat."

Strange suddenly ceased nodding and looked sharply at Elliott. "What?"

"The, you know, submarine vessel. In the bay."

"What *do* ya know about it?"

"Not a lot, really." Strange frowned angrily, leaving Elliott grasping for something to mollify him. This wasn't going as well as he thought it might. "It's part of some scheme of your Wellborn Trust. I don't know what their true intentions are, though."

"Mah Wellborn Trust. Well, Elliott, it's not mahn anymore. That's the nub of the issue. Ah was found wantin', ya see. Lackin' in that superiority which marks the membership of the Trust. Ya know why?"

"They found out you weren't a real professor?"

"No, Elliott. They found out that Ah'd bin confounded an' impoverished by some brats."

Right. Elliott could see how that might irk Strange. "So that's why you…"

"That's why Ah set out to erase Elliott Graven from this world, son. Not to mention because of this vendetta y'all've been pursuin' against me. Rewards, and wanted posters. Not very friendly, Elliott, not very friendly. But," said Strange, smiling in a way that communicated nothing of pleasure to Elliott, "Ah had a change o' heart. Ah'm gonna let ya live, Elliott."

Strange kept smiling as he walked past Elliott to the table bearing the luggage, and fiddled with the straps and latches on one piece until he got it open. Elliott, though breathing a little easier after his reprieve, was wondering darkly what he'd been spared to do. Serve as bait for someone else? Deliver Paisley so that she could join McKelvie as one of Strange's research animals? Whatever it was, he'd refuse. Or… should he pretend to go along with it, long enough to escape?

Strange came around the chair holding a weird hemispherical metal frame covered in bolts and wires and leather straps. It was about the size of a watermelon.

"Ya know what this is, Elliott?"

Elliott examined it. "If it's your latest Eel King crown for the Spohrville Eel Fair, I think last year's version was better."

"Well, ya might call it that, since you and an eel'll have about the same amount o' brains after this's worked on you for an hour or so. Ya see,

Elliott, this is what Ah created to rehabilitate Union soldiers back in the war." Strange pointed out the evenly-spaced needle-like projections pointing inward from the frame, rather like an iron maiden. "Ya see these? They work in pairs. One on either side o' your head. That way, Ah can send current from one side o' your brain t'other, an' pick which part t'electrifah. Ah never was able to turn it into an exact science, but for mah purposes it'll be jus' fine."

Elliott felt his brain had had enough to cope with for one week. This was a bit much. There had been permanent damage when Strange had used these things on Gibson and Elliott's mother. He remembered Strange's description the previous year of these so-called "rehabilitations": *twenty percent forgot which side they were on, rather than forgettin' how to hold a musket, or stand up, or breathe, for example.* Elliott felt cold sweat trickling down his sides, and contorted against the straps holding him to the chair as Strange, humming again, began fitting the metal frame over his skull and tightened the pins until they pricked his scalp.

"So..." said Elliott, his jaw clenched against the pain, "what are you planning to turn me into? Some sort of assassin, or slave?"

Strange, made a few more adjustments before interrupting his humming. "The purpose o' this here procedure is to make a change in the subject. The subject will be changed from an irritatin', meddlin' know-it-all, to a dribblin', mindless know-nothin'."

Strange resumed his humming while he strung wires from Elliott's head to something behind the chair.

"But..." Elliott couldn't think of a but. What did you say to someone whose fondest wish is to electrocute your brain?

"Generally," said Strange, "subjects have one o' these in their mouth," he said, indicating a sort of black rubber stopper on a string, "to make everyone more comfortable."

"Oh."

"Ah find the screams distractin' from mah work. Gives me headache. Today, though, as there is a special subject, and there's nobody in earshot, Ah think we can dispense with the mouthpiece. It'll be like the sweet music o' those birdies outside, twitterin' merrily, don't ya think?"

Elliott ran wildly from room to room inside his head, searching for something, anything to keep Strange talking, to get him onto some other subject besides the one strapped in the chair. Something to keep Strange from emptying all of those rooms with galvanic current, leaving them ruined nightmares like the rooms in this farmhouse. He was getting dizzy already, but he hadn't even felt the current yet. He realized he was hyperventilating, and tried to calm down. He couldn't think. His brain felt like treacle, from the concussion.

"After considerable deliberation," said Strange, "Ah decided that simply killin' the subject was too simple. Unartistic. The Gravens would, naturally, be distressed at their only child bein' blown up, or otherwise put out o' commission, as would his chums. But they'd get over it. But," he said, taking a cigar from his breast pocket and lighting it, "but, just imagine if they got back, not a body that they could bury, and blubber over, and remember as a nobly fallen fellah, but instead got an empty starin' piece o' nothin' that looked just like their boy, but had no-one inside. An obscene mockery of their only son, that they'd have to look at, and be horrified bah, every day for the rest of their lives." Strange puffed out a cloud of smoke. "Now that's somethin' that's gonna give me a warm feelin' for a long time to come."

Elliott tried to swallow the lump in his throat, but couldn't. "I was going to tell you some interesting facts about werewolves. But I don't think I will, now."

Strange stooped to look closely at Elliott and blow smoke into his face. "No, Ah reckon you won't."

Elliott didn't flinch or look away, even though he had to blink because of the smoke; Strange wasn't going to catch him crying.

A slightly puzzled look crossed Strange's face. He inclined his head slightly to one side and narrowed his eyes. "Ah'd forgot those eyes. One green. One blue. Ah remember wantin' to add those to mah collection. Well, no time like the present."

Strange walked around the chair again, to where Elliott could hear him rummaging in his luggage with the spine-chilling clanks and rattles of surgical instruments. Elliott pressed his eyes shut. *No...no...no.*

Strange clinked and clattered sickeningly until he emitted an exasperated sound and stamped out of the room past Elliott, who struggled again, futilely, against the chair. Across the room, McKelvie had woken and, mumbling through the gag Strange had put over his mouth, was fighting against the knots. There were more clatterings from elsewhere in the house. Then returning footsteps.

"This'll jus' have to do," said Strange, as though he'd been forced to use a brick for a hammer. He drew to a halt in front of Elliott. He was holding a spoon. "This was the sharpest one Ah could find." He stooped over Elliott again before stopping to think. "Ah wonder. Is it better to take 'em out now, when ya still have some self-control, or later, when yer a mindless, gibberin' animal?" Strange considered this. Elliott could see past him to where McKelvie was thrashing and staring with protruding eyes. "Well, Ah'm a man for compromise. One now, one later. The blue one, now." He raised the worn spoon, and pressed the cold edge tentatively into the soft flesh under

Elliott's eye orbit. Then above his eye. McKelvie was screaming into his gag. Elliott felt every muscle in his body as rigid as steel.

"Only a charlatan," croaked Elliott, "would perform an enucleation of the eye with a spoon."

Strange straightened his back and looked stung, as though he had bitten his cheek. Anyone like him could hardly have gone thought life without occasionally being shamed as a faker, and a deranged impostor.

McKelvie had gone quiet. In the stillness, Elliott heard a sound. A wail. A... an eerie, rising wolf's howl. It stopped, then started again, low and building to high moan that made Elliott's hair bristle. Strange looked at McKelvie, then Elliott, then went quickly to the window.

"Another one," he said, and left the room again.

Run away. Get away.

He could hear Strange's steps receding. Elliott strained as hard as he could against the fetters, only succeeding in making the chair creak, and his hands go purple. He listened. A door was thrown open. Strange shouted. A gun fired. That was when things became confusing.

The window nearest Elliott shattered inwards, and something stuck into the room. A ladder. It jiggled, then steadied. A girl ran up, using it as a ramp, and launched herself inside, landing in a crouch. Alison straightened, turned her appalled face first to Elliott, then McKelvie, and reached under the hem of her dress to draw a knife from her boot.

"It's all right," she said, and cut McKelvie's bonds before coming to undo the straps holding Elliott's body in the chair, and his head in the machine. Only a minute earlier he'd been bending his bones trying to get out of it, but now he just sat in the chair and watched. Dr Maddox entered the room via the ladder next. There were sounds in the hall. Strange stumbled into the room, his face scarlet with rage; behind him — where his hands were tied — followed Lady Beauchamp with two revolvers, accompanied by Paisley's aunt brandishing her *Peabody's Patented Parasol.*

Elliott launched himself out of the chair, hardly noticing a body racked with pain. "Where's Paisley?"

"Paisley?" said Miss Hayward. "She's fine..."

Elliott ran from the house, pausing only to grab a long canvas duster that was hanging on the coat rack by the door. He lurched from place to place in the yard, on tenterhooks, hoping she was safe, and found her examining the pump, seemingly working out how to operate it with her paws. Elliott knelt to throw his arms around her.

"It really is you?" he asked. He didn't know if she could even understand him. He looked into the small, strange eyes. "Paisley?"

The wolf whined. She grinned, and panted.

"Oh. You're thirsty." Elliott pumped the handle, bringing up some brownish water that he caught in his hand for her. It took quite a few repetitions to satisfy her thirst. Only when she stopped drinking did he stick his head under the pump and drench it, drinking as the water gushed past.

It helped the throbbing in his head, a little. He held out the duster. The coat was for someone a lot bigger than Paisley, but this was an emergency. "I brought this, in case... you needed it."

Paisley stopped panting, as though to give her full attention to reasoning out this proposition. Perhaps reaching a conclusion, she opened her mouth again and took the coat, carrying it away into the lilacs.

For what could have been hours, Elliott lay by the pump, shaking, staring at the clouds drifting overhead. Raised voices argued in the house. Birds sang. The lilacs rustled. A girl hugging a duster around her slim body looked down at him. She looked pale and worn out.

"Are you all right?" asked Paisley.

Elliott nodded.

"Let's go inside and finish this. We need to go home and get some rest."

Elliott nodded again and heaved his reluctant body to its feet.

A ROOMFUL OF people, some standing, some sitting on crates, were still discussing something when Elliott and Paisley entered. Strange was strapped into the same chair that Elliott had so recently vacated. The mere sight of it made his skin crawl. Fortunately McKelvie had found some clothes, probably in Strange's suitcases. It seemed that Strange was doomed to forever have people taking his luggage.

"There you are," said Paisley's aunt. "We were just discussing what to do with Mr Strange, or Slack, or whatever he calls himself. In some ways, I regret that I did not swing my parasol harder, so that the question would be moot. Mr McKelvie seems to be of the opinion that he is insane. Then, of course, there are the various outstanding warrants for his arrest in divers nations. There is a minority opinion," she added, glancing at Alison, who was fingering the point of her dagger, "that he should meet with an accident. But one can't allow one's prisoners to come to mischief."

Elliott went over to Strange, picking up the electric crown from the floor on his way. He held it up in front of Strange, who flinched, unable to move any further. Elliott placed it on his head. He grunted as the points dug into his scalp, as they had into Elliott's.

"How does it feel, Strange?"

Strange squirmed. His eyes flashed madly to others in the room. "Ya can't. Ya can't let him..." A keening groan came from somewhere in his throat as he jerked against the leather restraints.

"Not very nice, is it?" said Elliott.

For a good five minutes as Elliott studied the electrical apparatus, Strange roared like an animal, kicked, whimpered, and fought with the chair until — his sweaty face an unhealthy colour — he wore himself out, and stared at the floor, breathing heavily. Eventually, he looked up at Elliott. There really was something missing, thought Elliott, behind those hateful eyes.

"So this is your revenge is it, boy? Use mah machine to leave me as Ah was gonna leave you, an empty husk?"

Elliott paused, almost too tired to continue. "No, Strange. Because we're different. I'm a gentleman. I don't know what you are. But I'm going to forgive you. Because a wise train porter once told me something Oscar Wilde said: *Always forgive your enemies; nothing annoys them so much.*"

Strange had nothing to say to that, so Dr Maddox came over and dropped a paper into his lap. "That, sir, is a writ of *capias*. With it, I have accomplished several things. I have placed you under arrest. I have earned my statutory fee of 20 cents for delivering the writ plus 5 cents per mile travelled to do so. And most importantly, I have finished this blasted press-ganged job of Special Constable. Good day to you."

Chapter Twenty
A Day of Rest

PAISLEY AWOKE ON June the 12th to a day of rest, and as far as she was concerned that was the ideal kind to wake to after a day like Saturday. If anything, she was regretting that there was only one Sunday per week, as she could have made good use of a month of them. Elliott had once told her that the human body contained six or seven hundred separate muscles, a fact that is difficult to appreciate until, like Paisley that morning, one has had the opportunity to enjoy the sensation of each of those muscles individually smarting. Even her hair ached. It was the sort of all-over soreness that, in all likelihood, can only be achieved by getting squeezed and warped by weird Scottish poisons into the shape of a wolf, and having to run several miles in hot weather, on all fours, with your nose in the dirt. And then changing back. Paisley was willing to concede that falling into a steam-powered laundry wringer might produce a similar effect, but she suspected that it would be less painful. Her only consolation was a cup of tea delivered by Mary who, Paisley thought, was reluctant to leave her with the spoon. Paisley pressed the metal to her temple and sank back against the pillows without feeling noticeably improved.

There was an indistinct quality to certain moments in Paisley's memory that made her uneasy. The whole period between guzzling McKelvie's elixir and turning up at an abandoned farmhouse wearing nothing but a canvas duster, for example. Only a blurry smear of smells that she couldn't name, and images that she couldn't credit. A particular type of horse sweat. Shouting pursuers. Licking Elliott's face. Moreover, something gave her the impression that her story of a dog named Paisley had been over-hastily improvised. Certain looks seemed to imply that Aunt Claudia harboured suspicions of unnatural goings-on. Paisley clung to the hope that it was only the spoons her aunt had cottoned on to.

Oh, the *spoons*.

She set aside her teaspoon and cup in dismay. "Oh, how it makes one a buffoon, When first we filch a silver spoon!" said Paisley, making a mess of Scott's *Marmion*.

There was a rap on the door, and Mary re-appeared. Probably to recover the spoon before it joined its fellows in Paisley's illicit collection.

"A visitor, miss," said Mary, ushering in Adelmo.

The submarine boat's engine installation was supposed to begin that day, impious as that was; perhaps he was calling on his way to the vessel. The maid, before departing, allowed herself a momentary frown over the impropriety of maidens entertaining swains in their bedchambers on Sunday mornings, no doubt deciding that unsupervised visits were the least of the strange happenings of late.

Adelmo carried a cheerful bouquet of flowers. "For you," he said, offering them with a cautious bow, and a smile. "You see, I am remembering to bow without danger."

Paisley worked herself painfully upright to accept the blooms, and sniff them. "If only I could live as you bow."

"Ah," said Adelmo, when he had finished knitting his brows over this. "I have been told of this danger you have met. This Herr Strange, this enemy of your family who is being held fast by the police. He sounds a most disagreeable man. A low-born fellow, putting on airs, who despises his own class and would elevate himself on a pyramid of slaves and skulls. No sense of duty, or service." Adelmo dropped to one knee by the bedside, his stricken blue eyes giving him the face of a woebegone husky. It took all of Paisley's forbearance not to pat him on the head. "I regret that I was not there to help you, dear Paisley. I vas, during ze festivities, on my motorwagon taking youngsters for rides, and removing toffee apples from ze controls."

"Please, don't be concerned. I was never in any real danger. It was Elliott whom Strange was trying to kill."

"So. Your young friend. He is well?"

"I think so. Though I gather it was quite shocking, what Strange tried to do to him. The man must be deranged. It's as well for everyone that he is safely in gaol now."

"He is telling very *extraordinary* tales."

"Oh?" Paisley didn't like the sound of that. She kept her eyes on the bouquet.

"Zey say in ze town zat a volf ran along ze streets. Zis man, Strange, is telling zat he saw volves become men. Most extraordinary. Do folk believe such zings here?"

"I... I really couldn't say. It sounds like something from a fairy tale, doesn't it?"

Adelmo frowned. "Never when I was young did I enjoy such stories."

"No?" Paisley pulled some blooms from the right side of the bouquet and stuck them into the left.

"It vas quite disgusting in stories, zis turning of men into animals, and animals into men. Hideous. Lower things into higher things, and ze reverse. A frightening deception for ze true humans. Imagine the repugnance of such a thing! How often in zese stories does some creature make itself human in form only to wed a true human. It is not entertaining, zese tales of defiling a family lineage with abominable things. Some persons have very strange tastes in stories. But, you grow pale. I am upsetting you with unsuitable talk." He reached out to touch her face, finding the bouquet in the way.

Paisley stared into the flowers. "Please go. I don't feel at all well."

"Do you need anything? Should I…"

"Just go."

Confused, he stood, hesitated, and then with a curt bow, left.

BY THE TIME the next knock came, Paisley was quite worn out with crying. Her aunt entered, shutting the door behind her.

"Paisley, I… are you all right?"

Paisley wiped her eyes.

"What a charming bouquet," said Aunt Claudia.

Paisley became aware that she was still holding it to her chest and threw it at the armoire, scattering flowers over the floor. Aunt Claudia came and sat on the edge of the bed. "Trouble with your German friend?" she asked.

Paisley stared bleakly out her window at the Bells' icehouse next door, feeling about as cold and lifeless. "Herr Hasselberg's eugenic beliefs make him feel ill when he imagines mixing his family's blood with that of…" Paisley looked at her aunt, who was raising her eyebrows expectantly. "… of unusual people."

Aunt Claudia patted Paisley's knee, as if to say, 'there, there,' leaving Paisley wondering if she really knew anything about werewolfism at all. Paisley didn't feel like volunteering any clarifications.

"Far be it from me, Paisley, a spinster of… well, shall we say past the first bloom of youth… to offer advice in connexion with your young men, but it did occur to me that your infatuation with this German was precipitate. It was barely a week ago that he shot you, and already you're disconsolate over his failure to appreciate your unique heritage."

"Mm," said Paisley. "What do you mean young *men*? There's only the one."

"I mean Elliott too, of course."

"Elliott isn't… I mean he isn't my…Elliott is a *friend*."

"I'm sure he is, but anyone could see that there is more than that."

"Whatever do you mean?" demanded Paisley.

"For Heaven's sake, Paisley, I've seen starving beasts look at food with less longing than that boy shows watching you, hoping for a smile or a kind word."

Paisley felt her face growing red hot. "I'm sure you're imagining things."

Aunt Claudia gave a dismissive sniff. "And for him to come all this way to be with you, after a year of constant worry about his poor mother — half-mad from what that man Strange did to her — getting beaten black and blue on the way, and nearly killed, only to find you more or less in the arms of a complete stranger... I am amazed that the poor boy has not sunk entirely into despair."

"I didn't think..." ...*he could care for me. Knowing what I am.*

"No, dear, I don't suppose you did, about anything but yourself, and your own misguided sense of inadequacy."

The embarrassment, and shame, came out in new tears. What an awful fool she had been. She felt Aunt Claudia patting her again.

"There, there," she actually said this time. "Believe it or not, Paisley, almost all of us get into some terrible mess of our own making at one time or other."

Paisley snuffled and used her damp handkerchief. "I suppose you're going tell me that you were similarly unwise in your girlhood?"

"Certainly not," said Aunt Claudia, sounding so affronted that Paisley couldn't help uttering a hiccupping laugh. "In fact," continued Aunt Claudia, looking even more put out, "It was not for the discussion of your romantic entanglements that I came to speak to you."

"No?"

"No."

Paisley drew in a long breath that made her shoulders shake. She felt so flat that it was like trying to re-inflate, from toes to nose, a collapsed Paisley-shaped balloon.

"All right, she said. "It was me. I took the spoons."

Aunt Claudia sat like a statue, except for occasional outbursts of blinking. Her eyes swivelled to the cup and saucer on the bedside table, then back to Paisley. "Spoons?"

Now Paisley was confused. "I thought... Well, you see, I took the spoons."

"*You* took the spoons. *Not* Mrs Leonowens."

"Yes. It's the silver. It does something or other. Like an opiate, perhaps. I was so anxious about Elliott coming to visit, that I needed to settle my nerves. It started with my silver locket. Then just the one teaspoon. Then

I was afraid Adelmo would… find out about, *things…* " And then she was worried about someone missing the spoons, and so needed some more to stop worrying…

When Aunt Claudia had rubbed her temples for a while, she nodded. "Your parents must be saints, Paisley. How am I going to apologize to Mrs Leonowens? Between Elliott accusing her of being a fraud, Lady Beauchamp snubbing her, and my insinuation that she was pilfering my spoons, she will not have left with entirely happy memories of her visit. What do I say? My niece is a kleptomaniacal spoon addict?"

"I'm so sorry. We don't use silverware at home. I'm not used to it. I will apologize to her."

"No, no. I will do it. After all, it was I who jumped to conclusions. I only wish she might have visited under better circumstances. She did wonders for the organization of the suffrage campaign."

"Yes. Very… diligent," suggested Paisley. "Efficient."

"Of course, she's still an insufferable woman."

Paisley laughed. "But if it wasn't about love or spoons that you're here, what is it?"

"I came about family secrets, Paisley."

"Oh."

"Except for occasionally disrobing and running through the streets as a wild animal, you seem to have been capable of protecting a secret."

This wasn't exactly how Paisley would have chosen to describe her past conduct, but she was fair enough to see some justice in the description.

"You, ah, *know* then."

"When presented by a Frenchman with a large dog named Paisley DeLoup, which leads me to Elliott, being held prisoner by a man claiming to have seen werewolves, I am able draw inferences. Normally I would leave such *outré* matters to Dr Maddox and his Etheric Explorers Club, but when they emerge in my own niece, I naturally take an interest."

"It's never happened before. I'm only part werewolf. One sixteenth, I believe."

"But since you were on holiday, you decided to make a special effort to run amok, is that it?"

"It was something Mr McKelvie gave me that made me change. And the moon was full that first time."

"When you tore that man's head nearly off by the apple tree."

"I wish people wouldn't keep describing it that way."

"He was trying to kill Elliott, of course."

"You knew?"

"I must say, Paisley, that when I invited you here I didn't exactly have this in mind. I had hoped that you might lend me some small assistance in another matter, as the accounts of events last summer in Spohrville made you sound reasonably resourceful. Getting besotted with Germans, intoxicated by spoons, and turning into a wild beast were not what I had anticipated."

"I did help with your suffrage campaign posters," said Paisley, feeling that they at least turned out better than expected.

"While I am interested in the suffrage question, that was primarily meant to distract from my real intentions. It was the exchange of submarine technology, mediated by Bell and the Wellborn Trust, which was my primary interest, and the reason why I rented this house for the summer in the first place."

"Oh." That would be why Aunt Claudia had been so vexed by her failure to cultivate the society of Mrs Sowerby. Though what she hoped to accomplish, Paisley couldn't fathom. "I don't know much about that."

"I don't suppose you do, given all of your gallivanting about."

"I was only able to find out that the *Paradoxo* was built in Kiel, has a range of several hundred kilometres, is powered by electricity, and will use an engine sold by Captain Rawlins, an engine which has no moving parts but moves the ship silently by employing a struggle of electric forces. The proposal is for it to be used in East Africa, to subdue the slave trade there. At any rate, that is what they say. Oh, and the crew will eat Johnston's Fluid Beef. No-one seems to know where Captain Rawlins obtained his engine, nor exactly how it functions. Until recently, the engine was hidden in Dr Bell's house next door, which accounts for the lights late at night that have been mistaken for ghosts. Those were merely the French spy, Monsieur Percheron of the *Deuxième Bureau*, who was looking for the machine until we alarmed him by hanging him over the banister until he told us everything. It is his opinion that the submarine ship may destabilize the European balance of power, rendering the British navy largely obsolete, though of course being French he may be biased. He does seem like a nice man, though. He was willing to drive my, ah, dog into town with no questions asked, even after we interrogated him, and made him and his watch fall into a hole."

Looking like a woman who has received a tidal wave when she asked for a glass of water, Aunt Claudia sat dumbstruck as Paisley, unhindered by spoons or anxiety, kept gushing out information.

"I had felt that the blood ties of our royal family to the German imperial family might preclude war, but the news of the Crown Prince's health suggests that he may not have long to live, while his heir is apparently being educated by a militaristic Prussian faction led by the Chancellor, Prince von Bismarck, who is seeking to undermine any English influence in court that might lead to the liberalization of the German state.

"Of course, that peculiar cypher that Lady Beauchamp received at dinner, means that the submarine agreement is to be announced at the Jubilee, and that her grandfather — whoever he is — wishes her to prevent the announcement, or otherwise hamper the Wellborn Trust's use of the submarine boat. Is she mad, by the way? I was wondering, when she was flirting with Elliott at dinner."

Aunt Claudia opened her mouth to reply, but Paisley remembered a few more things.

"Monsieur Percheron suggests that discrediting the Wellborn Trust somehow before the announcement might forestall matters. Unfortunately, I don't know of any scandals. Mr Strange — or Slack, as his real name is — was connected to the Wellborn Trust, which supposedly aims to improve the world through eugenics. That is, ensuring that only superior people have children, whatever happens to be what *they* think is superior. I believe they have wide-ranging business interests, which fund their programme of so-called progress. And the Minister of Justice, Mr Thompson, believes that this foolish scheme and the inconsiderate manner in which it has been conducted on Canadian soil without the Imperial Cabinet offering the courtesy of informing Ottawa, may lend aid to those in the Liberal party in favour of commercial union or outright annexation to the United States. Mr Thompson said that it was probably some plot of Lord Salisbury's — he's the British Premier. Mr Thompson doesn't seem to think very much of him. He says this is merely 'the latest act of what I regard as a very stupid and worthless life'. A bit hard on Lord Salisbury, I thought. I prefer Bismarck's assessment of him: 'Lath painted to look like iron'.

"Oh, and I have a key to the submarine boat," added Paisley, touching where it hung on a cord around her neck. Feeling short of breath, and sadly reminded of Adelmo by the key, she lay back on the pillows to take stock of her aches and pains.

Aunt Claudia, unusually for her, was wearing her bewildered expression again. Her fingers fidgeted as though suppressing an impulse to take notes. When she had recovered her normal, calculatingly energetic bearing, Aunt Claudia regarded Paisley silently until she felt the need to creep defensively farther under the quilt.

"Paisley, when I invited you here, it was partly to assess your suitability to join an organization I belong to."

"Is it this Fenian Society that you mentioned?"

"*Fabian*, Paisley, for Heaven's sake. No, not that."

"The Salvation Army?"

"No..."

"The Y.W.C.A.?"

"No, Paisley. Would you please just listen? You've been picking up bad habits from Elliott. It is an association formed in the 1820s, after the wars with France at the turn of the last century, and is devoted to avoiding another catastrophic European conflict. It is an association of young women who work towards this goal, begun by Dr Maddox's grandfather."

"Why young women?"

"John Maddox believed they were an untapped resource, with different avenues through which to influence affairs."

"But I thought that you wanted to win the vote and have women take part in all of the regular institutions of society, just like men."

"Well, of course I do, Paisley. There may be a day in the future, perhaps a hundred years hence, when we will not need our own segregated organizations, our own schools and scholarships and prizes. Books for girls, and so on. When we have equality, we will not need these crutches and ghettoes. But we do not have equality yet."

"And you wanted me to join this group?"

"Only if your aptitudes and inclinations were in that direction. I can see that, despite your amorous and argentine intoxications, you have not been idle, and have shown some initiative. Should you prove able to exercise some self-control, you might yet find a place with us."

After seeing Strange safely ensconced in the local gaol, Paisley had been looking forward to ordinary life. Or as ordinary as could be managed. Joining another vigilante conspiracy hadn't been on her list of summer amusements.

"Lady Beauchamp isn't connected with this group, is she?" Alison, she could understand; the sort of girl who dashes about with knives in her boots was probably cut out for the type of group Aunt Claudia described. But Lady Beauchamp?

"She is, as a matter of fact."

"But isn't she rather..." Cuckoo, or barmy might cover it.

"Lady Beauchamp was *acting*, Paisley. For the most part. Dissembling is often necessary, in our work."

"There don't seem to be very many of you, for such an important problem."

"Alison is helping also. But you must take into consideration that we are more concerned at the moment with the assassination attempt that will be made on the Queen at her Jubilee."

"What!" Paisley shot up in her bed.

Aunt Claudia held her palm up for calm. "It is being seen to, Paisley. But you can imagine the repercussions if the Queen were to be assassinated, and the blame were traced to some other power. War could easily ensue. So, the situation in London takes priority over ours here."

"I will have to think about joining."

"Very well, Paisley," said Aunt Claudia, getting up from the bed. "I needn't tell you that you should not discuss this with anyone."

"And please do not discuss my... hereditary condition... with anyone."

Aunt Claudia nodded and turned to leave.

"Aunt Claudia? What is this group called?"

"Its name is *The Athenian League*, Paisley," said Claudia, suddenly opening the door and checking to see that no-one had been lurking at the keyhole, before departing.

IT WASN'T UNTIL half-past noon or so that Paisley's weariness of her flower-strewn bedroom overcame all of her other wearinesses. She drooped out of bed, washed, brushed and dressed, every motion rediscovering a monster in her menagerie of aches. To be safe, she checked her teeth to make sure they hadn't grown longer or sharper during the recent unpleasantness. Assured of her presentability, she set a course for the library for an afternoon of conva-lescence that would, she hoped, be full of distractions from everything she'd spent the morning brooding upon.

There was a queer stillness about the house that was evident even be-fore she descended the stairs. The electioneering, debating, and so on had stopped. Aunt Claudia and her guests might be calming their democratic fervour our of consideration for Paisley and Elliott, the temporary invalids — assuming they hadn't already given up their façade of rabble-rousing — but Paisley doubted it. More likely that they were just off saving the Empire. It was doubtless Paisley's duty to do the same; at the moment, however, she felt that the Empire was bigger and older than she, not to mention in finer fettle, and it could take care of itself for one afternoon. If not, it had no-one to blame but itself.

Elliott, wearing a strange blobby hat and swaddled in his heavy green bathrobe, was already installed in the wing chair in which Paisley usually read. He was well engrossed in his book, for Paisley had nearly reached the chair opposite before he caught sight of her — it wasn't the first time her cat-like tread had caught someone unawares. He politely stood to greet her, when suddenly he uttered a weird groan or cry that halted Paisley in her tracks. A horrible grimace disfigured his face. He flailed his arms about un-til both hands had latched onto his neck as if he were in desperate combat, trying to throttle himself. Paisley could only surmise that Strange had suc-ceeded, during the short time he had had Elliott under his power, in twisting his mind to implant this last, dreadful urge toward self-destruction.

Paisley was desperate; in any other circumstance, she would have asked Elliott for medical advice, his father being a doctor, but that was obviously out of the question. What could be done? Hitting him on the head might be fatal after his previous concussions. There was no ether. Paisley took the only alternative that presented itself — she pinned his arms to his sides by wrapping her own around him with all of her strength.

The treatment was effective almost at once. Though confused, his eyes focussed on hers, only inches away. He stopped writhing. Paisley hoped that he was now lucid enough to advise her.

"Elliott! What do I do next?" she asked.

"I... I was... also," he said, a little wonderingly, "asking myself what you were planning to do next." Elliott seemed to be having trouble breathing. "I don't know exactly what you're doing now."

"I am restraining you. You were having a fit. Strange must have placed an impulse in your mind to strangle yourself."

"Um... the ice, from the ice-bag. It fell down my back when I got up."

While they were digesting this, Mary hurtled through the door to an abrupt stop, as if she'd reached the end of her rope. "What! What was that yell?"

Paisley, tangled with the belt of his dressing-gown, released Elliott from her embrace and lurched away in an unexpected paroxysm of propriety, one which like most paroxysms did more harm than good, at least from the standpoint of propriety. She was pulled up short in her sudden recoil. Elliott was pulled off balance. He toppled into Paisley. They both toppled into the wing chair. The wing chair collapsed. Mary screamed, and Paisley found herself, not for the first time in the past week, in a confounding heap with an indeterminate number of arms and legs protruding at all angles, the only difference being that this time many of them belonged to a chair.

Chapter Twenty-One
POLLING DAY

ELLIOTT COULD HAVE saved himself a lot of trouble by resorting to the back door. It was the niggling concern about going native that prevented him from taking the easier path. Who knew where it might lead once a fellow started adopting Maritimer habits? It would begin innocently enough with ignoring the existence of the front door, or calling the maid "the girl", but how long would it be before Elliott found himself eating dulse and salted codfish, and saying things like "Holy jumpins! That weather, she's some nice today, why I think I'll jig school." He'd even heard that cheated carpenters got their revenge here by leaving herring boarded up in people's walls. It was a strange, fishy land.

His negotiations with the jammed portal having passed the yanking stage, but not quite reached the whimpering-with-impotent-rage-and-looking-for-an-axe stage, he was trying his luck with clenched fists and blasphemy. At least there was no obstacle to giving his imagination free rein, since the household had long ere that day taken to ignoring signs of battle coming from the front door. The outside world was another matter. Someone out there murmured, and knocked. Elliott composed himself and suggested that the caller pull while he shoved. Then he suggested the reverse, once he remembered that the door opened the other way. Surrounded and outnumbered, the door gave up.

"Good morning," said Elliott to the woman on the porch. There was something familiar about the scene; the stack of folded clothes, carried by the woman, topped by a pair of shoes, were the spitting image of the ones Paisley had been wearing a few days earlier. "Mrs McKelvie?" guessed Elliott.

"Aye, and you would be Elliott?" She passed him the bundle.

"Would you care to come in? Do we, um, owe you anything for the laundry?" Elliott had no idea whether Mrs McKelvie genuinely washed clothes for Paisley, or if she was only tidying up after one of Paisley's... *changes*. Nobly, he tried to push the whole subject around a corner of his thoughts, to someplace where his mind's eye couldn't peek.

"Nay, I was only come to leave these things on the porch, when I heard your struggles. I must go back to Mungo. He still feels poorly." She silenced Elliott's concern with a shake of the hand. "Naught a few days' rest won't set right, and we'll get used to the ear."

"Please tell Mr McKelvie how grateful I am for his help the other day."

"Ach, he's a fool, is my Mungo. But a brave fool. He would nae be Mungo had he not lent a hand."

"And thank you," said Elliott, whispering now, "for helping Paisley with her condition."

"Tis but Mungo's Christian duty to come to th'aid of another werewolf," whispered back Mrs McKelvie.

Elliott, his mind already reeling from a head full of other imponderables, set aside for another day this remarkable morsel of theology.

"She's a good lass," continued Mrs McKelvie. "I would have Mungo do what he could no matter what."

"Is there anything she needs?"

"Why do we whisper? Do ye nay want someone to listen?"

A good question. Elliott had gotten used to conspiring about everything. But most of the neighbourhood appeared to already be apprised of Paisley's nature. "I suppose so Paisley won't overhear."

"Ah. Well, as to your question. She wants learning about herself. Mungo'll give her that." Mrs McKelvie pondered for a moment. "There is one thing. It's what Mungo needed when we were first courting."

"Yes?" Elliott leant closer.

"What he needed was what I said then. That I didn't care if he was man or beast, but that whatever he was, he was all I wanted."

WHEN HE'D STASHED Paisley's things inside, Elliott resumed his interrupted walk into town for some much-needed air after his Sunday of convalescence inside. Or *hobble* into town, as Paisley had landed rather heavily on his ankle in the library. On such a day, it was better to be out in nature, like the crows that were sporting about in the road, making weird noises and doing whatever it is that crows do all day. Eating rubbish and carrion? Perhaps one could go too far in imitating crows. The exercise, though, and sunlight, and the fresh breeze off the lake went to work on his brain, blowing out the cobwebs and balming the bruises. There was a lot to think over, things that were difficult to concentrate on while cooped up in the library. And anyway, there were fewer places to recline when Paisley was reading, now that the second chair was smashed to kindling. She had been uncommonly with-drawn, too, ever since they extracted themselves from the wreckage, and Paisley picked up his book, *Strange Case of Dr Jekyll and Mr Hyde.*

His nemesis was in gaol. It was all over. Assassins and detectives, want-ed posters and rewards. It was all in the past now. Really, he should feel re-lieved. Even elated. It was victory pulled from the jaws of defeat, after all. Or something along those lines. He really ought to feel more than what he *did* feel, which was like a migraine sufferer.

He rubbed the slowly shrinking lump that Strange's pistol butt had made on his occipital bone. There was still time left in the summer to have a nor-mal holiday, which was some consolation. He needed one rather more now than he had a week or so ago. It wasn't going to be the holiday he'd had in mind, but... But nature abhors a vacuum. Now that Strange was locked away, what would rush in to fill the void? There could be little doubt that it would be something terrible. Even the crows seemed to concur. They'd been following him since he left the house, gurgling and cawing impatient-ly, as though they'd been looking forward to picking his bones clean once Strange was finished with them, and were relying now on some new deadly event to finish him off.

"Sorry," he told one of the crows who was giving him the beady eye, "I still need this carcass for a while yet."

"Erk," said the crow.

Elliott was on the verge of saying "Pardon me?" when he decided that fun was fun, but if he made a habit of talking to birds people might get the wrong idea and lock him up with Strange. Then again, if Paisley could turn into a wolf, perhaps the crows might be people too?

Though a casual acquaintance would have been unable to tell by her looks alone, Paisley was full of surprises. Not least was that tendency of hers to turn into a wolf on occasions, and howl, or tear people to pieces. The other day, her reaction to Elliott having what felt like half the Beaufort Sea cascading down his back in an icy wave had also been surprising. Pleasantly surprising. It had been an agreeable antidote to death by icewater, having Paisley seize him in an embrace warm enough to melt a glacier. He only wished that her motivation had been something other than the notion that he'd been in a suicidal fit of insanity. That had sapped some of the romance of the situation. Still, in this life one couldn't be too choosy about one's cherished memories.

It begged the question, though: "What next?"

Much as he respected Mrs McKelvie's opinion, Elliott could hardly con-template sidling up to Paisley to announce that she was "all he wanted". She might laugh. Worse, she might look at him with a blank pity that would be the end of any chance of a normal friendship. Though if Paisley married a German submarine captain and emigrated to Zanzibar, or some such place, that would be pretty final too. Looking back, Elliott had to admit that he hadn't exactly exhausted himself with romantic overtures. The German had gone to the effort of shooting Paisley, and bringing her flowers and whatnot. But what could Elliott do now? He couldn't very well challenge the blighter to a duel. Apart from anything else, he'd most likely lose.

Fate, Elliott decided, had gotten used to carrying its jokes too far, and if fate ever came within swinging distance it would be lucky to get away with just a punch in the nose.

As ELLIOTT WAS turning onto Water Street, the ample figure of the Hon. Mr Thompson, Minister of Justice, hove into view, hailing him jovially, evidently fully revived after the weekend's crimes, riots, and politics.

"Good Morning, Elliott! Out to witness the voting? You look a little lame today. I hope that limp isn't anything serious."

"No, sir. Just a little trouble yesterday, with a chair."

Thompson nodded like an understanding man of the world who had seen a few chairs in his day. Or had not seen them in time.

"And with a girl," added Elliott, who was fastidious about accuracy.

Thompson's sage-like brow wrinkled up.

"And a dressing-gown belt."

The brow hovered uncertainly between wonder and disapproval.

"And a bag of ice," said Elliott.

"Hmm. None of my business, I'm sure, but if you'll take my advice, I suggest you abandon this wild life of yours, Elliott, if you're looking forward to a long and prosperous future. Now, shall we stroll past the polling place, to see how lively the voting is? I can't vote in this riding, myself, of course, but I like to see a good turnout."

Fed up as he was with things political, Elliott's only other plans were to wander about aimlessly, brooding. "All right," he agreed, "if you think it worthwhile, what with we being like most of the people in the country: ineligible to vote."

"You mustn't give in to cynicism, Elliott," said Thompson, smiling almost imperceptibly as they set off. "Great progress has been made in our Dominion. Greater progress is yet to come. It won't be long before woman are enfranchised."

"One day, maybe even lunatics and civil servants will have the vote."

"Now you're waxing fanciful. On the subject of lunacy, I was meaning to tell you that we shall be having Mr Strange, or Slack, examined by several physicians, to determine the state of his mind, establishing whether he is fit to stand trial."

"And if he isn't?"

"Most likely committal to an institution for the criminally insane. Do you think him mad, yourself?"

What was insanity? Where was one to draw the line between cruelty and madness? It was a question that could never be answered with perfect precision. Elliott was willing to hazard a guess, though, that it should be drawn somewhere in the vicinity of scooping out eyes with spoons.

"I really don't know."

"His ramblings about werewolves are suggestive."

Not suggestive of werewolves, Elliott hoped. "He has a good deal of cunning, to evade capture for so long."

"Cunning, but not wisdom. Men are never wise when they resort to crime. Innocence is the only wisdom."

A short walk had brought them to a spot across the street from the polling place, where citizens were flowing to and fro like purposeful ants. Except that ants didn't vote for their queen. Come to think of it, Canadians didn't vote for their queen either. Nor even for their premier. They just voted for some local dud like… whatever his name was. The fellow who got hit by the egg. Ogilvie. It was the party who chose the premier.

Now Elliott didn't know whether the electors of Victoria County were like ants or not. If they were, they were like ants who'd lived a rough life. Many of them looked worse than Elliott, having partaken on Saturday of one cup too many of the Democratic Spirit. The moral seemed to be that everyone gets bruised, regardless of whether the punch is Liberal or Conservative, especially if the punch is spiked. On the bright side, Elliott didn't stand out so much now amid the general display of cuts and contusions.

Thompson, from his beaming countenance, was evidently gratified by the show of public-spiritedness demonstrated in this sad assembly of battered invalids who had managed to drag themselves to the polls for the sake of democracy. It was meat and drink to a statesman like himself, ever concerned with the common man and the public good. Not that meat and drink weren't also meat and drink to Thompson, to judge by his girth.

"Look at that poor cripple on crutches," said Thompson, shaking his head. "Imagine the suffering he went through to exercise his right to vote today."

Elliott watched the righteous citizen hopping away painfully, on his props, clutching a slip of paper in one hand. He looked rather like Elliott felt. Looking closer, he looked rather like someone Elliott had seen on Saturday doing an impression of a bandsman playing the cymbals, only with a Cadet of Temperance in each hand.

"Impressive determination, that," said Thompson. "I want to meet him, and shake his hand. Even if he voted for that fool, Ogilvie."

Thompson strode out into the street after the rapidly-shambling elector, with Elliott tagging along half-heartedly behind. Even if he didn't feel overwhelming loyalty to the Sons of Temperance, it wasn't his idea of a well-spent morning to chase around after the dregs of Baddeck society to shake their hands. Being in little better condition than their quarry, Elliott tended to slow the chase. After a few corners and a block or two, they saw the man nip down an alley. Thompson and Elliott followed, emerging into a little yard behind some shops, where the man on crutches had halted at a wagon attended by a few restlessly smoking men, one of whom was Ogilvie's campaign manager. He was receiving the paper Elliott had noticed earlier, and handing over a bottle.

"What's this?" said Thompson, approaching the little assembly. The elector on crutches guiltily slipped a bottle of rum into his pocket, while the campaign manager tried futilely to block their view of a crate of further bottles on the wagon with the word "LEMONS" stencilled across it in black letters. Thompson snatched the paper from the man's hand. "A ballot! You," said Thompson," prodding a finger into the other man's chest, "are in serious trouble, sir." He held the ballot up for Elliott to see. It was blank. "It's the old game — giving out a marked ballot to vote with, and letting their... accomplices... trade the unmarked ones from the poll for bottles of rum. Well," he said, jabbing the man again, "you won't get away with it."

Thompson heaved the crate off the cart and let it drop in a smashed heap before marching out the alley a few steps ahead of Elliott, almost bowling over a couple of respectable citizens who were suddenly reminded that they had taken a wrong turn.

It put a considerable strain on Elliott's ankle, trying to keep up with the bull-like figure of Thompson, who was cutting a wide swath though the pedestrian traffic. Every so often he caught a bit of Thompson's muttering.

"As bad as Antigonish," puffed Thompson, growing winded from his furious pace.

"Antigonish?" Elliott sprinted even with the Minister, ignoring the twinges from his ankle. Thompson's red face was making Elliott worry about apoplexy and the man's heart.

"My riding. Antigonish. If ever there was a county flowing with rum and whisky, cards and fiddles, it was Antigonish."

"Sir, shouldn't you calm down? Where are we going?"

Thompson came to a halt and puffed to get his breath. "You're right. I'm sorry, Elliott. I forgot your limp. I despise this sort of corruption. Foolish to become upset though. In the law, the passions must be crushed and subdued by the will until the head is as cool and steady as a surgeon's hand."

"Yes, sir." Elliott had seen his father's hand in emergencies. It was invariably steady.

"I must inform my candidate of the Liberals' bribery. You were a witness. Please come along to the party offices, won't you?"

They set off again, Elliott experiencing a vague unease about the crates. Crates labelled "LEMONS". They bore a marked resemblance to the crates Denis had been selling from his boat, earlier in the week.

Grant Street was a mere minute or two away, bringing them to the Conservative Party headquarters. Thompson, his old calm jurisprudential self again, excused himself politely as he edged though the throng of party supporters packing the office. He saw the Conservative candidate towards the back.

"Ah, Borden," said Thompson. "You won't believe what we…"

Thompson stopped. Borden was behind a table covered in ballots, with a lemon crate on either side of him, and a whisky bottle in his hand. Thompson pounded the table — not like a bull, now. More like a judge swinging a very weighty gavel.

"This election," he boomed, "is null and void!"

Chapter Twenty-Two
THE PAPER CHASE

ELLIOTT'S RETURN ON Monday afternoon was heralded by a din of thumps and raised voices that roused in Paisley the fear that Strange had somehow mustered a new mob of mushroom-addled automata to lay siege to the house, just as he'd done in Spohrville. Seizing the stuffed owl in a firm grip for defence, she stepped half out of the library for a view down the hall towards the door. At the end of the passage a steamer trunk appeared to be attacking George, the telegram boy, in its furious bid to gain entry to the house, and the trunk clearly had the upper hand. Dismissing the idea of luggage riots, Paisley went to help, so startling George with the owl that he dropped his end of the trunk on his toes.

"Oh, hello, Mr Gibson," said Paisley, when he lowered his end of the trunk. "Don't tell me you're moving into Aunt Claudia's house as well?" Elliott was holding back the door and shoring up the trunk's middle.

"No, Miss DeLoup," said Gibson, dusting off his hands. "Elliott here wanted to go through my files on Strange and the Wellborn Trust."

Paisley took George away to the kitchen to treat his toes while the other two edged the box along the hall. She had been ruminating, ever since Aunt Claudia's revelations yesterday, on whether there was anything she might usefully contribute in connexion to the submarine vessel and its impending completion, due to be announced to the world in about a week, on the Jubilee. Sorting these papers might be one way. Seeing George had planted another in her mind: a way to delay the announcement, if that turned out to be essential. She checked that Mary was still outside, in the kitchen garden.

"George," said Paisley, depositing on his bare feet a cold bag filled from the ice house, and putting it back on after he jerked his feet away, "is there any way that the telegraph can be — temporarily — disabled?"

In his element, George tipped back his chair and held forth on the technicalities of telegraphic communication, in greater detail than was strictly required, until Paisley's impatience forced him to sum up. "Sure, it's not too hard to throw a spanner in the works and keep it from transmitting for a few hours." His face waited questioningly for Paisley to explain her curiosity. Paisley established again that they were alone.

"George, how would you like to do your country, and the Empire, a great service?"

Twiddling his toes under the ice, George gazed meditatively out of the kitchen window, no doubt envisioning himself striking a bold attitude in a red coat, holding a torn but proud Union Jack aloft, undaunted amid a sea of fallen foes. His eyes returned to Paisley.

"Will you give me a dollar for it?"

"Okay."

Paisley explained, in general terms, the dangers brewing around the submarine boat, and the gist of her plan to delay any announcement of the agreement between the various parties involved.

"Crikey," said George, "it's sabotage!" This time *he* raked the kitchen for eavesdroppers, and Paisley marvelled at what a cauldron of suspicion the sleepy village of Baddeck had become within a few short days. "Will you put in a good word for me with Mary?"

"What kind of good word?"

"Well, you know. Sort of, 'That fellow George, he's a swell chap, isn't he? Did you know that he rendered a great and heroic service to the Empire, saving us all from certain doom.' Something along those lines."

"I'll see what I can do, George. You're very fond of Mary, aren't you?"

George blushed, and as he contemplated the object of his affections his face took on a beatific look. Or possibly his toes were throbbing. "She's swell. I want to marry her some day. She's so... I don't know. Exotic. Mysterious."

It could well be, thought Paisley, the first time that a cockney housemaid had ever been thus described. Still, she was happy to agree. It was a small-enough price for saving the world from war.

IN SETTING ABOUT the task of sorting through Gibson's mass of files, Paisley was not insensible of the fact that confinement for several days in a small room with someone who may — or may not — be in love with you, will inevitably present some interesting situations. Particularly when you may — or may not — be in love with that person. In one respect she was more fortunate than many who find themselves in this situation, which so quickly exhausts their conversational resources: there were piles of things to discuss that would help them to avoid talking about what was most on their minds. It had to be admitted, though, that the perfect backdrop for the cultivation by two young hearts of the tenderer feelings does not usually include a bureaucratic nightmare of the sort with which Paisley and Elliott had to contend. Thousands of papers — many of them needed to hang a man, or even forestall a war — were liable to give rise not so much to amorous goofiness as disquieting fretfulness.

With the chest of documents installed in the middle of the library, a table, and the addition of a couple of chairs, they settled in for a long ordeal of re-organization on a scale that called for someone like Mrs Leonowens. Surveillance notes were mixed up with newspaper clippings. There were sworn affidavits by victims of Strange's experiments; Paisley soon learnt not to read too far into any of those. She wanted to be able to sleep at night. Then there were reports to and from authorities that took forty pages to say nothing of consequence. Pots of tea and plates of lemon pie came and went as stacks of documents built up on every surface. Paisley found herself playing with the teaspoons more than was strictly necessary for mixing sugar into her tea, which was permitted now that Lady Beauchamp was relaxing her dietary despotism.

INITIALLY, GIBSON HELPED out, in a half-hearted way. After the first day, he spent more and more time on the porch, smoking.

"I, uh, expect," said Elliott, on one of Gibson's re-appearances, "that it's not too agreeable for you, going through all of this again."

The ex-Marshal surveyed the papers bleakly, and shook his head. "It's the wreckage of my life, all this."

"I was thinking," continued Elliott, "that you might travel up to Kingston, to see my father. He is trying to understand this electro-chemical hypnosis that Strange used. He might be able to help you to return to work; to heal whatever it was that was done to you."

Gibson seemed dubious. Whether he didn't like the idea of being the object of more experiments, or thought he had unfinished business at Strange's trial, he only fiddled pointlessly with a pile of papers.

"It would be a great help," continued Elliott, "if he could have someone else to work with. There's so much about my mother's condition that he still can't figure out. I'd... pay your expenses, of course..."

So Gibson agreed. Secretly, Paisley was pleased that Elliott had been able to manoeuvre him towards accepting the offer for the sake of helping Mrs Graven, for it would have been awkward to have had to say that, when Strange's trial finally came, Gibson would be a liability as much as anything else. Justice being what it was, the credibility of an ex-U.S. Marshal

— sacked for stealing watches — was going to be questioned in court, even if making him into a thief had been one of Strange's own crimes.

Something occurred to Paisley when the former Marshal was leaving.

"Mr Gibson? What exactly is a trust? The Wellborn Trust, I mean.

Gibson scratched the back of his neck and thought. "It's a sort of business venture. Companies are divided up into shares, owned by the shareholders. In a trust, all the shareholders in a bunch of related companies give over their shares to a gang of trustees, who run the companies and channel some of the profits back to the former shareholders. For instance, you might get a railroad trust that combines all of the railways in a state. It *looks* like there's still a lot of different railroads, but they're all run by the same trustees."

"And that's what the Wellborn Trust does?"

"That's right. Mining. Chemicals. Steel mills. Shipyards. They're putting together a load of industries with the help of people who think like they do."

"So," said Elliott, "they're mostly a business?"

"Mostly. Not just a business, though. Trusts aim to get monopolies. They take over all the iron mines, and then charge what they like for iron, because there's no competition any more. I reckon they're skimming off some of the profits for this eugenics stuff, too." Gibson stuck out his jaw, as if he were ruminating on something bitter. "They talk a lot about competition, the marketplace, and struggle, and the best coming out on top, but when it comes to their own business, they use every trick in the book to make sure they don't have to compete with anybody."

Paisley liked the Trust less and less, the more she learnt of them. "And now they want to sell submarine boats."

"Looks like. Y'see, miss, there's only so many useful things a fellow needs. You can sell him food, clothes, a house, books, a telephone, a locomotive ticket. But sooner or later, he's got all he requires. Then, you've got to start selling him what he *doesn't* need. A new style of clothes. A fancier house. A better class of ticket. You make him want something else. Doesn't matter what it is. You sell him rum and cigars to make him sick, and sell him patent medicines to cure him. You make a man want war, then sell him the battleships and guns to fight it with. I reckon that's about the size of it."

The ex-marshal's departure wasn't followed by any noticeable slackening in the pace of sorting, and between bundling up documents to send to Mr Thompson for Strange's trial, and putting the rest into some kind of order, Paisley occupied herself with the more important matter of divining the feelings that skulked under Elliott's enigmatic exterior. Aunt Claudia might believe there were hidden romantic passions seething in there someplace, but then it had to be borne in mind that Aunt Claudia was a politically-minded old spinster who didn't like cats, and spent her days surrounded by very peculiar women. As an authority on *amours*, she lacked credibility. It was plain that Paisley was going to have to make up her own mind about the question. There was no contesting the fact that she very frequently caught Elliott looking at her. The possibility existed, of course, that he was doing so merely to watch for further symptoms of lycanthropy. It would be the sort of thing that he *would* do.

Paisley kept a close eye on him as he shuffled paper across the table from her. Something, perhaps even something trivial, was bound to reveal the true nature of their relationship, one way or another. What she mostly observed was that he would periodically swell up with a deep breath and compose his features, only to look at Paisley and deflate back into the guise of a faintly bored clerk who had seen better days, almost as if he were awaiting someone on a train platform, and kept mistaking strangers for his visitor.

With one eye stuck to Elliott, she added a letter to this stack, a notebook to that heap, a laundry bill to the teetering mound reserved for "miscellaneous". His bruises were improving, she noticed. And she was glad that his nose hadn't been broken and bent like Mr Gibson's, Elliott's being a nice sort of nose which, like a necktie, wouldn't have been improved by looking as if he'd carelessly stuck it on crooked at the last minute as he rushed out, late for an appointment.

It did seem, though, that the cut under his left eye was going to leave a scar. At least it would be a proper scar, one born in deadly, virtuous combat. Not one of those silly just-for-show scars that all of the young German fellows got from their play-duelling at university. Elliott's would be quite a handsome scar.

She decided that she liked his hair as well. Chestnut brown. Slightly wavy. From the way he kept brushing it back with one hand, it was getting too long. It was the sort of hair that you wanted to run your fingers through, and when he leant forward over the table, his forehead twitching yet again from a ticklish hair, that was exactly the impulse to which Paisley yielded.

Elliott goggled at her across the paper-strewn table. He couldn't have appeared more surprised had she smitten him with an eel.

Paisley was taken aback too, having not really been properly paying attention.

"Your hair," she said, floundering back from her daydreaming, "it wants cutting."

"Oh," said Elliott. "Right."

Paisley forced her attention away from cataloguing Elliott's finer points, back to sorting documents, and afternoon faded into evening without either of them taking any notice until Lady Beauchamp appeared in the doorway, with Alison hovering impatiently behind almost out of sight.

"And how is you work progressing, my dears?" asked Lady Beauchamp, tugging on a long pair of silk gloves. "Have you made any discoveries?"

Elliott and Paisley looked blearily up from their files.

"Not really," said Elliott.

"Persevere," encouraged Lady Beauchamp. "I am off to dine with Captain Rawlins."

"Is Alison dining with you also?" asked Paisley.

"No, she will be burgling his rooms. Good night — don't wait up for us."

FOR THREE MORE days they followed Lady Beauchamp's advice and persevered, the ordeal punctuated by Elliott regularly sneezing over mouldy papers, afterwards holding his concussed head and groaning. Paisley intermittently felt as if things were crawling under her skin. Her fingers still lingered longingly over the teaspoons, looking for relief.

The morass absorbed them while one by one the things of the ordinary world melted silently away like false friends when the money runs out. The pattern of the day, with its meals and tasks and diversions, gave way to the longer timeline of years that framed the jigsaw of documents. Even the glass-eyed owl on the bookshelf ceased to exercise its sinister mesmerism on Paisley.

They missed the departure of Mr Thompson and Dr Maddox for Halifax. The motorwagon noisily approached and departed several times, repulsed each time by the news that Miss DeLoup was not at home to visitors. There was the to and fro of the household to break up the monotony, and the regular arrival of tea. Aunt Claudia would pop in to brief them of her progress in soothing Mrs Sowerby's temper. Claudia had managed to wheedle her into delivering another lecture on Saturday, "on condition that Elliott will, under no circumstances, be present, or within a mile of the hall," she said. Alison too was abroad, skulking in and out of the house at odd hours, probably unaware that Paisley could hear her creeping about.

Amid the gradual lessening of paper chaos, Tuesday imperceptibly turned to Wednesday. Wednesday turned to Thursday. Paisley turned to Elliott on Friday night around eight: "How much more of this is there to sort through?"

"It's like a paper chase, isn't it," said Elliott, rubbing his eyes. He'd abandoned his shirt collar some time ago, and they were both slumped in their chairs on one of their tea breaks. The organizing seemed as endless as counting stars. "The kind of paper chase Pheidippides would run…"

"What do you mean?"

"Pheidippides? He was that Greek who ran for days to get help from Sparta when the Persians landed at Marathon, and later died of exhaustion."

"I know *that*." Only deafness could have prevented Paisley from picking up from her father's impromptu lectures the details of nearly every battle since the dawn of time. She got to her feet, stretched, and retrieved a volume from the bookshelf. "Browning wrote a poem about him. *Pheidippides…*

…Ran and raced: like stubble, some field which a fire runs through,
Was the space between city and city: two days, two nights did I burn
Over the hills, under the dales, down pits and up peaks.
Into their midst I broke: breath served but for 'Persia has come!'

She flipped a page. "After the battle, he ran again to thank the god Pan,

'Athens is saved, thank Pan, go shout!' He flung down his shield,
Ran like fire once more: and the space 'twixt the Fennel-field
And Athens was stubble again, a field which a fire runs through,
Till in he broke: 'Rejoice, we conquer!' Like wine thro' clay,
Joy in his blood bursting his heart, he died—the bliss!"

They silently reflected on joy. For her part, Paisley found it hard to credit that a broken heart could be all that blissful, patriotic ecstasy notwithstanding. Elliott shifted in his chair.

"Well, I hope we come out of this chase better than poor old Pheidippides did."

Paisley nodded. "What I meant, though, is what is a 'paper chase'?"

"Oh." Elliott pushed back his roving hair again. "I suppose you didn't have many friends to play games with in Spohrville. It's a chasing game, you see. One person, the *hare*, lays a trail with bits of paper, which often get blown about in the wind, like a scent trail. The others, the *hounds*, try to follow the trail. This seems a little like that. Trails of paper left by Strange, and the Wellborn Trust. And we're the, ah, hounds."

Hounds. *Something* dog-like, anyway… Paisley was reminded of her last encounter with the French spy, Monsieur Percheron. Getting up to stretch and groan even more extravagantly, she suggested that they pull out all of the copies of *The Journal of Modern Eugenics*, and look through it for anything that might make the Wellborn Trust uncomfortable. And still having beasts on the brain, it struck her that no-one had been feeding Elliott's cat, Sniggler, of late. She went and scrounged up some fish scraps in the kitchen, and a few minutes later was hastening back to the library.

"Did you know," she said to Elliott, who was engrossed in one of the paper-bound journals, "that Denis is living in the woodshed with Sniggler?"

Elliott looked up blankly. "Hmm? Listen to this," he said, turning to a page he'd bookmarked in the journal. "This is by someone from the Wellborn Trust, in an essay about slavery. He writes,

It has been the custom in the past to import slaves from the African continent to labor in the agricultural industries of the American south, giving rise to considerable profits. However, the Wellborn Trust is unreservedly opposed to this practice."

Paisley retook her place at the table. "That explains why they're involved with the submarine device, to stop the slave trade in East Africa. I mean, if they oppose slavery, it makes sense."

"Ah. But listen. He goes on to say,

The transportation of the lesser races to serve as slave labor introduces a number of problems. Firstly, the danger of the mixing of the races, and the potential creation of inferior offspring. Secondly, the necessity of feeding, housing, and providing for the slaves. A more rational, profitable method would be to leave Africans in Africa, and exploit their industry there. This system has been successfully begun by the Belgians in the Congo Free State, where quotas for rubber and ivory are set, and the natives are given incentives to meet them. With the employment of native militias to oversee and enforce quotas, a profitable industry may develop, as in Belgian territories, with the corollary benefit of improving the native stock by weeding out the weak and unproductive."

"Oh," said Paisley. So that was their attitude. Eugenics again. And a different type of slavery. The story about using submarine ships to help the British and Germans suppress the slave trade was all a sham.

Elliott looked uncomfortable. He touched the page. "Gibson has made a note in the margin. He says that if people don't meet their rubber-gathering quotas in the Congo, the *Force Publique* punishes them..."

"I shouldn't wonder," said Paisley. "It must be a cruel regime if the Wellborn Trust approves of it."

"The *Force Publique* punishes them," repeated Elliott, "by cutting off their hands."

Their eyes met. To say "how terrible" was not quite enough. No words could be.

"We had better keep going with this, then," said Paisley.

Abandoning the rest of the paperwork for another day, they divided up the back issues of *The Modern Journal of Eugenics*, which was evidently meant to be one of the Wellborn Trust's private publications for its members. Filled with tedious, pseudoscientific essays on why the Trust members — and their friends and relations — were superior to everyone else in the world, the journals made for dreary and rather irritating reading. Nevertheless, Elliott and Paisley ploughed stoically on through the reams of blather.

An hour or so later, Elliott sneezed the dust off yet another volume. Opening the cover, he blurted out "Hey! *Mrs Sowerby* has an article in this one."

It was all about the ancient Lacedaemonian practice of disposing of unfit children by hurling them from a mountain into a pit called Ceadas, which was not so alarming in itself; everyone knew that in antiquity they did plenty of things that would be frowned upon today in polite society. No, the unsettling part was the way Mrs Sowerby described the ancients as "possessing healthy instincts". In other words, they had the right idea.

"Check the rest," suggested Paisley. "See if there are any more pieces written by her."

Thumbing through her stack, Paisley spotted the name in one of the tables of contents. "Here's one. It's called, *The Regressive Selective Pressure of Prolonged Martial Desuetude*...What on earth does that mean?"

Neither Paisley nor Elliott was in peak form, mentally, both being a bit numb after their immersion in a chilling paper quagmire. Getting this title into the brain was like trying to fit a sea urchin into hole meant for a square peg.

"It's jargon," said Elliott. "Like when someone says 'hedonic' for 'pleasant'. It lets them pretend to be scientific, and makes what they say sound more important than it really is. Like that schoolmaster, Benjamin Partridge, in *Tom Jones*, using Latin all of the time. Of course he *was* a Latin master, even if he wasn't a very good one."

"You've read *Tom Jones*?" asked Paisley, scandalized and intrigued.

"Um," said Elliott. "What about the journal? What, ah, else does she say?"

Elliott was right. There would be chances to make circumspect inquiries about Fielding's novel later, at some more convenient moment.

"She says," read Paisley,

"In this century there has come into being a general pacification of the

world, brought about principally by the British Empire. Its great extent and prosperity have resulted in what has been variously called the 'the British Peace', 'the Pax Britannica', or 'the Roman Peace', the latter by analogy with an ancient period of warlessness in the Roman empire. It is the assertion of the author that nothing has been more injurious to the character, morals, and vitality of the races than this elimination of the healthy influence of conflict. Just as Rome was weakened, and finally fell, owing to decadence and the avoidance of bellicose pursuits, so in the current peace is civilization sickening for want of battle. There is no greater danger to the improvement of mankind than the avoidance of war, and no greater mission than to ensure that the so-called Pax Britannica is brought to an immediate end."

There was much more, about the decline of France, and the invigorating benefits of the United States' Civil War. Paisley sensed, though, this was enough. It was a virtual declaration of war.

Aunt Claudia, when she had been tracked down and led to the library, glanced over the journals without much eagerness at first. Then she re-read the two passages, checked the authors' names, and looked at the title pages of the journals. She tapped her lips, thinking.

"Yes," she said at last. "This has a promising air about it. A scent of scandal. Well done." She patted Paisley's shoulder. "Well done, both of you. My excellent bloodhounds…" Aunt Claudia gathered up the journals and was on the way out the door, vague and preoccupied, when she paused to tell Paisley and Elliott to quit for the night. "You've done quite enough already."

"That's true," agreed Paisley, as they both slouched into their chairs in a sort of daze. From the other side of the quiet house, Paisley could dimly hear Aunt Claudia in discussion with Lady Beauchamp.

"Did you say something about Denis?" asked Elliott, his eyelids drooping now that there was no more work to be done.

"He's hiding in the woodshed. From the Customs Detectives, apparently. His ship has been impounded for smuggling bootleg liquor."

"Yes?" said Elliott, dreamily. Then he sat up, looking out the window in the general direction of the outbuildings. "What!"

"Don't rush out. He doesn't want to attract attention."

Elliott sank back into the chair cushions. "Huh. I knew he was selling liquor to the politicians. To both parties, in fact. But I never guessed it was *smuggled*."

"Oh well," said Paisley. One crisis per day should be as much as any of us are called upon to solve. Denis' predicament could wait until tomorrow. Perhaps some time alone with his conscience, in a woodshed full of Sniggler's mouse-tails and fish scraps, would make him repent of his wayward life.

Elliott seemed lost in thought. Paisley, too, was pondering things. Such as what Aunt Claudia had said on Sunday about Elliott. Was this the moment to raise the subject of what they meant to each other? Paisley looked to the stuffed owl for guidance. Owls were supposed to symbolize wisdom. How did one broach such a delicate matter?

Slowly and obliquely. That was surely the best way.

The owl was no great help. It merely looked taken aback, no doubt because someone had hollowed it out and filled it with sawdust, which is enough to make any of us feel unhelpful. Paisley decided that it would be safe for her to mention that she was no longer associating with Herr Hasselberg. That would suggest... something. It would be less abrupt if the remark could appear to be inspired by, say, the sound of the motorwagon's engine passing yet again. Paisley waited. Nerves tried in vain to tell muscles that weren't there to swivel ears that were now firmly stuck to either side of her head. There was only more silence. Feeling that the world was becoming very lazy about coordinating things, she faced Elliott.

"I...," she said. And stopped. His eyes were shut. His breathing was regular. He had fallen asleep.

Chapter Twenty-Three
KNIGHTS OF THE TEA

NOW THIS WAS more Elliott's idea of a holiday: the honeysuckle humming with bees, the croquet hoops laid out in a labyrinth across the sunny west lawn, Paisley looking merry as a dandelion in her summer frock and straw hat, and nary a murderous villain or folder of documents to be seen at any point of the compass.

Saturday had dawned with a chill fog, which might have dampened Elliott's outlook on the day had he not recalled that, in the Maritimes, the weather never made its mind up until noon. And often not even then. By its second cup of tea, this Saturday had cast off its grumpiness in favour of clear skies and a wind strong enough to ruffle the young leaves on the trees, but not enough to endanger anyone's headgear.

Not that getting the holiday going had been entirely straightforward, even after the weather accepted their petition for clemency. Their first attempt to relax, by playing backgammon on the front porch, had had to be abandoned when the sight of the submarine boat bobbing in Baddeck Bay had given Paisley the pip. Moving to the east lawn hadn't been much better; between the hammering of carpenters at the Bells' house next door, and the doleful countenance of Denis at the shed window, peeping out like a condemned prisoner, the atmosphere had proven singularly unrestful. Not to mention the apple tree of gory memory putting Paisley off her watercress sandwiches, and making Elliott feel dangerously exposed out in the open air, with nothing solid between him and the next bullet; that rainy night held a number of disconcerting memories best forgotten on a day like this one.

With nothing objectionable on the west lawn aside from a few repulsive grey grubs in the grass, they blithely bashed and thwacked the striped balls with their mallets for the better part of an hour. Paisley's condition had improved measurably, Elliott was pleased to note. No longer harried and drawn — chewing on silverware and jumping at the smallest noise — she was quite transformed. Mind you, it was as well that they were having sandwiches for afternoon tea. What with Paisley's compulsive spoon poisoning, and Elliott nearly having his eyes scooped out, it would be many a moon before either of them could look a bowl of soup in the face again.

"Hard to believe," said Paisley, stooping to better appreciate the disgusting grubs in the turf, "that they'll be bobble-flies in a few months."

"Bobble flies?"

"You know. Like mosquitoes, only not biting. With very long legs." She twiddled her fingers in the air like a flailing insect.

"Crane flies?" guessed Elliott, after wracking his brains to work out what species of creature she meant. Notwithstanding her skill at drawing from nature, some of Paisley's biological nomenclature could be... *unconventional*.

"That's right. I think some people call them crane flies. They're similar to the floaty ones you see in swamps in summer. The spectral ghastly-flies. They have a lot of thin feathery legs. Like horse radish."

"Horse radish...?" They were going to have to repair to the library for field guides if the conversation stayed with entomology for too much longer. Fluffy. Like horse radish... "Horsetails, you mean?"

"Mmm."

Elliott gave his mallet a measured swing that carried the ball through two hoops with gratifying accuracy. This gauging of the forces and angles to use on the wooden balls quite brought back old times, of being on the beach at Spohrville, flourishing sabres with Paisley, armed men storming ashore in an open boat, cannon balls hurtling down in fire and thunder from where Paisley's parents practised their artillery trajectories, and certain death looming in the air. Happy days. It seemed like practically anything could be an occasion for happiness, so long as Paisley was involved too.

"That looks like Aunt Claudia returning," said Paisley, drawing Elliott's attention to a buggy coming along the road from Baddeck. Suppose they had failed in their efforts to confound the submarine plot, what then? One half-holiday of croquet hardly seemed sufficient recuperation to prepare either him or Paisley for an international crisis. Besides, wasn't all of this Paisley's aunt's responsibility, in some cryptic and semi-legal sense? Now that he thought about it, Elliott wondered just who she and Lady Beauchamp *were* working for. Perhaps there was a secret British espionage service employing unscrupulous widows and spinsters to keep the Empire safe from naughty foreigners and incompetent prime ministers? If so, he wished they would get on with it without his and Paisley's assistance.

Before long, the buggy was drawing up in the drive at the other side of their croquet court, Alison being left to stable the horse once Lady

Beauchamp and Paisley's aunt had dismounted. The two older women, glowing in triumph, threaded their way gracefully between the hoops.

"The meeting," asked Paisley, "went well?"

Her aunt clapped her hands together and rubbed them. "Splendid, splendid!"

"Most satisfactory," concurred Lady Beauchamp.

"Marred solely," added Paisley's aunt, waxing serious, "by the members of the press, who somehow obtained compromising statements written by Mrs Sowerby, statements which made her ill at ease."

Lady Beauchamp nodded. "Markedly so. She stormed out in a huff, swearing formidable oaths."

"…After Mr Garrity inquired as to the amount of profit she expected to make from the wholesale destruction of the British Empire, and the incitement of a catastrophic general war. With quotes from her article."

"And then there was that man from one of the local papers, who asked that she expand upon her views in support of killing babies."

"Splendid…" said Paisley's aunt again, summing up the event.

"Aunt Claudia," said Paisley, interrupting her relative's reveries. "I meant to speak to you about our friend, Denis."

"Yes?"

Elliott gave Paisley a slight nod when she looked uncertainly at him. Presumably, in fairness to her aunt, she meant to confess to hiding an uninvited criminal on the premises.

"Denis has had a spot of trouble with the Customs Department about some rum, or whisky, or something. He has temporarily taken up residence in your woodshed."

"This would be in connexion with that election bootlegging that is the talk of the town? As usual, business and politics are working together in perfect partnership. In the shed, is he? The more the merrier, I suppose," said Paisley's aunt. She inclined her head, thoughtfully. "Denis… his name comes from Dionysus?"

Lady Beauchamp stepped forward to dissent. "Oh, no, Claudia. Saint Denis, surely. The patron saint of headaches. The boy must be named after Saint Denis."

Paisley's aunt threw up her hands at the conundrum. "Either way, a most appropriate name in the circumstances. And speaking of Dionysus, what say we close this *very* agreeable afternoon with a drop of sherry?"

"Capital!" agreed Lady Beauchamp.

"Actually," said Elliott, after the two ladies departed for their refreshment, "he was named after his maternal grandfather."

So that was settled. There was nothing to worry about, except for the possibility of Denis being arrested, and he had no-one to blame for that but himself. He had thousands of dollars taken from Strange's retirement hoard; was that not enough? No, he had to become a smuggler too. Perhaps smuggling was one of those inexplicable cultural traditions one kept hearing about, like eating cod tongues. And goose tongues. It was difficult to argue with anything that had acquired the sanctity of a cultural tradition, no matter how idiotic it was. Sadly, there was most likely also a tradition of hunting down smugglers and throwing them in gaol for a long time.

And Paisley might still decide to elope with the German.

Now that he thought about it, things weren't as bright as they at first appeared. Paisley's voice jostled him out of his black mood.

"What would you like to do for the rest of the summer?"

"Convalesce? My plans for the future don't go much beyond, oh, being installed with a rug and regular cups of beef tea on the porch, from where I'll have a good view if civilization decides to collapse all around me."

"No, really. We must do *something*."

When Elliott could offer no suggestions, Paisley rolled her eyes. "There's the Jubilee for a start. It's only a few days away, and now that we don't have impending unpleasantness to contend with it should be fun, don't you think?"

"I hope it will be better than the election."

"Now that everyone has spent their violence and lunacy on the election, they should be in a better temper for the Jubilee. It's not political, after all. There'll be music, and games, and races, and sports, and bonfires in the evening, and *fireworks*. I love fireworks, don't you?"

In a burst of crackling that sounded almost like one of the bonfires, Paisley writhed onto her side in the big wicker chair to beam a grin like a spotlight onto him. Had he been one of Madame Tussauds' wax figures who, in a foolhardy moment, decided to open a furnace door to see what was inside, he could hardly have felt more like being about to melt into a puddle.

"Mmm," was all Elliott could say.

"Even the ones that go BOOM, as long as I plug my ears ahead of time."

"Paisley," said Elliott.

"Yes?"

"I..." Oh, dashed cowardice. He couldn't say it. "I like fireworks too."

"We can watch them together, then, at the Jubilee on Tuesday."

Paisley twisted back upright in her chair, leaving Elliott more like a congealing mass now, ruing his spinelessness.

"Dr Maddox's wife," he said, "knows all about rockets, apparently."

"Oh?"

"She used to fire them at drowning sailors."

This startled Paisley out of her cheerful contemplation of future fireworks. "That doesn't sound very nice."

"They had ropes attached. For rescues. Her father was the light-keeper on Sable Island. I gather plenty of ships get wrecked there, so they do a good deal of rescuing."

"Well, fireworks are rather jollier than that." Paisley seemed struck with an inspiration. "I know. Why don't you make us some tea with that thing you got in Halifax. A samovar, was it?"

Elliott readily agreed. He'd been itching to have a go with the contraption ever since Starko had given it to him in recompense for Elliott's paying his hotel bill. He retrieved it from his room and they cleared off the dining room table to accommodate it. From their chairs on opposite sides they studied the samovar.

Paisley at length passed judgement upon the tea machine. "It looks like a steam powered beetle."

There was something not wholly inaccurate in Paisley's appraisal. Elliott, though, would have said it had been designed by someone of very mercurial temperament, who had set out to build an ormolu clock, only to change his mind mid-way and start making a small locomotive on legs, then taking a final stab at a kettle before giving the whole thing up as a bad job. There was a tap in the front, and a short baroque chimney on the top, with a small brass teapot crowning the smokestack. Elliott rubbed his chin. It would be *interesting* to combine an alarm clock with an automatic tea kettle that would have the tea ready the moment one woke up. An Autokettle, it could be called. Or the Horolopot...

"How does it work?" asked Paisley.

Starko's grasp of English had been slippery. Even when he'd explained the basics of samovars several times, Elliott had continued to feel that something was missing.

"We need some fuel. Would you collect some pine cones?"

While Paisley was outside filling a basket, Elliott filled the samovar with water. Upon her return, she watched with polite interest as he endeavoured to get the tap to stop dripping all over the table. The cones presented a partial solution when the tap responded somewhat to careful pounding with one of them. Elliott then went to get a cloth to mop up the water.

"And we need cups, too, of course."

He found some in the china cabinet, and laid out one for each of them, and one for the pot, under the now only slowly-dripping spout.

They studied the samovar. Paisley had propped her head on her hands for a closer look at the thing. "I expect we'll need some tea, too," she said.

Elliott retraced his steps to the kitchen, where Mary provided him with a box of *Morse's Tea*, and a spoon.

"Right," said Elliott, satisfied at last that they had amassed all of the needful elements of a nice cup of Russian tea, and for safety's sake keeping the spoon on *his* side of the table. "Now, to heat the water…" He stuffed a few pine cones down the chimney, and cast about for something to light them with. "Matches…matches…"

In the kitchen, Mary, looking increasingly apprehensive, provided a box. Elliott proceeded to stuff lit matches down the chimney after the pine cones. One and all, they fizzled out in sad little wisps of smoke.

Paisley had by now brought her head to rest on the table top, from where she wiggled her eyebrows up and down questioningly. "Tea?" she implored, not very hopefully.

"Soon. I just have to get the fire going."

While Elliott tried various ingenious methods of inserting matches, or lighting pine cones and then inserting those, Paisley found a large sketching pad and some pencils. Elliott paused in his incendiary experiments to wonder what she was up to.

"Carry on," said Paisley. "I am going to sketch a likeness, which I shall call *Scientific Man Preparing Tea*."

The pine cones were not co-operating at all. Most likely they were damp. He would have liked to brood upon the unfairness of this for a little while, but Paisley was scribbling audibly, and it's well nigh impossible to brood properly when someone is drawing the scene. Looking about for inspiration — as have many men of science over the aeons — he discovered some, and lifted down a lamp from the mantle of the fireplace. Unscrewing the wick apparatus, he decanted a few drams of kerosene into the samovar chimney.

"That ought to do it," he said, dropping another match down the tube. A gratifying whoosh of oily fire shot out. In a minute, the pine cones were crackling enough to kindle optimism that there might one day be something resembling tea.

Paisley drew on, peeking around the pad less and less frequently, as though afraid of what she might see next. Elliott kept carefully cramming pine cones into the now blazing chimney. Every so often he gave the tap a cautious turn, checking whether the water had grown more than lukewarm yet. It hadn't. And the basket of cones was getting low.

"Your aunt doesn't have any coal, does she?" he inquired.

A smudged hand emerged around the sketch pad, pointing to the scuttle by the shallow hearth. When the last of the pine cones went in, Elliott chased them with some lumps of bituminous coal, giving rise to a nice steady glow inside the samovar, the sides of which were growing warmer now, even if the atmosphere in the dining room was getting a bit thick. He heaved open one of the windows and waved ineffectually at the sea of smoke, coughing and feeling rather like Canute trying to get the tide to shove off home again. Leaving such things to a Higher Power — namely convection — Elliott set about the next stage of the process.

"I wonder," said Paisley over the top of the paper, "if the Russians learnt tea-making from the Byzantines."

Starko hadn't mentioned. Elliott only knew that he was supposed to put about a dozen spoonfuls of tea into the diminutive pot.

"Won't that be too strong?" asked Paisley.

"Ah, this is the *zvarka*," explained Elliott, in a commendable simulation of competence. Starko had called it something like that. "You must never, on any account, drink the *zvarka*."

"I see."

"If you drink it, it will drive you mad, or be mortally dangerous."

"Of course."

"A Russian duke once drank a pot of *zvarka* and went raving mad. He had to be taken away and strangled for his own good."

Paisley was watching him silently now, with narrowing eyes. Possibly because of the sulphurous smoke billowing out of the samovar's chimney. Though, now that he came to repeat this particular story of Starko's, there did seem to be something not quite right about it.

"So," said Paisley, "We've spent the better part of an hour making a form of tea which we mustn't on any account drink."

"It's all right diluted with hot water. That's why the samovar holds so much."

Paisley, slightly re-assured, went back to sketching the great tea project, leaving Elliott to stoke the machine and cope with any further nonsense.

Absorbed in the complexities of coddling the machine, Elliott was weighing the interesting question of how one knew if a samovar were about to explode — would it leak? more? would steam shoot out? would it bulge like a balloon before bursting? — when Paisley's aunt stepped in. If he was ignorant of the signs foretelling tea disasters, Elliott was at least confident of his ability to recognize an aunt about to go off like a bomb. The sudden, unnatural stillness, as in the centre of a cyclone. The look of speechless wonder as she drank in the scene, of soot snowing gently down upon her dining room furniture, almost as if her house had become a charming domestic diorama inside a photographic-negative of a snow globe. Elliott smiled, welcomingly, and awaited further developments; like the samovar, the situation was now largely out of his control.

Paisley laid down her pencil to add her full attention to her aunt, whose opening salvo was a squib-like cough.

"I do trust," said Paisley's aunt, "that you have not also turned to moonshining."

"Excuse me?"

"You seem to be distilling something on my dining table."

"Sss..," said Elliott. "Certainly... ah...ahhh... not," he got out with difficulty, as a smoke-induced sneeze built up deep inside his sinuses. Was this how the samovar felt? "I am a teetotaller," and offered up by way of evidence a series of colossal sneezes.

"Scientific research, then?" Paisley's aunt sniffed the atmosphere, which compelled her to place a handkerchief over her face. "The distillation of kerosene, à la Gesner, or perhaps the refinement of coal tars?"

"I'm making tea," explained Elliott. Paisley's aunt greeted this revelation in blank silence. "Would you like some?" he added, feeling that some overture on his part was called for to overcome any little tensions that may have arisen.

Paisley's aunt pressed the handkerchief even tighter over her face. "I was only popping in to see if the two of you were... I have already... I must be going," she said, seeming a trifle confused to Elliott. She appeared to pull herself together. "I am definitely dining out tonight. With Lady Beauchamp. Somewhere." Turning to go, she paused. "Good luck with the tea," she said, rather forlornly, as though she might not see either of them again.

In the fullness of time, the samovar came to a boil without any loss of life, and the tea proved to be not only not fatal, but rather tasty with a spot of cream. Suitably diluted, it did not even drive them mad. In the clearing smoke of evening, Elliott and Paisley sat drinking it, returning to the subject of what to do for the rest of summer.

"Dr Bell might," said Paisley, smiling encouragingly, "show you some of his inventions when he returns from New York, or wherever he went. He has made machines for transmitting messages by light, and for listening to sounds underwater."

Elliott turned the tap to dribble some more steaming water into his tea. Certain signs of impending madness suggested that the tea might be still too strong.

"I've gone off inventions in the past fortnight. Too many submarine boats and motorwagons."

Paisley's smile faded, and she hunched back into her chair. "Herr Hasselberg and I are no longer associating."

Elliott lost track of what he was doing and scalded himself on the metal. "What?" He sucked his finger and waved it in the air to cool it off. "If he's...

insulted you, I'll…"

"No. We simply have irreconcilable differences," said Paisley in the rapid staccato people usually use for things they want to get said as quickly as possible.

This put a different complexion on things. It bore thinking about.

Elliott pondered this development, and they both sipped strong tea until Paisley sat up with a jolt. For a few moments he thought that the tea hadn't been watered enough and that she was about to ramble maniacally. Then he heard the engine too. The motorwagon, coming down the Baddeck Road.

They settled back with their tea, listening to the growl, waiting for it to pass. Instead it approached, growing louder, finally turning into the drive to reach a crescendo of noise before stopping. The bell rang, the visitor was admitted, and they found themselves assaulted by a hodgepodge of excited German and English.

"What is the matter?" asked Paisley.

"They are taking it!" said Hasselberg. "Even now!"

"Taking what?" demanded Elliott.

Hasselberg was pacing frantically to and fro. "*Das Unterseeboot!* The submarine boat! And the engine is not even finished the installation."

Elliott and Paisley — with Hasselberg on their heels babbling about hunting near Macaulay's Hill and returning to find the vessel departing, and a cheque left for him — went to the front room for a view of Baddeck Bay. There was a ship under steam, funnel smoking like a samovar… towing something. The submarine boat.

Paisley turned to Hasselberg. "If they paid you, though, it's not stealing…"

"But my shipyard is meant to manufacture them! They have all ze plans. Ze engine. I was meant to study and test ze engine. Zat vas our agreement."

The Wellborn Trust was obviously cutting its losses and taking away the engine for themselves, to disassemble, study, and copy. Powerless, they watched as the two ships moved ever farther away, towards the mouth of the bay and the lake beyond.

"They mustn't take it," said Elliott. "If they start producing submarine vessels, who knows to whom they'll sell them, and for what purpose."

"Not for anything good," said Paisley.

"Aren't there locks at the canal, at St. Peters? We could wire ahead to have them closed," suggested Elliott.

Hasselberg shook his head. "No, zere is a channel to ze zea just around ze headland zere. Zey will go zat way, I am sure."

"Then we will have to find out where they are going."

"But how?"

"Follow them," said Elliott, heading for the door of the front room, where he bowled over the crouching and listening Alison.

Alison came stammering to her feet. "I have to tell the others about this," she said.

"Come along then," said Elliott, carrying on towards the porch.

On the front steps, he found they had no need to roust Denis out of his shed; he had already presented himself and was examining the motorwagon engine.

"We need your boat," Elliott told him.

"Ship," said Denis. "And so do I. She's impounded. Some cove's always guarding her."

"We're taking it anyway," said Elliott as the others caught up. "someone has to find out where they're taking that thing."

Denis gloomily changed the object of his studies from the motorwagon to the dirt at his feet. "No point. The crew's all flitted off someplace, soon as they got wind of the Customs men."

"Well," said Elliott. He hadn't though of that. "I can sail." He'd never sailed an eighty-ton schooner, of course…

Alison stepped forward. "I can sail," she said.

"You can?" several people chorused at once.

"How about you?" Denis asked Hasselberg.

The German recoiled as though someone had inquired of his ability to tie his own shoes. "Of course. I am from *Kiel*."

Denis turned to Paisley.

"I can't even fly a kite," she said.

Rubbing his chin, Denis pondered. "I suppose we could sail her with a crew of four," he decided.

"Come on, then," urged Elliott, climbing onto the motorwagon.

Once Hasselberg had gotten the machine running again, the five of them clung onto it as best they could as the German sent them hurtling towards Baddeck at ten miles per hour.

The trip afforded Elliott a few minutes to think, when not holding on for dear life, and when the outskirts hove into sight he directed Hasselberg towards the gaol, where he hopped off to rattle the bars of a familiar window. "Hello? Are you still in there?"

The incarcerated former Customs official gave Elliott a cheerful wave from the dank, medieval interior of his cell. "Still here," he said.

"Listen," said Elliott softly, pressing against the bars. "If I send the Customs detective at the dock up here, can you keep him busy for a while? Tell him where you buried the bodies, or whatever it is you're supposed to have done?"

"Oh, sure, I'm a great talker. I'm known for it. I could talk all day. Why, one time I..."

"Never mind. Look," said Elliott, digging into his wallet, "Take this." He handed over a handful of banknotes. "Get yourself a good barrister." And before the other could do anything but gawp incredulously, Elliott was back on the thrumming motorwagon and speeding away towards the harbour.

Almost at Water Street, Elliott tapped Hasselberg's shoulder and told him to stop.

"Someone needs to run down to the dock to tell the Customs detective he's wanted at the gaol."

"I'll go," offered Alison. "I need to tell Lady Beauchamp what has happened, also."

"Where are they?"

Alison hesitated. "I don't know exactly. They must be at one of the hotels. Unless they're dining at someone's house."

"Never mind, then. Just get to the dock and back. Hurry."

Alison sped off at a semi-dignified trot towards the waterfront.

"All right," said Elliott, "let's follow."

They abandoned the motorwagon so as not to attract any more attention than Denis already was, with his hat pulled down as far as possible while he hid behind his smouldering pipe. No-one seemed to take much noticed of them, except briefly when George, the telegram boy, was passing and Paisley sent a flurry of waves and winks in his direction, only to say cryptically that she needed him to "do that thing we discussed", whereupon he responded with his own fit of winks, and took the dollar Paisley offered.

But there was no time to chat about Paisley's telegram accounts. They were at the corner overlooking the docks, with Alison pointing the Customs guard towards the gaol. He seemed to be hesitating. Alison wrang her hands, and the man set off.

"Let's go. And walk naturally," Elliott added, as the others threatened to break into a run.

After an agonizing minute or two, they reached the dockside.

"Right," said Elliott. "Denis, get us away from here as fast as you can."

Denis emptied his pipe and assumed a captainly air on deck, checking the wind, which was north-westerly. "You, German fellah. Haul the mainsail throat halyard. That one," he pointed out, "in case you don't know the English. I'll haul the peak. Alison, Elliott, haul up the foresail gaff. Paisley, cast off, and as soon as we're free jump aboard."

In a few agonizing minutes the gaff sails were set and the halyards belayed. Always imagining the Customs detective's return, they were inching away from the dock with Denis at the wheel, and gaining speed.

Chapter Twenty-Four
SUB DIVO, SUB FINEM

LACKING ANY SEAFARING skills, Paisley kept out of the way at the stern, looking over her smoked glasses back towards the receding port for any signs of pursuit, leaving the others to scurry about the deck performing their mysterious nautical deeds with rope and sail.

"Anyone after us?" asked Denis, smoking his pipe at the wheel.

"Not that I can see." She sidled to starboard to be upwind from the tobacco.

"That Customs fellah may wire to Sydney. Have a Dominion cutter, or the Fisheries Police, out to seize us."

Paisley hugged herself against the evening breeze, chillier now that the first fever of excitement at sneaking away was fading. "Oh, I don't think he will. I had a friend disable the telegraph for a few hours."

Denis tapped the peak of his cap with his pipe stem in a salute to Paisley's forethought. He then aimed it at the headland past which the steamer had gone with the submarine boat in tow. "May be why they're taking the Great Bras d'Or channel instead of the canal — thinking someone might've telegraphed to the lock-keeper to stop them."

It was a moot point whether the Wellborn Trust had committed any crimes in taking the submarine boat away. "What we're doing may be more illegal. The law may not be able to touch them."

"The law…" said Denis, derisively.

Perhaps he'd learnt nothing after all. Already feeling reckless for having flitted out of town on a smuggler's schooner, under the nose of Customs, not to mention feeling a trifle queasy from the waves, Denis' lack of repentance made Paisley feel even worse.

"You ought never to have done it, you know, smuggling all that rum and whatnot. It was foolish. Whatever were you thinking?"

Denis chewed on his pipe awhile, gradually adjusting the wheel to turn towards the channel and pass around Red Head. After a minute, he took his pipe in his wheel hand and cupped the other to shout.

"Alison! Elliott! Haul the mainsheet! German, haul the foresheet! Ready to gybe!"

The crew rushed to pull on their assigned ropes to rein in the sail booms as they swept over the deck, the sails first flapping loose when the ship crossed the wind, then filling again on the other side.

"The German's name is Adelmo von Hasselberg," said Paisley.

"Anyways, I reckoned I didn't care much for the law, since the law didn't care much for me. Me, or anybody."

"That Justice of the Peace, you mean. The one that didn't listen."

Denis nodded. "When they let murder and slavery go on, and turn a blind eye, why respect 'em?"

"Strange *is* in gaol now. Mr Thompson *is* investigating."

"Finally." He puffed and chewed on the pipe, overseeing from a distance the belaying of the sheets. "Thanks. For getting me out of it. That was my own fault, getting into such a fool mess. It's good to see the back of it. No more, though. Wherever we make land, I'll sell *The Avenger* and get into some honest line of work."

Now, at last, Denis was truly penitent. He stared wistfully down the channel towards the sea, and to the steamer far ahead, perhaps imploring forgiveness from a Law greater than man's. It was worth risking life and limb in the hazard, judged Paisley, and worth the flouting of Customs, if only to lead back a friend from the bitter, self-destructive path that he had unwisely started down.

"I only wish…" muttered Denis, his attention grimly redirected into his extinguished pipe-bowl now, as if into the pit of cinders that awaits the unrepentant sinner.

"Yes?"

"I only wish I'd been able to shift the rest of the booze. I'm still stuck with crates and crates of it. And all those *bloody* lemons…"

Paisley scowled as though she'd bitten into one of them.

Denis looked up, brightening. "I'll throw 'em in when I sell the ship, to sweeten the deal. I'll turn a profit yet," he said, poking at her with the pipe stem, "You'll see."

Any hope Paisley retained for mankind was ebbing away, along with her appetite. Like Lord Talbot, she now felt compelled to proclaim,

> "*O, too much folly is it, well I wot,*
> *To hazard all our lives in one small boat!*"

"That doesn't rhyme. And it's a ship," protested Denis, more out of reflex than from any real ire at the world's unfathomable belittlement of his vessel. He was paying more heed to something forward, nodding appreciatively at it. "Looks some good in trousers," he said, startling Paisley out of her ill-humour. The solution to the remark presented itself when she saw Alison, emerging from below decks, dressed in what must have been the cast-offs of one of the former crew — black trousers and a striped white blouse — with her fair hair loose over her shoulders. Catching sight of them watching, Alison broke into a sailor's hornpipe dance, hopping ludicrously about on alternate legs while miming rope pulling, and saluting, and folding her arms, and any number of other things. Mercifully, she broke off as abruptly as she began and skipped over to them like a Maenad from an operetta, glowing with what Paisley took to be exertion, until closer inspection proved it to be pleasure.

"This is the life, isn't it!" declared Alison. "The open sea, the wind, chasing villains, no-one giving orders..."

Denis cleared his throat. "'cept for the *captain* of course, ah, able seaman Stiles. I'd ask that you not set a bad example to the lubbers aboard," he said, eyes pivoting in Paisley's direction.

"Aye, cap'n," said Alison, snapping a salute, then steaming past them to the small bronze swivel gun mounted on the stern railing "Ooh, and you have a cannon!"

"That," said Paisley, "was my parents' cannon. If anyone fires it, it will be I."

Captain Ludlow then announced that he'd decided to relocate the cannon, as he was now chasing someone rather than worried about being chased by the Customs men, at whom he'd planned to fire rotten potatoes and lemons had the ultimate extremity of capture arisen. The stern chaser would become a bow chaser, and Paisley, as *The Avenger*'s self-appointed Gunnery Officer, was in charge of moving it.

"She's stronger than she looks," said Alison, as Paisley staggered forward lugging the cannon.

Paisley left them discussing the relative merits of tar and ribbons for holding back the hair, and followed a wobbly course generally in the direction of the bowsprit, the details of which were dictated by the vagaries of the sea and the availability of handholds to keep her from toppling over at each lurch of the deck. Midway, Herr Hasselberg accosted her with effusive Teutonic exclamations and offers of aid, which she politely declined. Elliott approached more cautiously, inquiring at whom she intended to fire the cannon.

"I haven't decided yet," said Paisley.

Together they settled the swivel-gun into a slot in the gunwale to one side of the bowsprit, where it wouldn't get fouled in the rigging.

"Do you think, Elliott," she asked, when the weapon was installed, "that we should be getting involved any further in this business?"

Whether it was mal-de-mer, or the waning moon, or waxing common sense, or having so suddenly divested herself of her hoard of inebriating silver, whenever Paisley turned around lately she found herself staring into the sour face of discretion. It was quite unlike her to be so unreckless. Or reckful, to be less negative about it. Surely it wasn't a result of growing up; one didn't grow up this quickly, even at sea. Perhaps it was the undeniable awkwardness of being aboard a small ship in the company of both Adelmo and Elliott, without so much as a change of clothes. Whatever it was, she was finding it hard to "stiffen the sinews, summon up the blood, disguise fair nature with hard-favour'd rage", and all the rest of it. Especially "Let pry through the portage of the head like the brass cannon," which had always puzzled her. At least she *had* a brass cannon, if she needed one. Or bronze, anyway.

"Who knows where they're going?" she continued. "They may head to Europe, or South America. We can't very well go chasing them around the globe. Apart from anything else, it won't be more than a few hours before that Customs Detective is wiring his superiors to alert every British port to be on the look out for this ship. Even if we follow them all the way to their destination — whatever that may be — if they remember that this ship was impounded, they might even have *us* arrested. It will worry our parents, too, if we disappear. At least, it will worry yours."

Elliott looked thoughtful, even through his wind-tousled hair, which Paisley was again tempted to brush out of his face. "We'll have to discuss it, with everyone," he said. "But unless we're to turn ourselves in, we at least need to get away from *here*."

They decided to consider the matter further tomorrow. Who knew how things might stand by then? They'd at least be away from the Bras d'Or Lakes, and the no-doubt frothing Customs agent who would, before long, be moving heaven and earth to avoid looking like a bungler.

A wave of sea-sickness sped Paisley to the gunwale as a precaution against anything unsightly happening on Elliott's shoes, making as if she were merely taking in the view. Beyond the black hull, to the west, the lake was falling away as they sailed into the long, wide, river-like channel. It was hard not to feel sorry for the huge, briny Bras d'Or Lakes, which would have had an even chance of being a sea if Canadians weren't such a prosaic, self-deprecating lot, used to oversized landscapes. This, thought Paisley, was the sort of country where what Europeans would call a forest was only a woodlot; where a great mountain range was considered an inconvenient bump under the railway; where the ocean, being merely local, was treated as a rather dull fish pond, kept out back for industrial purposes, with a handy regular tide to carry the trash away. The Dominion's people might be many things — earnest, pious, polite, prudent, moderately corrupt and moralizing — but *romantic*... not romantic. Alas.

"I hope there won't be trouble," said Paisley. It's hard to face trouble on an empty stomach that's determined to make itself even emptier.

Elliott leant over the rail beside her. "I'm tired of fighting too. Awfully tired. The problem is, they seem obsessed with starting a war. If there's any way we can help prevent that, to frustrate them, we pretty much have to."

"Mmm."

"I... I wish you were home, safe," said Elliott.

Paisley looked at Elliott, her nausea fleetingly forgotten. He was examining the water rather shyly.

"I wish," he said, "I were there with you. But if we *have* to do this, there's... no-one I'd rather have beside me."

Perhaps not entirely unromantic.

Elliott had to return to folding sheets, or whatever it was that Denis was shouting about, and once Paisley had charged the little cannon with powder, wadding, and real iron shot, cramming a wooden plug in the barrel and a cap for the frizzen-pan to keep it dry, she went back to drooping dismally over the side, waiting to be sick and watching the wooded green banks of the channel slip past. It widened and narrowed, villages drifted by, and occasional ferries crossed their path. When the sun was low enough that even Paisley felt her dark glasses superfluous, and she was wondering whether the channel was going to go on forever, they passed a little headland, opening the vista out to a grey wedge of waves vanishing at the horizon. The Cabot Strait, and beyond it, Newfoundland. And the French islands of Saint Pierre and Miquelon. Paisley stiffened. Could the Wellborn Trust steamer be going there? Had they made some arrangement with the French government for the submarine technology?

She meandered aft to raise her suspicions with Denis and Elliott, receiving a laconic "We'll see" from the captain, who assigned her to hang out *The Avenger*'s lights, now that night was coming on. Red on the port side, green on the starboard.

The deck was livelier than ever, making her feel like a string puppet that several rival puppeteers were fighting over. Back at the wheel, she clutched for support at a stubby post like a fire hydrant.

"Isn't it getting too rough for sailing?" asked Paisley.

"Don't mess with the binnacle," replied Denis, rather cryptically to

Paisley's thinking. Denis lit a match and touched it to a lamp inside the post, illuminating a compass. "And this ain't rough. We're at sea. It don't get much smoother than this, 'less you're becalmed in the Sargasso."

"Oh. Oh no…"

"Get some sleep below," suggested Denis. Or more likely ordered, he being captain. "We take shifts from here on out. You and Alison are off first. There're hammocks in the crew's cabin. Hasselberg is off too. He's in charge while I'm off-shift. He can sleep in my cabin."

Seeing the state she was in, Elliott helped Paisley down the companion-way to the cabins.

"It's only sea-sickness," Paisley assured him. Elliott darted out of the cabin, promising a sure treatment, leaving Paisley to accustom herself to life as a pendulum. On her left, Alison was swaying sickeningly in her own hammock.

"Comfy," said Alison, bouncing to illustrate her point.

Paisley groaned. She was concentrating enviously on the gimballed wall-lamps, which stayed upright no matter how the ship moved. When Elliott returned — it was hard to tell how much later, as the lamps were having a hypnotic effect — he seemed to be carrying an armload of remedies. "Have some of this," he suggested, handing her a tin mug and tucking a woollen blanket in around her.

It smelt citrusish. "Were you squeezing lemons?"

"They're excellent for sea-sickness. Also for preventing scurvy."

Paisley sipped some, cautiously, amid the rocking. She was glad he'd remembered to add a little sugar.

"I should get back on deck," said Elliott. Surveying Paisley's wobbly nest, he took off his jacket, rolled it into a bundle, and slipped it behind her head. "I'm afraid there aren't any pillows. Try to get some rest. I'll leave this under the hammock, in case, um…" Setting down a galvanized pail, he headed back up the companionway.

"Thoughtful boy," said Alison, when Elliott was gone. "You're lucky."

"Elliott is very medically inclined. He would do the same for anyone."

"Hmph. I got knocked on the head with a boom earlier, and he didn't tuck *me* into bed with his coat for a pillow. He just felt my skull and said I'd be fine. He said he'd been knocked on the head more times than he could remember."

Alison hopped out of her hammock, turned the lamps down, and threw herself back into the network sling like a suicidal fish.

"Though somehow that isn't very reassuring. Good night."

STARTING AT FOUR a.m., Sunday was broken up into six-hour shifts. Fortified by regular draughts of lemon juice, Paisley helped out by preparing in the galley what passed for meals; there wasn't much to work with. As Denis had said, to be a sailor you needed a strong stomach, and stronger teeth. Something of an expert in the field of pies, she set about creating one out of potatoes, smoked mackerel, and anything she could find. In the intervals between baking, Alison showed her the ropes of seafaring. Learnt, apparently from her grandfather, on his yacht on the English Channel.

"Does he know Lady Beauchamp's grandfather, the one who sent the telegram?" asked Paisley, after Alison had shown her how to set the staysail, a smaller triangular one ahead of the foresail. The English girl gave her a canny look.

"You're in the know, aren't you. About the Athenian League," she said. "Grandfather isn't related to either of us. It's he who started the League. Mind you, he *is* a grandfather. He's Dr Maddox's. Grandfather is *John* Maddox." She grew confidential, edging closer to Paisley, even with Adelmo unable to overhear at the other end of the ship. "They say he was once a pirate, though I think that's all stuff. There can't have been pirates any more, even back then. But he really did fight at Navarino, the great sea battle that freed Greece from the Turks. He loves sailing, ancient as he is. You *must* come over and meet him," she said, with such passion that Paisley half expected her to produce an ocean-liner timetable to arrange a travel schedule. Alison obviously worshipped the old man.

By noon it was obvious — at least to Denis who, with his binnacles and his sailor's wiles, had some idea of where they were — that the Wellborn ship was not bound for Newfoundland, the French isles, or anywhere across the ocean to the east; they were turning southwards; it was to keep pace with them the staysail had been set. In a lull in activity, with a steady course, there was a meeting of the whole crew on deck by the wheel, seated on lemon crates, or on the overturned dory that was *The Avenger*'s ship's boat. Paisley had brewed up the stale old coffee, hoping it was moderately palatable even without cream.

"What now?" asked Elliott. "Shall we follow until they make landfall and observe them?"

"Since we haven't been arrested yet," said Denis, "I'd say things are proceeding pretty good so far."

Herr Hasselberg seemed dubious of his coffee. "This is not like the coffee in Germany," he declared, in a tone darker than the gritty brew.

"I did my best with what was available," said Paisley, casting a new light on the coffee in the opinion of Hasselberg, who put on a forced smile to assure Paisley that it was not so bad after all.

"The Wellborn Trust has paid my expenses, of course," said Hasselberg after forcing down some more coffee. "It was not our understanding, however. My business, the Hasselbergwerke, was meant to manufacture more undersea vessels. And I have grown most fond of the *Paradoxo*. She is the favourite of my ships. I should not wish to bid her goodbye forever. Also, they have taken my entire supply of *Johnston's Fluid Beef*, for which they did not provide me recompense."

"In my opinion," said Alison, interrupting everyone's reluctant contemplation of Fluid Beef, "the submarine boat must be destroyed before, or immediately after the steamer docks. The engine, in particular, must not remain in the possession of the Wellborn Trust. They will inevitably disassemble, study, and learn to reproduce it. The consequences of their producing and selling submarine craft with such an engine are…" she grasped in the air for a word, "…incalculable. I suggest following the steamer into harbour, and dropping a firebomb through the hatch of the submarine boat, or scuttling…"

"Excuse, please," interrupted Adelmo. "Are you not a maidservant?"

"Not *exactly*, Mr Hasselberg. You will recall my previous attempt to destroy your submarine boat with a bomb which, sadly, failed to rupture the hull. I believe you mistook it for a lightning strike."

Adelmo looked from face to face, smiling uncertainly at what must have sounded like a joke being played on the German.

Denis shook his head, grinning. "These modern girls, eh?"

Paisley felt compelled to disillusion Adelmo.

"I am afraid it is true," she said. "Miss Stiles, with others, has been attempting for some time to disrupt your co-operation with the Wellborn Trust."

"But your government approves… why?" he asked, bewildered.

"Our government," said Paisley, "is complicated. There are local governments, provincial governments, the Dominion government, and the Imperial government. The Imperial government is misguided in this, and has acted without consulting the Parliament of the Dominion. They have not correctly assessed British interests. Or yours."

Adelmo remained incredulous. Elliott seemed about to offer his own argument, but Paisley caught his eye and signalled to him to keep quiet.

Adelmo would be more likely to believe her than Elliott.

"We know," she said, "something of the Wellborn Trust. They are connected to the man who tried to kill Elliott. We have been hiring a private detective, for some time, who has gathered information about the man, Strange, and the Wellborn Trust. Mrs Sowerby, in one of the organization's own publications, professes a belief that the most charitable act towards mankind is to foment war, for the improvement of the race. Your submarine boat is how she, and they, intend to do that. They wish to bring about a war as great as those with France and Napoleon, to destroy the British Empire, and draw Europe and America into a conflict that would cost countless lives. They never had any intention of using your machine for benevolent purposes. In fact, the reason they fled with it is that their true intentions were revealed in public."

Frowning in thought, Adelmo pressed a fist to his lips.

"I cannot ask," said Alison, a fearsome gravity coming over her, "Miss DeLoup or her friends to endanger themselves further in this matter — it is a task that I have been given, and that I have accepted; the responsibility is mine. It is very likely that I shall be arrested should I attempt to destroy the submarine boat in harbour. I feel it only proper to warn you that I intend to accomplish this undertaking, no matter the consequences. I must ask that you not interfere in any way with the destruction of the *Paradoxo*. I should not wish any harm to come to you."

Adelmo looked up from the deck. "You are in earnest? You will do this?"

"Nothing in my life shall ever be more significant than this task."

Scowling, Adelmo rose slowly, like a wrathful whale surfacing. Alison's hand went to her pocket and half withdrew a small pistol.

"I shall destroy *Paradoxo*," said Adelmo. "It is simple. I shall open the hatch, and let the waves fill her." He took from his pocket the cheque that the Wellborn Trust had left for him, and tore it to shreds.

"But... how can you open it at sea?" asked Alison, hiding the pistol again.

"Ah. That is not so simple."

The substance of his plan was straightforward enough, if fraught with danger in the execution. To board another ship is no easy chore, not when both are in motion on the open ocean; hence piracy's reputation for being a risky profession. Adding the hostility of the opposing crew, and a moonless night, made the troubles sound insurmountable. Even more so when Adelmo realized that he had neglected to bring the submarine boat's hatch key. Paisley, however, had hers.

At ten o'clock, with a hint of twilight still in the western sky, the topsails and jibs were set to close the distance between *The Avenger* and the steamer, visible at the base of the emerging Milky Way as a far-away smudge of smoke, coming and going from sight with the swell. They were just now lighting their lamps; *The Avenger*'s own would stay dark that night.

The most keen-eyed of anyone aboard, Paisley watched from the bow to ensure that they didn't lose sight of their prey. It was a tense job, and the spray made it a wet one, slightly improved by a long oilskin coat and her growing immunity to sea sickness. Twice, she nearly became confused when the lights of other passing ships joined those of the steamer — had the Wellborn ship extinguished its own, she might well have told Denis to follow the wrong ship altogether.

The fish pie of dinner was a fading memory by the time the steamer began to seem any closer. At an hour past midnight, they were all growing impatient as the distance closed. Denis, loath to lose any of his remaining cargo, reluctantly gave the order to haul up crates of lemons to dump overboard to lighten the ship a little. Whether it was that, or a change of wind, their speed picked up. Paisley hoped that Elliott and Alison's continuing stream of lemons from the hold to the sea would miss a few for the good of her stomach. Denis must have had thousands of them down there, soon to be enjoyed only by the fish.

She could clearly make out the silhouette of the steamer rising regularly against the pale starlit sky, a white light on its mast and coloured sidelights, a black fishlike shape trailing perhaps ten boat-lengths behind it on a cable or chain, stirring up pale trails of foam and phosphorescence. They would have to manoeuvre almost beside the towed submarine boat for Adelmo to have a chance.

Closer now, Adelmo was preparing near the relatively uncluttered base of the mainmast. It looked as if he were tying himself up, which wasn't too far off the truth. Paisley went aft to wish him luck — they wouldn't lose sight of the steamer at this distance.

"This will save me if I should fall into ze sea," he explained, looping a rope around himself and securing it with knots that he tested with a few sharp yanks. "It vill be tied to ze ship. Zis," indicating another coil of line also tied to a cleat on the gunwale, but with a hook at the other end instead of a man, "I vill throw to ze *Paradoxo*, to…"

"Snag? Grab?" suggested Paisley.

"*Greifen, ja.* Grab. To grab the railing of the *Paradoxo*. I will then climb across."

Paisley offered him the key, and he bowed low so she could hang the cord around his neck. "Be careful," she said.

"*Natürlich!* From you I have learnt to be careful when bowing — you see? I have concussed no-one."

Paisley returned to *The Avenger*'s bow to watch for any changes of course in the steamer, leaving Adelmo to make some practice twirls and swings of the hook. She could hear the steamer's engines now, thrumming. They were almost upon the submarine boat. Elliott and Alison were adjusting sails to match the speed of the steamer.

The schooner slid abreast of the *Paradoxo* in the darkness, the two hardly much different in length. With each rise and fall of the ship, Adelmo swung his hook like a lasso, changed his mind, and waited for the next wave. Then out the hook flew, finally, in a wild arc with rope, ship, and submarine boat each dancing to a different tune.

The hook overshot the *Paradoxo*. Adelmo hauled on the rope to try again. No — it had snagged the railing on the way back! He secured the rope, threw one leg over the gunwale, and began climbing hand over hand across the wave-tossed gulf between the two vessels.

When Adelmo was nearly to the *Paradoxo*, a spark caught Paisley's eye, followed by a bang from the steamer. Then more. A wave burst over her, and when she had wiped her eyes she could just see a black figure at the stern of the black steamer, holding a flashing revolver. Adelmo — he was all right, surely a pistol couldn't hit anything at that distance, not at night. That evidently wasn't the thinking of the pistolier. The pause had only been to reload. The flashes and bangs came again. Then from behind, closer — Alison was firing back at the steamer from the foresail mast. On the *Paradoxo*, a small figure clung to the hatch, waves smashing over it with a wrath that made the pistols seem ridiculous toys. Poor Adelmo had enough to contend with without being shot at as well. Paisley swung the swivel gun towards the steamer, dug inside her coat for matches, and when the ship rose with the next wave struck one straight into the touch-hole, aimed, and gritted her teeth. A fountain of dazzling sparks shot from the touch-hole. The gun rocked with a deafening report and burst of… something.

She'd forgotten to take the plug out of the barrel.

The wind whipped away the gun-smoke. A sepulchral *bong*, like a funeral bell, chimed from the direction of the other vessel. The iron round-shot had struck a plate on the steamer. Probably only denting it. She was considering reloading the swivel gun for another go, when she noticed that the firing has stopped. Unless she'd gone deaf. No, there were no flashes either. Except… there was one off in the east. A ship's light? All they needed now was to be run down by an ocean liner. No. It was gone now. Far away, on the horizon, whatever it was.

Adelmo was… still there! He had the hatch open, and was wedging it in place with something. Hours seemed to have passed, her mind telling her it was only moments. He was taking so long. He didn't… surely he didn't mean to go down with the *Paradoxo*? That would be insane, it would be too horrible, it would be… impossible, after he'd lashed himself so thoroughly to *The Avenger*. Paisley sighed, relieved. Too early for relief, though. Adelmo still had to climb back. He was gripping the line again now, dangling over a dark seething abyss of waves.

There was a change in the note of the steamer's engines, drawing Paisley's attention to it. Gone! The lights were out. They were all racing into a thin fog, making the steamer increasingly hard to separate from the darkness. Now there was only a cable from the submarine boat, vanishing into murk, and Adelmo's line, sagging… dropping him into the sea.

Paisley raced midshipward, found the rope and hauled frantically on it, reeling in more and more slack. No tension. There was no-one one on the other end. It was the hook rope. Elliott appeared beside her, then Alison. All at once the three pounced on the safety line and dragged on it. It took a lot of effort, for someone was attached to this one. Hauling yard after yard of line over the gunwale, it became suddenly even tougher work when there was a thump on the hull, scraping, dragging, and a spluttering, coughing body tumbled onto the deck.

"Turning," gasped Adelmo, when he could speak, "They are turning! Why are we not turning?"

The engines. The slack rope. The steamer was turning across their path to shake Adelmo off the *Paradoxo*. Which might get pulled into the side of the schooner. Paisley ran to the stern, babbling rather incoherently.

"Port!" she said, and then turned to look at the ship. Or was that stage left. "Starboard! Right! That way," she pointed. "Turn!"

Imperturbably gripping the wheel, Denis grumbled around his pipe stem. "I *am* turning… It wasn't easy, y'know, keeping that rope taut, but not so tight it'd snap. You got 'im back aboard?"

"Yes, yes, but the steamer, it's turning, east, right, whatever…"

The fog was dissipating already, the stars growing sharp and bright again.

"Reef the foresail!" hollered Denis. "They can go if they like. That submarine boat'll make 'em a fine anchor when it fills up."

They'd done it. The *Paradoxo* was doomed. They could go home.

Ahead, the fog was lifting patchily. Another band of it lay across their path. Of fog, and stormier-looking water. Whiter, though really a paler shade of black. It sounded rougher. And a black shape.

"What's that?" said Paisley, grabbing Denis' shoulder and pointing.

He squinted. His face fell. "Oh my God."

Paisley strained to see the thing again. On their port side the *Paradoxo* had slipped past, its cable gone, or slack in the sea. The black shape was the steamer, tipping as if to capsize. It seemed to be sailing backwards to ram them. Or *they* had put on speed. Or..."

"She's aground," said Denis, turning harder to port.

The bowsprit exploded in splinters like a thunder clap as *The Avenger* ploughed into the steamer's stern. The next she knew, Paisley was sprawled on the deck half-buried in lemons, feeling like Jumbo the elephant the day he got a speeding locomotive in the small of the back. Wood was cracking. The steamer's engines were roaring nearby in the night, and even ignoring Paisley's aversion to the way ships moved, the schooner was not moving well at all. Its unpleasant but reliable rise and fall had given way to lurches, judders, and sways. What followed was a shadowy nightmare of confused crawling, hunting for Elliott with the ship wrenching itself to pieces all around. Freeing him from a tangle of ropes, they scrambled up a deck growing ever more steeply angled, joined by Alison and Adelmo.

"She's had it," said Denis.

He went to the dory, which they worked madly to right and launch. Waves spilt across the deck, clawing at their legs, eager for the little boat, or their lives. At the last moment, Adelmo, still wrapped in rope, lashed each of them to the boat's thwarts, and they plunged with it into the sea, making barely a ship-length from the wreck before the churning waters overturned them, leaving them clinging to the dory's gunwales with little besides hempen umbilicals between them and death.

They floated, exhausted, for some time. The submerged sand bar and the wrecks fell away and with them the wild, roaring surf. Only thick, rolling waves of ink remained on every side, rising and falling like a giant's breathing. It was impossible to climb atop the dory, but at least they could cling to the edge, or an oarlock.

"Everyone still here?" asked Denis from past Elliott, towards the back of the overturned boat.

"Yes," said Paisley. Elliott, beside her, added his own "Yes". From the other side came a "Yes", and a "Yes", and a "*Ja*".

"Right," said Denis. They sank back into silence, apart from the wind and the gurgle of water around the boat.

"Hold on," said Elliott a while later. "Miss Stiles?"

"Still here," came a voice from the far side.

"Did you say 'yes' twice?"

She hadn't, but thinking back, Paisley also felt that the numbers didn't quite tally.

"There's myself, Elliott, Denis, Adelmo, and Alison. That's five."

"The other 'yes'," said a girl's voice, "I think was mine. My name is Ellen."

Five voices competed to ask questions — who the girl was, whether any more escaped the steamer.

"I was wrecked too, like you. There were no survivors," she said. "I am so glad I am no longer alone."

They had had some luck, then, to be yet alive. For how long they would remain so in the cold water, Paisley hated to think. "What are we to do now, Denis?" she asked. He surely knew something about staying alive at sea.

"Well," he said, "we could sing, I guess."

Paisley didn't know about the others, but breaking into song was not her dearest desire at that moment. "I mean, how shall we live?"

"If they'd seen us — the lifesaving crews, I mean, on Sable Island... that was Sable Island we ran into, or an outer bar of it. If they'd seen us, they'd've signalled. Sent out a boat. But I didn't even spot the light. We've got to be ten, fifteen miles from land at least. And drifting."

"Drifting where?"

"Currents round here... probably down the coast."

"That's good, isn't it?" asked Elliott. "Someone's sure to see us along the coast."

"The island's more'n a hundred miles from the nearest land. The cold'll get us 'fore we're anywhere's near land."

So that was that.

At least there would be no war. That would be some consolation as they perished, one by one, in the cold sea. She didn't regret it, not really. Only it would have been nice to settle things with Elliott. An understanding. She groped along the edge of the boat to where he was holding on, and clenched her hand over his. She'd been such a fool to waste the last few weeks on a silly infatuation. At least they would be together, eternally, in Heaven.

Or would they? It felt as if seawater had seeped into her and chilled her heart. What exactly *would* it be like? Would... they even be allowed to be together? One couldn't even stay at an hotel with a young man one wasn't married to. Heaven would certainly be more strict than an hotel. How could they possibly enter Heaven and stay there together forever without being so much as betrothed? It would be... improper.

"Elliott," she said, her voice shaky despite her best efforts, "we must get married."

"What?"

"You can do it, can't you Denis? You're a sea captain."

"Well...um... I don't exactly have a ship any more."

"You must. Before we die. Please…" In the faint starlight, Elliott's face was dumbstricken and, Paisley was fairly sure, pleased.

"I, um," said Denis, "I don't know how it goes. The vows and things."

"Doesn't anyone know the words for a wedding service at sea?" asked Paisley, shouting urgently to be heard around the hull.

"I'm sorry," said Alison.

"It would be a pleasure," said Ellen, "to be a witness, but I regret…"

"This," asked Adelmo, "is what you wish?"

"It is. I *am* sorry. I was confused before, but I see now where my affections have always lain."

"I know a service. But solely in German."

That would have to do. It was an emergency, after all.

"Captain Ludlow," said Adelmo, "you must say ze names of ze bride and *Bräutigams*. Bridegroom, zat is."

"Elliott and, um, Paisley," said Denis, uncertainly.

"*Sind Sie*," continued Adelmo, "*freiwillig und bereiten Herzens gekommen, um miteinander die Ehe einzugehen?*"

"Er," said Denis, "Sin sea, um, freewheeling underwriting hurtsens gecomen, um, mitten an der dea aya ine sooga hen?"

"Ze bride and groom say *Ja*."

Elliott and Paisley looked at each other in the dark. "Yeah," they said together.

"Now, ze captain says, '*Wollen Sie einander lieben und achten und die Treue halten bis dass der Tod euch scheidet?*'"

Denis cleared his throat a few times. "Woollen sea, ine ander leave a nun actin' undie troya halting bees disaster toad ook shy debt. Is that right?"

"*Herr Gott*," muttered Adelmo. "Now… now you answer, *Ja*".

"Yeah," repeated Paisley and Elliott.

"You are *Mann und Frau. Glückwünsche.*"

Congratulations came from around the dory. Elliott shifted closer to Paisley. She stretched to receive his kiss. The boat slid into a trough, and Elliott's nose went into Paisley's eye.

"Ah!" they both shouted, heads crashing together.

Well, thought Paisley, winking but still gripping Elliott's hand. And now we die.

"My best wishes," said Ellen, "for a long and happy life together."

Not quite in the best of taste, it seemed to Paisley.

"When you see him, give him my love," continued Ellen. "Tell him to be patient, and not to fret. We'll meet again at the right time."

"See whom?" asked Elliott. There was no reply.

"Ellen?" said Paisley. "Are you all right?" Again, there was no answer.

"Alison? Adelmo? She's on your side. Is she all right?"

"She isn't," said Alison. "She's on your side."

Denis swore she was never near his end.

"She's washed away," said Denis. "Ellen!"

Paisley shifted to search the heaving blackness around her for a face in the water, a hand, anything. There was nothing. She looked about again. At least, now that the moon was out, shining on the surface, they might have a chance…

There was no moon tonight. Even had she not know from the calendar, she would have felt it. Paisley gazed up at the sky.

"Look," she said.

Elliott and the others all chorused, "Where?"

"Up."

Perhaps a hundred yards above, or two, was a white figure, like a girl in a shaft of moonlight, her arms outstretched. Paisley stifled a sob and turned to Elliott. "What's happening? Are we dying?" They watched, silent, as the girl hung there in air precisely above them as they drifted through the long, chilling night.

SLOWLY, IMPERCEPTIBLY, LIGHT returned to the world, the grey foredawn giving the shapeless sea back its form, its texture, and its vast expanse. The girl dimmed, and dimmed, until she was almost an afterimage floating at the edge of vision. With the first rays of sun over the horizon, she was gone.

O day and night, but this is wondrous strange…

Had she not been so very drained, or so cold, the sunrise might have brought renewed hope. Instead, the marvellous vision of the girl in the sky had utterly flummoxed Paisley. Had she had the strength, she might have asked the others their opinions on it. For her part, Paisley felt a little put out, if anything. What was the sense in a miracle that had no effect whatsoever, except to shut people up in stunned disbelief. She supposed she shouldn't complain. No doubt it was well meant. But really, a freak wave turning the dory upright would have been far more practical. Perhaps it was someone else's miracle, and their boat just happened to be floating by at the wrong moment.

Elliott hadn't said anything since the apparition. When he did, his teeth chattered from the uncontrolled shivering. "I-I-I'm g-glad. Ab-b-out the wedding."

It made Paisley feel a degree or two warmer. There had still been a niggling doubt in the back of her mind that Elliott might have gone along with it to humour her, to be nice before they drowned.

"I-I always l-loved you. I n-never cared about your… c-c-condition."

Someone coughed on the other side of the boat. "Please?" said Adelmo. "What is this condition?"

Elliott ignored the interruption, and continued chattering, wonderfully. "I know I p-p-put off t-telling you how I f-felt... to the l-last minute... b-but, well... there you are."

Aching and numb, she worked her hand around Elliott's again from where it had slid off. His flesh was cold as the wooden hull of the dory.

"Yes. Here we are," she said.

With a little effort, they both managed to form a pair of shaky smiles.

"And," came another intrusion, from Denis this time, "th-there's a b-boat."

This took a moment to be absorbed by some rather strained and frozen brains. There was some jibbering and indiscriminate gawping in all direction until at the top of a swell Paisley spied the sails of a square-rigged ship in the distance, reappearing periodically as they rose and fell. Spontaneously, they all bawled for help until they were hoarse. A longboat hove into view, full of men pulling oars. Alongside, they all seemed to be yammering in some foreign tongue, crossing themselves, and flailing boat-hooks towards the dory. Paisley couldn't even wave. Her strength was spent. She found herself being violently rubbed in the bottom of the longboat, a blanket thrust around her, and noxious hot brandy poured down her throat making her choke. The others were jumbled in beside her in a heap. A huge man in a dark coat and beard loomed over them all. His grave countenance turned into a gape of wonder, and then an equally gaping grin.

"*Vsemogushchiĭ Bog!* First, saint in sky, then trails of lemons in sea, and now this! Eeliott, my friend, is bloody damn good to see you again!" said the giant, just as Paisley fell unconscious.

Chapter Twenty-Five
A Warm Welcome

An unlit lamp swung over the creaking bunk, light streaming instead through a glazed porthole. On the wall an exotically primitive painting — liberal in its use of gold-leaf — hung. Formless snippets of dreams wafted through Elliott's mind, hampering his efforts to work out where he was. Drowning. Faceless things chasing him through the dark. More water. Nameless catastrophes.

Popular belief would have it that the sea has a wholesome effect on convalescents, rendering the most stubborn patient hale and hearty whether he likes it or not. Without any formal medical qualifications, Elliott was willing to concede that there might be a few grains or minims of truth in this; lately hay fever had been very low on his list of troubles. It was, nevertheless, also true that the devil is in the dose, as the apothecaries say. Elliott had received, by all accounts, one devil of a dose of ocean. Enough, surely, to tide him over for a lifetime.

Thinking to get up and find out how soon he could look forward to putting the sea behind him forever, he found to his horror that he couldn't, no matter how he thrashed about. It was like Strange's chair all over again. Arms. Legs. Trapped. In the midst of his woolly-minded half-asleep despair, it struck him that the lumpy mountain of blankets piled atop him might be acting like a strait jacket, and he squirmed an arm to the surface, bumping it painfully on something in the process. He plunged the hand warily back into the heap, feeling an angular impediment in the way. It proved, when he dragged it to the surface, to be a brick. Elliott studied it, but whoever had left it in his bed had neglected to attach an explanation.

As he dragged his other arm into the air, it encountered something rounder, and he drew out a large, corked bottle this time, full of clear liquid. He studied it minutely without illumination before setting it on the floor beside the brick, and wriggled free enough of the blankets to sit upright, emerging with a heavy knitted sock on his chest. Inside was a silver flask.

"Curiouser and curiouser. What on earth was I doing last night?"

Finding himself uncommonly thirsty, he unstoppered the flask even though, like the brick, it failed to bear any helpful label, such as "DRINK ME". A sniff of the contents revealed no scent, and sipping showed it to contain water. When he'd drunk off half the flask to slake the great thirst he'd woken with, he set it, too, aside with the other inexplicable items.

The whole holiday — this morning not excluded — seemed to stretch back like one of those peculiar nightmares he sometimes had from reading too much Jules Verne; like the one with the clockwork men who kidnapped him, leading him away to thraldom in a sinister undersea city where he was forced to share a cell with a codfish whose only interest was discussing cricket teams. Except, of course, that none of those things had happened on *this* trip. Yet. Perhaps the events of the past few weeks would conclude like one of those exasperating books where the last chapter reveals everything to have been a dream. Episodes thus far had left him prepared for almost anything, but he hoped that the Author of events would have more sense than to use a cheap trick like that. Steering himself away from such blasphemies, he heartily thanked heaven that he was no longer hopelessly adrift in the frigid sea, and that... that... that...

Startling images were coming back to him. Some officious and panicked clerk deep in his brain kept stamping the memories "Dream — Please Disregard", but a more competent authority was swearing oaths as to their veracity.

"Great Scott... I'm married!"

Elliott thrashed again to free himself from the blankets and get to his feet, only avoiding a tumble from the bunk due to a wooden barrier meant for keeping sailors in bed in high seas. He sank back onto the mattress.

"Married. I'm *married.*"

That was *good*, wasn't it? It was what he'd hoped would happen. *Eventually.* But eventually was a long way off when you were sixteen. At least, until you woke up one day to find that it wasn't any more.

Ye gods. He wasn't even finished school yet. A fellow was supposed to find employment before a wife. What would he do? What would *they* do? It wasn't as if you could say that it didn't count because you were still alive.

And it wasn't going to be easy to explain all this to his parents. He could imagine them, meeting him at the station in Kingston.

"Welcome home, Elliott, dear! I trust your trip was refreshing."

"Oh, yes. Someone left a bomb in my compartment on the train. Then, when it didn't blow up, he tried to beat me to death and throw me off, but

that turned out all right because the Minister of Justice killed him. Later, a lunatic tied me up and tried to scoop out my eyes with a spoon. We took an impounded smuggler's ship from Customs detectives, chased some of the lunatic's associates, exchanged gunfire with them, and finally rammed their ship, whereupon we sank and nearly drowned."

"And... Miss DeLoup has come for a visit...?"

"Actually, um, she's come to stay. And she isn't Miss DeLoup any more..."

ELLIOTT WAS ALMOST coming to grips with this unsettling development, when an even greater one struck him in the form of a clammy foot suddenly pressed against his own. His recoil made him stub his big toe painfully against the wooden barrier, thus finishing off one of the few parts of his body that had survived the holiday intact.

It had to have been another brick. That was it. A brick. He shakily probed about under the covers with a hesitant and throbbing toe. Nothing. It was bricks. Or imagination.

The foot twitched into his again.

No shock of natural or artificial origin, inside or outside of a laboratory, had ever sent a mollusc reeling back into its shell with the hastiness deployed by Elliott as he withdrew all of his limbs into a ball to consider matters further.

The situation seemed to stand thus: he had been shipwrecked. Somehow, as a consequence of this, he had gotten married. Unexpectedly, they had been rescued from almost certain death. Even more unexpectedly, he had woken up in a bed containing not only uncanny bits of junk, but also... Paisley. Oh, dear Lord. Obviously, he knew that weddings were meant to lead to... to... this sort of thing. But really. A fellow needed at least a day or two to get used to the idea.

Elliott's mind, finding the main thoroughfare too disturbing, wandered off down a harmless cul-de-sac alley to consider what kind of junk Paisley might have on her side of the bed. Doorknobs? A set of dishes? They couldn't be wedding presents; no-one would give a couple a brick for their wedding. Unless... no, even as a joke it made no sense.

No, this wouldn't do. There was no escaping it — he was going to have to say "Good morning" or something. He took a deep breath to settle his nerves and leant across, to find only a featureless mass of quilt.

"P-Paisley?" he whispered.

There was no reply. Elliott tugged back the cover and got as far as emitting another "P—" when the departing blanket revealed a familiar but slack-jawed and unconscious submariner.

"…aysleeah!", blurted Elliott, not quite getting either name right.

This time the raised side was no obstacle to Elliott's bound out of bed. He retreated until his back hit the wall.

Iarik Starko stepped through the cabin door, expressing mild surprise to find Elliott pop-eyed and flattened against the panelling, in a set of long underwear.

"Eeliott, so goot seeink you oot and aboot. Were frozen last night like Siberian mushroom at Christmas. How you feelink?"

"All right, but… but… my bed. It's full of things. Germans. Bricks."

"You dyink of cold. We put hot water bottles and thinks in bed with you. Double you up for warmink."

Ah. This prod had stirred the still-slumbering medical lobe of Elliott's brain into motion. Cold. Exposure. Extreme loss of body heat. "So… Paisley and Alison are in a bed somewhere? They're well?" Though that would leave Denis, the odd man out, in a bed alone. At least, he had better be alone.

"Eeliot's *oboroten* sweet-heart!" exclaimed Starko, elbowing Elliott hard enough to propel him to the floor.

"Apollo-geese," said Starko, giving Elliott a hand up. "Am forgetink you are in-valid. Da, she ees fine, fine. *Kak krasivo!* Paysle-ee, she is wery loverly-lookink girl. Such beautiful fair hair. And such quantity of knives and pistols she keep about her person…"

"That's Alison. Paisley has dark hair." Auburn, to be precise.

"Ah. She ees nice also," conceded Starko, gravely nodding his beard. "Ees less dangerous lookink."

"Looks can be deceiving. She's, um, actually my wife now."

Starko blew out his breath in an appreciative puff. "Here am thinkink you British is such reserved slowcoaches in romantics, and you go jumpink into wed at drop of hat."

"Or at sink of ship, anyway. We were wrecked during our attack on a submarine boat, and got married while adrift."

"Oy! You must take up quieter life, my friend."

"It is my solemn vow, Iarik, never to do anything exciting ever again," said Elliott with conviction. "Is this *your* ship, Iarik?"

"Da!" said Starko, pounding a proud fist into the wooden panelling, and cracking it, making him suddenly remorseful. "Now First Mate will have peeves, for breaking his cabin wall. Da, she is my ship, a brigantine. The *Krasnaya Luna.* How would you call… the *Red Moon.*"

Much as Elliott would have liked to yarn away with Iarik about the jolly seafaring life aboard his old bilge-bucket, the *Krasnaya Luna*, they were interrupted by a crewman carrying a tray of cups.

"Here is tea," said Starko. "You drink. Do you goot. See you later. Must go do captainy thinks.

"It's not *zvarka*, is it?"

Starko gave a somewhat sinister laugh before departing. "No, would not give *zavarka* to my dearest foe. *Do svidaniya!*"

Looking for a place to set down the tray, Elliott noticed some clothes slung over a chair, and left the tea there while he got dressed, hurrying as groans and writhing from the direction of the bed suggested that something was awakening. He was sneaking doorwards with his cup of tea, when accosted by a voice from the depths of the mound.

"*Wo bin ich? Warum kann ich nicht bewegen?*"

An arm and a head broke the surface. "Graven? Ist zat you?"

Too late to escape, Elliott offered the German his cup of tea.

"Ah. *Danke schön*. Thank you," said Hasselberg, repeating Elliott's own ordeal of extracting himself from the woollen quicksand in order to be able to accept the tea. Elliott handed over the cup, taking the brick that Hasselberg was studying with furrowed brow.

Elliott got himself another cup from the tray and made a second attempt to escape while Hasselberg was grimacing at the taste of his tea, again failing to make it out in time.

"The others — they are safe?" asked Hasselberg.

Elliott assured him that they were, at least according to Starko. Sipping his tea, he could understand Hasselberg's reaction; it was about half sugar.

"Allow me," said Hasselberg, dragging himself into a slightly more dignified position, "to offer my congratulations properly for your and Mrs Graven's recent wedding. I trust you both shall be very happy."

"Thank-you. I, um, I'm very sorry about your losing the *Paradoxo*. It must have been... difficult."

Had Elliott been in the same boat, or rather the same dilemma, he wasn't sure but that he might have come up instead with some far-fetched scheme for getting his submarine boat back, probably leading to utter failure. He felt pretty childish for having refused to tour the machine when he'd been offered the chance. Now he never would.

"*Ja*. I shall miss her. I shall miss them both." Hasselberg looked up from his cup. "You would not object, I hope, if I should say good-bye to Miss... to Mrs Graven... before I return to Germany?"

Had Hasselberg been a more puffed-up, arrogant fellow, Elliott might have felt justified in a spot of gloating over the way in which fortune, and more importantly Paisley, had smiled on him instead of on the German. As it was, Elliott felt almost as if he'd cheated somehow. Hasselberg, bolder and braver than he — and so much better at wooing — had willingly sunk his extraordinary vessel at the peril of his own life, and had ended up with only a broken heart.

"Of course," said Elliott. "I hope we might all be friends. And that there are no hard feelings." When Hasselberg looked puzzled, he added "I mean, no anger. Resentment. Bitterness."

Hasselberg looked bleak for a moment, but then shook his head. "No. No hard feelings."

Elliott drank some more tea, filling time, not knowing quite what to say. "I... I've loved Paisley for a long time. Though I didn't always show it. I'm sorry that my... ah... happiness had to bring disappointment for you."

"Very kind of you to say."

Elliott nodded. Perhaps there wasn't anything more that needed saying. He turned to leave, and remembered one of Paisley's remarks when they were walking into Baddeck. "Paisley once compared you to Lochinvar. Do you know the poem? By Sir Walter Scott?"

"Yes," said Hasselberg wistfully. "*Marmion*."

"From what I've seen, I would say that it suited you quite well —

> *So faithful in love, and so dauntless in war,*
> *There never was knight like the young Lochinvar.*

"I hope, if I ever need to be, that I might be as courageous."

BAD FEELINGS THREATENED to arise again a little later when Elliott, who was indeed wondering the time, was presented with his watch by a helpful crewman who had pickled it in a jar. Why anyone should have chosen to do this, Elliott had been unable to say. From the sailor's encouraging expression, he seemed to consider it a nice achievement. It principally had the effect of confirming Elliott's growing impression that, wherever one travelled, there was sure to be found a modicum of madness. It was not until Starko, some while later, inquired confusingly as to whether the vodka had washed the salt from his watch, that it dawned on Elliott that if there were a fool on board, it was he.

In fact, he'd slept in until afternoon, hardly feeling refreshed at all. It seemed that nearly dying in several different ways, and getting married, can take it out of a fellow. Paisley, when he found her cabin, was still abed, tea untouched, locket broken on a chair beside the cup. Or... he looked closer, and picked it up... open to dry. There was a little picture on each side of the locket's interior. Photographs. Faces, cut from the Sporeville Eel Fair photograph. Him. And Paisley. He returned the locket in a flash at the first signs of the blanket-mound stirring. Paisley's head protruded sleepily into the air. She really was all right. They'd survived. Weak from relief, Elliott sat with a thump on the edge of the bed to watch, spellbound, as she blinked and yawned.

Assuming that Alison was also buried inside the bed somewhere, Elliott had to be circumspect in his conversation, which stuck mainly to Paisley's well-being, checking that she had no fevers, or chills, or any other dire symptoms. She was, as Starko had said, fine, but having not had the advantage, like Elliott, of a series of nervous shocks and divers alarums to drive away the effects of slumber, she was set on getting a few more hours of rest before the next horrifying experience came upon them. Out of a charitable impulse, Elliott rummaged in the covers before leaving to settle the question of whether Alison had succumbed to suffocation under the burden of wool, and bricks, and eiderdowns, finding her looking uncharacteristically peaceful, though in a drowse rather than anything more worrisome.

The crew, as Elliott pottered about aimlessly, seemed to regard him with a superstitious awe. In the beginning this added harmless amusement to his day, but the more he considered it, the more he came to believe that he would have to discover the truth of their miraculous rescue. Perhaps Dr Maddox and the Etheric Explorers Club might be able to shed light on the happenings of that uncanny night.

The *Krasnaya Luna* had anchored off Sable Island to inform the life-saving station of the wreck, and to help in the search for survivors, but by Tuesday night they had found no traces of the steamer, and at sunset they weighed anchor to head back to Halifax.

WHAT WITH GOING ashore on Sable, and helping where he could, it wasn't until Wednesday morning that Elliott was able to find enough time and privacy to have a good chat with Paisley, sheltered on the leeward side of one of the many deck structures, the names of which his limited sailing education had failed to teach him. Paisley, squinting from the loss of her smoked glasses in the wreck, still looked slightly self-conscious dressed in a sailor's loose jersey and trousers as they huddled together shoulder to shoulder, out of the wind, watching the mouth of Halifax harbour gradually rise above the cloudless horizon. A new day. A new life.

"I hope," ventured Elliott, who had been agonizing for some time over how to broach the subject, "that your family won't be upset. About not being invited to the wedding."

Before replying, Paisley finished swallowing a piece of the crystallized ginger she'd been given by Starko for her seasickness. "I expect they'll be glad to have missed it, considering the circumstances. We couldn't have fit many more guests around the dory."

"You don't regret it?"

"No," said Paisley, turning to Elliott. "Do you?"

"No! It's only, you know, going to be difficult. To explain."

There was unspoken agreement that this was an understatement.

"I think Aunt Claudia," said Paisley, "will find it most extraordinary. She has lived twice as long as I have, and yet in all that time *she* has never managed to get married. I don't know how it will affect the... the vocation she proposed I take up."

"Vocation?"

Paisley explained that her aunt was connected with something called the Athenian League, which went about meddling in hazardous goings-on with a view to preventing wars from happening.

"Do you really want to do this sort of thing all the time?" asked Elliott.

Paisley didn't answer right away. "I'm not sure."

"Might you put it off for a few months? I was looking forward to spending the rest of the summer not doing anything exciting whatsoever. Aside from, um, being with you, of course."

Paisley leant harder against his shoulder. "I'd like that. I believe we *deserve* a holiday. Two months without guns, or bombs, or ships, or spore-mad sleepwalkers. I will suggest most strongly to Aunt Claudia that she provide us with a proper holiday. As a wedding present."

They bantered happily on a host of important matters relating in one way or another to their not unhappy predicament. Such as whether they could, in fact, expect wedding gifts after such an irregular marriage. Whether getting presents would require entertaining hordes of relatives. And whether being married meant that they now were adults, and could begin wearing their hair up (in Paisley's case), or could grow an imperial-style beard (in Elliott's case), this latter idea being one that Paisley, after careful scrutiny of Elliott's features, begged him to reconsider.

"I still have most of my share of the money from Strange," said Paisley, "so we shan't starve."

"I haven't spent all of mine either. We could get a good-sized house."

"Sniggler could catch the mice..."

"There would be a nice kitchen where you could chop up eels for your pies, and sharpen daggers for your madcap adventures..."

"And a surgery on the ground floor where you could saw off people's gangrenous arms and legs..."

"I *would* have to study medicine first," said Elliott, detecting a hurdle that would need to be leapt prior to wallowing in this domestic idyll.

"You could study in Halifax. They have a medical school there. And with plague ships arriving, the harbour full of filth, drunken sailors killing each other and so on, there should be no shortage of bodies to anatomize for your studies."

They sighed in harmony, basking in the morning sun. The future looked bright indeed.

Something caused an eclipse. Something Denis-shaped.

"Uh, morning," said Denis. He was twisting his cap in his hands and kicking at a tuft of oakum that was sticking out between two deck-planks. "Guess we'll be in Town soon." He surveyed the coast and McNabs Island, nodding vaguely as if everything was as it should be.

"We were thinking," said Elliott, "of buying a house in Halifax."

"Oh." He kicked at the oakum some more in what seemed to Elliott, even from his limited acquaintance with ships, a manner calculated to defeat its purpose of caulking the deck. "I, ah, got to confess," said Denis.

Paisley sat upright. "Oh, Denis. You haven't committed *another* crime?"

Denis grew alarmed, as though this was a side of the affair he hadn't considered.

"I dunno… maybe it is a crime. Anyways, the thing is, I don't have my papers."

Elliott and Paisley glanced at each other questioningly.

"You mean, your passport?" asked Elliott, taking a random guess. Presumably Denis didn't mean newspapers.

Denis shook his head. He was still looking at anything but them. "My Master Mariner's papers. I was just the owner, y'see. I hired a crew."

"I wouldn't worry about that," Paisley reassured him, "the smuggling was much more illegal than that."

"The thing is, I was never *really* a captain. Not *legally*. So… you're not *really* married."

"Oh," said Paisley and Elliott.

Denis smiled nervously, and stepped out of the sun, momentarily blinding them. "Sorry," he said, before making his escape, crabwise.

Not married. They weren't married at all, and never had been.

"Do you need to look so relieved?" asked Paisley abruptly.

"What?"

Paisley looked offended.

"No, I'm not," said Elliott quickly. "It's just…" What was it? Being married hadn't been so bad, for a day or two. And the future hadn't been the problem. So why this flood of relief?

"It's just…" Elliott tried again, "…we're too young." That wasn't quite it. There was more to it. "We should enjoy *this* for a while," he added.

Paisley didn't appear entirely convinced. He hoped she understood that by *this* he didn't mean the tar-reeking deck, and the unprepossessing sight of McNab's Island.

"I mean," he tried again, "you know. Playing croquet. Picnicking. Going on long carriage rides to look at boring local attractions that are only nice because we're seeing them together. I, um, I want to spend the summer together, like we planned. And then go home, and write long letters to you every day, about what I'm doing, and thinking, and how much I miss you, and wait every day for the postman to come with letters from you, and read every word again and again until the next letter comes, and count off the days on the calendar until... I can see you again."

Elliott stopped, afraid he was babbling. Beside him, Paisley was awfully quiet. She probably thought he was just making up a lot of lame excuses. Then a shadow fell across him. She kissed him on the cheek.

"That sounds wonderful," she said.

Elliott thought so too, and they both settled back to enjoy a spot of *this*ness.

But just as a comfortable rest is always ruined by an itch or a cramp, so is contentment usually upset by a nagging question that the intellect refuses to leave unanswered. The irksome intruder into Elliott's bliss was the small matter of why they had gotten married in the first place. Paisley had seemed to think it essential when they were drifting towards certain doom. Doubtless it had been one of those panic-stricken losses of reason that afflict victims of calamities. Though, everyone had been reasonably calm when the ship went down...

"Paisley," he said, not too loudly, as she seemed to have fallen asleep on his shoulder, "why was it so urgent that we get married, when we were shipwrecked?"

"You won't laugh?"

"No, of course not."

She explained — with a few confusing asides about hotels which he didn't entirely follow — about being afraid that they wouldn't be together in Heaven unless they were decently married before drowning.

"Oh."

The trouble wasn't one that had ever occurred to Elliott, so his mind was still not completely at ease. On those rare occasions on which Heaven had occupied his thoughts, it was a place he imagined as a kind of garden, rather than an hotel. A garden with an elaborate wrought-iron gate, like the Halifax Public Gardens, only with more gilt attached — especially to the interview with St. Peter. Surely they didn't segregate everybody into walled-off areas reserved for boys or girls who had failed to arrange a death-bed wedding. If anything were to get in the way of eternal bliss, he was more inclined to think that it would be the gatekeeper looking askance at Elliott trying to get inside with a werewolf. He could picture the great saintly fellow in his snowy beard frowning when they got to the head of the queue, and pointing first to Paisley, and then to a sign on the gate saying *Dogs Must Remain on a Leash at All Times.*

Elliott snickered.

"You beast," said Paisley, "You promised you wouldn't laugh."

This had the effect of making Elliott laugh all the harder.

"What?" demanded Paisley, digging Elliott in the ribs to make him tell her.

He revealed his glorious vision of the Afterlife.

"You have offended me, Mr Graven," said Paisley, stiffening.

Elliott, worried now, turned to apologize, but her seriousness was belied by the pretty wrinkling of her nose in amusement. She burst into laughter too.

"If you buy me a muzzle, I shall be very cross indeed. And I'm still not sleeping well on ships, so I've been getting cross easily lately."

"On my first morning on the *Krasnaya Luna*, I woke up crushed under a hill of blankets, with a German and a load of bric-a-brac."

"I woke up with a bomb-throwing lady's maid."

"Well, tonight we can take rooms at the Ivanhoe Inn. Separate rooms, I mean," he added hastily, not wanting to get into a discussion of theology again. "We should be able make up for lost sleep. Halifax seems a nice quiet town. If we see Dr Maddox again, I'll recommend that his next invention be a recombobulator for the treatment of weary travellers like us."

Nearly inside the harbour now, they got up and went to lean on the gunwale to watch the city come into view.

"Do you know Halifax?" asked Elliott.

"Pretty well. You know Papa — he had us tour all of the fortifications, thoroughly."

"Is that a Martello Tower?" asked Elliott, pointing starboard to a squat stone structure at the end of a long spit of land that jutted away from McNab's Island. They had Martello Towers in Kingston, too, so it gave Elliott a twinge of homesickness to see one here, in unfamiliar surroundings.

"It was. It's used as a lighthouse, now. That's where Dr Gesner — you know, the man who invented kerosene — tested it as a fuel for signal lights."

"Nice pebbly beach," said Elliott.

"Mmm. That's where the Navy used to hang deserters' bodies, and leave them to rot."

"Oh."

"Fort Ives is at the end of the island. That," said Paisley, pointing over the port side to the mainland on the opposite side of the channel, "is York Redoubt. Straight ahead, in Point Pleasant Park, is another Martello Tower — the Prince of Wales tower — and the Point Pleasant Battery. That's Fort George, high up on the Citadel. George's Island is that little one in the harbour off to the right. It has Fort Charlotte on it. And across the harbour, on the Dartmouth side, that's Fort Clarence. You can just see it now."

"They're pretty well supplied with forts, then."

"Never used, of course. And now that a war has been averted, hopefully they never will be."

To the port side a black warship was steaming into harbour puffing black smoke, its skeletal masts bare of sails. When she'd studied it, Paisley declared that it was a corvette, originally a sloop before it was reclassified. Part iron, part wood — part sail, part steam — it was halfway between the old ships of the Napoleonic Wars, and the new capital ships that relied solely on coal and steel.

"They have fourteen breech-loading cannon, and eight Nordenfeldt machine guns," explained Paisley.

At the citadel, a puff of smoke appeared, then a *boom* after a delay.

"It's not noon already, is it?" asked Elliott. Being from near Fort Henry, and therefore used to people using cannons instead of bells for timekeeping, he hadn't been surprised on his first visit to Halifax to see people setting their watches by firearms. He pulled out his own and shook it a few times. It said the time was only about half past ten. Perhaps the diet of seawater and vodka hadn't agreed with it.

It was just when Elliott was tucking his watch back into his waistcoat that the Point Pleasant Battery opened fire. York Redoubt, behind them, was the next to erupt in a cannonade, blasting towards them with every gun. The corvette was returning fire, veiling herself in a cloud of fumes from her five inch guns, the haze flashing with countless pencil-thin flames from her multibarelled machine guns, blazing away at the forts. Paisley gaped at Elliott and they both dropped to the deck, suddenly alive with stamping, shouting Russian feet. More cannon fire sounded from ahead, and deafening shots from the right, on McNab's Island. A cross-fire. Surrounded. The firing rose to a pounding, non-stop roar, reeking of gun-smoke. Elliott lifted his head just long enough to see that all of the forts were now bombarding with every gun at their disposal, but the corvette was still putting up a good fight.

"But we stopped the war," bellowed Elliott over the din, "didn't we?"

Paisley's face was ashen. "The Queen!" she shouted. "The assassins have killed the Queen! It must have started a war!"

This was the first Elliott had heard of assassination plots, and he silently wished that Paisley would try to keep him better informed. Life was confusing enough without these sorts of surprises being thrown into the mix as well. War or no, there was little they could do to sway history at the moment other than to keep their heads down and hope that the mob of cursing, crossing, hysterical Russians could steer the ship enough to keep from running into anything. Like a cannon shell.

As the brutal racket went on and on, it became evident that whatever everyone was shooting at, it was not them, unless the artillery men were badly out of practice. Still, Halifax harbour was hardly a safe place to be at the moment. They were meekly peeking past the gunwale again during a lull in the fighting, to see if they were leaving the scene of battle yet, when a colossal explosion hurled them onto their backs. Elliott, in what was now becoming a habit, flung himself on Paisley. A pillar of water had been blasted into the air like a vast fountain, rising and spreading into a bloom of foam. The ship heeled to port as if a gale had struck out of the blue, and then bobbed sluggishly back and forth as they were pelted first with briny rain, then mist, then a scattering of fish, slapping dead onto the deck.

Paisley squirmed out from under Elliott and crawled to the railing again. "What's happening? Is it over?"

Whatever it was — a civil war? An attempt by the Wellborn Trust to provoke a conflict? — the warship seemed as if she had been silenced, but abruptly she sent forth a massive broadside, every gun firing simultaneously. It was an immense roar, sending Elliott and Paisley cringing below the dubious protection of the gunwale. But it was only a hopeless parting shot. Beaten at last by the overwhelming firepower of the city's countless batteries and forts, the corvette began to back out of the harbour through a fog of smoke towards the open sea.

But what was this? A steam launch was steaming past the corvette, towing a barge. The men aboard were rushing about, obviously up to something. They dropped one long cylinder after another into the water. The water churned and foamed around them, and the shapes sped off through the waves leaving white trails behind. They were heading roughly towards the *Krasnaya Luna*.

"They're like little submarine boats," said Elliott, interested in this latest, less dangerous looking turn of events. Paisley's mouth was hanging open. Elliott found it a pleasant discovery that even with that expression her face was no less charming.

"They're torpedoes!" said Paisley, red-faced and wide-eyed "What are we to do?"

"Should we get married again?" suggested Elliott.

Paisley laughed, a trifle crazily. "Eels…" she muttered. "In German they call torpedoes… eels…"

They flung themselves to the deck yet again to await the unavoidable blast. They were helpless — even leaping overboard would only be to jump into a worse maelstrom. Despite this, there were one or two splashes as crewmen dove off. Elliott took Paisley's hand.

There was a dull thud that he felt through the decking. Something had struck the hull, but… not exploded?

"It was a dud?" said Elliott, lifting his head off a seam of oakum.

There were no more explosions. The cannon were silent all around the harbour, and the smoke was beginning to thin. His ears were ringing like fire-bells, but it seemed as if he could hear something coming from the shore. It sounded like a ragged cheer. They rose cautiously from the deck.

"Did we win?" he asked.

"Someone did. I hope it was us."

Faintly, sounding wobbly with the wind, there came the strains of a brass band. It was playing… something familiar…

Rule, Britannia.

Paisley gave a joyous shout and jump.

"We won! We…" The clouds drifted apart. As the view opened up, they could see crowds lining the bunting-hung waterfront, all applauding and harrahing, and waving flags. It was a jubilee celebration. A naval display. Paisley's face dropped. "Why couldn't they have had a parade, like everyone else?"

Elliott shook his head. "You did say you loved fireworks."

Chapter Twenty-Six
Χαίρετε, νικωμεν
(REJOICE, WE CONQUER)

IT SHOULDN'T HAVE been a surprise to find, when they descended dazed and deafened from the *Krasnaya Luna* onto a Halifax dock, that their acquaintance, the Hon. Mr Thompson, was there installed in a prominent place on a review stand with his family. He was, after all, one of the city's leading citizens, and as such was entitled to the best view of any torpedo attacks being offered up as entertainment. Whatever the others felt about the meeting, it was one jolt too many for Denis's nerves — coming hard upon his recent forays into the professions of smuggling, piracy, and illegal weddings — to find himself face to face with the country's Minister of Justice. Denis dissolved into the merrymaking crowds before Thompson could sharpen his arrest-warrant pen. Herr Hasselberg likewise went his own way, to begin arrangements for his return to Germany.

Amongst the plug-hatted dignitaries and their richly-attired wives was a portly woman built along capital ship lines whom Paisley rightly took to be Mrs Thompson, partly on the grounds of her proximity to the Minister, and partly on resemblance to him. As soon as her husband had explained who the new arrivals were, Mrs Thompson abandoned all thoughts of royal revelry and bore them away to cabs, bowling aside MPs, MLAs, mayors, honourables, and patricians like a battleship running down a fleet of squid-boats. Around her as she left swarmed her brood of ice-cream-armed destroyers, helping to keep the dignitaries at a safe distance, while her husband was towed along in the wake of the fleet, issuing orders and apologies like a rear admiral whenever someone's ice cream landed on the Lieutenant-Governor.

Along with the Thompsons' guests, the Maddoxes, they set off for the Minister's two acres at the corner of Windsor & Almon Street. The younger Thompsons at first complained bitterly at the injustice of retreating from the show so early, when there might yet be mayhem to enjoy. But the mere sight of two girls dressed in sailors' togs, hair wild with sea-foam and gun-smoke, smelling of harbour-brine and adventure, was enough to whet their interest. When they grasped that the three had not only sailed through the thick of the mock battle, mistaken for one of the "attacking ships", but had in fact been wrecked only the other day, the junior Thompsons (except for the eldest, John, who had only just returned from Lancashire — whither he had been sent to learn French — and who at fifteen was too dignified to partake of his siblings' zeal or their confections) were able to forego further treats and cannonades with clear consciences. Obviously something even more exciting had landed in their laps.

June sunshine notwithstanding, Paisley huddled for warmth against Elliott in the cab as snugly as decorum would allow. The fishy downpour from the exploding mine in the harbour and the anticipation of being questioned by Mr Thompson were combining to give her the chills. Ever a dutiful niece, she shiveringly begged that they pause briefly en route at a telegraph office to reassure her Aunt Claudia that nothing too dreadful had happened to her wayward relation. With any luck, Claudia would have done nothing more than panic, and would yet to have contacted Paisley's parents about her disappearance.

Shock and exhaustion, if not her on-again off-again wedding, had returned Paisley's mind to a spoony, porridgey state, so she sent off the first thing that occurred to her, in keeping with Lady Beauchamp's telegraphic style. She felt very much as she imagined the swift-running Greek messenger must have, shortly before he expired, and so took the pencil at the telegraph wicket and filled out the form with

REJOICE WE CONQUER ATHENS IS SAVED PHEIDIPPIDES

"You didn't mention Denis, did you?" asked Elliott, on the way out of the telegraph bureau. Paisley told him what she'd sent.

"Won't that make her suspect you've dropped dead at the end of your journey?" objected Elliott. "And tell them to feed Sniggler."

They returned to the wicket where, for slightly more money, she appended STOP REALLY ALL WELL STOP TELL MARY CONTINUE SARDINES AND GEORGE SAVED EMPIRE PAISLEY to the first message, and they continued on their way to the Thompson residence, hoping that the telegram would not be set aside with the usual nonsense from her father.

It was a fairly plain clapboard house, enlivened with a grand entrance reached by a flight of stairs, and an elaborate first storey veranda or balcony from which the Thompsons might take in a view of the glasshouse across the street at Hornsby's Nursery. The entire mob settled into chairs around the parlour, neat and tidy apart from an incongruous tin bucket positioned under a stain in the ceiling, suggestive of a leaky roof. Bowls of strawberries and scones swimming in cream appeared, and Paisley found she was ravenous after countless hours of queasy horrors.

"We made a speaking tube out of lamp chimneys," said Frankie, the youngest, as she scooped up spilt strawberries from her dress.

This led — presumably building on the theme of telecommunication — to Mrs Thompson asking whether Alison and Paisley were dressed as boys as a result of Dr Bell's influence. "Mrs Bell does have a habit of fitting out her daughters that way, when she can get away with it."

"Are you pirates?" interrupted Frankie brightly, only to be shushed by her older, more sensible sisters, who were inconveniently both named Mary. Or conveniently, depending on how one viewed these things. Paisley was quickly coming to understand how young Frankie had come to be nicknamed "the dizzle-dazzle".

"Mr Garrity's articles," said Thompson, getting down to business "have been appearing in the Halifax papers. A good deal has happened since I left Baddeck. I take it there was more than luck involved in his knowledge of certain embarrassing statements by that Mrs Sowerby?"

"Oh, yes, sir," sighed Elliott. "Much more than luck. It took Paisley and me days of research to find those quotes. But I'm afraid Mrs Sowerby has died."

This was it. Elliott had touched off the fizzing fuse leading to the obligatory explanation: what exactly they had been up to. Ever since catching sight of the Minister of Justice, Paisley had been dreading the inevitable questions, but had been borne along helplessly. He was, perhaps, the greatest legal mind in the Dominion. Paisley, by contrast, had all but lost count of the number of people whose deaths she directly or indirectly had a hand in. Or a fang in, as the case might be. It made for a most awkward situation.

Paisley, her mouth full of scone and strawberry, was powerless to intervene at the point where the story began to sound like a confession, but Alison hastily took over the narrative from Elliott, emphasizing the exciting parts at the expense of the ones associated with long prison terms, and omitting — somewhat to her disappointment — Paisley's successful cannon-shot.

"And then the Russian ship rescued us," concluded Alison.

Elliott, from his expression, found the expurgated version of their escapades too thin. "There was the girl, too. I'll never forget *her*."

"Girl?" asked Joe, the second oldest Thompson offspring.

"When we were adrift," said Elliott, "we were clinging to an overturned boat in the pitch black, and discovered there was an extra person with us. We assumed she was from the steamer that sank. She was even a witness at Paisley's and my... well, anyhow, she was there, but we weren't sure exactly where because we couldn't see. Then she said something. She said, 'When you see him, give him my love.'"

"When you see whom?" asked Mrs Thompson.

"I don't know. She never mentioned what 'his' name was. Then she said…" Elliott frowned, trying to remember.

Paisley set aside her bowl. "She said, 'Tell him to be patient, and not to fret. We'll meet again at the right time.' And then she was gone."

"Drowned?" said Mrs Maddox. "Poor girl."

Paisley studied the pattern of the carpet. Beside her, Elliott was doing the same, and their hosts respectfully allowed them a moment of sombre remembrance.

"That's what we thought," said Elliott. "I… I don't blame you if you find it incredible. I know I would, hearing anyone else say it. But when we looked up, there she was in the night sky above us, bright as the stars."

There were several intakes of breath from the listeners. Dr Maddox, on the chesterfield opposite, leant forward. "What do you mean?" he asked.

Paisley looked Dr Maddox in the eye. "Just what Elliott said, sir. I don't know what she was, but she hung there, above us, until dawn. The Russian ship only found us because they saw her and changed course."

"And this was near Sable Island?"

"About ten or fifteen miles," said Elliott, "east of the lighthouse. That's what we guessed, anyway. We never saw the island. We struck a sandbar. Or rather the steamer did. Then we struck the steamer."

"Did she say nothing else? Her name?" asked Dr Maddox, so interested now that the Thompsons were holding their tongues, though they seemed to be bursting with questions.

"Yes," said Paisley. "Just her given name. She said it was *Ellen*."

Dr Maddox fell back against the chesterfield cushions. Mrs Maddox took his hand. "Rafe had a…" said Mrs Maddox, her voice catching. "He had a sister named Ellen. She was lost, very near where your ship went down."

Elliott cleared his throat. "We're truly grateful to her."

Dr Maddox nodded silently.

A HEAVY LUNCHEON left Paisley more in the mood for a nap than for anything so weighty as further discussion of the past few weeks' labours. Putting paid to Strange and the Wellborn Trust and the rest was long overdue, except that there were too many loose ends threatening to unravel the victory. There was Strange's trial. And the matter of pinching *The Avenger* from under the nose of Customs. That too might end up in the courts.

The Thompson children were being kept amused by Alison behind the barn, where she was giving fencing lessons with their toy swords, while

Elliott and the Maddoxes were discussing the unfathomable mysteries of the etheric realm, leaving Paisley free to have a private chat with Mr Thompson, who had changed into a less formal suit now that there were no more public events to attend. As he was accustomed to a stroll whenever needing to think, he suggested walking to the Commons.

"If ever I needed to mull over anything, I certainly have reason now. I'll have to talk to Bishop Cameron about this ghost. It is the most extraordinary thing I have ever heard."

Paisley agree that she had never experienced anything quite like it.

"Normally I like to walk about Point Pleasant Park. It will be too crowded today to find any peace, particularly with the gunfire of the batteries. Here, put this on," he suggested, giving Paisley his black homburg to wear when a passing couple shot a disapproving look at Paisley's attire. When she'd tucked her hair up into it, the hat fit. More or less. "I'm afraid," said Thompson, "that you're still too pretty to be a young man in a Homburg, but if no-one looks too closely you may pass muster. Now, what was it that you wished to discuss, Miss DeLoup?"

It would come out sooner or later, when the Customs Department contacted the courts. Better to be forthright. "It's about the ship we were travelling on, sir. It was the same one used to smuggle the rum for the election."

Thompson's face umbered. "The by-election. I haven't forgotten that bit of knavery. There will be yet another by-election, once we've cleaned up the muck from the last one. Do you mean to say that you took the smuggler's boat?"

"Yes, sir. The smuggler was a friend of ours, you see."

"Hmm."

They walked on down Windsor Street while Thompson ruminated on this.

"There has been a good deal of talk about these Wellborn people wanting to cause a war, and this submarine vessel — the one that sank — being the instrument meant to bring that war about. I suppose that you mean to suggest that these are extenuating circumstances, and that the smuggling should be overlooked?"

Thompson was certainly as quick as Paisley had been led to believe. There would be no pulling the wool over his eyes.

"Not exactly, sir. It's true that the threat of a war coming from the submarine boat was real. Miss Stiles was quite prepared to sacrifice her freedom, and her life if necessary, to avert the danger of it." They had all been, if it came to that. "But the smuggling was nothing to do with it, really. Denis didn't even know about the *Paradoxo* at the time."

"If you mean to be your friend's advocate, Paisley, I must tell you that you don't paint a very sympathetic portrait."

"No sir. It was a most foolish thing for him to do. But he has suffered. He lost his ship. And he promised me, I think sincerely, that he means to take up a proper line of work from now on. Do you remember the motorwagon of the German gentleman? He gave it to our friend. Perhaps he will turn his talents to manufacturing them."

"I am sorry, Paisley, but there are legal processes that must apply to everyone. Remorse mitigates the crime, but does not erase it."

She had so hoped there would be a way to avoid gaol for Denis. He hadn't hurt anything, not really, except the coffers of the Customs Department.

"There were no legal processes when we needed them," she said bitterly. "This never would have happened if the courts weren't so... corrupt."

"To which courts are you referring?"

"The county magistrate, of course," snapped Paisley. "Denis' town — my town — was virtually enslaved last year. His father lost his leg as a result, and can hardly work any longer. He had friends, and neighbours, and relatives killed, or crippled, or driven mad, and we had to solve the problem ourselves. Afterwards, the magistrate did nothing. He wouldn't even listen, and interfered with any efforts we made to contact other authorities, discrediting us. Is it any wonder that Denis was cynical about the law and flouted it after it deserted him when he needed it most? That magistrate may even have colluded with Strange. Denis never would have been smuggling had the courts not been so corrupt and incompetent. He didn't even profit from his mistake, or really hurt anyone, and now he's sorry, and *now* the law goes into action. Against him. It's not fair."

They turned onto Cunard Street. "This Spohrville affair again," said Thompson. "That is a good example of why efficient and trustworthy courts are so important. Without them, people are left to their own devices. Frequently, that means violent, vigilante devices. Order breaks down. We no longer have civilization, only individuals acting in their own interest, not the common interest." After they had waited for a carriage to pass and crossed the street, he continued. "Have your friend come to see me before I return to Ottawa. If his character is as reformed as you say, then perhaps nothing will be served by depriving his family of another wage-earner."

"Oh, thank you so much, sir!" Paisley almost wept with relief. Impulsively, she took Thompson's arm and kissed him on the cheek, earning another peculiar look, from a delivery boy this time.

Thompson chuckled, before growing serious again. "There is no need for thanks. Miss DeLoup. This is not a favour, you understand. Law must be universal, but it must be tempered by fairness, and reason. Besides, if I were to arrest your friend, I would necessarily have to arrest half of Victoria

County, for participating in the perversion of the by-election with liquor, bribery, and evasion of customs duties. Frankly, I do not believe that our penitentiaries have the capacity to hold all of the offenders in that county, much less in the Dominion. Circumstances demand that we be selective."

The Commons, Paisley discovered when they arrived, was little more than a few empty triangles of field between roads, with a some not very impressive trees along the edges. The best view was of Fort George, its guns now happily done their duty for the day; Paisley had had enough of cannons for a while. Thompson strode along beside her, looking abstracted, in what must have been his pensive walking mood. Anyone with as much to think about as he had could probably walk from dawn to dusk without working out all of his problems.

"This Miss Stiles," said Thompson, just as Paisley herself was letting her thoughts wander. "What has she to do with the Wellborn Trust. Isn't she a lady's maid? For that very peculiar Lady Beauchamp? How does she come to be applying herself to averting wars?"

Paisley kicked herself for not seeing this coming. Thompson's was the sort of penetrating mind for which the slightest crack might as well be an open barn door.

"Ah, Miss Stiles," said Paisley. Alison wasn't easy to explain. Then Paisley hit upon a fortuitous comparison. "Just as the Wellborn Trust is interested in bringing about a war, because of their theories of eugenics and of improving the race, so there is another organization devoted to preventing wars from taking place. Miss Stiles belongs to this organization."

Thompson walked on, but was clearly cogitating.

"And this Lady Beauchamp. Is she involved in the other organization? Surely that woman's ridiculous pomposity was some sort of act, to distract from her true intentions?"

"I believe so, sir, yes. On both counts."

"Officially, of course, wars are the responsibility of the Imperial Government. Not that it isn't high time we began to play a larger role in Imperial affairs. I take it that this organization is not connected with the government?"

"Not that I know of."

"I cannot," said Thompson, "feel wholly at ease with these secret societies, doing who knows what behind a veil of deception. Then again, war is, in a way, the border of law, where it ends. We have seen in our neighbours' civil war how terrible it can be. To incite a war needlessly is surely the greatest of all crimes. Do you trust Miss Stiles, and her associates?"

"Yes, sir. In fact, if there has been no alarming news today, I believe that they have successfully foiled an attempt in London to assassinate Her

Majesty, the Queen."

Thompson stumbled to a halt. "Are you being serious?"

"Quite serious. That was why the submarine boat did not receive their full attention."

Paisley waited for Thompson to regain command of himself. He was staring vacantly across the Commons.

"Clearly," said Thompson, "there is a good deal in the world of which I am unaware."

That was often Paisley's impression of the world. "Sir," she said, "there is another question that has been troubling me. If you could give me your opinion, I would appreciate it very much." Even Thompson's political enemies generally acknowledged his dispassionate wisdom on thorny issues. She was not likely to find better advice anywhere. "This organization that Lady Beauchamp belongs to... it has been proposed that I might be considered for membership in it. Can you see any objection to me entertaining such a course?"

Thompson led them off on their walk again. "As I said, there are certain aspects to secret societies of which I cannot approve. They may, for example, decide to become a law unto themselves, in which case they make themselves the enemies of law and order. There are any number of associations today. Odd Fellows. Masons. The Orange Order. The Knights of Columbus in the United States. There have been some, like the Hunters' Lodges, that have dedicated themselves to the conquest of this country, and which therefore needed to be fought and eradicated. I know almost nothing of the organization that you propose to join. If what you tell me of them is true, then it sounds as if what they do needs to be done by someone. It would be preferable that it were done by an official body, such as the police."

There had been times when Paisley would have agreed without reservation that she was being called upon to do things better performed by the police, or by anyone else if it came to that. There were also other times, and those were the reason she still gave the proposal serious consideration. Times when she felt that she was in the right place, at the right time, and was the right person to be there. Those times were not always pleasant, but they *were* exhilarating.

"There seem," said Paisley, "to be occasions when there is no appropriate authority to step in. Given your experience with government, sir, which would you, in an emergency, prefer to rely upon? A dedicated hellion like Miss Stiles, or the Circumlocution Office?"

Thompson guffawed. "Yes, I can see your point. The fact remains that you are very young. I could not in good conscience counsel you to undertake any dangerous activity."

"Even a very important task? One at which I might be capable of succeeding."

"If you were my daughter… well, we all have to learn to make our own way in the world sooner or later. Annie — Mrs Thompson — would likely say that you never know what you are capable of until you test yourself. At least, that's what she keeps telling me whenever I grumble about politics, and propose to go back to the Supreme Court bench. If she had her way, I would keep on taking tests until I graduated and became Premier of the Dominion." Thompson laughed again. "God forbid! Being a Minister already feels like the work of ten men. As for *your* tests, I would surmise from recent results that you are capable of a good deal, Paisley. It would be a shame for that capability to never be tried, and applied to some good service."

Yes, thought Paisley. It would be a shame. And very dull, too.

Thompson, until now carrying his side of the conversation with the rich, confident voice of a man who had spent his life using language like a surgeon's scalpel — to cut through rhetoric, bluster, and sentiment — became hesitant.

"Should you decide to join this society, whatever it is, you may well be privy to information of a very valuable kind. Even on the periphery of it, you clearly have learnt of matters of which I, and the Dominion government, were completely ignorant. Without influencing your decision in any way, I would like to express my hope that you might, should you encounter facts of direct import to the safety or welfare of this Dominion and its people, share with me those facts."

This was unforeseen. "You want me to be a spy?" asked Paisley.

Thompson waved the notion aside. "No, no, nothing so cloak-and-dagger as that. Merely a passing along of observations, information, and the like. Anything that you feel I should, in my position, know. You are under no obligation, naturally."

"I…" *Good heavens. What next.* "I cannot promise to do anything that would compromise any oaths, or confidences that I might accept."

"Of course not. Unless they involve a criminal act of which it would be your duty to inform me."

"Well… I think that would be acceptable."

"Good," said Thompson. "You understand, there would be no remuneration. This is not an office of profit under the crown. And you would be under no obligation."

That was hardly shocking. If one wanted to do anything really worthwhile in this country, one needed to be prepared to do it *pro bono publico*, as Mr Thompson would put it. Even the Minister himself, one of the most distinguished statesmen of the Dominion, lived in a leaky house better suited to the junior partner of a law firm.

"It would be my pleasure, sir," said Paisley.

"Excellent!" said Thompson with more enthusiasm. He extended a large hand that swallowed up Paisley's, and cast his gaze around, apparently surprised that they had run out of Commons to pace, having reached the base of Fort George. "What do you say to tea and macaroons at Wilson's restaurant on Hollis Street?"

"Ready, aye, ready!" agreed Paisley, her mind awhirl as they turned their feet towards town and refreshments. An agent of the Dominion... and a member of this so-called Athenian League. What next? One intriguing thing after another seemed to be queueing up to keep the future from growing stale. But they would all have to wait patiently until after the summer. Come war, conspiracy, or stratagems of aunts, Paisley had promised Elliott, and they could both *definitely* use a holiday.

ABOUT THE AUTHOR.
AND ALSO ABOUT BOATS, CONSTITUTIONAL HISTORY, TOPONYMY, HOLIDAYS, CORGIS, RADIO, & MADHOUSES.

PAUL MARLOWE IS a man of the world. *This* world, that is, mainly be-cause he hasn't had the opportunity to travel to any *other* worlds, apart from fictional ones. Sticklers may wish to know that the particular patch of the world that he most often sees outside his window is the province of New Brunswick, Canada. To those unfamiliar with the kingdom of Canada: it is this world's largest constitutional monarchy. Or monarchy of any sort, if it comes to that. Possibly the coldest kingdom also, though parts of Sweden are rather chilly, and Denmark does include Greenland. In fact, originally it had been planned to officially call the country the *Kingdom of Canada*, but there were those who felt that this name might upset Americans (some-one on the names-committee doubtless heard that our southern neighbours were republicans, or democrats, or something like that, and wouldn't take kindly to kings…). They finally decided on the name *Dominion of Canada* as one that would be acceptable to everyone, since it didn't mean anything at all, and we can feel justified in rejoicing every year at their decision (on Canada Day, or Dominion Day, or Victoria Day, depending on your choice of holidays and/or names), considering some of the other names that were mooted and, mercifully, rejected: Tupona, Efisga, Albertoria, New Albion, Victorialia, Transatlantica, Vesperia, or Albionara. Though it would have been amusing if they had gone with *Transylvania*.

Canada actually became a separate kingdom, independent of the UK, in 1931 (with the Statute of Westminster), but as with most of our system of government, no-one knows this fact aside from a few constitutional ex-perts. Which is odd, really, because it simply means that the Queen — like so many of us in these days of recession and belt-tightening — has to hold down several unrelated part-time jobs, most of them unpaid. One day, she's Queen of Canada. The next, she's Queen of the Bahamas. Then she puts in some evenings as the Queen of the UK, or Australia. Weekends as Queen of Jamaica, and New Zealand, with odd hours here and there devoted to being

Queen of Saint Kitts and Nevis, Belize, Barbados, etc., and any spare minutes filled up being Lord of Mann and Duke of Normandy. With that many separate jobs to attend to, it's a wonder she ever has the time to take the corgis for walkies.

And speaking of our sovereigns, as an indication of how fond we Canadians are of one of the earlier models, Queen Victoria, consider the fact that, not content with staging a furious naval battle in Halifax to honour her Golden Jubilee (yes, that part of the story *was* true to life), we still celebrate her birthday every year in May, over a hundred years after she died. Of course, being Canadians and therefore feeling vaguely embarrassed about our history and culture, we occasionally have fits of considering it to be just another bland, meaningless holiday like the first Monday in August, or Labour Day — "the long weekend" instead of Victoria Day — though in the province of Québec a *Parti Québécois* government was so overwhelmed with royal loyalty that they decided they'd call Victoria Day the *Journée nationale des patriotes*, which is jolly nice of them, really, to feel so patriotic about the old Queen's birthday.

Getting back to Mr Marlowe... his short stories have been published practically everywhere else except at home, including in Australia, Africa, Europe, and the United States. *Knights of the Sea* is his second novel. His most recent project prior to *Knights of the Sea* was "The Resident Member", a humorous Victorian ghost story which has been broadcast as a radio play on stations in Canada and the United States, and was called by Sonic Society "an instant classic".

Genuine seadogs have the author's apologies for any nautical howlers that he may have inadvertently committed. As fully one third of his own sailing adventures have ended in the sinking of the boat, it goes without saying that his expertise has certain limitations, even if he can claim some familiarity with maritime disasters.

FOR THE BENEFIT of the inmates of schools, madhouses, prisons, and other facilities devoted to the welfare of our youth, a series of educational historical notes for *Knights of the Sea* has been prepared which may be read and, where appropriate, snickered over, at *www.PaulMarlowe.com*

Questions, praise, greetings, corrections, grievances and other communiqués can be delivered via the same web site. Vexatious criticism may be sent to the Devil by whatever means the writer wishes.

THIS VOLUME IS dedicated to the memory of *Pippin,* the best of pals, who saw its beginning but not its end, and who

> delighted in each new road,
> remembered every old friend,
> met enemies with noise, not teeth,
> had mischief, but never malice,
> had fears, but always humour too,
> hated loneliness,
> loved without reserve,
> was eager to learn,
> taught us what joy was,
> endured pain with courage,
> met each dawn like the first,
> and lit the world with a better light.

We shall not look upon his like again.

Pippin — after death, Aug 5, 2007 — Upper Kennetcook

ALSO FROM SYBERTOOTH INC.

WWW.SYBERTOOTH.CA

DONALD JACK

BY 3-TIME LEACOCK award winner Donald Jack: *The Bandy Papers* series, about First World War ace Bartholomew Bandy.

THREE CHEERS FOR ME: VOLUME I OF THE BANDY PAPERS (E-BOOK)
ISBN: 9780986497414

THE LEACOCK WINNING classic: Bartholomew Wolfe Bandy abandons medical school for the Victorian Light Infantry. He survives the trenches only to be transferred to the Royal Flying Corps after capturing his own colonel in a daring raid on his own lines. (forthcoming, 2010)

IT's ME AGAIN: VOLUME III OF THE BANDY PAPERS
ISBN-10: 097395051X • ISBN-13: 9780973950519

IN THIS CLASSIC novel of the First World War, ace pilot Bartholomew Bandy struggles against his adjutant, his adjutant's pigeon, a defective parachute design, a new German bi-plane, and the Bolshevik army, managing to get promoted to general in the process... (Also available as an e-book.)

ME BANDY, YOU CISSIE: VOLUME IV OF THE BANDY PAPERS
ISBN: 9780973950571

WINNER OF THE Leacock Medal for Humour. The Great War may be finished, but Bartholomew Bandy isn't. After not quite succeeding in defeating communism in Russia, he returns to the New World, but what with carrying airmail and trying to start his own aviation business while dodging flappers and bootleggers, Bandy hardly has time to be a silent movie star... This edition includes the radio play "Banner's Headline". (Also available as an e-book.)

ME TOO: VOLUME V OF THE BANDY PAPERS
(forthcoming, 2010)

THIS ONE'S ON ME: VOLUME VI OF THE BANDY PAPERS
ISBN 9780973950557

IT'S 1924, AND Bandy is making a solo flight across the Atlantic in the Gander, a seaplane of his own design. Not for fame though – he's fleeing from arrest for train robbery, from his job as Minister of Defence, and from his would-be assassin and friend George Garanine. (Also available as an e-book.)

ME SO FAR: VOLUME VII OF THE BANDY PAPERS
ISBN: 9780973950502

BANDY HAS FINALLY found a secure post-war job, as commander of the Maharajah of Jhamjarh's new air force. The only problem is, the British Raj are not so happy with him for setting up a rival air power inside British India.

Hitler Versus Me: Volume VIII of the Bandy Papers
(includes the novelette "Where Did Rafe Madison Go?")
ISBN-10: 0968802486 • ISBN-13: 9780968802489
It's 1940, and the intrepid air ace of WWI is eager to join the fight against Germany. Unfortunately, everyone seems to think Bandy is too old to be flying Spitfires, and should go quietly into retirement to polish his medals. Bandy, however, has other ideas, and uses his friends and/or enemies in high places to manoeuvre himself into the Battle of Britain.

Stalin Versus Me: Volume IX of The Bandy Papers
ISBN-10: 0968802478 • ISBN-13: 9780968802472
In the aftermath of the Normandy invasion, Bandy continues to bob through the ranks like a cork at sea, persecuted by one of his pilots and pursued by Gwinny, who just can't understand why her attempt to have him convicted of treason has soured their relationship.

And also:
The Canvas Barricade
ISBN-10: 0968802494 • ISBN-13: 9780968802496
In print for the first time, Donald Jack's comedy *The Canvas Barricade* was the first modern play performed on the main stage of the Stratford Festival (1961).

The Captain Star Omnibus
By Steven Appleby
ISBN: 9780973950564
From the creator of the cult-classic *Captain Star* TV cartoon series: the first collection of comic strips tracing the strange but illustrious career of Captain Jim Star – the greatest hero any world has ever known – from its surreal beginnings to its improbable middle. Witness his triumphs, learn from his words of wisdom, and meet his crew on the Boiling Hell: Navigator Black, Officer Scarlette, and Atomic Engine Stoker "Limbs" Jones.

Letters from Helen
By Helen VanWart, edited by Douglas Lochhead
A collection of letters and photographs from a New Brunswick girl travelling to Leipzig, Germany to study music just before the outbreak of the First World War. (forthcoming, 2010)

Quests and Kingdoms
A Grown-Up's Guide to Children's Fantasy Literature
By K.V. Johansen
ISBN-10: 0968802443 • ISBN-13: 9780968802441
"... THIS IS not only a fine reference tool but a finely-written book...This is undoubtedly a seminal work guaranteed to stimulate discussion on children's literature..." *–Books in Canada*

"WHAT TRULY AMAZES, though, is Johansen's reliability and depth of knowledge...and her accuracy with facts...The sheer volume of knowledge on display here could earn Johansen honors for scholarship. This is a truly useful reference book..." -*Mythprint* (Bulletin of the Mythopoeic Society)
"...A LIVELY, THOUGHTFUL read, and a useful reference volume." - Terri Windling

BEYOND WINDOW-DRESSING?
CANADIAN CHILDREN'S FANTASY AT THE MILLENNIUM
BY K.V. JOHANSEN
ISBN: 9780968802458
"BEYOND WINDOW-DRESSING SHOULD be of particular interest to public and school librarians, and academic librarians in institutions offering courses in children's literature. It should serve as an inspirational tool for seeking out, selecting, and retaining exemplary fantasy literature in our library collections." –The Canadian Library Association's journal *Feliciter*
"I APPLAUD THE honesty and forthrightness of her analyses. Far too often, reviews of children's books provide little more than vague plot summaries with very little, if any, questioning of the aesthetic or literary value of a text. Not so with Johansen's analyses. She has her opinions and she quite adroitly defends them. She establishes clear criteria for what she considers a valid and valuable fantasy, and judges each text accordingly. And, I must admit, I found her criticism of even some of Canada's literary icons both refreshing and, more significantly, quite convincing." –*Canadian Literature*

LOVE ON THE MARSH: A LONG POEM
BY DOUGLAS LOCHHEAD
ISBN: 9780973950533
LOVE ON THE Marsh, a long poem in 100 stanzas, is described by Lochhead as "an extension of *High Marsh Road*" and "brother and sister to it". The diary-like entries, a form to which Lochhead has frequently returned over the years, can also be compared to his work in *The Panic Field*. By turns earthy and ethereal, a pilgrimage through a landscape of grass and sky and tumultuous emotions, *Love on the Marsh* revisits the *High Marsh Road* with a new eye and finds in it the self-examining, self-discovering heart.

LOOKING INTO TREES: POEMS BY DOUGLAS LOCHHEAD
ISBN: 9780981024431
"WHAT LOCHHEAD'S POEMS achieve, virtually effortlessly, is an aural and imagist immediacy without sacrificing the richness of layering. Metaphors are repeated, and there is a cyclical nature to these connections - we keep returning to dreams and prayers, memory and the insistence of love - but the immediacy is tangible. These poems engage the senses and the heart." - Heather Craig, *The Telegraph Journal*

SPOREVILLE: BOOK I OF THE WELLBORN CONSPIRACY
BY PAUL MARLOWE
ISBN-13: 9780973950540

ELLIOTT GRAVEN WAS prepared to be bored by Spohrville, and prepared to be annoyed by it. After all, it was a run-down fishing village in the back woods, and moving there suddenly had been his father's idea, not Elliott's. But he wasn't prepared for the sleepwalkers. Or the mushrooms. Or the jars of eyes. At least the werewolves seemed to be on his side...

"FANS OF PHILIP Pullman's *His Dark Materials* trilogy will certainly enjoy this novel. In fact, readers who like gothic literature, science fiction, fantasy, and history will all relish this book... I cannot wait for the sequel...It was absolutely the best, most delicious thing I have read in some time." –Bonnie Campbell, *Resource Links* - (Also available as an e-book.)

THE STORYTELLER AND OTHER TALES
BY K.V. JOHANSEN
ISBN: 9780973950588

A COLLECTION FOR adults and older teens, *The Storyteller and Other Tales* will take you on a journey through exotic worlds and times.

"...PERFECT FIRESIDE READING, full of bravery, tragedy, belief and treachery." - FantasyBookReview.co.uk

AND NOW ... HERE'S MAX
BY MAX FERGUSON
ISBN: 9780981024479

THE LEACOCK AWARD-WINNING memoir of his life at the CBC, by the legendary Max Ferguson. With an introduction by Shelagh Rogers. (Also forthcoming as an e-book, 2010.)

THE DRONE WAR: A CASSANDRA VIRUS NOVEL
BY K.V. JOHANSEN
ISBN-10: 0973950528 • ISBN-13: 9780973950526

JORDAN O'BLENIS MAY be a genius when it comes to computers, but with spies after his sister's research in unmanned aerial vehicles and artificial intelligence, he needs all the help he can get from Cassandra the virtual supercomputer to keep her safe and save BWB Aerospace's top secret drone project.

"THIS BOOK IS a non-stop adventure...It's a very fun, often funny, intelligent read. I highly recommend it." –Carrie Spellman, *Teens Read Too*

THE BLACK BOX: A CASSANDRA VIRUS NOVEL
BY K.V. JOHANSEN *Coming soon ...*

www.ingramcontent.com/pod-product-compliance
Lightning Source LLC
Chambersburg PA
CBHW022009010726
47494CB00003B/965